OMELET ENDGAME

COOKING WITH DISASTER
BOOK 3

DAKOTA KROUT

This is a work of fiction. Names, characters, places, and incidents either are the products of the author's imagination or are used fictitiously. Any resemblance to actual persons, living or dead, businesses, companies, events, or locales is entirely coincidental.

ACKNOWLEDGMENTS

Wow! The end of the trilogy already! It's amazing, and so are you.

Thank you all for reading this novel. It's a massive blessing to bring you joy and cool stories. I hope you'll come and read Everything soon.

My lovely wife, many thanks for being there with me for all the sleepless nights and distracted days I had while thinking through what needed to happen here.

Aaron Michael Ritchey, thanks for all of your input on this work. I know things have been hard for you, but I know things are going to be looking up soon.

The same goes for the rest of you: better days are on the way, and they're coming fast.

May your future be delicious.

PROLOGUE

PROBABILITY VISION

Arriod QuaJohn of A-One District's Ultra Unit Strike Force stood just behind the tree line. As the Ultra Commanding Overlord of the Ideal CruxTerran Unified Peoples—better known as the ICUP—Arriod knew all of his commanders and soldiers were waiting on his signal. He waited patiently in the shadows, with one hand on his very special, very deadly katana.

His sunglasses were pushed up on his head to keep his thick black hair back, and as always, a lower-face cloth covered his chin, mouth and cheeks. He wanted to see with his own eyes that the famed Assassin, Eli 'Nacho' Naches—better known as 'the Shadow Killer'—was being led through the gates of Richard Crave's compound.

"These humans are very bizarre, sir." One of Arriod's subordinates shuddered as she watched the basic humans with disdain. The observation made the leader frown, but he allowed her to speak so long as she maintained proper standards of stealth. "Not only do they only have *one* stomach, but the pupils of their eyes are disgusting. Round? It's unnerving and unattractive."

Arriod, his entire generation of soldiers, and everyone currently alive on their world had grown up with the cross-shaped pupils, even though they were relatively new. For most of their shared history, CruxTerrans had been born with vertical pupils. About a hundred years ago, horizontal slits were added, and it had revolutionized civilization in all sorts of important ways.

During the original ICUP surgeries, back when the initiative began, some very effective propaganda had been turned into a proverb to encourage people to get the surgery. He breathed it now, earning looks of admiration from all sides. "The eyes are a window into the soul, and every soul is a crossroads."

Most of the time, Arriod didn't care much for proverbs. Their financial or strategic value couldn't be graphed. They were pretty, but pretty didn't keep a fighter alive. But propaganda? Arriod understood propaganda exceedingly well. It was both a carrot and a stick for the lowly and the ignorant. It created obedience. If the CruxTerrans were obedient, they would crush these round-eyed Earthlings.

Arriod breathed in the night air, preparing himself to act when the humans were at their weakest. "This night is another crossroads."

"Sir!" His people's admiration was near reverent.

Two of the most powerful guilds on the Earth's Starter World were merging—the Final Victory and the Gorged. It seemed impossible, but Richard Crave and Kala the Death Knight had come to an agreement and would be using the momentum of their union to counterattack the CruxTerrans. Only one fact had been able to delay the ambush the CruxTerrans had planned to crush both guilds: one requirement of the merger was that Nacho—the Shadow Killer—had to die.

More than just being an Assassin with an *astounding* kill count and mission success ratio, Arriod had disturbing dreams of Nacho. He didn't know if they were a boon or not, as the dreams didn't seem to have any strategic value. They seemed like simple, troubling visions. But that was all over now, if his intel was correct.

Nacho was scheduled to die at first light, which would weaken the human forces and practically assure the safety of Arriod's political backers and various VIP's in the bunkers. As soon as the death was confirmed, both the Final Victory and the Gorged would be destroyed. Even now, Arriod's well-equipped and well-fed army—a collection of UltraUnits, G-Units, and Total Units—filled the forests around the compound. The soldiers were silently killing any scouts and stragglers, which would allow the CruxTerran cooks to provide them *quite* the victory breakfast after Crave fell.

They would have enough meat for a long, *long* time.

Human breakfast sausage added a certain… *something* to the scrambled eggs that Arriod enjoyed. His mouth watered at just *thinking* of scrambled eggs, and even mediocre ones reminded him of nice vacations he'd taken as a boy. He'd grown up visiting the plastic pebble beaches on the Eastern Glory Sea. What could be more beautiful than the radioactive glow of the factories lining the swampy rivers as industrialization reached new heights?

Arriod toyed with his sword, idly slipping it a few inches in and out of its sheath at his side. The humans called it a 'katana'. It seemed to be a foreign word—the Roundies had all sorts of nations, countries, states, and provinces. Theirs was a foolish method of governance, one that had been stomped out of his world centuries ago. The ICUP had divided the seven continents into districts and subdistricts for maximum efficiency; it worked perfectly.

The Earthlings were chaotic creatures with faintly amusing ideas on personal freedom with a utilitarian bent. It was probably why they had so many different kinds of foods all around their world—or what had been their world before the Juxtaposition. That was one of their only redeeming features, in his mind: the sheer decadence of their foodstuffs. It didn't matter though—not anymore.

Arriod mostly got his information from hungry people, and hungry people talked about food. A lot. Many mentioned something called 'tacos'. From what he understood, it was meat inside a fried shell. Then someone explained to him that the shell didn't *need* to be fried. As he had come to understand it, they just did it to increase the flavor and calorie count. Shaking his head, he muttered disdainfully, "Incredibly wasteful."

The Patrons had given both the humans and CruxTerrans a new language to use: Juxtaposition tongue, or Patronese. Even so, some words didn't translate well. For example, back on CruxTerra, there had been the word 'Eejailspee'. As he had explained to captive humans during his clinical trials on determining the limits of their subpar minds, 'Eejailspee' was the fear a person felt when their government had imprisoned or killed all of their friends, and they were next on the list.

Arriod had not experienced Eejailspee himself. From an early age, he knew that it was better to be the jailor than the jailed, so he'd risen as fast in the ranks of the ICUP as he could manage. Questions were often punished, so he learned to keep his curiosity to himself. One of the reasons he had been promoted so rapidly was because, unlike so many others, *he* could control himself. Another reason? He loved games, all kinds of games, as much as he enjoyed breakfast. What was survival and political power, other than the most dangerous game that he could attempt to play?

It had been three years since he'd emerged from the Evaluation World, having scored nearly perfectly. He'd perused the Evaluation Mall for a very long time, since time had stopped meaning anything, and the Patrons had seemed perfectly willing to let him shop forever. In fact, he had considered shopping forever as a possible strategy. How angry would the Patrons be if he sat out their entire game in the Evaluation Mall?

Although it had taken a bit, Arriod's curiosity had eventually gotten the better of him. He did take the time to read every single description of every single class, and every single skill in those classes. He'd thought he'd compiled a good working knowledge of the Juxtaposition's game elements, but he hadn't been completely certain why anyone would choose to spend their Evaluation Points on being a Satiation Player. He'd been slightly tempted, since judging by the Evaluation World, food was certainly going to be important. Both Hunger and Thirst were tracked on their Stat Sheets, and both were necessary in using one's Skills.

Arriod could've even become a Common Cook, the most expensive class available. The Patrons thought they were clever, assuming they had successfully hidden the importance of the class. But it wasn't *their* call to ignore the class; it was his. In the end, since he was sure he didn't truly comprehend all the variables, he decided to go with the most powerful Body Player class: a Paladin. In the Juxtaposition, his military skills would be the most useful tool at his disposal. A soldier didn't rise through the ranks of the ICUP without winning the military games between the districts, and that meant excruciating training. He wasn't about to waste all that effort on a class with weaker combat potential.

There was one final *glaring* difference between the CruxTerran and the earthlings. On the Earth's Starter World, pockets of people had organized themselves into various guilds. On CruxTerra, the ICUP took control immediately, killed anyone who disagreed with their methods, and brought the entire globe back under control in about six months. Since then, UltraUnits had been plundering dungeons with ruthless efficiency and working for the benefit of the ICUP, which acted as a single massive guild with an Ideal Leader at the top.

Regardless, Arriod knew what that man really was: a figurehead. Arriod was the voice of the military, and he held true authority for his people. A smile that no one could see graced his lips at that moment. He had won the game before; now he just needed to do it again.

As projected, the CruxTerrans had discovered some rebels,

some martyrs, and a whole faction that had tried to form a guild and live underground. Just people being troublesome people. In that behavior, the Roundies and the CruxTerrans were the same —both races did crazy things when not properly guided.

Well, once Arriod and his men slaughtered the Roundies, he could see about exploring this planet's history from whatever scraps of human civilization they allowed to survive. For now, all he had to do was wait at the edge of the forest.

Or so he thought.

Something flickered to Arriod's right. His Patron appeared without warning in his old CruxTerra cooking whites, wearing a Quack Ball helmet—the Juxtaposition was jarring like that.

'Hey, Arri!" the god-like being boomed, the curve of his thick pink lips revealing a humorless smile full of bright white teeth. Chubby flushed cheeks lay under small eyes and pencil-thin eyebrows, and a simple bamboo toothpick jutted out of the corner of those hamburger-colored lips.

"Johnny Meat." Arriod nodded solemnly at the Patron. No one had dared to call him 'Arri' since the fifth year of his SubSchooling, and that had included his mother, who was wise enough to know to stop at that point. He could recognize a power play, and he wouldn't let it fluster him.

Johnny Meat plucked his toothpick out and tapped it against Arriod's sword. "You love that sword, don't you? I know it's probably hungry for a bunch of action in the morning."

"Indeed." Arriod backed up and leaned against a tree. On more than one occasion, he'd thought about drawing the so-called katana to see if he could carve some ounces of breakfast sausage out of his Patron, though the objective part of his brain acknowledged that the attempt would not be in his best interest. So far, Johnny Meat had helped him on numerous occasions, though an attitude of chaos always seemed to be included.

Arriod casually kept his hand on the hilt of his blade. "You're not here to talk about the sword or my many deadly Skills. What are you doing here?"

"Such a blunt instrument. Do you mean that in an existential way?" The Patron toyed with his words. "Like, why is *anyone* doing anything? In this case, I'm a Patron of this round of the Juxtaposition, and I just got some news that is messing with every single Patron that is placing bets. I came here to personally deliver that news."

"Do tell." Arriod was somewhat intrigued, but he knew better than to broadcast his emotions to this being. He and his troops were but entertainment, and watching him squirm would bring too much pleasure to the higher entity. He was surprised—they seemed to be firmly in control of the Juxtaposition, down to every person, every detail; all of reality. The Roundies found such power and knowledge an invasion of privacy. For Arriod and the rest of the CruxTerrans, it was just a Toozday—same scrutiny, same manipulations, just a different face at the top level.

Johnny Meat squinted one eye shut. "I'd say I have some good news, and I have some bad news. Sadly for you, you might not actually exist. So… the flavor of the news probably isn't so important."

A shiver went through Arriod, but he tried not to show it. "I was looking forward to a trencher of approved victory food at the dining facility."

"As we all were." The god waved his toothpick like an orchestral baton. "I'm not saying you'll never get CruxTerran breakfast food again. It's just probably not going to be *you*."

"Because I won't, or don't currently, exist." Arriod didn't understand, but this conversation didn't bode well for his future. Futures, like pasts, required an existence. He *thought* he was real. He seemed real. But he was dealing with near-omnipotent people who could shape reality at a whim.

"Because you probably *don't* exist," Johnny Meat agreed easily as he gestured with his toothpick. "To get the probabilities nailed down, old Kronos really had to go all out. I mean, giving his chosen guy an extra life only to take it away would've been brave, but the probabilities wouldn't have really been there. But to give *two whole worlds* life so he could give his guy that one boon? There you go, boy. That takes a big bloody bull's heart brimming with bravery."

"Bulls are male peefs, right?" Arriod's sword still remained in its sheath. If he didn't exist, nothing that he did mattered. He slowly widened his stance, hand on the hilt, ready to draw the powerful blade once he got a complete picture of the situation.

"That'd be *beef*," Johnny corrected as he pulled a face. "Bulls, cows, beef, hamburger, steak—lots of different words here on the Earth's Starter World for all that. Kronos gave his guy, Nacho, a boon. Once that guy gets his throat cut, all of this ends. That includes you, Mr. QuaJohn. You, the sword, it all goes back into the big unknown until version two-point-oh hits us with its strangeness. I took notes of some things, so when I do talk to the real you next time, we can work some pretty big magic and get you to the endgame faster. This round took *forever*. Next round is going to be over in months, definitely less than a year, if I'm right. There's been talk of using the Starvation Dungeon to speed things along."

Arriod wasn't going to waste a second trying to argue with the Patron or beg for his life, or do any such thing. He would take what Johnny Meat was saying at face value. When Nacho died, both worlds would die, since this 'game' seemed to have been an entire simulation for one man to learn from. Sliding his sword out a few inches… he let it drop back into its sheath. He didn't draw the weapon; he didn't attack the Patron. No.

Once Arriod died, another version of him would come into being. If he attacked Johnny, or admitted he'd wanted to murder the Patron since the first moment he'd laid eyes on him, then Johnny would have that information. Worse, he could use it against Arriod's next iteration, his real self. He'd give himself a break this time around.

However, Arriod was desperate to know the exact nature of the Juxtaposition. What was it for? What was the end game like? Was it solely designed to amuse gods? Or did it have a higher purpose?

"Johnny," Arriod slowly let the question creep from his lips, "since I'm about to snap out of existence, tell me all the big secrets. It won't matter if I know them, since I'll be gone. There is no reason why you shouldn't tell me."

Johnny Meat laughed and stuck his toothpick between his front teeth. "The opposite is also true there, Arri. There's not a single reason why I should risk the other Patrons overhearing and busting me. It's too risky. How about I answer three 'yes or no' questions? Go. Better hurry. Crave is about to hit Nacho with that feather of his."

"Is the Juxtaposition only for the Patrons to bet on?"

"No." Johnny Meat rewarded him with a big toothy smile that showed all of his pearly white teeth.

Arriod tried not to get upset. "Do you want to add anything to that?"

"No." Johnny giggled. "That should be the second question, but I'll go easy on you. You only have a few more minutes of existence left."

"Thank you for your kindness. I'm assuming it is because we've known each other long enough to give each other a bit of leeway." Arriod paused. In the three years since he'd left the Evaluation Mall, he'd suspected that the game was more than just sport for the Patrons. Now, he'd gotten that confirmed.

"Better hurry, pal," the Patron prodded. "Pokey-poke time over there."

"Is the war between the CruxTerrans and the Roundies a zero-sum game?"

Johnny waggled the toothpick at Arriod. "Oh, you're clever. There're a couple different questions there. Is there a war? Can there only be one winner? Or in essence, can only one world win? I'll say yes, there is a war. Given what you know about the game after your three years here, I would assume you'd know the answer to the other question. I prefer to let your future self figure out how that all works."

Arriod knew his time was short, and so far, the questions had gone fairly easily. "If I win the game, would I get to become a Patron?"

Johnny raised a finger. "Hold on one moment, wouldja? Incoming message on Patron radio. Nacho is unconscious. The blade is at his throat."

"Oh, Johnny." Arriod sighed and shook his head. "Mr. Meat. Right up until the end, you are toying with me. Just tell me."

He felt the terror coiling heavily in his gut. Regardless he didn't show the god in a sports helmet a single spark of emotion. Johnny threw his toothpick away, and his face lost all expression. "Yeah, QuaJohn, yeah. Be a good little player long enough, across enough worlds, and you get to become a good little Patron."

Arriod felt relief flood through every part of him. One of his biggest fears had been that the Juxtaposition was unwinnable, that even if the CruxTerrans destroyed every last one of the Roundies, it wouldn't matter. But no, there was a point to the game. One could win it and ultimately become one of the gods that controlled it.

"Last question… do the Patrons control the system?" That iteration of Arriod would never know the answer.

Sheer annoyance filled the eyes of Johnny Meat a millisecond before the entire land around them turned to dust, then turned to nothing. Arriod didn't get to witness the phenomenon… because *he* was already dust.

"We sure don't, Arriod."

CHAPTER ONE

Eli 'Nacho' Naches stood at the edge of the forest holding his Skillet of Turtling. Reuben and Brie flanked him, hidden in the trees. The Dinner Party gazed with astonishment at the field of vicious millet, misshapen stalks heavy with monstrous grains of epic proportions. It was a farming nightmare; a bedtime story wild-eyed vegans told about what would happen if people didn't stop eating meat. "Guess they ended up being right in the end, though, so what do I know?"

Fifteen feet of open field lay between the forest and the first row of the millet monsters, so the cook started moving. It felt good to be out adventuring with his two best friends. Nacho had decided that he needed a break from the kitchen after spending so long working for the benefit of his guild once they had returned triumphantly from the UnderFun. "See the world, kill some monsters, just relax a bit. What better way to unwind than to push our limits?"

"You're mumbling again." Reuben called out his friend's bad habit cheerfully, seemingly not at all worried about the upcoming fight. The mood made sense, as each of them bore the natural confidence that came from long hours of deadly combat against enemies so powerful that none of them had ever expected to walk away. If they played it smart, they would take care of these monsters, process the plants, and wind up with some real flour to use for all *sorts* of yummy things.

"Don't sass me… *you.* I've got the right kind of grease for donuts, and I'm not afraid to use it." Nacho had stowed his Gauntlets of Oven Taming and was trying to hide his blush from his failed comeback against Reuben. Pretending that he needed to inspect his equipment so he could ignore the chuckling at his expense, Nacho ended up actually looking over his gear in earnest.

His Wok of Blocking covered his chest, while the Helm of Boiling protected his head, just as the Pauldrons of Frying protected his shoulders. His feet and legs were guarded by the Gravy Boots, which contained a mysterious ability he had yet to unlock. Sheathed at his sides hung the HungerCry Knives—the Hunger Cleaver and the Cry Chef's Knife.

They were his steel babies, and he loved them.

He might look silly, but as far as kitchen combat was concerned, he was dressed to the nines. Each article of his equipment was a Tier one item, except for his armored boots. A glance at Reuben gave him a glimpse of a wide, happy smile, along with confirming the fact that it was unlikely that the Healer would ever part with his leather Helmet of Helming. Reuben's fashion disaster didn't end with his headgear, but also fully encompassed his wrists, where the Sausage Clips of Striking jingled. The metal bands made his hands indestructible when he attacked and allowed him to clobber monsters with unholy amounts of fisty damage.

In the weeks since they'd won the Sewer Skewers, Reuben had also picked up a sleeveless red leather brigandine reinforced with oblong pieces of metal underneath. It was magical, allowing him to wear it at all times, since it felt like a T-shirt and cleaned itself. The fact that he *did* wear it at all times made Nacho consider his friend in a completely different light.

Looking the effusive man over more closely, Nacho had to

admit that Reuben had taken to their new life in the Juxtaposition rather nicely. He'd slimmed down, bulked up, and when he flexed, it was Bicep City: Population Two. The Tricep Suburbs were easily accessible by train, and too many times, the cook had seen Brie's fingers trailing along the tracks.

Arguably the most eye-catching item that he had recently acquired was a pair of leather disco pants, which acted as Tier one armor. The metal boots he had looted off a dead Final Victory guild member in the sewers could have belonged to Frankenstein's monster, or a clown, depending on which one scared an opponent the most. All in all, the Healer looked absolutely terrifying. This was clearly a man that cared only for functionality and would discard a matched set item for a ridiculous piece that offered a one-percent better boost.

Their team's main damage dealer, resident Berserker Brie McCurdy, had grown increasingly unhappy with the state of her new husband's wardrobe. The helm was bad, but his sabatons were especially ungainly. The entire team was fairly certain that the Patrons had begun to intentionally harass Brie with magical armor that didn't match. Her Lacrosse Stick was black and gold, a gorgeous piece of sports-equipment-turned-medieval-weapon. She'd been on the hunt for armor, any kind of armor, that might match it.

So far, she'd unearthed a pair of reinforced neon green metal boots, a weathered crimson leather skirt that protected her legs, and an eye-searing purple tunic of magical chainmail. A mustard-yellow satchel from the Store held her lacrosse balls, which she could hurl from a distance to effect substantial damage. Her helmet was brass, making those two pieces the only articles that matched in the slightest. The final statement piece hung around her waist; a custom-made belt of Cow Poke leather holding yellow and red tubes of Life Hack Yogurt—an odd-textured combination of plain Greek yogurt, strawberry jelly, and cottage cheese.

All in all, she looked like a lacrosse clown at the epicenter of an atomic fashion disaster. Even so, as her delighted husband was quick to point out, she was *protected* by the armor, and that was all that mattered at the end of the day.

The three had come an incredible distance from their first days in the Juxtaposition. The summer had flown by, and their one-year anniversary was barely more than a month away.

Nacho shook off the nostalgia as he refocused on the monsters at hand. Reuben had been the one to discover the field of monstrous millet. The grains exhibited no discernible mouths, but the gnarled stalks sent spiked vines crawling across the ground, which was littered with decomposing flesh, which filled the air with a sharp, sweet, and very unpleasant smell.

The top of each plant bore a big cylinder of millet, covered in a layer of silk so fine that it almost looked like spider's webs. Truthfully, they hadn't *seen* any spiders… yet. They couldn't rule the possibility out, though. Each of the plant monsters ranged from tall—about six feet—to gigantic—a whopping twelve feet above the soil. The heads of grain on the biggest ones were a good two feet in diameter, making Nacho lick his lips in anticipation.

That was going to be a whole lotta flour once they managed to bring the beasties down. Brie, in charge of their combat strategy, voiced a few observations. "I don't see any fangs. I'm wondering how they eat, and that makes me worried about the vines. Be careful not to get taken down and reduced to nutrients."

"I don't know about you guys, but I can't wait to use my Splatter Millet for the first time." Nacho patted his pack, where the Warhammer-turned-cooking-utensil waited for its first victim.

Reuben rumbled with laughter. "That's right… I think it was the day after we got here, Brie got the Splatter Mallet, and you got the Splatter *Millet*. Man, that takes me back."

About fifty of the silken stalks had risen out of the mess of decay and produced spiked vines. Nacho got a System View on the biggest of the plants, which was a good fifty feet across when all the leaves and tangled roots were taken into account.

. . .

Massive Millet Stalker
Effective Level: ???
HP: ?

"Oh, boy," Nacho breathed, nearly coming to a complete stop. "I'm about ninety percent certain that we have ourselves a Tier two field of dreams here. We need to be careful."

"Field of nightmares, more like." Reuben grinned as he attempted to negate Nacho's worries. "If you build it, they will come… to eat you."

"Am I missing something?" Brie nimbly spun her lacrosse stick in her fingers. "I get the outdated movie reference, but not all of the monsters are Tier two. Some are also some zeroes and ones—seems like Tier and level depend on how big they are? It doesn't matter to me, since they can't move. I'll Combat Dash within fifteen feet of them, then throw my distance attack into one to see if I can hit it. If I can't, I Combat Dash away. Too easy."

Nacho held up a hand to forestall any more conversation, his mind racing. "Hold up. Let's think about this. We're about a six hour walk from Armor Mountain, and people from the Chips Guild have come this way before, but no one has reported these monsters. The Millet Stalkers must've either sprouted up within a day or two, some faster than others, or they killed anyone that found them previously. My bet is that the entire crop is absorbing a dense concentration of Putrid Mana. The Juxtaposition works like that sometimes—things sprout up, sometimes literally overnight."

"Sorry, I can't hear your worry," Brie calmly stated as she targeted the largest monster in sight. "I'm too busy… staying fresh, cheese bag."

"Wait, hold on! If we run out there to attack them, we might fall into a hidden pit, and then those vines eat us."

Nacho barely managed to keep her back, literally dragging her almost to the ground through sheer stats in order to inhibit her initial charge. She did *not* appreciate his interference.

"Did you see anything like this in the Probability Vision?" Reuben questioned in an attempt to save his friend from being mauled by his wife.

Nacho shook his head and let go of Brie's arm. He had done everything he could to protect her without resorting to fisticuffs. "No, but monsters grow, evolve, and change. Some are repeat offenders, but others are brand new. When I was an Assassin, I wasn't exactly looking to backstab wheat fields. I only went after people and monsters… sometimes."

He regretted that last word. Most days, he could forget about what he had needed to do to survive. Other days, it was… harder. Only the fact that all of his sins had been the product of a Patron-induced fever dream let him sleep through the night, otherwise the sheer variety of murder and cannibalism would've given him a chronic case of insomnia.

Reuben patted the cook's back, carefully ignoring Brie preparing to attack, warning or no. "It's okay, man. Let's just focus on the moment, like how if you tackle Brie without a really good reason in the future, I'm going to have to side with her and beat you until I've achieved blood and cheese."

"Um," came Nacho's eloquent reply. "Pitfall traps aren't a good reason?"

"It might be. Ooh! Idea!" The incumbent Merchant of Soothing brightened. "Brie, can you toss a ball into one of those things from here and see if you can hit it? If you can't, then we can plan a new strategy from there. Maybe we can toss some credits against this issue and blow holes in the dirt to check for pits?"

Nacho tapped his own nose, then pointed at Reuben. "There's my buddy, always thinking with his noggin."

"Fine. Do *you* have any ranged attacks?" Brie produced a golden ball—which matched her lacrosse stick perfectly—and dropped it in the net. "These things are not cheap, you know. They run forty credits a shot."

"Unfortunately, no." Nacho's inner skinflint screamed and fell to its knees at the reminder. "It's gotta be you, Brie. Can you throw that far?"

"Easily. I'm accurate with my stick to about sixty or seventy yards. Even better if I boost real quick." Brie was already munching an Uncommon pocket pancake, chasing it down with a Rare Life Hack yogurt. By eating quickly, she could replenish a full portion of Hunger Points as well as basically doubling her Fitness.

"Let's give you some Positive Vibes to help with your damage. If this doesn't affect them, we *absolutely* need to run away." A golden glow covered the trio as the Healer's main damage-dealing buff was activated.

Reuben—like both Nacho and Brie—had bought his way to level fourteen, but their Skills were all at level nineteen. Leveling Skills was far cheaper than upgrading a Character Class, and thanks to Nacho's warning, they hadn't fallen for the trap. Beyond allowing them to be more conservative with their credits, it had enabled them to become a far more effective combat team.

Not that they were being austerely conservative with their finances anymore. With how successful the Chips Guild had become, credits were rolling in all the time. Realistically, the only natural limits to how much cash they could access were Kala the Death Knight and Old Bill.

Kala watched the finances like a vindictive hawk, her black sword and nearly impenetrable armor ready to leap to the defense of the tax revenue, unafraid to fight The Dinner Party to the death if they took too much for themselves. Old Bill was a geezer in a Royals cap who insisted on doing everything for himself, to such a degree that he tried not to spend a single credit at the Store, and he wanted to hold them to that same standard. Even so, both of them were easier to deal with than a new addition to the guild: Zack Puck.

The loud-mouth had joined them from the Final Victory, and he was not someone that Nacho could tolerate for very long without longing to stab him. Brie shared the same class—both were Berserkers—which she felt was an embarrassment. With a herculean effort of will, Nacho put the annoyance out of his mind and focused on the issues at hand just as Brie hurled the lacrosse ball into the nearest plant creature.

The System immediately threw them a message:

Welcome to Active Combat! It's not very fair to throw stuff at plants, but we understand that you're not here for fairness. You're here to kick the ever-lovin' excrement out of the local foliage. While you commit acts of atrocity on the flora, you cannot access the Store, and your Regens have been paused. May your future be delicious!

Brie's ball struck the thing's silken stalk with a dull **thwack**. The plant shuddered, but not a single grain of millet fell to the ground. The monstrosity flung up its leafy fronds and lashed out blindly with its spiky vines—sending the whole field into a frenzy, fluttering their papery blades and shaking their cylinder heads. The trio collectively held their breath, but Brie shook her head after squinting in annoyance at the System View. "No damage done. They have four hundred and twenty Health Points. I can't deal permanent damage without using Combat Dash."

"I could try using the Sewer Skewers again," Nacho suggested easily, practically *itching* to take out the long lances that were currently filling one of his Storage Slots. After a few rounds of testing in combat, the team had determined that the skewers were far more effective as a 'finisher', unless he had the opportunity to use them as a surprise weapon. His knife blades were more effective by far in general combat, mainly thanks to his Skills and the experience he had in using them.

"Look, you have so many good qualities… maybe one of

them that you could work on is your skewer use," Reuben stated in a mild tone, as though he were trying hard not to hurt his friend's feelings. "Even when they make sense, they aren't great weapons."

Brie agreed readily. "The fact that you can use them even decently well in combat is a testament to your skill, and I think you use them the best way that you can, but the things you can do with a knife versus the things you can do with the little pokey sticks? I agree that they're closer to punch daggers than anything else. Too bad only S-classers can wield 'em, or they'd be really useful."

"Fair enough." Nacho didn't bother to correct her terminology. For some reason, some random guild member had decided that saying 'Satiation player' was too much of a mouthful, and had opted to call them 'S-classers' instead. The concept had spread like a wildfire, with Body and Mind players soon becoming 'B-classers' and 'M-classers' respectively. Nacho had tried to point out that it was inefficient, since each class of player branched into seven different starting choices, but it was far too late to stop it at that point.

Beyond the newfangled slang that he wasn't sure he liked, he was actually fairly decent at using the Sewer Skewers. He tended to hold off, since they always put him in a bad position during combat. Because he was used to flowing from one move to another and attempting to deal death via a thousand cuts, switching over to a straightforward attacking style of 'insert rod into enemy, now do it again' was not in his future. "Wanna try again, Brie?"

"I think we just go for some of the smaller ones." Reuben shrugged his shoulders, getting a nod of approval from Brie. "We're not going to walk away from a field of easy credits. Credits that grow on vines? Awesome. Turning your back on them? Not a chance. It's in their name; these are *Stalkers*. Can't just walk away from stalkers. They'll stay on your mind and show up when you least expect it."

Nacho quickly ate a quarter portion of his own food and

chose to boost his Fitness. Finding that he was sitting at fifty-eight points, thanks to his bonuses—just a touch less than what a level sixty version of himself would be able to muster naturally—he grinned and started some completely unnecessary stretching. "How much damage are you doing with your adjusted strength?"

Brie's eyes skimmed across her internal calculator before she answered. "Both the pancake and yogurt together increase my Fitness by about forty Points. I'm hitting with a Fitness of sixty-one, so when it's combined with Reuben's Positive Vibes, I'm dealing fifty-five damage with the ranged attack. If I use my Combat Dash, that increases to seventy-five. You guys ready? I'm going."

Reuben, like Nacho, clearly wanted her to be careful, but he was also better equipped not to put his foot in his mouth due to how he went about it. "There's something rotten here, Brie. I don't mean the corpses, and I think we should proceed with caution."

"I would, I really would, but I'm far too busy…"

"No. Brie. *Brie*!" With a sinking feeling in his gut, Reuben knew what was coming.

"...Staying fresh, cheese bags!" Brie burst from the grass, laughing maniacally.

Nacho shook his head and patted his crestfallen friend on the arm. "You were the one that was pushy about her deciding on a catchphrase."

"Be quiet and help me help her!" the disgruntled Healer demanded as they started chasing after her.

CHAPTER TWO

Brie flashed like lightning through the meadow grasses. When she got in range of the grain monsters, a wave of energy tore across the meadow and struck the first Massive Millet Stalker. The resulting explosion of millet and black sap splashed across the ground while Brie was still fifteen feet away. She'd hit one of the plants and reduced its total Health from four hundred and twenty, to three hundred and forty-five.

"I'll have to hit it six more times to kill it!" She whirled her weapon around. "As a bonus, no pits opened up under my feet."

So far, combat seemed like it would be fairly easy and straightforward, as the Millet Stalkers didn't appear to be mobile. That hope was promptly defenestrated as the ground behind Brie boiled and green vines shot up from the soil. A concealed Millet Stalker burst from the midst of the writhing tendrils in a cloud of dust and grass and immediately threw vines around Brie.

She was so surprised that she didn't have time to activate her Defensive Whirl. One set of vines bound her limbs while another vine, full of spikes, did what it could to shred her armor. As she howled in pain, everything that wasn't a system-recognized armor was stripped from her—namely, the yellow satchel of lacrosse balls and her belt of Life Hack yogurt.

Nacho watched in horror at the scene as it unfolded. These things didn't *need* to eat people: they only needed to strip the flesh from a person's bones, then let that flesh decompose into fertilizer for their roots. That explained the field of fetid decay and the plants' lack of mouths.

Their name—Stalkers—suddenly made far too much sense. They had undeniably stalked Nacho and his friends; the entire discovery had been a trap. The monsters had known they were coming and pretended to be immobile, though it seemed that the pernicious grasses could only move when underground. One by one, the entire field of stalks started to force their vines and leaves back under the surface. Nacho knew right then that if he and his friends didn't get out of there immediately, they'd find themselves in a hopeless situation.

Nacho caught a glimpse of gore-splattered skeletons and the leftovers of armor and clothing peeking out from under the residual vines. These monsters had definitely done well against other players: they were smart, and they clearly used the fact that humans weren't used to plants being self-propelled to their advantage. "It's a colony of genius grains."

The cook's mind sharpened to a razor's edge as another of the creatures started to erupt from the ground behind them, though he couldn't suppress a hint of begrudging respect for such a well-planned ambush. Regardless, he wasn't going to worry about defense for the moment. Nacho gripped his cleaver and prepared to start choppin'. Thanks to the magic of the HungerCry knives, he would be able to damage the Tier two monsters—but he tempered that assumption with caution, as the Patrons had thrown him curve balls before.

Nacho's Small Blades ability provided him with two useful perks. First, it increased his damage when using his blades by thirty-eight percent and allowed him to strike successfully from a distance of six inches. Based on an upgrade he had gotten when increasing the Tier of his weapons, the HungerCry

Knives hit with double the normal damage expected of daggers—ten instead of five. Altogether, when Nacho hit, he hit *hard.* Adding in his food-based boosts and Reuben's Positive Vibes, he was slashing for twenty-five health… times four.

He shredded the Millet Monster attacking Brie like a renegade lawn mower, focused only on freeing his friend. Thankfully, he tore away the flaying vines in time, so she was still able to run. They retreated in hasty unison but were forced to stay in range because too many of the Millet Stalkers were rising out of the ground in their way. "What is this, a millet palisade?"

They turned just as a second Stalker Millet reached for Reuben, who had been throwing punches against the initial ambushing shoot. Sadly, his attacks weren't inflicting damage. Even though these things were technically food, enabling him to deal more damage per punch thanks to his Sausage Clips of Striking, it just wasn't enough to break through the fifteen percent mark required to deal lasting damage to a Tiered creature's health.

Brie dove in to save him as a thorn slashed at his leg from an unseen angle. Taking advantage of the fact that raising her Skills to Tier one resulted in ranged options, she flung out her hands and sent a tornado of her Defensive Whirl spinning furiously across the ground. The blast of whirling energy orbited Reuben protectively, blocking the vines and strikes of the two Millet Stalkers from landing.

Nacho couldn't help but appreciate how effective her ranged Defensive Whirl was at protecting her target from harm. It used fifteen percent of her total Hunger Points, but it could block ten attacks before wearing off. The brief respite allowed Reuben to escape to the forest, but it also meant that Nacho and Brie were effectively cut off from retreat.

Both of them found this situation perfectly acceptable.

Reuben threw his arms around himself. He didn't glow, but Brie did. The damage she'd taken from Millet Stalker healed over immediately, and she glared at him. At level nineteen, the Merchant of Soothing restored ninety-five Health with a single spell, which had come in *really* handy once they had started increasing their Fitness.

"Nacho! I don't think they can't travel through the ground if other roots are present. Get to the forest!" Once again, Reuben's ability to notice details astounded the cook.

Brie quickly threw her hands and set a second Defensive Whirl on Nacho. He wasn't about to complain, as it allowed him to put his entire attention on dealing damage.

He raced forward and ran *through* a smaller Stalker that sprang up out of the ground, his knives carving a path through its papery stem. It took him a moment to cut all the way to the other side, but the vines couldn't grab him because of the whirlwind protecting him. As the grain-heavy head crashed to the ground, he shot forward and reached the forest within a few strides, then whirled around and managed to get a System View on the smaller monster as he skidded to a stop.

Mini Millet Stalker

Effective Tier/Level:?

HP:?

Reuben had the same idea and called over with his information. "The Medium Millet Stalkers are Tier one, so we're facing a variety of giant, large, medium, and small."

Nacho dropped the System View and turned to his friend, aghast at the words he had just heard. "You're not saying there's a Tier *three* out there?"

Brie was still trapped in the middle of the literal killing field, but she charged the Mini Millet Stalker and hit it with her normal damage, opting not to activate her Combat Dash. The small Stalker's silken sack exploded and loose grain rained down. Nacho ran to the fallen kernels and started collecting them before the other monsters could close off their exit.

With a shout, Reuben danced forward from the trees, fists

raised, and struck once, twice… and the thing was down to one hundred and thirty-nine Health. Nacho sprang up, whisking the last handfuls of grain into a Storage Slot as he hacked into it twice with his cleaver; removing chunks large enough to keep a fire going for three hours at a time.

Damage dealt: 115/210.

"The small Tier zero have half the Health of the Tier twos!" he called out, attempting to raise their combat awareness.

"Good to know!" Reuben slammed his fists in a one-two punch that knocked the Tier zero Stalker for a loop. The second hit dropped the plant onto the ground in a detonation of grains. "Oh, look! We managed to kill *one* of the nasty weeds."

"Only twenty credits? This system is so unbalanced!" Brie thundered in frustration.

A Medium Millet Stalker grabbed Nacho from behind with a vine, trapping his arms against his sides, while another spiked version tried to rip off his armor. Failing at wedging its tendril beneath the metal edges, it instead attempted to shred his flesh like a shark. Even though his Skillet of Turtling nearly slipped off his back, he felt a rush of relief as the rest of his armor held. One thorn gashed him down his arm as another ripped through his jeans, opening a terrible jagged laceration in his thigh.

Health remaining: 68/126! Direct hits and glancing blows, into the ground you soon will go!

"*Abyss*, that hurt!" Bloodied and shaking with pain, he realized that the shredding vines were dealing thirty-four damage a pop. No wonder the field was littered with decaying bodies. If the

Tier one version did that amount of damage, how much did the Tier twos do?

Brie streaked forward, yelling insults and ducking vines as she threw her boosted damage against the Medium monster. The pulpy stem of the flora was blasted into soggy shreds, freeing Nacho from its vines. The cook should have run at that moment, but he wanted to make sure Brie didn't get trapped. He retreated slowly, his back to the woods, hacking and slashing until everything around him was raining green.

The entangling vines attempted to snag him again, but two things happened almost simultaneously. First, his body glowed, and Nacho felt the ghostly form of Reuben hugging him as his Health Points were restored to full.

Second, Brie's Defensive Whirl blocked the other plant monsters from hurting him, giving him the option of running to safety.

Regardless, he couldn't and *wouldn't* leave Brie. He turned and attacked more Stalkers from behind, creating a slashing flurry with his cleaver and chef's knife that generated a rain of green and grain snowflakes.

"Abyss, Nacho! Just leave so *I* can leave!" Brie was forced to slam her stick into the wounded Medium Millet, reducing its Health even further. If Nacho's math was right, the Medium Millet Stalker only had sixty-five Health Points left.

Before Brie could run to the edge of the forest, a pair of vines grabbed her ankles and dragged her back into the middle of a group of Stalkers, impervious to her furious struggles. "I'm at ten Health, people! I can't hurt the Tier twos without using my Skills, and I can't use my Skills again, or I'll go negative on Hunger!"

Brie had Athletic Endurance, which reduced all her Hunger Point costs by thirty-eight percent, but she'd been using her Skills near-constantly, with all of her combat snacks lying on the ground, far out of reach. Nacho finished off his target, leaving a splash of millet, leaves, and black blood in the process of collapsing as he rushed to her aid.

. . .

Congratulations! You have killed a Medium Millet Stalker
Tier 1 Creature = 0 Credits
Very palatable work!

Nacho raced forward and drew a Life Hack yogurt from his Storage Slot, tossing it to Brie, then stepped into harm's way. "Reuben! Keep me healed; this is gonna hurt!"

Two of the massive monsters and one of the mini monsters flogged him with their spiked vines, enraged that their original target of the fallen Berserker had been saved by his intercession.

Health remaining: 24/126!

Brie sucked down the yogurt and kicked her feet harder. Reuben hit Nacho with another heal just in time to save his life. Nacho's Health shot up to one hundred and twenty-six, only to be immediately sapped again as three of the angry grainy plants whipped him mercilessly.

Health remaining: 24/126! Wait, didn't we just *give you this message?*

While Nacho was shredded and healed, then shredded and healed again, he traded blows with the wounded Tier two, reducing it to forty-five Health Points.

"I got twenty-five Hunger back!" Brie yelled at him as she struggled to her feet. "Have I told you how much I hate eating and fighting at the same time? Get ready to run, Nacho, and this time, *stay* saved!"

In a final burst, thanks to the quarter portion of food, Brie used her Combat Dash on the heavily wounded Massive Millet Stalker. She hit the monster so hard that she burst through its main trunk, killing it and sprinting for the tree line without pausing. Unwilling to expend her efforts to bushwhack, the Berserker threw her Defensive Whirl in front of her to clear a path. She and Nacho bolted down the makeshift path, barely managing to escape and reach Reuben in the forest.

"I was wrong. I should have listened, and I am so sorry." Brie hunched over, gasping for breath, sweating, and clearly upset. "I thought the plants wouldn't be able to move."

"Talk later, move now." Nacho directed them deeper into the woods as monster after monster erupted from the noxious soil until the entire meadow had shifted to the edge of the forest. The vines had begun wiggling between the trees, grasping for fresh meat.

The System finally gave them some good news.

Congratulations, Player! Active Combat is over! That certainly was an exciting battle! There was blood, pain, and millet. Now, fighting Millet Stalkers might seem like a waste of time, but so does most of the farming you humans used to do… all the way until the harvest. Have fun shopping, and enjoy your Health and Mana Regen!

Nacho was intrigued by the idea of a harvest. Before satisfying his curiosity, he led his friends slightly south, where they sat on fallen trees and watched the Stalkers return to the center of the field and gather around the large piles of decayed meat.

"I feel terrible. I lost my lacrosse balls, my yogurt belt, and… I nearly got us killed." Brie shook her head and groaned as she habitually reached for a snack, only to remember that all of her extraneous gear had been stripped away. That hand instead shot out to grip Nacho near the elbow. "You have to forgive me. We've been fighting such easy Tier zeros lately that I forgot what the real monsters can do."

Nacho pulled her in for an awkward half-hug. "It's okay, Brie. We made it out alive, and that's the only important thing. Now… you guys stay here. Since the herd has returned to the middle of the meadow, I want to go gather those dead monsters and process out the Putrid Mana. Maybe that will make all of this worth it."

Reuben blinked owlishly as he tried to parse what had just entered his ear-holes. "Are you seriously going to sit there and tell me you're going back into the killing fields?"

"I refuse to miss out on the chance to make an Epic donut." His peak examples of culinary creations had been stuck at 'Rare' for so long that he assumed the quality of his ingredients had to be what was holding him back. "I want to get Taye and Kristie up here. Now that we know the Millet Stalkers' secret, we can take them out from a distance. Well… at least the weaker ones. Once we level the playing field, we can annihilate the rest of them."

Reuben started clapping in admiration. "That's why we love you, Nacho. One minute you're talking about forgiveness, and the next… *annihilation*. What's *not* to love?"

Nacho gave them a wolfish grin and crept back toward the fields, staying low. He did not know whether hiding behind the underbrush would help, as the monsters had no discernible sensory organs, but he was going to lean into his stealth as much as he possibly could.

"This harvest is long past due. Imma make a donut outta you."

CHAPTER THREE

Since Nacho had upgraded his Ingredient Processing ability to Tier one, specifically level nineteen, he didn't need to pull the Tier two Massive Millet Stalker into the relative safety of the forest. He could process the Putrid Mana out of the grains remotely. He bought bright yellow sacks from the Store with 'It's Juxta-bag' written on the front in big red letters.

Brie was clearly still feeling concerned about their reactions to her reckless charge, so she didn't say a word against his request for her to keep watch. There was a good chance that they were going to be ambushed by other monsters, or by any of the Millet Stalkers that might've found a way through the roots covering the ground. The cook had to work quickly, because he only had a certain amount of time before the monstrous grain liquified—and he had no idea when that would happen.

To turn the grain into food, he needed to have at least three ingredients. Nacho knew that he planned to make donuts from the millet flour, but which recipe should he use? In his *All Things Chicken and Breakfast Happiness* chapters, there was a recipe for chicken donuts, but Nacho wasn't feeling that adventurous. He turned to the section on *Jimmy's Fast Food for Everyone* and decided upon 'Jimmy's Belly Bombers', a yeasty raised donut with a sugary glaze.

Nacho flopped his *Aria* onto a rock and started reading over the ingredient list for the Belly Bombers. Wizards might have spell books, but he only had access to a cookbook. Thus far, he had incorporated three full cookbooks into his *Aria*: *Colonel White Beard's All Things Chicken and Breakfast Happiness*, *Jimmy Fast Food for Everyone*, and *Hiccup's Cantina Cuisine*. He had his eye on one more, *Insect Eats: Delicious Bug Recipes*, since they kept encountering bug monsters. He shook his head and grimaced. "Somehow I know if I get that, I wouldn't see another insect for weeks…"

Even though he was on a time limit, running a test on the grain was an important step. If he didn't have a recipe that could actually make use of the millet flour like he hoped, then going out and harvesting it was going to be a waste. More than that, it was going to be a threat against his very life, thanks to the monsters. Nacho shook his head and muttered, "All of this… for a *chance* at an Epic donut. Is this reality insane or what?"

His basic strategy was to process four cups of millet at a time, or at least enough to get four cups of the crushed millet. Thanks to his constant testing of his abilities, Nacho was almost certain he could get the Putrid Mana out and *then* pound the grains into flour. To be fair, he wasn't absolutely certain, as sometimes the rules were funky when it came to things that the Patrons didn't want players to be able to do. For some reason… they *hated* the fact that he was a Satiation Player, especially that he had maxed out the class line by becoming a Common Cook.

Nacho clanged his knives together—he didn't need to do it to get the Juxtaposition's attention, since the Patrons were always watching, but he liked the symbolism of it. It reminded him of his purpose.

"Here we go." He could remove the Putrid Mana from ingredients at a maximum distance of fifteen feet. He crouched, waiting for the perfect moment to strike, watching for the wind to shift in his favor, the monsters in the area to move in a specific manner, and *ju~ust* the correct angle—*there*! His cleaver slashed seemingly lazily to his front, but nearly fifteen feet away, a grain spike was shaved off a Tier two monster they had slain.

Reuben held a bag open, and the enormous seed head that Nacho had targeted split off the mangled stem and bounced across the ground like a fumbled football. It took a little bit of finagling, but the Healer was able to catch it directly in the sack. Reuben gasped as he hefted the bag. "That was wild! Also, this is abyssally *heavy*. Tier two stuff gets heavy real quick, huh? Is it more dense, or is it the magic?"

"Couldn't tell you for sure." Nacho felt like a real sorcerer as he processed out Putrid Mana and swept the millet seeds from one of the garishly colorful Juxtaposition sacks into another. He managed to get nineteen rounds of the seeds processed before he approached the danger zone for Mana loss, yielding him eighty cups of whole millet.

Four cups of the millet weighed six-point-two-eight pounds, so he would end up with a little over six *hundred* pounds of flour, thanks to its strange weight. The System kindly let him store the twenty sacks in his Storage Slots; an extra-dimensional space which the Patrons allowed Players to stuff with the same basic items. Yet for some strange reason, Nacho wouldn't have been able to wedge even one single stalk of wheat in with the millet. Stacking in a single slot was exclusive to each item, or type of item.

"This is crazy, man. Last time you tried something wild like processing at a distance, all you did was get in the way." Reuben laughed as millet seeds practically *hopped* into his garish bag. "What changed?"

"Practice makes better, my friend." Nacho was almost *always* practicing at least *some* portion of his skills or thinking of a way to use them in a better, more efficient manner. Nineteen rounds of Ingredient Processing later, the level twenty-one ingredients, at fifty credits per every four cups, had earned Nacho a total of nine hundred and fifty credits.

When he informed his team of the windfall, it was clear that Brie was trying not to be jealous over it. She had received a mere sixty credits for killing the Tier two monster, and Nacho perfectly understood her frustrations. "I know that you're upset about the credit scaling, but you need to remember that we're *wild* outliers. The fact that all three of us can hit above our Tier is already fairly unique. We aren't supposed to be fighting monsters this strong, not in a serious way. We should, if we are following the scripted plan, be currently working our way through hordes of Tier *one* creatures."

"I'm not *mad*, I just think it's completely ridiculous that you are able to pull in so many credits from a single kill like this." Brie clearly wasn't getting it, and combined with her earlier recklessness, it was clear that she needed a reality check on. "Just doesn't seem fair."

"*Fair*, is it, Brie?" The cook impaled her with a stone cold glare, making her freeze in her tracks for just an instant; a trick he had learned during his life of killing people for profit. "The Juxtaposition isn't *fair*. End of story. I chose a class that only one percent of the population had the option to select. How many of those people in the same position would have taken it? A fraction of a *fraction*. Add that on to the fact that I should be almost *entirely* a support class, unable to fight at all, with no credits for any kills I make, not to mention how quickly the ingredients go bad?"

Nacho tried to rein in his anger, so he took a deep, controlled breath before continuing. "I would say most cooks get to process maybe—*maybe*—one kill a day. Our team is ahead of the curve in almost every single area. Get your head out of the clouds, and try not to get us killed because you're mad that we aren't going 'fast enough'."

That was the end of any conversation for *quite* a while, he was sure. Even so, the situation reminded Nacho that he was glad he'd chosen to be a Satiation Player. More than that, he was happy that he had been able to spend a few years as a fighter and knew how best to utilize the choices he had been given.

"Should we be worried about those?" While Nacho and Brie worked in silence to package everything up, Reuben had kept an eye on the shifting Stalkers. "Most of the time, they stay in the center of the meadow, but it looks like a few found a passage between the trees on the other side of the forest. If we want to keep the monsters bottled up, do you think we should dig out the space between the trees to block their escape? It's already getting dark."

"Better now than after they get somewhere else and make a mess," Nacho agreed calmly as they purchased shovels from the Store. Reuben had gone cheap; he had purchased a Common Tier zero shovel for twenty credits, and it showed. The red metal tip was poorly attached to the yellow handle, wobbling slightly as it appeared in the Healer's hand. When he drove it into the ground the very first time, the handle snapped.

"Cheap and useless?" Reuben wiped sweat off his head.

"The Patrons won't remind you to buy Tier one stuff now that you're Tier one. They'll just mess with you." Nacho raised up his own red and yellow spade. "I got a Very Uncommon Tier one shovel for only forty credits. It's super dull, and the handle is splintery, but it should work."

Brie nodded and decided to break her silence. "I went with Nacho's recommendation."

"Sure," Reuben erupted good-naturedly, throwing his hands and busted shovel into the air. "Here's the guy trying to save us some money, and all I get is 'you should know better'. I see how it is. You're conspiring against me."

"Yes." Nacho admitted freely, earning himself some side-eye as Reuben bought an upgraded tool. From there, they all worked quickly. Since they were all Tier one, they were far beyond the human limits of strength from old Earth. They didn't stop digging until their trench had reached bedrock, which they hoped would prevent the Stalkers from escaping, just as the tree roots seemed to do.

The sun had fully set by the time the culvert was done, and neither Nacho nor his friends wanted to stay in the forest near Murdering Millet Meadow. The regrettable alternative was a hard march back to a river to set up camp on the beach, and agreeing upon watch rotations. The worst part was that there was no way to get a message confirming their wellbeing to the Chips Guild, or to warn their people to watch out for plant monsters.

Nacho knew that those he'd left in charge would worry, as his team was supposed to have returned by now. Still, there was nothing to be done, since no one who wanted to see the morning would travel through unfamiliar territory at night. The Dinner Party would just need to camp out and walk back the next morning, hopefully early enough to calm the masses.

The Guild Leader rested with his back propped against a dead tree, a pretty good seat that gave him an excellent view of his surroundings. He'd stowed his Sunday Brunch Armor and was lounging in his boots, jeans, and hoodie. He scanned the area nearly unconsciously as he started thinking back to the Probability Vision. It felt good to be out hunting with his friends again, just the three of them, like their first weeks in the Juxtaposition. That had been what he'd wanted more than anything else during the three long years he'd been alone as the Shadow Killer.

"Why did I mess that all up by starting a guild?" He shook his head at his previous actions, trying to remember the logic that had dragged him from 'I will keep us alive at all costs' over to 'I should take responsibility for a bunch of random people'. Most of the time, he wasn't bothered; being allowed to test and experiment as much as he wanted was a pretty worthwhile perk. Most of the time, that meant that Nacho was in his kitchen cooking a dozen things at once, and had to pretend not to be annoyed by the intermittent interruptions.

Assassinations had been a *stupendous* teacher of focus, but in the kitchen with pasta boiling, sauce reducing, and bread baking? He could have any number of dishes going all at once, and if he didn't address each one with a certain amount of aplomb and attention to minutiae, the food would be ruined. Any loss further cost him whatever amount of credits he had invested in the process, as well as the time he had spent.

Then there were 'the Brittanys', his new kitchen assistants that always pointed out his mistakes before he served the food. Even now, he wasn't entirely certain how those two teens had ended up as his kitchen staff, but Britt and Brittany loved to cook and had dreamed of opening a restaurant. Who said dreams didn't come true in the Juxtaposition? They had certainly been a lifesaver for him, the guy who had survived on Earth only thanks to pre-packaged food.

Now the Brittanys organized the weekly menus, took care of the logistics, and were in charge of hiring additional help as needed so that the huge number of guild members didn't starve to death waiting for him to make meals or return from missions. They couldn't *make* the food, but they kept things running smoothly by rationing out the vast quantities of prepared dishes that he left for their usage.

That reminded him that it had been weeks since he looked over his guild status, and he pulled it up to take a quick peek.

Chips Guild Stat Sheet

Total Guild Credits: 859,993 credits

Total Number of Members: 5,536

Guild Master: Eli Naches

Alternate Guild Master: Daniel Chronour

Third Alternate: Reuben Colby

Settlements controlled: Armor Mountain, Jalapeño Town, Tortilla Flats.

. . .

Reuben was attempting to relax next to the fire on a Common Tier one camping chair, constantly having to adjust his balance because it was so uncomfortable and rickety. At any moment, it could snap and send him tumbling to the ground, but he didn't seem to mind. He was savoring a root beer from his white and yellow Yeti horn, but his eyes snapped over when Nacho let out a pained grunt. "Whatcha looking at, Nacho? Doing some shopping, or are you still waffling on that insect cookbook? If you want my two credits in warning… no one is going to want to eat bug gyros."

"You know nothing!" Nacho shot back without thinking about it. "I've been adding bugs to your meals for days, and you never said a word. Still, that's not the issue right now. I'm actually looking at the Chips Guild Stat Sheet."

"I *knew* that was a cockroach," Reuben mumbled as he spat a wad of phlegm into the fire. "Brie tried to convince me it was a date. I *knew* it."

"When should I start taking benefits from the Guild?" Nacho desperately wanted to get a handle on the conversation, and that manifested itself by the words tumbling out of his mouth in a rush. His friends stared at him with concern, and he coughed lightly to try to cover his embarrassment. "Sorry if that was a little... explosive, but it's been on my mind for a while. At some stage, we're going to have to grab credits from the guild's coffers and start leveling ourselves again. We need to get to Tier two, even though that'll make life harder, but we're not getting there without outside financial support. That's what the guild really needs to do: support us until we are essentially nuclear deterrents for other guilds."

Yet despite the need to level, the idea of having so many Tiers of people to feed exhausted him. He'd have to prepare *three* different ranks of the same food—Tier zero, one, and two—to safely sustain everyone. It wasn't like he could skip the weaker people; most players in this hostile world were still Tier zero, not to mention the main source of their guild's income.

"We could level ourselves now," Reuben suggested eagerly,

not wanting to put off gaining power for even a moment when it was offered. "We have enough. For the three of us, at seventy-five thousand credits each, we could do it. If Old Bill, Kala, or Zack complains... we give them the bird."

"Obscene finger gestures?" Nacho queried after Reuben paused leadingly, clearly hoping someone would bite.

"Au *contraire*!" Reuben tipped his bottle toward Nacho in thanks for the opening. "Not a rude gesture; a polite one! You cook up some fried chicken, Colonel's original recipe. We *literally* give them the bird, deep-fried to perfection in a special blend of herbs and spices."

"I... fail to see your point." Nacho rubbed at the stubble that had grown in on his chin, an uneven mess that he wasn't able to do anything about while they were in the field. "Because you failed to convince *me*, how would you present your case to the people holding the purse strings and pitchforks, so they don't incite an angry mob? Let's just talk to the council when we get back."

"*Boo~oo*, my way is better." Reuben clicked his tongue, though he gave up without another complaint. "On the plus side, we *are* getting the ambitious types, thanks to my Marketing ability. Not only did we win the Dragon Spear—excuse me—the *Sewer Skewers*, but we're really starting to have an impressive city."

"Three cities, or settlements, at least." Nacho leaned back against the dead tree and scooped up some sand to let it fall between his fingers. "I'm not sure how much I like all of the... people. That is, the problems all the people bring."

"So give up and leave them to fend for themselves," Brie called from the darkness, knowing that he would never do something so callous, despite all his complaints. "No? Didn't think so. You might as well stick to worrying about problems you can *solve*. On that note, should we have tried to use the Sewer Skewers in the Millet fight? Would those have helped?"

Reuben laughed at the thought of the cook trying to stab the wiggly monsters with a thin, pointy object. "It might've helped Nacho stab *himself*. I've only ever seen him successfully fight with the skewers against rats."

"I'm amazing with them in enclosed spaces where my enemies can't get away very easily." Nacho let conversation die off, knowing that he had nothing to explain. He was great with the weapons, compared to what anyone else could do with them.

He smirked, knowing that it wasn't a fair comparison. Only Satiation players could use the Sewer Skewers, and he was the only S-classer that had survived this long. The subconscious use of the slang term caused Nacho to shake his head and grimace. "Aw, man. Now *I'm* calling them that? This reeks of a Marketing Skill... Reuben, did you have something to do with people calling Satiation players S-classers?"

"Snore, snore," Reuben stated aloud, attempting to avoid the conversation.

"You can't just say 'snore' and actually expect me to think you're asleep!" Nacho threw a moist pancake at his snickering friend, resigning himself to the fact that the conversation would just need to wait until another day.

CHAPTER FOUR

"Before we decide to make a whole proposal for raising the three of us to Tier two…" In the predawn light, Nacho added another stick to the fire and stood, brushing his hands off. Sweet smoke filled the air, and the river bordering their camp gurgled over smooth stones. Everyone was awake and wanted to continue the discussion from the previous night with a clear head. "…let's talk cash flow. We're receiving ten credits a day per member on average. That means most people are earning one hundred credits before taxes kick in, and ninety credits just isn't that much once they get to a certain level. Since tax percentages haven't increased by any perceptible amounts, the large majority are evidently hunting only until their daily needs are met, then stopping."

"We need to incentivize growth without throwing them to the wolves. Is that what you're saying?" Reuben stood and moved his terrible camping chair to a different spot, as if a different patch of dirt would help the rickety perch feel more comfortable. "Too easy. For people that are already searching after success, we offer a lot of money for leveling classes and Skills. People with more power die less and earn more. It's a win-win. Aggregate success, baby. By being successful now, they'll be more successful in the future."

"If we're helping Tier zeroes to level, then *we* should be fine getting some help with reaching Tier two," Brie insisted from the tree line. "We have to start preparing for the war with the CrossHumans, and that reminds me… we need to talk to the Brittanys. The last time I spoke to them, they mentioned they might have a lead on a Brewer. If we had a source of Mana in Active Combat, more spell support suddenly becomes possible."

"A Brewer? Why am I just hearing about this now?" Nacho felt frozen in place. If a Brewer existed, that would *radically* change combat for them going forward.

"You heard all of this before; you just weren't *listening*," Brie told him matter-of-factly, pointing her lacrosse stick at him accusingly. "Before they came to us, the Brittanys had been searching for an alleged Brewer in their area, but they were attacked by CrossHumans and needed to escape to Armor Mountain for safety instead. We had this conversation right next to you when you were preparing breakfast, probably a week ago?"

"Can confirm," Reuben informed Nacho dryly.

"Was this when they were rehashing that ghost story the Patrons were trying to foist off on us? The Walking Freds?" Nacho questioned them uneasily. He still wasn't sure what to make of the tall tales of a guild full of necromancers and zombies. There just weren't enough people with a class like that for it to be a real thing. Probably. "I tend to zone out whenever someone talks about that."

Who had time for sensationalist gossip when they had *actual* threats to be concerned with? There were two big guilds in the surrounding area that the Chips had to consider: the Midnight Fist, and the Credit Machine. So far, no violence had occurred, but neither guild had reached out to talk about joining, let alone agreed to their proposed treaty of non-aggression. Nacho wasn't sure how to approach the other guilds—other than the runners he had sent with letters that went unanswered—and he had enough work to do. Just the idea of all that was left to accomplish made him dizzy with the possibilities.

"I give up!" Reuben burst to his feet, grabbed his chair, and tossed it in the fire hard enough to scatter the coals. "I hate this chair, and I'd rather sit on the ground."

"Doing alright there, friend?" Nacho chuckled at the seething Healer.

"That's enough out of you." Reuben tried to be serious about his order, but the smile twitching just under the surface showed what he really thought of the situation. "I think we've given enough proof that you need to buy that Skill… um. What was it—right! Feasting Feats? I think you've earned it, and it'll help out a lot, right?"

Nacho threw his head back and groaned. "Picking out a new Skill is risky and expensive. You have *no* idea if it'll be useful, and neither do I. The information on it is lackluster at best, and purposefully misleading at worst. Do we really want to do this right now?"

"Yes!" Reuben and Brie agreed vehemently at the same time, giving each other a rare smile at the unusual perfect synchronization of their responses. Reuben sank into the dirt next to the fire. "Dude, if you could increase your food output, we'd get more credits. Then you wouldn't even need to be 'embezzling' from the guild, like Old Bill whines about. We have over five *thousand* people to feed. If it'll make you feel better, tell us about this Feasting Feats Skill one *last* time."

"No! I'm so sick of-" Brie was cut off as Nacho launched into an explanation.

"Here's the thing." Nacho drew a hand through his hair. "Buying a Skill is expensive if you want to buy something that is guaranteed to be useful. As an example of what not to do, Reuben's chair, or his shovel from last night. You buy the cheap stuff, and it's terrible."

"How is it that *I'm* being insulted for being frugal when *you're* so worried about every little credit? For shame!" Reuben gasped dramatically and blinked his eyes at Nacho, pretending to be on the verge of crying.

"Nice try. I know for a fact that your eyes stop producing tears as soon as you hit Tier one." Nacho continued without missing a beat as Reuben wiped at his own eyes in sudden concern. "If you *don't* spend a bunch of credits on a powerful Skill, you wind up having to buy a potion that removes the Skill. The base cost of a Skill-removal potion is a *thousand* credits. To buy another Skill Slot is five thousand credits the first time around. Then there's the real reason I've been dragging my feet on purchasing another Skill… Skill Boxes in dungeons will give you Rare skills for a reduced cost. So far, we haven't run into any, but at the rate we're going, I have high hopes that we will soon."

"You can't pin your hopes on that. You're getting practically no sleep these days." Brie approached the edge of the fire light with her shovel, and put the smoldering coals out with a scoop of wet dirt. "You've been needing the Feasting Feats for a while now. We have enough credits, so don't worry about being careful with money. You'll earn it back, and faster than before."

"Ugh… as always, your arguments are good, and you know I *want* it. If it's gonna be like this, I just can't keep saying no." Nacho accessed the Store and found the Feasting Feats Skill, reading it over one last time as he hoped for the best.

FEASTING FEATS: Have to cook for a battalion? Need to feed an army? This Skill will spread out the joy of cooking and feed the multitudes with a limited amount of food, as long as your guests have some credits to spare. Make a little go a long way, through the power of money!

"Do it," Brie demanded when she caught him still hesitating. "You should've bought this a long time ago. You've been cooking up a storm, and now you can finally get something from it."

"Okay. I'll buy it, um, right now." Nacho spoke the words, but he didn't really mean them. Not yet. He stalled by checking the Store for prices instead. For the Common Tier one Feasting Feats Skill, it was four hundred credits. The top-Tier Epic version would be eight hundred credits just to get it at level zero.

Screaming internally, he spent the requisite credits to buy the best version of it, and added what the Store required to bring it to level nineteen before reading the notifications that had popped up.

Wow, CookMeister McMoneybags! You're finally buying another ability? It took you long enough. Congratulations on taking this important and brave step toward self-improvement. Now, you can inflict your iffy cooking on more people at once! We feel for them, but it'll be fun to watch!

Would you like to know more about your Feasting Feats ability?

Yes / No

Nacho chose 'yes', glaring at the message.

With the Epic rarity, Feasting Feasts multiplies the amount of food you create by the level of the Skill! For example, at Level 2, the amount of food is doubled. Already, your HungerCry knives are doubling your yield when you chop, chop! Now, you get even more out of every bite!

We saw you cranked this skill up to Level 19, sight unseen! That's a lot of trust in your Skill selecting skills. Should we see if it paid off? … It did! Now if you make a dozen eggs, you'll end up with 228 eggcellent edibles.

Best of all, here's your Tier 1 bonus: you can choose up to five places where people can access the food! At the low, low cost of 15% of the sale price, you become a vending machine, and people no longer need to come bother you directly for food. It'll just appear in front of them, wherever you specify, within 500 feet.

Caution! As this is meant to generate a feast for many, and not for one, only a single portion of each meal created through the use of this Skill can be eaten by each person!

Note: Hooray! Now you can be shoved into a small room and forced to cook for a whole guild without them ever needing to interact with you! Perhaps you want to keep some of your Skill's usefulness to yourself, hmm?

Reuben snapped his fingers as Nacho stopped staring blankly into the distance. "All right, Nacho. Let's see your character sheet. I want to see all your slots filled."

"That's what she…" Brie abruptly cleared her throat and halted her own joke. "Yeah, Nacho, let's see it."

With a shrug, Nacho showed them his entire Stat Sheet.

Eli 'Nacho' Naches
Class: Junior League Chef
Level: 14
Experience Points: 98700 to Level 15!
Current Credits: 6337 (19017 total Dinner Party pool)

Build Type: Balanced, Delayed
Body:

- *Fitness: 20*
- *Metabolic Efficiency: 20*

Mind:

- *Mental Energy: 20*
- *Circuit: 20*

Satiation:

- *Hunger: 100*
- *Thirst: 100*

Health Points: 50
Bonus Physical Damage: 10%
Health Regen: 20% Health Regen/minute
Total Mana Pool: 40
Bonus Spell Damage: 10%
Mana Pool Regen: 20% Mana Regen/minute

Skill Slots (4/4)

- *Small Blades (Passive) Level 19: 38% bonus damage on all knife attacks.*

Tier 1 Enhancement: Your blades can slice from up to 6 inches away from their edge!

No Mana, Hydration, or Metabolic Cost

- *Ingredient Processing (Active) Level 19: Remove Putrid Mana from monsters up to Level 21.*

Tier 1 Enhancement: Process ingredients from 15 feet away!

Mana Cost = 5%
Hydration Cost = 5%
Metabolic Cost = 5%

- *Cooking Magic (Active) Level 19: Create food that enhances a single stat by 95% of maximum.*

Tier 1 Enhancement: Throw magic into a food item you cooked from 15 feet away!

Mana Cost = 5%
Hydration Cost = 5%
Metabolic Cost = 5%

- *Feasting Feats (Active) Level 19: Cook 19 times the food you're currently preparing!*

Tier 1 Enhancement: you can choose up to five places which people can use like a vending machine! At the low, low cost of 15% of the sale price, people no longer need to come bother you directly for food. It'll just appear in front of them, wherever you specify, within 500 feet of the food source.

Caution! As this is meant as a feast for many, and not for one, only a single portion of each meal created through the use of this skill can be eaten by each person!
Mana Cost = 10%
Hydration Cost = 10%
Metabolic Cost = 10%

Nacho was a little troubled by the realization that Feasting Feats used so many Mana, Thirst Points, and Hunger Points simultaneously. Hopefully that was just when setting the pickup points, and not for each individual portion he made. Even so, he took a moment to marvel over how much easier it would make his life. Namely: no more constant interruptions from hungry people. If he could cook the same amount of food, but generate nineteen times the portions, even with losing a fifteen percent tax, it *should* make him a lot more money. "That's still a net increase of over sixteen hundred percent."

"Seems like that was *totally* worth it," Reuben gleefully announced. "We should *lock* you in the kitchen with how useful this is gonna be!"

That earned the Healer a sharp look from the cook, even though he knew that Reuben had not been able to see the flavor text that had warned about that exact scenario.

They started walking toward home, discussing what other Skills they might want, but Nacho convinced the other two to wait. He just *knew* that they'd find a Skill Box in a dungeon eventually, but his arguments weren't what put an end to the conversation. No, the conversation died because Brie hoisted her weapon and started yelling. "We have people coming. Look alive!"

Their heightened awareness lasted only until a familiar voice reached them, as Taye shouted a happy, "*There* you are!"

Kristie's voice followed. "We were so worried! No way would we leave you out here on your own."

"Hey there, buckos! That was pretty rude of you to make us worry about you like that." Abby was with them as well, sending a mock glare their way. "Running off without your Brunch Force buddies?"

A good-natured clamor arose as everyone tried to speak at once, but Taye forestalled it with a wave to grab their attention. "Listen, it's good to see you, but we have to get back to Armor Mountain and make a stop at the Tortilla Flats on the way. We have some, uh, *issues*."

CHAPTER FIVE

Nacho couldn't get many specifics about the situation from the Breakfast Club. All three said it was a 'see for yourself' situation and were hesitant to share too many details. Nacho pushed, but Brie eventually told him to drop it. "Why? Why can't I just know ahead of time?"

"We don't want to push you one way or the other. We want you to make your own decision," Abby insisted in an attempt to soothe his troubled mind.

The cook wasn't enjoying the deflections. "At this point, I'm thinking that I'm going to need to be ready to fight. Is that better?"

They could only shrug helplessly, and all too soon, it was time for them to part ways. Taye, Kristie, and Abby needed to get back to the Bove's Lair, but they had detoured in order to seek out the missing chef. There were reports of a new dungeon, as well as hints that the CrossWorld Portal had been found, and they had been tasked with checking both out.

"Shoot, I forgot that we need to clearly mark the path back to the Millet Meadow." Nacho put action to words and started slicing lines into the trees as they walked to make sure they could come back and clean the place out with a large group of volunteers looking to earn credits. "We're gonna get our best warriors in there, kill those plants, and process millet until I've milked every credit out of these monsters."

As he reached to cut into a tree, a small face popped out of the underbrush. Nacho barely kept himself from throwing a knife into it, until he recognized the green-hued fur and markings. "You… the plant-dog hybrid. You've gotten big; are you hostile yet?"

In reply, the sad-faced dog rolled over and offered him a green belly in a sign of submission. Nacho narrowed his eyes and growled, "I don't believe you. There aren't any monsters out there that *aren't* hostile. Not without a Skill to tame them."

"Who are you talking to, Nacho?" Brie ran over when she noticed his defensive posture, ready to take the fight to whoever was coming after them. Once she saw the dog, she froze in place. "Is that *the* green dog? The one that loves you? I haven't seen that since we rescued you from Crave!"

"No," Nacho firmly replied. "That is a green *monster* that looks like a dog."

Reuben came over to join the conversation, and tapped on his chin as he heard their debate. "Easy way to check… here, pooch."

The dog looked from Nacho to Reuben, clearly nervous. After a moment of hesitation, it rolled to its feet and slowly belly-crawled over, its vine-like tail wagging uncertainly. Reuben kept his hand out and gently scratched the dog behind the ear, both of them gradually relaxing. "You know what's going on with this little fella, Nacho?"

"Yes. It's been following me practically since the Juxtaposition began," Nacho stated harshly, not taking his eyes off the creature for a moment. "It's been waiting for the right moment to strike, I'm sure of it."

"Any reason you think that way, beyond it being a wild creature?" Brie wondered as she also scratched the dog. The verdant canine leaned into her hand with a satisfied chuff, and a happy smile took over her face. "I can't believe I never realized how much I miss dogs."

"A mental attack?" Knives spun into Nacho's hands as he eyed the dog warily. "Do you feel a compulsion to take it back to base? To do what it wants? Is it in your head?"

"'Course not," Reuben scoffed, patting the dog and stepping away. "We'd never risk our people, no matter how cute this little gal is. Would we? No we *wouldn't.*"

"See? You're losing your mental faculties! You're acting like a child!" Nacho raised his cleaver and stepped forward to put an end to the threat once and for all, only to be blocked by Brie.

"That's baby talk, and it's something people did with animals even *before* the world ended." The Berserker stared at him coldly. "I'm not going to stand by and watch you kill a non-hostile dog."

"It's a Tier *one* monster at this point!" Nacho pointed his knife at the beast, which even the System View couldn't identify. All it gave him was question marks for its name, level, and Tier. "When are we going to take it seriously? When it hits Tier two and goes on a rampage? I knew I should have taken care of this before you ever got involved."

The little dog scampered backward into the underbrush with a whine at the naked hostility in Nacho's face. In a flash, it had vanished. No matter how carefully he searched, he couldn't find it again. "Great. Just great. Now there's a stealth-specialized Tier one monster hunting me, which can seemingly find me no matter where I go."

Reuben glanced at Brie, spinning his index finger around his temple. "Something tells me the paranoia is getting to you, man. That thing clearly only wanted to be your friend. Maybe it's a type that can be domesticated."

"I'm not letting it get away next time," Nacho promised them, only to get shaking heads and hints of anger in reply. He grumbled at their foolish stubbornness, feeling put-upon. "My paranoia is what's kept us alive this long."

Awkward silence surrounded them as they continued traveling homeward. He didn't mind; he knew that he was in the right. For now, Nacho wanted to get back to his people, figure out the problem, and make some definite decisions about their next move. Not counting the green dog—even though he *wanted* to—they had three big issues: the CrossWorld Portal and Cross-Humans, the possible trouble with other guilds, and finally whatever was happening within his own guild.

The three of them crossed the distance back to Armor Mountain as rapidly as possible, managing the trek in just shy of six hours. With their stats, that meant that they had just been nearly fifty miles from home. They approached from the north, bringing them through one of their new settlements: the Tortilla Flats.

The town had been established on the northern slope of the hill known as Armor Mountain; in fact one of its 'walls' was the sheer face of the 'mountain'. The area had been fairly well wooded, but many of the trees had been chopped down to make way for tents and houses. They'd named the northern wall the 'Tortilla Shell', and while the original northern ramparts of the core guild area were still present, they'd added a gate. Combining fortifications with apartments had allowed them to hack the system once again, just as they had done with the Great Wall Apartments surrounding the original guildhall on the eastern limestone cliffs.

The Tortilla Shell was pretty impressive, even if no one would ever know it without seeing the inner workings. Beyond the arrow slits stood apartments where the remnants of the Final Victory Guild had come to live, along with some other members who could tolerate Zack Puck's leadership style. While the Chips guild had annexed the guild through the death of the previous leader and winning the remainder from the bet that Crave had made against the System, Nacho had foolishly allowed himself to be swayed into allowing them to self-govern, which had translated into Zack having a say in the big decisions made by the guild at large.

Normally, that wouldn't have been a terrible issue, but it

turned out that Zack was neither a nice nor a reasonable person. He was more a 'collect skull trophies of your enemies for decor' type of man.

As their luck would have it, Zack himself waited by the drawbridge as it was lowered over the trench in front of the Tortilla Shell. "Ay, Na-chode! Ha, just kiddin', bud. Know what I realized? We need a crazy moat, man. With alligators and stuff in it. Didja know we can buy alligators from the Store? I checked. It would be awesome."

Nacho pulled sharply at the shoulder straps of his gigantic mobile kitchen backpack, tightening them so that he wouldn't be tempted to take a swing at the eminently punchable person. Pots swayed. Pans clanked. Zack watched the obvious fidgeting with a sneer and a dark look in his eye.

The bellicose man possessed tall, beefy features, with jet-black hair and dark brown eyes. If a particular trigger-happy, egg-guzzling fairytale villain were brought to life, about fifty percent more narcissism and gym-bro would need to be inserted to accurately capture this man that was able to forcibly influence the decisions of the guild council.

Reuben stepped in before his lovely wife could deploy what was about to pop out of her mouth. Brie loathed Zack. Although both were Berserkers, all similarities ended there. "You know, Zack, if you want to buy the Moat Alligator Info Pack and study up, no one here would stop you. If you want to finance your alligator moat with Tortilla Flat money, that might be great. We're not the sort of people to shoot down your ideas."

Brie tapped her weapon on the drawbridge. "How are you going to ensure the alligators stay in the trench? How do you stop them from attacking other guild members who come walking up?"

"I'd just *reason* with them, pretty lady. Like any other beast, they'll follow their alpha." Zack exhaled heavily, as though explaining himself was a personal trial. He paused and snapped his fingers, and Nacho could practically see the candle light up above his head as an idea struck. "Or I'd give them meat! Like, feed them in the same places so they would stay around. Maybe I *could* train them to not attack the people I like."

"Reuben had a great idea. The Alligator Training Info Pack might give you the solution." Nacho gripped the backpack straps tightly, channeling his annoyance into his clutch as he walked past the combative town leader. "Perhaps run it by Kala and see what she has to say."

"Kala?" Zack somehow managed to inject his laughter with sneering. "I know we're supposed to be something like co-leaders, but it's never going to happen. I mean… look at me. *This* is who people want to follow, for all sorts of reasons. *Ladies*."

Brie let out a disgusted grunt as he winked at them.

Zack wasn't the best leader, but oddly enough, he wasn't the worst in the guild either. Kala over in Jalapeño Town *should* have earned that distinction. There had been… complaints. It didn't help that the people following Kala had made a game of pushing her buttons, though Iron Becky had been trying to explain to her that beating people into submission wasn't the best way to lead them down the path she wanted them to follow.

Kala just wasn't getting it.

Becky had come into the Juxtaposition with a counseling skill, and she'd freely spent credits to level it. The higher her counseling level, the healthier she could help someone become —if they wanted to get there. For Kala and Zack, she'd had to buy her way to Tier one, then shell out more credits to max it out at level nineteen. Even then, the pair pushed Iron Becky's abilities to their limits.

The entire cyclical struggle did beg the question: were there limits to how many Tiers they could climb? Were the Patrons just players who had advanced to Tier ten, or were they something else entirely? Nacho didn't have the answer, and nothing he'd ever read in the Store, nor any rumor he'd ever heard, gave him that answer. For all they knew, the Patrons were bored interdimensional beings looking for a good time by playing games of chance and genocide.

"I heard there was a problem? Where do I need to go?" Nacho didn't like that he needed to directly engage with this guy, but the troublemaker had answers.

"Guildhall, bud. But listen, we need to talk about upgrading the cistern and doing some stuff with the water system in Tortilla Flats. You said when you had enough money, we'd figure it out. *Becky* said it could wait, but I say it can't. We all know she's just trying to play mind games."

Finally at her limit, Brie decided not to stick around and stomped off. The sheer fact that she could leave so angrily without causing some kind of political incident left Nacho feeling jealous down to his bones. Reuben stayed with Nacho, and he appreciated the support.

The cook gritted his teeth into an off-brand smile and reached out to pat Zack's arm. It felt like patting skin which had been stretched over concrete and oiled to glisten in the sun. "Yeah, Zack, I hear you. Look, I'm kinda tired. Let me get settled, and then we can work on your water issues."

"A moat is *full* of water. Just sayin', water in a cistern, water in a moat… think about it!" Zack wasn't about to just let the Guild Master walk away. He followed along and went on a rant about the leaky tents, how he needed to advance to Tier two faster than anyone else, and eventually raved about a new dungeon that one of his crew had found, called the 'Grotto of Grunt'. They hadn't been able to figure out what was producing the grunting, but it sounded pretty intense. Out of nowhere, the man said something that caught Nacho's attention fully.

"Apparently there's a bonus for running the dungeon without speaking or making any loud sounds. Everyone who's tried has failed because it was too tricky to fight silently." Zack shook his head and laughed bitterly. "People are so bad at fighting that they have to call out their attacks or something? Weak sauce."

"Reuben. Dungeons that are offering clear challenges are

appearing." Nacho tried to tamp his excitement down. He had been waiting for this, knowing that it was likely that the advanced timeline would mean that they'd start appearing sooner than they had in his Probability Vision. The discovery was a good thing, though it was also something that made him nervous. The challenges were designed to make it harder to survive the dungeon, but in return, they produced impressive rewards if the distinct conditions were met. "That's a hallmark of dungeons that will offer not-yet-available skills as a reward for success."

"Got it, boss man." Their side conversation was so quiet that Zack didn't even notice as he continued prattling on.

Many of the Final Victory's former members had taken up residence in the Tortilla Shell apartments, but a healthy portion had opted to remain in tents. That had worked fine over these last few summer months, but with fall—and the one year anniversary of the arrival of the Juxtaposition—coming all too soon, the guild wanted to transition everyone into living in more permanent structures. As with any other major guild benefits, the optimal solution required credits, planning, and a frankly ridiculous amount of water.

Nacho was itching to finish the Market Apartments on the Main Street, but that was just one of many pending construction projects. For instance, Old Bill was working on getting a proper smithy up and running, since he hated spending money at the Store. Matt Martinez was setting up a farming site on the southern end of the plateau, just south of the guildhall. They hadn't found someone with a Farmer class yet, but they had decided to prepare everything on the off chance they did, just so they could entice them with a functional farm already awaiting their attention.

The Tortilla Flats also included a few completed structures just beyond the walls. In the middle of the tent city rose a secondary guildhall that included an auxiliary kitchen, an oven, some stoves, and a sink. Nacho cooked there only under duress, as he much preferred using his main kitchen connected to the

Armor Mountain guildhall and then sending the food down. To transport meals, Matt had designated a cart pulled by an old man that was too fussy to be trained on the main Human Treadmills that composed the Bove's lair convoy.

Eyeballing the distance, Nacho had to concede that there was no part of the Tortilla Flats that was within five hundred feet of his main kitchen. If it had been, Nacho could have set a 'vending' point to send food over to Zack and his people and would never need to show his face here again.

He could only mumble hopefully, "Maybe when the skill hits Tier two?"

CHAPTER SIX

When they reached the apartment Reuben shared with Brie in the primary guild area atop Armor Mountain, Nacho thought his friend would bail. When he didn't make the move to go inside, the cook realized that Reuben likely wanted to get to the bottom of this 'problem' business as well.

As if she had been summoned, Kala came marching down Main Street in her black armor, her huge sword sheathed on her back. "You're gonna do it? You're just gonna let him make a challenge like that? I can't believe you're that easy."

"What?" Nacho wondered out loud, getting a shrug from Reuben as the Death Knight stormed past them, refusing to pause and elaborate. It was clear she was on her way back to Jalapeño Town, as they'd extended the Eastern Road down to the southern boundary, where the big Oilbark Tree straddled the entrance to the Deep Buggy Darkness. They'd set up a system of ropes and pulleys to create an elevator that descended to Jalapeño Town, which followed the curve of the mountain to the south and to the west.

Another wall had been constructed at the outskirts, called the Habañero Heights. The Heights had its own trench in front and was the final fallback of the guild in case something was attacking from the air.

Before she could get out of sight, Kala stiffened, turned, and marched back to them. “Look. Becky said I shouldn’t take out my frustrations on you, or Reuben, or Gustav and Gary.”

“I hope you mean to say…” Reuben lifted his fist. “The Ghost Pepper Brigade!”

The GG’s—Gustav and Gary—were new to the guild, but the two had brought a whole squad of warriors who were very committed to combining the spirit of Sparta with that of a community college’s fraternity.

Zack particularly wanted to get along with Gustav and Gary, but the GG’s took neither him nor their present situation seriously. In many ways, the Ghost Pepper Brigade was… not meshing with their new reality. For one, they didn’t discuss their Tiers and level. Instead, they’d translated the whole thing into the Scoville Scale, which measured spiciness, and Nacho hadn’t been able to figure it out. To be fair, he hadn’t put in a lot of effort, especially since they already had such a clear method of understanding.

Nacho had decided to think of them more as a mercenary group than any regular fighting force. The strangest thing about their entire cadre, and the reason the Death Knight hadn’t lost her leadership role even when administering extra-judicial punishments in the form of beatings… was that they were completely *enamored* by Kala.

They went out of their way to complete *any* task she gave them in an over the top fashion, often to their detriment. She had once told them to leave her apartment ‘right now’, and a trio had thrown themselves out of the window… over the cliff. Only the fact that regeneration was active had kept them alive to brag about the feat of idiocy.

“Right. Becky also said that talking to people through my helmet might be off-putting.” Kala inhaled and removed her helmet, letting her short black hair free. “Fine. The situation made me angry… wait. Did anyone tell you yet?”

"They didn't!" Reuben lifted a hand to forestall any new information. "Wait. I'm kind of enjoying the mystery. Don't tell me too much. I want to be kept in suspense a little while longer."

"That's stupid." Kala grimaced and pointed a finger at Nacho accusingly. "He's after *you*."

"Me? Why, and in what way?" Nacho was completely taken aback by the strange glare that she was giving him.

"He is invoking one of your foolish rules in the guild charter. It's not a good one, and I think you're a fool for allowing it to be added in the first place." Kala replaced her helmet, and the eye holes darkened unnaturally. "I'm going to go down into the Deep Buggy Darkness to work off some… emotions. Also, there's new stuff spawning on the fourth level. Big beetles, Tier zero."

"Save the meat!" Nacho couldn't hide his excitement. "I want to try bug gyros."

"No." Kala rejected his request with a disgusted grunt and strode off.

"Becky does good work." Reuben squinted at the departing Death Knight. "I think she's making progress. That was an apology. Or close to it."

"Yeah, I think it was." Nacho turned to his buddy. "So… someone is after me."

"A universally *loved* S-classer." Reuben wiggled his eyebrows. "Who could be after you, and why isn't he already six feet under?"

"Nice. People are allowed to dissent, it keeps things from getting out of hand." With a shrug, Nacho turned and headed toward the Guildhall. He was dying to try out his Splatter Millet on the grains waiting in his Storage Slots, but first… he had to deal with whatever this was. Patting his stomach, he muttered, "I haven't forgotten about you, donuts. Don't you worry one little bit."

Reuben followed along as he continued down Main Street, where a market had popped up on either side. With over five thousand people now in the guild, vendors had begun selling any number of things, from clay plates that weren't made of yellow and red Juxtaposition plastic, to handmade furniture by Old Bill himself. He was bizarrely great at designing and creating wicker chairs in particular.

Nacho had big plans for the Main Street market, but he was re-evaluating it after his fight in the Millet Meadows. That battle had driven home the very real possibility of his entire guild being wiped out. Too many people were looking inward, wanting creature comforts instead of progressing, and this market proved that all too clearly.

Maybe he had known that, deep in his subconscious. Perhaps that was why he hadn't pushed for anything to be done about it yet. "More raw truth to face. What a day. All I wanted to do was to figure out the Splatter Millet, pound out some flour, and get to making donuts."

"Talking to people is hard for you, huh?" Reuben poked Nacho in the sides to shock him, then stepped away as a knife slashed through the air where his hands had been a moment previously. "Don't worry. I have your back. If things go south, you can always kill him and eat him, whoever 'he' is. No? I saw you wince. Was that too soon? Can we not joke about cannibalism yet?"

Nacho shrugged, even though he was feeling significant discomfort over the direction of the banter. "If you can't joke about cannibalism, what can you joke about? Just not with Brie, or you'll get to join me in sleeping like a princess on my kitchen shelves instead of in some bed like a sucker."

"With my *wife*," Reuben pointed out.

"Meh." Nacho slapped a bored look on his face. "If I wanted a wife, I would just bake one. Then I'd know she was sweet."

"Oh, what-*ever*." Reuben's snort went unanswered as Nacho pushed through the front doors of his guildhall. The breakfast fires were dark and cool, as no one else could cook in this world without getting a potentially lethal dose of Putrid Mana. In the back kitchen, the Brittanys were busy getting lunch ready—which meant repackaging the leftovers that Nacho had prepped before leaving. Fast-food chili, in this case, which he'd left in his icebox room to keep it cool.

That was another issue he had to figure out, and soon. The ice was melting too fast. It just wasn't efficient. There had to be a better way to keep things cold—his thoughts were interrupted as a voice boomed through the gloomy hall.

"I'm invoking my right as a member of the Guild to call a vote of no confidence against Guild Leader Nacho!" Reuben and Nacho both turned to stare at the person that had shouted. There had been no reason to be so loud, as the man had walked in with them. Zack smiled back at them as he held out his hands for his weapon. "I call for a trial by combat!"

"You can't *possibly* think that this is a good idea, Zack," Nacho informed him calmly, even as he undid the straps of his mobile kitchen and let the backpack fall to the floor. "Plus, *you* can't initiate a vote like that. Not on your own, and also because-"

"I represent almost a thousand people, everyone brought in by our Guild *Master*," Zack retorted as a massive Greatsword appeared in his hands. "That's plenty of people that agree with me. I read the rules."

"You clearly *didn't*, Zack." Nacho continued to keep his voice calm, hoping that he would be able to deescalate the situation. "The guideline requires the challenger to represent *twenty* percent of the *Chips Guild's* total population in order to call for a vote of no confidence on their own. Even if you represent almost a thousand people, that's still not one in five, nor is it the correct Guild that you're representing. Drop the sword or face the consequences."

All the command did was make the muscular man laugh. "What can you do? Sitting back in your comfortable kitchen while the rest of us do *men's* work! You know what? Fine, you think that you can take me? I don't even need to represent people, I'll just take you down, and anyone else who stands in my way. This guild is going to be *my* guild, and we're going to do what I want to do with this guild!"

"I'm going to report you to the Department of Redundancy Department," Reuben softly muttered, thinking he wouldn't be heard.

"Quiet down and get ready to work, *Healer*," Zack demanded as he attempted to dash forward and cut Nacho in half. The Guild Leader swayed out of the way, smiling the entire time. It was not a happy smile; rather, it was a tight-lipped, ghoulish facsimile of a grin.

"You just attempted an unprovoked attack on your Guild Leader," Nacho informed Zack quietly. "I only wish there were more people around to witness what happens when people do the dumb."

The Berserker screamed in sudden pain as black markings started to sear themselves into his wrists. They were forming words, but currently they were unrecognizable. In an attempt to escape the inescapable torment, he threw everything he had into trying to bring Nacho down for good.

The cook, for his part, merely avoided each of the attacks in an almost bored fashion. Massive sword swings came at him one after another, and he dodged them smoothly with inches to spare. "Looks like you're used to throwing your weight around. No technique, no training, clearly no real skill. Just a heavy sword and an impressionable audience. However, you forgot one very important thing, Zack."

"Stay still so I can hit you!" Zack grunted hoarsely, clearly thinking that Nacho was the source of his pain. In a way, he was right, but not in a way that mattered. He hoisted the enormous blade overhead with a wrathful shout, and his skin turned a dark Crimson as his heart began to beat erratically. "Berserker's Rage!"

Seeing the man use a Skill that allowed him to ignore pain in order to continue his onslaught, Nacho finally decided to take him more seriously. With a quick gulp of a Life Hack smoothie, his Fitness score increased by nearly fifty percent. There was no way a single Skill from a fresh Tier one combatant was going to be able to match that increase, so he simply continued evading attacks until the Berserker's Rage wore off.

Finally, Zack could no longer keep up the effort and was forced to let the tip of his sword fall to the ground. He stood there, heaving for air and glaring at Nacho. Clearly stalling for time, he managed to speak around the pain of markings being burned into both of his arms. "Fine, Nacho-chode. Tell me what I forgot."

"Fact of the matter is, *you* can't challenge me," Nacho explained with a sad smile. "You aren't a member of the Chips. I essentially run two guilds. In one, I'm a Guild Leader. In the other guild, which I won in a bet, I'm still the Guild *Master*. Tell me how much Hunger and Thirst you have. How much Hunger does that Skill take?"

"Ten percent and twenty percent remaining. Berserker's Rage takes Fifteen Hunger." Zack replied instantly, the color draining from his face. "How did you… I didn't want to tell you that!"

"Activate Berserker's Rage," Nacho ordered the huge man. Without a second of hesitation, the other man complied, attacking him once more. Again, Nacho held him off, though he amped up the show by using his knives to parry the attacks as needed. When the Skill wore off once more, Nacho gave another order. "Stay right there and don't move. Don't access the Store; don't eat or drink anything. Brittany!"

"Yes, Chef!" the Kitchen assistant squeaked out, eyes wide at the sudden violence that had come to the Guildhall.

"I want you to go outside and call everyone to assemble here. As fast as possible." Nacho turned back to face Zack, crossing his arms and watching the exhausted man.

Brittany hesitated, then finally worked up the courage to ask, "Why?"

"We don't have the capability to jail people," Nacho informed her heavily. "I want people to see what will happen if they break the law. There are no second chances in this world. More than that…"

Zack audibly swallowed, and sweat poured off his forehead as Nacho finished his explanation.

"There are most certainly *not* repeat offenders."

CHAPTER SEVEN

No matter how disappointed Nacho was with the way Zack had chosen to live and the decisions that had led him to this point, the fact remained that he *had* made those choices. It was astounding how little time it took for the rumor mill to convince people to swarm into the guildhall, though Nacho was in the process of grilling steak to hurry that along. Soon, anyone who didn't follow their ears ended up following their nose.

One of the Ghost Pepper Brigade brawlers had killed something called a Steer Clear, a mountainous blue cow with spiked forelegs and sword-like bone spurs jutting from expansive shoulders. Steer Clear charged through forests as it pleased, felling entire swaths of trees with its astonishingly keen-edged shoulder swords. Usually the gargantuan beasts were left alone to roam, as they didn't actively hunt people.

As a general rule… it was best to steer clear.

The beast was a level eleven monster—pretty tough for someone outside of the Brunch Force—but the Ghost Pepper Brigade had come to Armor Mountain already at Tier one. One of the reasons that Nacho had suggested they go live in Jalapeño Town was that their initial party name was terrible:

Gustav and Gary's Good Guy Gang. He had wanted to see their true colors, and… well, now Kala had to deal with them.

The other reason was that he had originally thought that the GG's team of warriors would keep Kala in check. That had backfired spectacularly, but in the best of ways. Both the Brigade and Kala worked well together when it came to running the town.

Nacho processed the Steer Clear, whisked up a simple recipe of salt, pepper, and meat, and chopped up five pounds of the beef with a few heavy **whacks** of his cleaver. There was no need to be super fancy, which reminded him to try out his Feasting Feats Skill. "Basic knife usage gives me seven and a half pounds… if I'm doing the math right, using the Skill will boost it to one hundred forty-two and a half pounds of meat."

Upon activating the Skill, the cook was given a System prompt regarding where to send the steak. It was surprisingly intuitive, allowing him to choose a location out in the hall, and he grinned excitedly as he set the point and walked out of the kitchen to investigate the results. It had only been a few minutes since he had cooked the steak to rare, but the hall was already packed near to bursting, although there was a clear, empty area around Zack.

He had hoped that the man would come around to see reason before it was too late, perhaps even to apologize and try to make amends. Instead, when Nacho emerged into the feasting hall, the loudest voice was Zack's as he begged for help against the 'tyrant' that was trying to kill him. "I'm literally starving to death right now! He needs to be stopped; somebody get me something to eat, quick!"

"Nobody help him." Even though Nacho kept his voice calm, it thundered through the hall and froze half a dozen people in their efforts to force-feed the man that had attacked him. "I'm sure you are all wondering why I have gathered you here today. Zack, be quiet. You are only allowed to speak if I say something that is *not* true."

The Berserker's teeth audibly **clicked** together as his jaw was forced shut. Nacho nodded slowly as he watched the compulsive response with a hollow glower. "I think some people have *forgotten* the situation that we are in. The fact remains that the world as we knew it has ended. Perhaps you have been able to convince yourself that you are safe, and that you can revert to old habits. I'm here to tell you that if you have started to backslide, you are not going to make it."

A disgruntled hubbub filled the room, and most of what he caught was angry retorts directed at him. "Today, I'm going to explain, in a way that everyone can understand, that actions have consequences. A short while ago, Zack Puck of the Final Victory Guild attempted to murder me. Because of that, under the terms of the guild contract he is bound by… he earned the Mark of Betrayal. If you examine his wrists, you will find tattoos that should say 'Oathbreaker'."

Multiple people approached the fuming dissenter and confirmed Nacho's claim as true, and the angry undercurrent turned into confused murmuring. Nacho allowed his fingers to lazily glide upward to point at the rest of Zack's arms. "Even after he started to feel the burn of his crime, he ignored the effects and continued in his attempts to kill me. *That* choice activated the second stage of the mark, which the Patrons refer to as 'did the dumb'. I'm explaining all of this so that you all understand what is happening."

"What are you going to do to him?" someone called out from the midst of the crowd. "Throw him in prison?"

"We don't have one of those, and we don't need one," Nacho stated solemnly. "Only one of two things can happen now, and I'll leave that for Zack to decide. Zack, answer truthfully: was anything I said a lie?"

"I did what I needed to—*aah*!" Zack screamed so hard that the entire hall went silent, drawing their attention to more black marks appearing on the man's face. He was forced to heave a few breaths before he could manage to speak again. "What… what's happening?"

"You're unable to lie right now, Zack. That will only bring pain. Every time you fail to follow a direct command, you're marching faster toward your death." Nacho didn't speak directly to him; he spoke to the room at large as the black marks wriggled up Zacks' neck. "There are no easy ways to punish people in this world. The Juxtaposition is already brutal, and there is no room for error. One person being selfish drags the rest of us down, and that leads us to *all* of us dying out. While Zack was attacking me, I assessed his combat capabilities. As far as I can tell, he has not earned his way to his current Tier and level through proficiency and accomplishment. It is clear that he has been extorting credits from other people and spending them to make himself stronger. Zack, do you have anything to say for yourself?"

Although the man was practically frothing at the mouth, he wisely chose not to lie and inflict more pain on himself. Nacho responded with a single solemn nod, then took a deep breath. "Then I judge you guilty. Your punishment is to stand motionless where you are for the next thirty minutes."

Nearly the whole room went pin-drop silent, and Zack laughed derisively as he scratched at the burning marks. "That's it? All that build up, just to tell me to stay in time out… not even for a whole hour? Fine by me!"

"Yes." The cook merely regarded him with serious eyes. "Your Hunger is negative. It's been thirteen minutes. I would guess that you have anywhere from eight to twelve minutes before your negative Health Regeneration kills you."

"W-what?" Zack blinked one eye, then the other, and shrugged, pulling up his character sheet, the blood draining from his face as he watched his Health tick away. "I'm standing here, actually dying! You're just going to… to let it *happen*?"

"I don't need to punish you, Zack," Nacho answered gently, shrugging as he watched the tattooed faction leader slowly lose the fight to remain calm. "In fact, I don't need to do anything right now. Frankly, it's a toss-up on what gets you first. The contract burnout, or starvation. I've seen both happen, and I highly recommend quietly starving to death. Lighting on fire and burning from the inside out doesn't seem like a pleasant way to go in comparison."

"You can't do this! Save me! Someone, help! Nacho! You can save me. *Please* save me!" Zack screamed at the crowd watching him with rapt, horrified attention. Since he had been ordered to stand in place, Zack couldn't even collapse to the ground to cry. Trying just sent the black marks spreading faster, inflicting further pain.

"I *am* sorry, Zack," Nacho informed the man, who looked at the cook hopefully… only to be met with eyes as cold and sharp as the knives he wielded. "But that was the cost of the contract you signed, and attempting to break it was your choice. It was your *choice* to think you could kill me with no repercussions, and to put actions to those thoughts. Here's today's life lesson, people. While everyone is free to think whatever they want… *actions have consequences*."

Just as Nacho concluded, the black marks scorched their way across the last of Zack's exposed skin. He grabbed at his abdomen, then crumpled in place as he was burned from the inside out. Nacho watched stoically until the entirety of the body had turned to ash, which blew away as though wind had swept through. Where Zack had fallen remained a pile of items that had burst from his Storage Slots, surrounding the words 'Did the Dumb', which was burned into the wood of the floor.

The room remained silent, but Nacho knew that it would stay that way only so long. He had nothing more to add to the conversation, and before anything else… lunch needed to get underway. He still had plenty of the Steer Clear left, and with his Feasting Feats, one hundred pounds of beef would become nearly three *thousand*. It was time to feed his guild.

The lunch rush was over before he knew it, though the story of what had happened spread throughout the encampments; the guildhall doors banged open constantly as more members rushed in to inspect the words burned into the floor. Brie even came to check up on the cook, but he sent her and Reuben away without taking the time to discuss the situation with them. Even though the man had earned his punishment, Nacho had been in charge of him.

The fact that the situation had dissolved that far was his fault, and it was his first major failing as a leader.

Nacho couldn't let it get him down, even though he knew he would need to spend some time thinking about ways to ensure something like this never again happened in his guild. Mercifully , he had plenty to be distracted by.

He had discovered a happy attribute of the Feasting Feats Skill: all he needed to do was make the food, and it could be sent to any five chosen locations within five hundred feet of the Skill *at the time of activation.* Best of all, that meant he could prepare the food, activate the Skill, and walk away.

His people were able to take care of themselves, and everything moved more smoothly than it had in weeks, even with the confusion over the change. Nacho didn't even care how much money he'd made from the steaks. He'd been able to feed everyone in his guild without a single personal interaction, which was very welcome after the morning he had just been through. Lunch had been over for him as soon as the food was complete.

The wave of relief was practically inconceivable: he had been able to buy back *hours* of his time for the day. As far as he was concerned, the Skill had already more than paid for itself. As he lay on the cold stone floor of his kitchen to cool down after the heat of slaving over his grills, he wondered how much money he'd need in order to turn the Millet Meadows into a safe and profitable hunting location. "Nah… they're too sneaky. We just need to wipe them out before they can spread."

With the food situation practically solving itself, he needed to turn his attention to providing a consistent water source. Early on, the Armor Mountain colony had bought a Tier zero water cistern. At the time, it had been serviceable and cheap, but Nacho knew they no longer had any choice but to start putting *serious* money behind their group survival needs. For him, a Tier zero water source was only worthwhile to keep around for showers, and to that end, they had built the bath and shower house to the west of the guildhall.

However, there were quite a few guild members who had risen above Tier zero, with more reaching that watershed level every day, and they all needed to be able to *drink* the water.

The problem was, the Store was charging them two hundred and seventy *thousand* credits for the Tier one cistern, and the same amount for pipes and plumbing to connect all the buildings to that water source. That cost *included* their ten percent guild discount for building supplies, else it would've been a grand total of six hundred thousand credits… for water that would be less useful than *air* to them in a few weeks.

Nacho grimaced at that realization. There were problems at the top. Even if they were problems he could handle, they were problems nonetheless. He banged his head against the ground, unable to damage himself even slightly. "We need a big win. Scraping together a couple grand in credits from processing Millet Stalkers just isn't doing much when we look at the bigger picture."

He lay there with his eyes closed, taking deep breaths as he tried to work through everything. Without warning, the world went quiet and eerily still. His eyes popped open, and he froze when he found a CrossHuman staring at him. With a predatory leer at the cook, Arriod spoke. "It's us or it's you, Nacho. This is a zero-sum game, and I can guarantee you… we are *not* going to lose."

Arriod charged Nacho with his sword raised. The deadly katana hit Nacho's flesh… and bad things happened.

Nacho awoke with a scream, lashing out with his knives like a startled blender before going limp. He was slick with sweat, and his heart was hammering in his chest. What little breeze his kitchen had was gone, and the place had become an oven.

"Mmkay. Need to fix the ventilation issues. Add it to the list of all the stuff that needs to be done."

He checked the time, finding that it was only a little past three. He had a few minutes before he needed to start prepping dinner, but only if he really *wanted* to make it. There was still plenty of food left over from lunch, and everyone had finally come around to the 'eat once a day or as needed' rule. No one got *hungry* anymore, not without using Skills or failing to eat for a full twenty-four hours. Still… the Ghost Pepper Brigade had found a whole herd of Steer Clears, and they had promised to bring back as many as possible.

The remainder of the steak feast had already turned into goo and drained down Nacho's sink. "Better to fill the freezer now, I suppose. Can't believe I got an actual break today; that was *awesome*."

Knowing it was better to stock up in anticipation of his next foray away from the guild, if nothing else, Nacho got to work, and as the afternoon progressed, all of the issues that had been swirling in his mind started to distill down to the main problem: Mana. Specifically, the lack of it. During Active Cooking, he ran out of Mana constantly. Large pauses when preparing his food became necessary if he wanted to imbue it with any kind of buffs.

Sure, he could eat and drink while he used his magic, but he had no way of refilling his Mana pool. They *needed* a Brewer, as Nacho was nearly certain that class would be able to generate homemade mana potions. "Why couldn't they just have named it something game-like? Alchemist, or something? I bet that would have been a class people *fought* to take."

There was an easy answer: the Patrons didn't want to make crafting classes obvious, let alone appealing. That line of thinking brought him directly to his almost-certainly-Patron-sent vision of Arriod. Kronos was working hard to make it clear that they couldn't just forget about the CrossHumans. The cannibalistic humanoid race was as much of a threat as their rival guilds in the area, and stagnation was death. Nacho *had* to continue upgrading his and his friends' classes to get them to Tier two. "Gotta get to level twenty so I can unlock the special Tier two option of my Gravy Boots. Can't forget to check those when possible."

Other than a general *desire* to do things, he was stumped on how to get there. That… was a relief, in some ways. "When there's no right place to start, there's also no *wrong* place to start."

Nacho knew he would enlist his friends in the decision-making process, and he actively chose to ignore everything else, except for how happy frying donuts for the next morning was going to make everyone involved. Crossing to the serving window, he called to the Brittanys, who were relaxing at a table in the main hall. "Hey, could you guys run and get Reuben and Brie? I need to talk with them."

"Sure thing, boss-man! We're on it!" Britt leapt to her feet and pulled Brittany after her. Nacho sat in a chair in his kitchen in the meantime, studying his hands and noticing that they were still a little shaky. Zack's death, followed by his dream of Arriod and the CrossWorld, still troubled him.

During Nacho's Probability Vision, very few people had survived the journey through the Portal to actually discover what the CrossWorld was all about. Some believed it to be a paradise, but Nacho couldn't imagine that was the case. If the CrossWorld was so great, the CrossHumans would've *stayed* there. In reality, they had come to the Earth's Starter World to find basic sustenance; the real issue was the fact that they ate humans for breakfast every day that they could get them.

"I'll see what Reuben and Brie have to say, but… maybe the next logical step is to find out what's on the other side of the Portal?" His head hung down as he took a few minutes for quiet introspection. He had no long-term plans. He was upgrading his class and Skills, however slowly that went. "What *is* the final goal? To survive, but what else?"

What if the Juxtaposition actually *was* a zero-sum game

between the Humans and CrossHumans? If there could only be one winner…

"We can't let them win." Nacho's eyes blazed as his will solidified around that single thought. "Humans need to go on the offensive and hit the CrossHumans before they can get their act together. We're going through that portal."

CHAPTER EIGHT

Reuben and Brie came into the kitchen, ready to help with dinner. The Healer pushed his leather helmet back to scratch under it, exaggerating his motions to draw attention to the item. He wore the helmet mostly to annoy the other two, and frankly it worked far too well. "About Zack-"

"Let's *not* talk about that right now. Give him some time." In an attempt to suggest *other* things, Brie called over to the cook, "Rumor has it Gustav and Gary are going to be taking down a herd of those Steer Clears. We might be up to our necks in missed steaks any minute now, depending on how fast you can get the meat processed."

"It's fine, Brie. I'll be ready." Nacho heaved himself up and pulled off the bar locking the door of his icebox room, then pulled the thick panel open. Most of his ice was gone, the only remaining evidence being a stagnant puddle glistening around the drain. "Ah, man… those pipes didn't work well."

A quick glance confirmed that he had the space for an influx of meat. That was the good news. The bad news was that he didn't think it was going to be useful to buy ice from the Store anymore. Tier zero ice melted almost immediately in the presence of Tier one food, so he was forced to buy Tier one ice, at ten credits per pound. Even with the sawdust Old Bill gave them to cover it, they were burning through four hundred credits a week.

Reuben and Brie flanked him to enjoy the cold draft wafting from the ice room. To prolong the experience, they ended up taking the chairs from his little table and putting them in the icebox room itself. While they had to sit in a few inches of water, it was still far more pleasant than sitting in the hot kitchen outside. The Healer inspected the floor and pointed at the drain. "I think the issue is that the grate is set in a block of stone, so the water needs to be higher than that to drain. Simple fix: get an earth elemental mage to sink that down a little."

"Not a bad idea at all. Way easier than what I had been planning." Nacho put away the chisel that he had bought for a single credit, hoping no one had seen it. "How about what we need to do next? First, I'm hoping to spend the night cooking Steer Clear meat, and then tomorrow morning… donuts."

"Meat and donuts." Reuben grabbed his gut and cheerfully groaned. "Slap those bad boys together, and I'll feel like a real American again."

"Hold on; I want to get this all out so that we can discuss everything." Nacho talked fast, knowing that his friend would want to make jokes the entire time. "We should get an extermination squad to the Millet Meadow, or at the very least, the Ghost Pepper Brigade. I'm pretty sure that Gustav and Gary can handle the Tier ones, and I think we killed the only Tier two. We can safely rule out a Tier three being a risk, as we are all still in one piece. That place is a hazard that we need to get cleared out as soon as possible."

"Is it actually that high of a priority?" Brie questioned him. "Didn't we cut them off from being able to escape?"

"The way they're growing… there's no way they'll stay in one spot for too long," Nacho informed her grimly. "If we leave it to spread unchecked, it could advance to a point that we *can't* clear it out without significant losses. Even with how far away it is, a species that wipes out everything else around it will just keep expanding. Now that we know it exists, we need to send someone to stop it."

Brie frowned as she tried to calculate all the work required to actually complete the process he was describing. "I'm still not sure the Millet Stalkers are worth it in the short term. We're collecting fifty thousand credits a day from taxes, so we have income. There's the new dungeon, the Grotto of Grunt, that our people are exploring. They're even progressing to the lower floors, which means more credits for them *and* us. If we focus on a general power-up for the guild, we can send less... *necessary* teams to deal with the issue."

Nacho didn't want to let go of his concern over the Stalkers, but he kept his mouth closed so he could formulate his reasoning more clearly. Reuben nodded and leaned forward, bracing his elbows on his knees. "Brie is right; you know she is. The Stalkers are low priority. Bringing in a Brewer is more important. We need a way to replenish Mana for our Mind Players during Active Combat. You know, what if there was a siege? Wouldn't we be in a constant state of Active Combat? For months on end? No Store, no Regen? I can only hug people so much before I run out of Mana and pass out."

"In almost any other context, that would be extremely creepy," his wife informed him primly. "I know you do that on purpose; you ought to start thinking about your social image a little bit more. You are a high level executive of the Chip's Guild. You don't get to represent only yourself anymore."

"Ah... huh." Nacho was still stuck on the concern of a siege. It was a sobering thought. He could easily see the Patrons gleefully keeping them in Active Combat as long as the enemy army was encamped outside their walls. Suddenly, finding a Brewer *did* seem like the next logical step, and something they should do as soon as possible.

That, and continuing the steep climb to Tier two. Nacho growled as he reflected on their only current option. "We need to put out help wanted ads."

"I volunteer Reuben to make them for us." Brie held up a hand to forestall any continuation, shooting her husband a sharp look as he grumbled about being talk-blocked. "Look, all of this is hypothetical. What we need to do right *now* is some shopping for ourselves. I think filling our fourth Skill Slot is something we should really look into. Upgrading Skills is cheap, comparatively, and since we're already Tier one, we could each upgrade a Tier zero skill all the way to level nineteen instantly.'

Reuben listened to his wife in rapt attention, fluttering his lashes flirtatiously at her. She rewarded him with a bored glance. "Yes, yes. I know. You have yourself a gamer girl—you're very proud, and I love you."

"She *loves* me." Reuben touched his chest and gasped with delight. "I knew it. Getting married didn't prove it half as much as this does. You love me with my helm and everything? So sweet."

"*Despite* the helmet, and everything else that goes with it. Nacho… you mentioned CrossWorld earlier." Brie leaned toward him, her sandal-clad feet splashing in the water covering the floor. "Are you serious about us going through the portal?"

"I am," Nacho stated with great hesitation. "We don't know for sure what is on the other side, but our next big threat is going to be the CrossHumans, I can tell you that much. In the Probability Vision, they had been building up an army, and it was only a matter of time before they attacked Crave's castle. That was one of the biggest reasons why he and Kala merged their guilds."

"Or maybe it was all just a misunderstanding, right?" Reuben laughed as he let his arms glow green. "Could be that it's not that the CrossHumans *want* to kill us. Maybe they just needed a hug."

"It's… *doubtful* that is the case." Nacho folded his hands behind his head, trying to put the truth into terms that his friend could not make into a joke. "I haven't talked to Kronos in a long time. I was hoping he'd show up, so I could ask him, but even if he did… he probably wouldn't tell me much."

Nacho stood with a sigh and sloshed his way out of the freezer, followed by his friends. He was getting chilly, and he needed to get back to work, if for no other reason than to clear his head. Crossing to a drawer where he kept various cooking implements, he retrieved the Splatter Millet and waggled the tiny hammer at his friends. "Remember this?"

Brie drew Mr. Lacrosse Stick out of the air and whirled it around, showcasing her restlessness. "I have a lot of fine memories of my Splatter Mallet, but I have to be honest, I'd rather have this bad boy."

"Mr. Lacrosse Stick, the implement of murder and mayhem," Reuben added in a dark tone, as though he were a narrator for a horror movie trailer.

"All this goes to say that, yes," Brie sent her weapon back into her Storage Slot as she rolled her eyes at her husband's theatrics, "we remember the hammer.'

"I've never really had a chance to use it." Nacho shook his head. "Frankly, it's not the right time to be messing around with this. It's not like upgrading a small hammer to pound grain would even make any sense."

"You can't be serious." Brie grimaced and folded her arms. Despite her cool tone, the finger irritably tapping her bicep gave away the degree of composure she was fighting to maintain. "Did you really call us in here to discuss the insecurities you have over your tiny hammer?"

"Wait just a moment, now." Reuben poked Brie in the ribs, getting no reaction at all. "Never refer to a man's hammer as tiny. We prefer the term 'average'."

"*Not* sure that's the term we prefer." Nacho waved the miniscule Warhammer. "For the record, I wanted you here because I had a vision of our impending doom at the hands of an invading alien army. The tiny hammer was an afterthought, but I'm pretty sure nobody ever used a grain hammer if they didn't have to. I'm pretty sure they used mills, like water wheels, to grind wheat into flour. Or on a smaller scaler, maybe a mortar and pestle."

Reuben tapped at the countertop he was leaning over. "You're not wrong about the grain mills. Even back before the Juxtaposition, there were hand-cranked mills for things like coffee. Brie showed me at least half a dozen when we were selecting kitchen appliances for our wedding registry. Put this in *game logic*, Nacho. Let's be real: if you had listened to common sense and the Patrons, you wouldn't have chosen the Common Cook class. But that turned out to be a very good move, didn't it? When it comes to magical gear for you, all naysaying should be yay-saying. Spend the money to upgrade it if you can, and let's see what this very small, but perfectly adequate for the task, hammer can do."

"I like that..." Nacho nodded at Brie, though his forehead still creased with concern. "I just can't make choices like this independently. It makes me feel too tyrannical to be spending credits on myself all the time."

"What can I say to that?" Brie lifted a fist halfheartedly, a baffled frown on her face. "Do you need motivation or something? Someone cheering you on? Yay. Woo. Spend the credits."

There wasn't much 'yay' there, but it was all he needed. "Okay, I've gone through the Store, I've found grain mills—everything from Common to Epic on the rarity chart—but I haven't found any other kind of grain hammer. I'm assuming, like the Sewer Skewers, that the Splatter Millet was created for the first time when a Satiation Player grabbed it. That means it's *unique*. I simply haven't had the time nor the inclination to actually research how much it would cost to upgrade it. Now that I think about it-"

Reuben snapped his fingers to cut off his friend. "No naysaying. I can see those evil naysaying thoughts in your noggin. Just get on with the shopping so I can go nab a steak."

Nacho grumbled under his breath but dutifully found the Upgrade option for magical items and sighed as the System started its usual antics.

. . .

Hello, Cookie!

From what you've been saying, it sounds like you want to upgrade the Splatter Millet from Tier 0 to Tier 1. Are you sure you want to waste the credits on such a useless magic item?

Yes / No

He had known that it wasn't going to be easy, assuming the System would throw him an impossible number and he'd walk away after tossing the tiny hammer over his shoulder. 'Ugh, the Patrons are messing with me. They're saying it's useless."

"Which is a good sign," Reuben insisted. "That means it's use-*full*. Must be opposite day!"

"Nay, nay, nay," Brie chanted under her breath, getting a wide smile from her husband.

Nacho chose 'yes' despite the Berserker's negative vibes.

Okay, look, Cook.

We want to give you a word of warning, since we're always so nice to our favorite players. The Splatter Millet will not become more of a threat to monsters. It's not an item for slaying monsters. It does only one thing, and it does that one thing well.

Would you like to continue?

Yes / No

"Yes," Nacho grumbled out loud, Relaying to Reuben and Brie what was going on in the prompts.

"Keep going, buddy." Reuben's encouragement was infectious, and Nacho mentally thanked him for the support as he selected 'yes' once again.

Abyss, Cookie, it sounds like either you want to waste credits on a hammer that only affects inert grains, or you are curious about what one thing the

Splatter Millet does well… which we assume you could guess, because you're not a complete fool. From our estimation, you're about a 51% fool—just enough in you for us to question your logic. Would you like to continue with more insults?

Yes / No

Nacho felt oddly relieved there were insults at all, which was practically the System's confirmation that he wasn't crazy for pursuing the upgrade. Reuben knew him well enough to recognize the expression on his face. "Nacho has them on the ropes. Go in for the kill!"

"Leave no grain unturned," Brie deadpanned, though it was clear that she was also starting to grow curious about the hammer.

Nacho chose the 'yes' option one final time and blinked in astonishment at the result. No more insults followed, and the upgrade was surprisingly inexpensive… and impressively powerful. "Huh."

CHAPTER NINE

The cook read through the latest message twice, knowing for a fact that he was going to buy the upgrade.

Okay, Cook, it seems you have fallen in love with this little hammer of worthlessness, so we'll give you a break. Upgrade it to Tier 1 for 5,000 credits. Not only will you double the flour produced with each strike—not unlike your HungerCry Knives—but the pulverized grain will also be reinforced with valuable nutrients and minerals. That's right: the grain will be armored, and so will you. Cooking with millet flour isn't easy, and people will complain, but you'll have thick skin. So thick, in fact, that all attacks against the person eating food made with the resulting flour will have their damage reduced by 10%. You can even bake with the slogan: Eat my bread to keep from being dead!

Note: There is a 25% chance that the upgrade will not work, and the Splatter Millet will explode. You're just going to have to take that chance if you're determined to continue. Also, if you drop the hammer during the upgrade process, it will automatically fail. It might not explode, but you'll be out the credits either way. Don't wimp out, is what we're basically saying.

Are you sure *you'd like to upgrade the Splatter Millet to Tier 1?*
Yes / No

Nacho didn't understand the line about people complaining about millet flour, but if he could bake something that could reduce the amount of damage from attacks, it would be worth it. They'd get a boon to their stats, as well as less severe wounds. It was a no-brainer.

Best of all, Nacho had the credits to pay for it all himself. He had nineteen times the cost in his personal funds, thanks to his Feasting Feats ability. His steak sandwiches had been a big hit, and he hadn't been forced to make individual sales. Even with a slight drop in total potential income, he had been able to bring in more during a single meal than he usually did over the course of two days.

Before Nacho chose 'yes', he pointed the Splatter Millet at the door. "You guys better get out of here. I've tied my fate to this tiny hammer, and there's a twenty-five percent chance that it will explode in my hand."

Brie knew he wasn't kidding, as did Reuben. Neither looked too happy about bailing on their friend, but Nacho wasn't budging. The Healer arched a brow at the cook. "I'll be standing right outside the door. If it explodes, I can and *will* hug you from a distance."

"Aren't you the best." Nacho waited until the kitchen door swung shut behind them, then started the upgrade. As the Splatter Millet started to glow with heat, he fought the urge to put it on the counter. Instead he focused on watching the hammer as it shifted, growing a bit bigger and changing shape before his eyes.

The glow and heat intensified until Nacho feared that the upgrade had certainly failed, but just as he prepared to fling the brilliant tool and cower behind a counter, it started to dim and cool. In seconds, it has reduced to a flat-headed kitchen hammer about the size of a meat tenderizer.

A new message appeared for the upgraded weapon:

The Splatter Millet

Tier 1 Weapon

Don't go to the mill. Instead, use this ultimate tool of grain destruction to produce quadruple the flour and leave behind a quarter of the mess. This grain-hating hammer will keep the fluffy white clouds to a minimum, so cleanup will be a snap!

Sounds too good to be true? Just wait, there's more! Any baked goods you create with millet flour will reduce damage taken by 10% while effects last. That's right. More pain (if you speak French) means less pain! Good luck baking with millet flour. You'll need it!

With the light show over, Reuben and Brie inched their way back into the kitchen. "How did it go?"

Nacho waved the small, flat-headed hammer at them. "It's expensive, not going to lie, but I'm also excited to use it. Not only will I make a ton of extra flour with each hit, but if you eat anything I cook with it, you'll take less damage. I don't get why the System keeps warning me about using the millet flour. Like it's hard to have around or something. It's just flour, right?"

"Like I have any idea about baking." Brie narrowed her eyes as she considered the man. "To be fair, you do have a history of having a… shall we say 'steep learning curve' when you start baking new things."

Nacho winced at the memory of their first few days in the Juxtaposition. "Ouch, Brie. Why must you hurt me so?"

Reuben interrupted and waved away the sting. "Use the thing already! You spent all this money, and I want to see you in your kitchen, doing battle against the most monstrous of grains—the evil millet, scourge of the local bulk food bins."

Nacho pulled the red and yellow sacks from his Storage Slot one at a time, handing them to Reuben, who laid them on the floor. Meanwhile, Brie cleared his main counter and wiped up some of the food remnants. Once his prep area was clean, the cook hefted a bag onto the table and sprinkled out a few cups of millet grain.

Raising the hammer high, he *smashed* the Splatter Millet down on the grains. The impact sent up a little puff of yellowish dust, but mostly flour spilled from the grains, easily generating a cup, if not two. He crushed more millet, **pow, pow, pow**, until his counter was covered in the yellow flour. It was easy to brush the pulverized grain into a big metal container, which he marked with 'Special: Ten Percent Damage Reduction'!

As he breezed through the tough grain, Nacho found that he was happy with the purchase, though he knew he'd be even happier when he perfected his millet-flour donuts and people started eating them before combat.

Brie seemed far less pleased than the cook. "You spent five grand on the hammer, which is fine... but we need to invest in our fourth Skill slots, maybe even buy a fifth for you, Nacho. I've been digging through the Store, and I've found a few things. There's this 'Yell' ability that would stun my opponents. Something like that can make a fight easy, or give me a moment to escape."

"We should wait for the Skills Box," Nacho stubbornly tried to deflect. "Just be patient."

"Says the guy with all four of his Skill Slots filled." Brie didn't try to hide the troubled look on her face. "Look, I get your point, but I'm also concerned. I don't want to die in this world, and I especially don't want you two to die. Having more, and better, Skills will help me feel a lot more comfortable."

Reuben pulled Brie close. Some yellow flour had landed on his nose, which sabotaged his tender expression with an air of silliness. Brie smiled in spite of herself as she reached up and gently brushed it off. He practically *radiated* positivity as he grinned down at her. "Don't worry. Let's do some leveling today. Since we're already spending money, let's get ourselves to level fifteen. That will increase our Fitness and Health Points, and we'll end up with a better Health Regen rate."

Brie shook her head. "We'll need to talk with the council first about collective expenditures and guild needs, before we propose more personal advancement. Frankly, we really have put off building the market apartments for too long. Let's get people eating Nacho's donuts, and then we'll make our case."

"Good call. I think that'll be the most effective way to get people on our side of things." Reuben squeezed his wife but looked at Nacho. "Depending on how good those donuts are, of course. I'll keep my fingers crossed."

Nacho had planned to get started right away, but he didn't get the chance. Gustav and Gary strolled in the kitchen door leading outside, followed closely by one of their new recruits, an excitable warrior named Simon Spear. His real last name wasn't 'Spear', but it had become a kind of nickname. He'd bought a magic spear and had both a defensive ability, enabling him to spin the weapon to avoid being attacked, as well as a hurl ability—which was where the magic spear really shone. He could throw the spear and call it back as soon as it impacted something.

Simon was a definite go-getter, probably because he didn't sleep much, talked fast, and fought furiously. He was roughly Nacho's age, if a little younger, but he had the temperament of a toddler on energy drinks. "Nacho! Hey, Nacho! We have beef. Like, a *lot* of beef. Tons of beef. Outside. The GG's and I brought up a bunch—we quartered it, like you showed us. Look… we want tacos. I know you might have some other plan for it, but we haven't had tacos since we came here, and since we brought the meat-"

Gustav lifted a hand and shook the spearman aggressively. "Easy, Simon. Go easy on Nacho."

The elder of the G's, Gustav had given up on fighting his encroaching baldness and just shaved his head. He was only thirty, a former high school football coach, and surprisingly chill. Gary, on the other hand, had a certain… intensity. He'd embraced his long hair and kept it back in a ponytail. Gary had played professional football for a while before blowing out his knee, which had inspired him to shift his knowledge into sports medicine. While Gary wasn't a Healer per se, he did provide his Ghost Pepper Brigade with some important basic medical services.

Gustav had a Motivation Skill, honed by his ability to get teenagers to actually practice and show up to games, and he fought with a two-handed claymore. His sword was almost as big as Kala's black blade, and it was coupled with a devastating Worldshaker Slash ability that used up the vast majority of his Hunger Points and Mana in one use, but he could oftentimes end a fight with a single blow.

"I love the sound of that!" Reuben clapped his hands. "Yes! Nacho! Tacos. It's been too long. I'll help with the tortillas. Good thinking, Simon."

"Did you fight plants, Reuben? We heard you fought 'millet', and we have no idea what that means!" Simon was practically shouting in enthusiasm, and when Reuben explained corrupted vegetation to him, the spearman went on a tear about predatory fruits and vegetables. Ultimately, he decided that he'd rather fight them than eat them. His friends had to physically block him from running off on his own to test his mettle against the nearest foliage.

Nacho left the kitchen with Gustav and Gary to take stock of the haunches they'd pulled off the downed Steer Clears. The quarters must've weighed a hundred pounds each, but Nacho didn't pause to calculate. If they wanted tacos, he'd have to begin processing the Putrid Mana out of the meat immediately; the timer had already begun. He called back through the doorway as he studied the piles of raw beef, "Reuben and Brie, if you can clear the flour off my counter, that'd help a lot. I'm going to haul this meat in and get started."

Nacho hoped against hope he'd be able to get every last credit for the slabs of Steer Clear. In the end, he went through one full quarter and part of another. He didn't get a full nineteen rounds, only sixteen before the second one dissolved, but that was still three hundred and fifty-two credits. Thanks to his knives, one hundred and twenty-five pounds of meat multiplied into one hundred eighty-seven and a half pounds… which Feasting Feats transformed into three thousand, five hundred, sixty-two and a half pounds.

Not everyone ate their allotted pound, but at the end of the day, he had sold one thousand eight hundred and eighty meals across Tortilla Flats, Armor Mountain Central, and Jalapeño Town. Newer residents were still getting used to the idea that Nacho could cook far more food than they could eat, and he was happy beyond words to be able to provide.

At the end of the night, Nacho and his friends had a ton of personal cash on hand to spend for their Skills, to level themselves, or to buy something from the Store. Nacho had also begun thinking of saving up for an actual room of his own, a little place outside of the kitchen. He still didn't mind sleeping on his shelf, but he had been thinking more and more that having a place overlooking the market might be fun. Or he could build a private tower right outside his kitchen—that would cut down on his walking time.

The massive windfall highlighted something important, however. Brie had been correct. They needed to start investing in themselves, and *heavily*. If he had been less of a miser, he could have purchased Feasting Feats months ago and would have progressed far beyond his current power level.

The bottom line was that with his cooking income, he needed to be more flexible when it came to shopping and leveling. It wouldn't do him any good to die with a bunch of credits to his name. Better to spend them and increase his Skills than to hoard them for no reason. On his way to bed, he promised Brie that they would do a ton of shopping the next day.

Nacho awoke at first light to get started on his donuts, finally ready to investigate the cryptic warning the system had given him about millet flour.

CHAPTER TEN

Nacho had been cleaning for *hours* after the morning's Great Donut Disaster. The Patrons had been right to warn him about the dangers of gluten-free cooking, and the logic that Reuben used to explain what he had been missing had finally clicked. The cook muttered that advice softly to himself, "If the warning seems vague and throwaway, it's deadly. If it's over the top, they're hiding a delicious secret."

The problem was twofold. When it came to making dough, the flour was so dry and volatile that it puffed up into a cloud, even upon impact with *water*. His first attempt had ended in absolutely coating the kitchen with the stuff, and the fine dust got into *all* of his other cooking supplies, which changed the Composition of the other dishes he was attempting to make by including itself as an additional ingredient. That eruption had cost him dozens of credits to replace every ingredient that had been left out, and forced him to clean all of his utensils and workspaces before making an attempt on any new dishes.

Nacho had originally assumed that he would be able to ignore the issue so long as he was already using that same ingredient, but millet was attracted to itself, and it ended up throwing the ratios off whenever he tried. Even when he finally managed to complete the first set, the donuts were so difficult to eat that anyone with fewer than thirteen points in Fitness was utterly unable to chew them.

The people that *could* eat them did not particularly *want* to do so. The fried disaster rings were tasteless, unpleasant things, and over thirty people had choked trying to swallow them—nearly to death in a few instances. Nacho hadn't planned any other food for breakfast, since he hadn't noticed any issues when munching on them himself, thanks to his inflated stats. When people practically started to riot about the 'tree bark circles', he hadn't been able to understand the issue at first.

It took nearly until lunch to get everything sorted out and make a new meal available to the guild. The Ghost Pepper Brigade had carted off most of his donuts and any leftovers available, but that was only because they were desperate for his food, both for the protection the millet flour offered, as well as his Cooking Magic that would improve their stats.

As lunchtime approached, shouts began erupting from the market. Several were calls for Nacho, and he could hear them without difficulty even from the depths of his kitchen. Fearing a resurgence of the food riots, he left the building with his HungerCry blades held loosely at his sides. He froze at the sight of the fear on Colleen's face as she came to find him.

She skidded to a stop as soon as she spotted him and motioned for him to follow her, then turned and took off down the stairs, racing along the well-worn path between the guildhall and the new eastern wing of the Citadel Apartments. Gustav and Gary were waiting for them in the center of a crowd, both unharmed but looking worried. As usual, Simon Spear was with them, though he was pale and seemed to be having trouble standing in one spot, weaving near-drunkenly from sheer exhaustion.

Amir, who had inherited the Gauntlets of Monster Destruction from Young Bill, looked the most ragged, but that made sense. He'd been regularly delving into the lower levels of the

Costco UnderFun. Taye had mentioned that he was going to grab Amir to help the Breakfast Club check out the new dungeon near the CrossWorld Portal. Amir wasn't one to take breaks, but at that moment, he looked like he needed a vacation.

Brie and Reuben were already present and deep in conversation, and Mayor Dan and Iron Becky stood with the crowd that was rapidly increasing in numbers. It seemed fortunate that Old Bill and Kala weren't present, but most likely, they'd show up once the news traveled through the community—it was clear that the report was bad.

Simon detonated like a volcano that had lay dormant for years before erupting out of nowhere. "Guild Leader! CrossHumans attacked! That's what happened, but we weren't there. It was Amir. He was watching the Portal, and nothing was coming out or going in. Like, not a thing. The CrossHumans just... appeared out of the forest, on our side. But Amir can tell you more."

Amir stepped forward wearily and opened his mouth, but Simon pounded his spear into the ground and kept going. "I guess there was this big, huge fight, and then someone materialized out of nowhere—we think it was teleportation. Some Mind Player who can teleport. He grabs Kristie and drags her through the Portal, which I guess smells terrible. That's my understanding, at any rate. Amir, *tell* him what happened!"

Amir squinted at Simon, managing to voice a single syllable, only for Simon to growl in frustration and begin shouting once more at how long the man was taking. "Kristie is gone, right? You can probably imagine what happens next. Abby isn't going to let her friend just be kidnapped. No, so she runs through the Portal."

Amir shrugged, clearly giving up and just waiting to let Simon finish the story. "Taye and some others go running after Abby. But Taye is bright enough to send someone to come and tell us. That was Amir's job. He races off, but then what does he find? Zombies! Like, actual reanimated corpses. He had to duck and dodge them, but Amir was good. He made it away from them. Anyway, he runs into us on the road. He told me the whole story, but you should probably hear it from him."

Nacho's stomach dropped at the idea of zombies around the Portal. "Were they Human or CrossHuman Zombies?"

"Does it matter?" Brie stood with her lacrosse stick across her shoulder, barely containing herself from smacking the chatterbox with it. "When did this all happen?"

Amir waved sourly at Simon. "I guess he can tell you."

"Thanks." Simon was oblivious to the undertone. "It was the day before today, so yesterday? Amir ran all night. He had to dodge some serious mobs, but he wanted to find us as soon as possible. We escorted him, me and the rest of the Ghost Pepper Brigade. Gustav and Gary wanted to come up with us to let you know we'll escort you back to the Portal and then to the other side. You'll need the best, and *we're* the best."

Nacho's mind churned through the story. Arriod had finally made a move. This had to be the first advance in a greater game. He had never heard of anyone being kidnapped by the CrossHumans before. Arriod and his goons had just killed people, collected their credits, had themselves a breakfast snack, and moved on. "This is something… different."

The commotion had drawn a huge contingent of residents, as well as some adventurers who were hauling huge caterpillar monsters that were obviously pretty high-value kills. Nacho kept his grin internal: he hadn't known what he was going to be making for dinner that night, but now they had some big old worms to cook up. The cook decided on the spot that no matter what anyone else said, he was going to buy that insect cookbook and add it to his *Aria*.

Even though he'd messed up the donuts, he'd redeem himself with a brand-new recipe that everyone would love. Nacho realized that he was stalling and shook off the daydream just in time for Colleen to surprise him by grabbing Amir and leading him into the guildhall.

"I'm so sorry, Amir. That sounds tough. Let's get you inside and sit you down. Nacho, do you have anything for Amir to eat?" In the next breath, she added with a wry grin, "You know… something good."

"Yeah, let's get Amir taken care of. We can talk in the kitchen while I start processing those big caterpillars." Nacho wasn't going to reveal what his gyro meat was made from. It would be seasoned so well that they would never know it had come from insect meat. For the time being, Nacho offered Amir some two-day-old tacos, wincing as the exhausted man wolfed down the sad, stale meal without flinching. "Does that taste okay?"

"Yeah," the fighter mumbled around bites. "Tastes just like everything else you make, so no issue here."

Not wanting Amir to see the discomfort Nacho felt at that moment—as the cook realized that the food being old and soggy didn't change the quality or taste—he retreated to his kitchen to be alone with the giant caterpillar he'd selected. Six feet long, and at least two hundred pounds, it would easily feed everyone by itself. He sneakily purchased *Insect Eats: Delicious Bug Recipes with a Middle Eastern Flair*, a Tier two Class Item, for six hundred credits. A glance around guaranteed that no one else was in his sanctum, so he openly read the gyro recipe and found that he needed coriander seed, which was the only ingredient he didn't have. He had all the optional ingredients on hand—thyme, paprika, garlic, oregano, peppercorns, sea salt, lemons, and olive oil; he simply needed to replenish all of his spices, thanks to the Donut Disaster.

He could peruse the rest of the recipe later—to process, he just needed to push the Putrid Mana out of the meat. As predicted, Old Bill and Kala burst into the kitchen just as black goop began to filter out of the spongy flesh. They grimaced and hastily retreated to join the rest of the crowd in the guildhall where Amir was retelling the story, with some unneeded help from Simon.

Turning his thoughts back to the meat, Nacho produced his knives and expertly carved away sizable chunks. The giant caterpillar was a level fifteen monster; if he got through twenty rounds of processing, he'd earn six hundred credits for the meat, which would be just enough to recover the cost of the cookbook.

On top of that, he could make ninety credits for a meal that served three. Multiplied by the thousands of guild members that would pay, it would grant him a hefty paycheck. The taxes would continue filling the guild coffers, and his cooking magic would linger for quite a while. He considered, then discarded, the idea of trying to use the millet for some kind of pita bread. He wasn't going to attempt any more gluten-free baking for a while; at least, not until he figured out the key to making it palatable. "I need to find someone that was a vegetarian back on earth. I bet they'd know what to do with this… demon grain."

It wasn't long before Reuben, Brie, and The Chips Guild's de facto ruling council came storming into Nacho's kitchen, still arguing amongst themselves about what to do about the Cross-Human situation. The sudden commotion put a small frown on the cook's face, as he preferred a calm and quiet workspace. He eyed the pile of clean caterpillar meat and decided that he had gotten through more than enough. Running his hands under some water to clean off the grime, he stood tall and cleared his throat to bring all eyes on him.

"Here's the deal."

Whether they would like it or not, he had been pondering the issue the entire time that he had been keeping his hands busy, and he had come to a decision. Nacho felt a thrill about the upcoming adventure, one that he hadn't even realized he'd been missing. His pronouncement echoed in the room. "We can't send half of our high-level players to rescue the other half. It doesn't make sense, and it would leave the majority of our guild unprotected. It just isn't feasible. I have an alternate proposition-"

He paused for a moment and glared until the last of the angry demands slowly died down. "You think I *want* to risk myself like this? Be real, people. Mayor Dan will take over running things on Armor Mountain. Kala and The Ghost Pepper Brigade all stay. Reuben, Brie, and I will spend the credits to level up, then go through the Portal after what I *hope* are captives… and not snacks. It *will* just be the three of us, so we can slip in quick and silent, and get out just as fast."

"All of this sounds like you planned it from the start," Kala disagreed with a snarl. "How do we know any of this is even real? That it isn't just you commandeering guild money to level yourselves up?"

"The fact that you ask that shows how little you know us. Frankly, it tells us more about you than what you're trying to imply. Notice that *no one* else even had that thought cross their mind." Nacho stared down the blustering Death Knight until she looked away, muttering under her breath. "That is a good point, however. We won't raise ourselves to Tier two with guild funds; we're just going to finish getting to level fifteen. I'm not going to explain why that's important, as it isn't knowledge everyone needs at the moment. On a related yet unrelated note, I can say that we're also on the lookout for dungeons that are… different."

"That was one thing that Simon forgot to mention." Gustav snapped his fingers as he spoke up. "There was a dungeon between the CrossWorld Portal and Muddy River. Except, it had already been plundered by the CrossHumans. I remember thinking that it was weird, because it said something about being their Welcome Dungeon, and had a line about the two worlds being connected."

"Or did it say the worlds were… *Juxtaposed*?" Reuben lifted an eyebrow and surreptitiously glanced around to see if anyone would comment on his genius.

"Mighta been something like that." Gary shrugged and kept his eyes on Nacho. "Not sure you'll have time to really look, but… then again, you might as well keep them peepers open. Whatever happened to our people might be a done deal by now, or they're keeping them alive for some reason. I guess it's either over, or you still have time."

"That's *very* helpful. Thanks for your input." Kala furrowed her brows at the man, who merely fluttered his eyelashes and subtly moved into different positions to flex for her. "I agree that I hate the idea of you three going off on your own."

"Because you care?" Reuben tried hopefully. "That's so sweet of you."

"Be realistic, hubby." Brie knew the truth, and she let it out with a huff. "She hates the idea of us finding treasure or skills that she won't get access to. Right, Kala?"

The Death Knight didn't bother to hide her smirk. "We also won't have Nacho cooking. Cheap, palatable food is something we can only get from him. Why is he going anyway?"

"My food is better than palatable," Nacho interjected mildly. "Also, I have a mission brief already laid out for the people that will be staying here. There's an entire field of millet that needs to be destroyed before it becomes a Catastrophe-level threat. Mayor Dan has the details for you."

"You of all people should know by now that he can do serious damage," Brie explained none too patiently. "If he comes with us, he can continue to cook for *us*. We'll need his magic. Lastly, he knows more about the CrossHumans than anyone else."

"I should come to protect him." Gustav was the only one who nodded at his own assertion. "Keep him alive. Protect his cooking hand. Wouldn't hurt me to collect some skull trophies along the way, either. Always looking to add to my collection."

Nacho was fairly certain Gustav's collection was small, if not completely non-existent. Wait… *monster* skulls turned into Putrid Mana. He made a note to look into whatever skulls the spicy warrior had managed to collect. He also subtly moved a few people between Brie and Gustav so that she didn't 'accidentally' collect a skull trophy of her own.

Mayor Dan put a hand on Nacho's shoulder as he walked back to his prep counter. "I don't like this plan much. If we lost you three, we'd lose a lot of the reason folks joined the Chips Guild in the first place. I do see your logic for only taking a small force, if we have to worry about zombies on top of everything else."

"Nacho and his friends shouldn't go alone. They should at least take Colleen and Simon with them," Iron Becky insisted, keeping an eye on Nacho's reaction.

"Sounds like a love triangle," Gary chuckled in a low voice. "How do you feel about making it into a square?"

"Get out of my kitchen, Gary." Nacho wasn't going to let that train of thought linger. "Enough. This is not up for discussion. Brie, Reuben, and I will leave tonight after making dinner available. See to your posts and your people. Remember that bread always falls on the buttered side, so expect—and be ready for—trouble."

"I guess we already *have* a square," Gary muttered as he rolled his eyes and stalked off as though Nacho were being unfair to him, getting plenty of laughter and high-fives from his Ghost Pepper group.

Kala eyed the mess of disintegrating caterpillar meat and fluid puddling on his counter and dripping onto the floor. "You're not going to be feeding that to us, are you?"

"Just processing it for the credits." Nacho didn't let himself flinch. People didn't need to know how sausages were made to enjoy them. Once they realized how delicious the food was, they wouldn't ask many questions. As his workspace emptied, he chuckled quietly to himself.

"Wouldn't answer those questions either way. Sorry, Kala… gotta work with what I've got."

CHAPTER ELEVEN

The Dinner Party hiked away from the guild as darkness settled over the land, following the **zip** and **snap** of Nacho's flickering Fireflies. He was down to eight little potstickers to light their way, and traveling at night in the Juxtaposition was a dangerous proposition. Beyond the standard threat of simply not seeing an incoming ambush, or the risk of stumbling into dangerous terrain, there were also high-Tier creatures that emerged from dungeons at night to snack on unsuspecting players.

Nacho knew that it was better to leave immediately to cut down on the chances of being followed, even if it was by someone well-meaning. They had the time and the necessary skill to get a few hours of travel in before they camped.

It had been a long time since he had been out in the darkness without a fire or a safe place to rest for the night. A smile that he hadn't felt since the last time he'd opened a few arteries started to invade his mouth. Instead of intimidating, the night felt *invigorating*. The forest air smelled of sweet suggestions, as predators that were new to this world tried to lure hapless creatures to their maw. Strange flowers blossomed in the moonlight, while *real* fireflies winked on and off, offering an open invitation to all suckers that would chase after them.

"Ahh… this is the life. Knowing everything wants to kill you, just *so bad*… and knowing that you can kill it first." He was feeling good, and he wanted to share that feeling with his friends. He couldn't tell if they agreed with him or not, as neither of them were talking to him currently.

Inconceivably, the caterpillar gyros had apparently been the biggest mistake of his culinary career, even taking into account the donuts. He didn't understand why people had such an issue with them; *he* thought they had tasted fine. Nacho nodded to himself as he worked out the *real* issue. "I see… people are getting too comfortable. Eh. They'll learn. Maybe I'll even extend this trip a bit, see how many people die of starvation? There might be a *tish* little bit of cannibalism that crops up, but we can stamp that out once we get back. I bet we won't have any objections after that."

"Let's not be too hasty!" Reuben nervously interrupted, breaking the silent vow of silence he had made with Brie. "That might backfire, and then people will try to keep you in the kitchen no matter what, right?"

"Hmm. You may have a point." Nacho lapsed into pensive silence as Reuben wiped away the sudden sweat that had appeared on his own forehead.

With the issue of 'silent treatment' taken care of with one clean kill shot, Nacho's thoughts turned to the credits he was planning to spend. He wanted to get to their cabin on Heartbreak Ridge before spending anything, as there was a chance that other Chips Guild members might be using it—either more people from Taye's Breakfast Club, or possibly one of the off-duty parties on rotation from the UnderFun.

About halfway to the cabin, Nacho lurched to a sudden halt, turned, and tackled his friends to the ground under the canopy of the whispering trees they were passing. Less than two seconds later, three enormous Vampire Owls floated above the branches overhead. Luckily for the humans, the leaves hadn't started to fall yet. Nacho had seen the creatures and scanned them in nearly the same moment, and moved as soon as it registered that they were Tier three.

The birds could have easily been mistaken for airplanes if someone were casually glancing upwards—except with talons that looked more akin to electrical poles than something attached to a living creature. Worst of all, instead of beaks, they possessed bat-like mouths full of fangs.

As a Tier Three creature, they were dangerous just to be *around.* As the deadly parliament passed over the trees, vitality drained from the leaves at the top. The foliage withered and started to drop as though winter had arrived early. Nacho shuddered at the thought of having to fight the creatures if they had come in for the kill.

Those Vampire Owls had been pretty high up, which was likely the only reason they hadn't seen Nacho's glowing potstickers, much less hear the clank of his mobile kitchen. The irony wasn't lost on him—in the Probability Vision, he'd moved silently—he had been the Shadow Killer, who appeared out of nowhere like a plague of knives.

Now? He clanked like a walking dishrack.

He'd have to fix that.

Once they were confident the Vampire Owls had moved on, Nacho and his friends sprinted until they were *sure* they were away from the terrifying creatures' habitat, then hustled the rest of the way to the cabin on Heartbreak Ridge, only to find it empty.

"Well *that* was terrifying. What do Tier three creatures have? Tier one gets the mana protection, two gets an aura effect; what about threes?" Brie openly addressed Nacho as she dropped her pack, while Reuben silently moved to get a fire going. "There's never been a better justification to get stronger. We have more than enough credits to level up our classes before we go to bed."

Reuben slumped over the sticks he was stacking and moaned, "Oh no, Brie. Don't. I say we do it in the morning."

"Did you say 'donuts in the morning'?" Nacho brightly questioned with a knowing smile.

"No!" Brie and Reuben answered in horrified unison.

The big guy followed their outburst with a last little quip. "We will revisit the Great Donut Disaster only when we are faced with imminent combat."

"Ouch. You *know* it's bad when people will only eat your food for combat purposes." Nacho clutched at his chest. "I can't help that cooking things that taste good doesn't come naturally. Also, Brie, I have no idea about Tier threes. When I saw them *back then*, they were something to run away from. Near the end, they were treated like natural disasters. I got to the peak of Tier two only because I kept killing people with fat wallets, like guild leaders that carried the entire guild's funds on their person. I never even *fought* a Tier three monster."

"Fair enough." Brie glanced between the other two, then shrugged slightly. "Should *I* level up first, or…?"

Nacho stretched, glad to have his mobile kitchen off his back, despite the fact that the weight was something he could easily manage, even in combat. "You're right. We should upgrade tonight. I got about twenty-five thousand credits from dinner."

"For your wormy gyros? Really?" Brie arched her eyebrows in astonishment. "You're not going to give that back to the people who ate… that?"

"All sales are final." Nacho shrugged away her concerns. "The meal worked as advertised. No Putrid Mana, refills Hunger points, affordable. I can't worry about everyone's delicate sensibilities. It wasn't people meat, and they should be grateful for that. If they don't want what's available, there's always Store food."

"I love it." Reuben pushed himself off the floor and tousled Nacho's hair. "Don't worry, buddy. I liked your weird bug tacos. It's just a shame that people figured it out like… the *second* they went up for sale."

"I blame the Brittanys. Pretty sure they let it slip that dinner was mostly caterpillar meat, and that started the… unrest. It was too bad people stopped buying them after that. I hate wasting food." Nacho paused to ponder whether he needed to create a non-disclosure agreement for his kitchen help.

"Old Bill didn't seem to mind them," Brie attempted to console her friend. "He said that your gyros were like ones he used to buy at the stand on the side of the road before the Juxtaposition. The one that always gave him food poisoning, but he bought from it every time. Well, after he found it. Something about how it had to be moved to a different street every few days to 'stay ahead of them', or something like that."

"Let's just… focus on successes? Start leveling up already," Nacho grumped at his friends as they chuckled at his expense. Trying to ignore them, he checked his Chips Guild Stat Sheet.

Chips Guild Stat Sheet

Total Guild Credits: 178,551 credits (an 80K Day x2! Keep the streak going!)

Total Number of Members: 6,136

Guild Master: Eli 'Nacho' Naches

Alternate Guild Master: Daniel 'Mayor Dan' Chronour

Third Alternate: Reuben 'Lactose Tolerant' Colby

To upgrade all three of them to level fifteen, they were going to have to pull in some cash from the guild coffers. At this point, Nacho wasn't going to worry about it. Mayor Dan would understand, and they hadn't heard any protests when they announced their plan before leaving. Nacho calculated the total credits required to bring Reuben to level fifteen and sent them along.

The big guy winced and grabbed at his ears. "*Ouch*, that **cha-ching** was loud. How many credits did you…? Oh, yikes. Yup, I'm gonna do this thing. Going first!"

Reuben started to convulse as his body was forcefully

mutated by the foreign energy that caused 'leveling up'. By the time the unnatural process was completed, he ended up on one of the bunk beds covered in sweat. Nacho wiped his friend's forehead with a cool, wet dish towel. "Okay, that was something. Feeling okay? Wanna share the results?"

The Healer closed his eyes and silently sent his status.

Reuben Colby
Class: Merchant of Soothing
Level: 15
Experience Points: 159,700 to Level 16!
Current Credits: 0 (342,817 total Dinner Party pool)

Build Type: Balanced, Instant
Body:

- *Fitness: 22*
- *Metabolic efficiency: 21*

Mind:

- *Mental energy: 21*
- *Circuit: 21*

Satiation:

- *Hunger: 100*
- *Thirst: 100*

Health Points: 54
Bonus Physical Damage: 11%
Health Regen: 21% Health Regen/minute
Total Mana Pool: 41.5
Bonus Spell Damage: 10.5%
Mana Pool Regen: 21% Mana Regen/minute

Skill Slots (3/4)

- *Healing Hugs (Active) Level 19: 95 Health Points Restored Upon Hugging.*

Tier 1 Enhancement: Hurl your hug 30 feet!

- *Positive Vibes (Active) Level 19: Weapon blessing: (applies to whole party, lasts 10 minutes) Adds 38% physical damage.*

Tier 1 Enhancement: Longer duration! Double the love!

- *Marketing (Active) Level 19: Able to lure creatures to a location. Impacts up to Level:20.*

Tier 1 Enhancement: Maximizes the four principles of marketing (Product, Price, Place, and Promotion).

- *Open slot*

"I figured out how to turn off the parts I don't want to share every single time. You know how much my abilities cost; it hasn't changed." Reuben plucked his Yeti drinking horn out of thin air and sucked down perfectly chilled root beer to cool himself down. "Know what I mean?"

The Healer seemed strangely dejected, and Nacho felt proud that he had been able to recognize the emotion. Now he needed to try to fix it. "What's wrong, Reuben? Other than the fact that your Marketing skill's Tier one Enhancement gives the 'awesome' combat bonus of letting you place a sign a little better."

"It's not that. Also, I'm not going to argue about how wrong you are. It is *super* useful." At least the Healer had begun chuckling and had his eyes open. "All those credits, and all I get are two extra Health Points and a bit more Mana? One and a half extra Mana? A *fraction* more Mana Regen? Just doesn't seem worth it."

"Don't think like that." Brie sat and leaned over to give him a warm hug. "It's a baby step toward Tier two. We can't just leap up levels anymore. There is no more sprinting; everything from here on out is going to be a marathon. All this does is convince me that we need to fill our last Skill Slot, and maybe buy another one each. Just like Nacho told us at the beginning, Skills are what matters the most."

"Once we find a Skills Box," Nacho deflected her attempt to get him to part with the funds she wanted, "I totally agree."

"So close." Brie snapped her fingers with a grimace. "Bah. Fine. We'll stick to levels, for now. Let's at least go at the same time? I'm going to handle this like the hardcore lacrosse player I am, and Reuben can watch the area while we upgrade."

"Good luck." Reuben pulled his wife in for a peck on the cheek as Nacho transferred the credits.

True to her word, she gritted her teeth and stared into her husband's eyes as she went through the process without making a sound, merely shivering intently and breaking into a feverish sweat. When she was finished, she started breathing like a bellows and glared at Nacho. "You were supposed to upgrade at the same time."

"Having two-thirds of our force out of commission would have been a foolish thing to do," the cook told her simply, ignoring the glare. She snorted, and without anyone requesting it, sent her Stat Sheet.

Brie McCurdy
Class: Battle Babe
Level: 15
Experience Points: 159,700 to Level 16!
Current Credits: 0 (145,417 total Dinner Party pool)

They skimmed through her information quickly. Nothing much had changed except for her Stats themselves, and since they were exactly the same as Reuben's, it was easy to gloss over them without spending too much time. The additional point in Fitness was the only thing that did anything useful, and it merely increased her Health Points from fifty-two to fifty-four.

Brie wiped a sweaty hand across her brow. "Okay, Nacho. It's your turn. Are you actually going to do it, or are you going to have some other excuse, like 'it's too dark to level me up tonight'?"

"No, nothing like that." Nacho would be going up to level fifteen, a big advancement for his build type. Each of his stats would jump by five, changing him further from human than any other person on the planet, so far as he knew. "Just trying to get ready for the pain."

CHAPTER TWELVE

Nacho threw another log on the fire, hoping that extra heat in the air would aid his skin in stretching with less tearing or pain as his muscles writhed.

The hard oak rapidly perfumed the cabin, along with the sweet smell of Reuben's root beer burps, as the Healer waxed eloquent. "I guess it's fair that spending credits on small steps isn't as exciting as getting those big, chunky upgrades. But those days are gone, unless we start earning and spending in the millions."

"Let's hope we get there someday," Nacho enthusiastically agreed, not at all matching the tone the Healer had been attempting to set. He dramatically lifted his arms toward Armor Mountain. "I'm going to need to borrow some credits from the Chips Guild Coffers. Forgive me, Old Bill!"

Once he transferred them to his personal account, he knew Mayor Dan would get a message. That wasn't an issue, since Mayor Dan trusted them. Nacho *did* suddenly wonder if they could use those messages to communicate. Could they somehow come up with a system of morse code by transferring credits in increments? Even something as simple as a specific amount that meant 'city is under attack'?

Nacho kicked off his shoes, bought and spent the requisite Experience Points, and was soon feeling the burn in his blood. His skin stung, and he didn't think the fire was helping whatsoever. He looked down in time to see the flesh over his bicep rip, and the adipose under the surface literally boiled and steamed as it was expended and removed, only for his skin to seamlessly heal over it. Nacho decided not to watch so closely anymore.

"That was truly disgusting. Thanks for the nightmare fuel." Brie gave him a thumbs up as he finished the process and collapsed in an exhausted heap. "I have to admit, I'm excited to see what your Balanced, Delayed Build type gave you."

Nacho shared his Stat Sheet silently, taking deep breaths in an effort to move past the mental component of leveling up. One nice benefit he immediately discovered was that he could inhale a *massive* volume of air and keep it in his lungs for longer than he really wanted to test. If he had to guess, he could likely survive nearly three-quarters of an hour underwater. Internally, he told himself, "It's the little things that make the boost that much more noticeable."

Eli 'Nacho' Naches
Class: Junior League Chef
Level: 15
Experience Points: 159,700 to Level 16!
Current Credits: 0 (0 total Dinner Party pool)

Build Type: Balanced, Delayed
Body:

- *Fitness: 25*
- *Metabolic Efficiency: 25*

Mind:

- *Mental Energy: 25*
- *Circuit: 25*

Satiation:

- *Hunger: 100*
- *Thirst: 100*

Health Points: 60
Bonus Physical Damage: 12.5%
Health Regen: 25% Health Regen/minute
Total Mana Pool: 47.5
Bonus Spell Damage: 12.5%
Mana Pool Regen: 25% Mana Regen/minute

Skill Slots (4/4)

- *Small Blades (Passive) Level 19: 38% bonus damage on all knife attacks.*

Tier 1 Enhancement: Your blades can slice from up to 6 inches away from their edge!

- *Ingredient Processing (Active) Level 19: Remove Putrid Mana from monsters up to Level 21.*

Tier 1 Enhancement: Process ingredients from 15 feet away!

- *Cooking Magic (Active) Level 19: Create food that enhances a single stat by 95% of maximum.*

Tier 1 Enhancement: Throw magic into a food item you cooked from 15 feet away!

- *Feasting Feats (Active) Level 19: Cook 19 times the food you're currently preparing!*

Tier 1 Enhancement: you can choose up to five locations where people can use you like a vending machine! At the low, low cost of 15% of the sale price, people no longer need to come bother you directly for their food. It'll just appear in front of them, at the location you specify, within 500 feet of the original food source.

Caution! As this is meant as a feast for many and not for one, only a single portion of each meal created through the use of this Skill can be eaten by each person!

Nacho had to wince at their current lack of credits. They were flat broke, which was beyond dangerous. They needed to have at least a bit of cash, so he transferred another fifteen hundred credits from the guild's coffers, just in case. He divided the extra money among his friends, so each of them were carrying five hundred, then focused on the changes that had resulted from his level increase.

Every fifth level, he reaped the benefits of his 'Balanced, Delayed Build'. In this instance, all of his Stats had jumped from twenty to twenty-five. The results were admittedly dramatic, and he had to stifle his elation over the boost. He had gained ten extra Health Points, and his Damage Bonus had jumped to twelve and a half percent.

His Mana Pool increased by seven and a half Points, and his Mana Regen was now at twelve and a half percent. "Every little bit helps."

Nacho shared his screen, as the others had, and all of their eyes glowed as they read over his Stat Sheet. Reuben started muttering to himself 'quietly'. "Don't be jealous of Nacho. Taking a bite of his arm won't increase any of my own stats. Just relax. Then again, one bite just to check wouldn't hurt *him* too much-"

"No. Bad Reuben." Brie slapped her husband's arm as he started reaching for the Guild Leader. "Don't blame Nacho for being able to plan ahead."

"This wouldn't have been possible for all of us." Nacho

blew out a breath, feeling a spike of regret despite knowing that he was right. "The incremental gains you guys get at every level is far better for staying at the top of your game as we fight through stuff on the daily. Otherwise we'd have to grind the same, safe, low-level creatures over and over until we reached our credit goal. Also, I had no idea back at the start that we would be able to pull in the number of credits that we're earning. It was the safest, best option, and I stand by it."

"Doesn't mean I don't want those thicc numbers, bud." Reuben studied Nacho one last time, searchingly, then grumbled and handed the cook the salt shaker he had grabbed. "It was just, you know... in case."

"In case I didn't stop you from biting him, and Nacho's skin needed salt?" Brie's query earned a guilty smile from the Healer. "Right; glad I'm here then. Any chance we can also shop for some Skills before we go to bed?"

"Not like I couldn't *heal* him," Reuben muttered as he waved off his wife's request. "No shopping, please. I'm beat. We should wait for this Skills Box thing that Nacho keeps practically drooling over."

The cook could easily understand why his friend was so tired. It was well past midnight, and they'd be up at first light to rush the rest of the way to the CrossWorld Portal. He turned to the Berserker. "Gustav mentioned something about a Skills dungeon near the CrossWorld Portal. Let's just wait a bit longer? Both because we're outta money, and because I truly think there are going to be better options."

Brie looked troubled and finally spat out the words that had been clawing their way up her throat. "We *have* to be at our best. I can't lose Reuben, and I can't lose you. You should know better than anyone that new Skills might keep us alive."

"No one is going to be dying. But..." Nacho dropped his eyes to the ground, lost in his thoughts for a long moment. "You're right. It's better to be ready for anything, and I agree that it'd be better to have Skills that will help in the short term, than to lose one of you because we wanted to be 'thrifty'."

Reuben called from his bunk. "I *know* for sure that a lack of sleep might kill me! Being distracted in combat is deadly, and all that."

"Thank you for seeing reason. Good night." Brie seemed willing to at least *try* sleeping, though like Nacho, she was clearly nervous about the upcoming day. It would mean fighting, and not just against Juxtaposition monsters, but against CrossHumans.

There was a side benefit to having leveled up: the massive stressors on their bodies—especially Nacho's—had worn them out. A good night of sleep, and a hearty meal in the morning, would enable them to utilize their new stats far better. The cook climbed into one of the bunk beds at the back of the cabin, suddenly missing his familiar kitchen shelf. Not that the shelf would be his bed anymore, as he'd be expected to sleep in the new tower that was being constructed for him while they were out and about.

"Ugh. People are getting too coddled already. Me too, I suppose." He nodded off in the process of muttering to himself.

As the first gleam of sunlight invaded the night sky, he was the first one up, pleased to find himself feeling completely refreshed. In a nod to their past camping adventures, he roused both his friends with the scent of freshly brewed coffee. While it was not something that was technically needed, old habits died hard. Old *addictions* died harder.

With how much cream, sugar, and Epic-grade Store vanilla syrup that Reuben added to his coffee, the beverage probably contained enough nutrients to replenish a quarter of his Hunger Points. Nacho could only watch on in disgust as Reuben shook the dregs from the bottle of sugary fluid, then took a sip of his.... abomination and exhaled a happy sigh.

After 'coffee', the trio packed up and were back on the road just as the sun crested the horizon. On the way to the portal, Nacho discussed his inspiration of being able to communicate long-range with the guild. By actively moving money in and out of the Chips Guild coffers, they could set up a code that would allow them to send messages. Automatic guild taxes hit without a notification, but any deposits or withdrawals were accompanied by careful accounting from the System for the top three people in the guild, which in this case was Nacho, Reuben, and Mayor Dan.

They discussed what each of the values could mean, and to no one's surprise, Reuben had a few excellent ideas and points that he was able to share. In practically no time at all, they had a rudimentary morse code set up between them. They never expected to have to use it, but it was a good way to pass the time as they moved.

Eventually they turned off their normal path to the Bove's Lair, instead following an understated game trail to the southeast that had been subtly marked by members of their guild. They only slowed, and eventually stopped, when Nacho caught the rank stench of the Portal blowing into their world. He dropped his pack, equipping his armor and weapons, though he kept his blades sheathed for maximum stealth.

The sky had been overtaken by a curtain of black clouds, and while it wasn't raining—yet—the smell of an imminent downpour had begun to mix with the rotten chemical smell seeping off the Portal. Nacho was grateful for the pseudo-darkness: he didn't have any special stealth abilities, but after spending three years skulking around in his Probability Vision, he knew his way around a shadow or two.

"Splitting the party isn't good," Brie argued futilely one last time. "You both told me that for *months* now, and here you go running off on your own."

"I'll be right back," Nacho stated with minimal exasperation. He was thankful that she was worried about him, and there was no reason to downplay that. "There's just no point in scouting if all of us are going at the same time. Don't worry… we can use our new System. If I transfer two credits, I'm fine. The second I need help, I'll transfer *three* credits, and you'll know to come running. Four credits means stay. Five credits means I need help, but approach with extreme caution. Six credits means I'm fine, but weirdness is afoot, so come but be careful. Seven credits means you should use Combat Dash to come and rescue me."

"Nothing that says don't come, but you're in trouble?" Reuben quirked an eyebrow with a troubled grin.

"No. Always make sure to save me at any cost," Nacho deadpanned in return.

"Nice." The Healer shook his head. "There's just one problem with our code. If you wind up in Active Combat, you won't be able to access the System. That means no credit transfers. Be careful, and don't take any unnecessary risks. After all, we *are* going to forgive you for dashing our hopes with the donuts… eventually."

"We'll forgive him when we're forced to use them and they actually help," Brie clarified, turning the mood somber. They all knew they'd be eating the deplorable donuts that very day.

Nacho nodded at his friends, then melted into the forest. His former Assassin instincts came flooding back as he focused on staying off the path and avoiding the tangles of thickets. With the thick layer of clouds, there were plenty of shadows for Nacho to use, and he was careful not to get entangled with any monster plants. Having been almost murdered by a basic millet, he didn't want to fall victim to any flora that had *started* dangerous, like poison ivy. "Leaves of three, don't devour me."

Nacho followed his nose to the Portal, pausing in confusion as he caught the scent of something else. A sweeter perfume than normal rot. "Zombies? I'd bet fifty credits that I just smelled zombies. Now *there's* a bet I'd be happy to lose."

He crept silently through the undergrowth, every one of his senses awake and alive. His heart was pounding, his lungs screaming for him to take deep breaths. Nacho crossed a dirt path marked by monster hooves but also by very human footprints. For a second, he felt the familiar thrill of battle, that heady intoxication of being in imminent danger.

Just then, the scent of a campfire filled his senses.

Creeping closer to his goal, Nacho approached the edge of

a glade, still a good ways away from the Portal itself. What made him freeze and hold his position was the numerous undead standing next to trees, motionless. Many were dressed in armor, surprisingly few held weapons, but *all* of them had rotting faces. To Nacho, that meant only one thing. "Someone *really* doesn't want to see these things as people."

He picked out a narrow path around the cluster of zombie thralls, making sure he could move without being seen. Getting back out would be tricky, but just like getting in, it wasn't impossible. Zombies were not good guards. Undoubtedly, it had something to do with necrosis frosting their eyes over.

Halfway around, Nacho spotted the woman in the glade, and all thoughts of reconnaissance left him. Actually, for several long seconds, he couldn't think at all. He was too stunned by what he saw.

She was *cooking*.

CHAPTER THIRTEEN

Nacho crouched in a thicket of bushes, barely breathing as he watched the woman work. He couldn't believe it. He'd found another Satiation Player, and it wasn't a hateful hermit who drank too much of his own hooch?

Or could this be… Nibbles? The mysterious player whom even the contemptible System seemed to speak deferentially toward? Nacho had heard of the Necromancer during both this version of the Starter World and in his Probability Vision. Most of the gossip described him as a tall, very thin man with a unique—very *human*—solution to the Juxtaposition's food problem. Was the gossip wrong?

Baffled, Nacho studied the woman as she stirred a massive cauldron over the smoky campfire. She wore standard leather armor, a thick shirt, a thick hood thrown back, and stylish pants. More to his annoyance, she wasn't using a typical spoon, and it didn't look like she was making soup or a stew. She had placed a table next to her fire, which held a variety of strange bowls and objects within easy reach.

Wrestling his brain back into investigative mode, he tried to take stock of the situation by scanning the area. The Portal appeared to be much farther south than this glade. A collection of tents and temporary buildings lay to the west. Some of the tents sported red letters; from his position, he could see a 'W' on one and an 'F' on another. Other structures had been marked with a clenched black fist. Had Nibbles destroyed, robbed, or teamed up with the Midnight Fist?

Nacho didn't know for certain, but this mysterious woman was alone for the moment. A couple of zombies loitered close by—a large dead man with his skull showing, as well as a wisp of a woman who probably couldn't see very well, thanks to the mass of blood-matted hair covering her face.

The enigmatic armored lady stirred her pot, then walked back to the table. A glint of light caught Nacho's eye, and he noticed a thick silver chain connecting her left leg to a nearby tree. She wasn't Nibbles; there was no way. She was a prisoner.

The epiphany was a great relief, but it made Nacho freeze to ponder his options for a minute. This woman likely wasn't a cook, which left… could she be the mysterious Brewer from the north? There was no way to know for sure, but he was hopeful that he could have just found a solution to several of his problems.

The cook needed to talk with her, but he had to be careful. Powerful Necromancers could see through the eyes of the undead to direct their movements, and it was likely that Nibbles was one of the top human powers in the world at the moment. That was a fight he did *not* want to start, not when he had a different goal in mind.

He fervently wished he had his old Assassin abilities. As the Shadow Killer, he could've easily melted into the shadows, as silent as a ghost. Nacho would've appeared right behind her before she knew he was there. He'd done such things often enough, though it usually ended in backstabbing, not chatting.

Nevertheless, he needed to work with the tool kit that he had. Nacho surveyed the underbrush surrounding the clearing, mapping a path that would take him near one of the undead guards. If he was quiet, he could slip by the zombies and sneak within earshot of the woman. She *had* to be a Brewer. Now that he was hunting for it, he smelled the unmistakable tang of barley malt in the air.

Creeping into the greenery of another bush, he managed to pick his way through the foliage and eased himself right next to some dead guy limply holding a brand-new sword that glimmered with magic. He grumbled at the sight internally. "Some corpses have all the luck."

Slipping past the unnaturally still sentinel, Nacho followed a row of hedges and came to a full stop as close to the table as he could go without being seen. Huddling behind the obscuring windbreak, he grabbed a rock and tossed it at the feet of the woman.

She whirled and her startled green eyes met his. Her expression filled with fear, then curiosity, hope, and finally bled back into fear once more. She blinked, and her face sank into a shadow of neutral impassivity.

Nacho put a finger to his lips.

The woman nodded and started whistling, then humming, and then finally began singing some old-timey sea shanty about pirates and bottles of rum. She sighed and skillfully wove purposeful words into her sing-song conversation starter.

"Oh, Brewing is such lonely work, such captive work indeed;

Brewing is such lonely work when one is out to sea.

If only a pleasant Necromancer would lend an ear for free,

Or perhaps a kindly Mind Player might keep me company."

She tapped her spoon rhythmically on the cauldron and continued humming the tune as she cautiously glanced around. Nacho followed suit, but *he* was holding a knife that was practically *crying* to be slammed into a Necromancer's tender flesh.

No one came.

"Might as well talk to myself, then." The Brewer seemed heartbroken over the idea. "Poor me, Jennifer Ales, chained up here against my will. Lost a lot of… a lot of friends to the Walking Fists. We had credits, boy. *Lots* of credits. Brewing up beer that restores people's Mana made us a lot of money. Too much. Brought the full might of the worst of humanity against us. Probably should've focused more on defense. There are some big guilds in Kansas City; they seem friendly. Chicago had… issues."

One of the zombies turned haltingly and pointed a withered green finger at her. The dead guy's jaws clicked and clacked as it mimicked speech.

"I'm not talking to you, tall, dark, and rotten," Jennifer evenly grumped. "Just complaining to myself. Talking to my shadow… makes me wonder what my shadow's name is."

The cook whispered as loud as he dared. "I'm Nacho. With the Chips Guild."

The Brewer kept chattering away, stirring as she muttered to herself. "You know, Jennifer 'ol gal, I used to hear good things about this Nacho from the Chips Guild. Won the Dragon Spear. I was kind of curious to see what he was like. He must be talented. To be a Common Cook? I know how much that cost in Evaluation Points."

"How many Players are keeping you chained up?" Nacho hissed the question.

"It was more than fifty Evaluation Points to become a Common Cook, back in the Evaluation. Probably closer to a hundred, now that I'm thinking of it; maybe two hundred if we're including the undead Evaluation Points." Jennifer shot him a quick glance, but smoothly went back to puttering at her Brewer's table and stirring her pot over the fire.

Nacho found her manipulation of idle dialogue pretty clever, and he wanted her to give them advice on the message system he was making with Reuben. More than just for her Brewing skills, he needed this person in his guild. The only thing stopping him from adding her right away was the fact that there were hundreds of enemies all around him.

"When will the other Players return?" Nacho's words carried along the wind, practically flying directly to Ms. Ale's ears. "How far away are they?"

"You've come a long way, Jennifer Ales," The Brewer continued rambling, tucking a strand of errant hair behind her ear as she bent to sip her brew from a wooden spoon. "At least a mile. You know, living in the Juxtaposition? It's like going through a portal. A big portal. Like that CrossHuman Portal. That's where all the cool kids are hanging out."

The Brewer sighed dramatically, setting down her spoon and pressing her knuckles into her lower back. "Too bad I'm chained here. I'd love to go take a look at the Portal myself. But this chain is thick, and I think it's magical, so I'm basically stuck here. At least I'm allowed to brew some delicious and powerful sodas for myself, and ciders for the others."

She had instinctively answered Nacho's next question. He'd needed to know the nature of the chains around her ankle. If he were rushed and absolutely needed to rescue her, he could cut off her foot to free her, grab her and her foot, and reattach it using Reuben's healing Skill. Even so, most people preferred to avoid amputations, even necessary ones. Nacho needed someone with a weapon that could break that chain, and he was betting that Mr. Lacrosse Stick would work.

Nacho opened up the Store interface and transferred six credits into the guild coffer. He was fine, but this definitely qualified as weirdness afoot, and they needed to approach with extreme caution. The transfer made him aware that they'd have to figure out a way to send morse code without having to spell out each word, which would take forever.

He sank lower and turned to retreat in order to meet his friends a little further away, but... Nacho couldn't leave without throwing her some hope. "I'll be back with someone who can destroy the chain. We'll get you out of here."

Jennifer laughed bitterly, sarcasm seeping from her pores. "Oh, who needs to see the Portal? I'm so happy here, brewing and helping out the thirsty players that keep the undead standing. I'm pretty sure that if I give them enough booze, they'll eventually upgrade my chains from silver to gold. If I'm *really* lucky, they'll give me some platinum. Fingers crossed. Who needs jewelry when you can just have the best prisoner accessories?"

Pretty, sarcastic, and a source of Mana beverages? Nacho was liking Jennifer Ales more and more. Also, what a *perfect* name for a Brewer. Before he could become *too* interested in her fate, Nacho turned and crept past the zombie, then hurried back the way he'd come. He stopped just before emerging onto a footpath and paused, hiding deeper in the thicket as a repetitive sound caught his ears.

Six soldiers in strange-looking chainmail shirts marched across the dirt. Each was armed with a short spear with an overlong blade. The weapons looked like Japanese naginatas, though something was *off* about them. Most likely, they were Cross-Human weapons, because all six of the soldiers were wearing sunglasses.

Strangely, their helmets were cheap Juxtaposition versions made from red and yellow plastic. The garish hues made them look rather ridiculous, and Nacho instinctively readied himself for battle, but the six walked past him without stopping. From the color of their skin, and their stink, they were resurrected CrossHuman zombies. These didn't shuffle, meaning they were at least Tier one undead —if not Tier two. He had no idea how that would impact their power level, but he also had no interest in finding out.

Luckily for him, he didn't need to fight. Nacho tried to access a System View on them, but nothing came up. These weren't Juxtaposition monsters; they were raised beings. Puppets, really, controlled at a distance by the pair of Mind Players that Nacho found walking a half-dozen paces behind them.

One was a fleshy guy whose head was tiny compared to his body, and it was clear he'd lost serious weight after society had collapsed. His brightly colored quilted armor didn't fit well, and the armored black fist that adorned his chest looked to be an odd choice. He wore a cloak with the hood down, not openly carrying any kind of weapon. Nacho assumed he was a Mind Player.

The other guy was tall, gaunt, and had a beard, but only on his chin. He resembled a goth Egyptian Pharaoh, with the bristly facial hair extending at least six inches from the tip of his triangular chin. The rest of his hair was buzzed to the scalp—but not with any skill. It looked as if he'd hired a Tier one Zombie to give him a haircut. He'd outfitted himself in a mismatched collection of armor pieces, none of it in good condition. Rusted chainmail, a big leather gauntlet, a bare hand with oversized rings, a left boot, and a right sandal had Nacho questioning the man's sanity, but the real kicker was the backpack.

The pack was most easily described as a knockoff hydration pack, complete with the plastic straw in red and yellow Juxtaposition colors twined through the strap.

While it made sense for a necromancer to keep hydrated, as thirst was such an issue, the Egyptian-looking guy had clearly solved the hunger problem as well… in a grotesque way that Nacho had been hoping was only a nasty rumor. Over one shoulder dangled the plastic straw. On the other, a human forearm had been tied to the backpack. The only thing that gave Nacho hope was that it wasn't the right color for actual meat, alive or dead.

The arm was the color of a birthday cake, bright pink and white.

Tiny Head Guy stopped his walking partner. "You know, Nibbles… at some point, we need to get through that Portal to get revenge. It was what Craig and Andrew would've wanted. Camping out here is fine, but it's only a matter of time before we either run into someone from the Chips Guild, or the katana-guy comes back through the Portal and attacks with an army."

Nibbles turned his head slightly and took a massive *chomp* out of the arm dangling next to his face. He chewed and swallowed loudly, clearly attempting and succeeding in unnerving his fellow player. When he eventually spoke, he didn't talk. He *shouted.* "Henry Star, we're going to win this game by conquering one world at a time! One guild at a time! Speaking of what Andrew would have wanted, want a bite? He loved making sure we were all fed."

Henry lifted a hand and weakly waved it, looking sick to his stomach. "No… I'm… full. What are we doing here, then, if not attacking?"

"We're *waiting*, Henry!" Nibbles bellowed, then boomed with laughter. "We're *watching*. The Chips Guild lost people. They're the most noble guild in the entire state, if rumors are to be believed. When they come, we'll want to be here. It's important we keep a presence here. It's a crossroads, and for every player we kill and turn, our army gets larger! The more credits we get! This is where we want to be: credits and death, death and credits. All the while, we have that Brewer giving us all the Mana soda we can drink!"

Tiny Head wheezed something akin to assent and the two continued walking along with the half-dozen zombies, only their loud volume allowing Nacho to hear them as they passed. Then he realized that the path must loop around to the camp where the Brewer was working. Things were getting dicey, and Nacho had to find his friends and rescue Jennifer before the two leaders returned.

Nacho had noticed how smoothly those six uber zombies moved, and he didn't like it. They wouldn't be easy kills. Now he had *two* missions to complete: rescue Jennifer Ales from the Necromancers, and rescue the missing members of the Brunch Force from the CrossWorld.

"Why can nothing ever be easy? I'd kill for a little easy right about now."

CHAPTER FOURTEEN

Nacho darted along the path without being seen. Brie and Reuben were about two hundred yards away, and he raced up to them so noiselessly that he had to duck a reactionary blow from Brie when she finally noticed him. Motioning them to the side, he directed them to a tiny clearing among three trees close together with enough foliage to hide among.

"Where's my pack?" Nacho peered around for the mobile kitchen. The looks of incredulousness on their faces told him everything.

Reuben wrinkled his nose and scoffed. "Uh, right, so, we tried to bring it with us, but it sounded like we were trying to walk around with a thrift store under our coats."

"*We* left it there for the same reason *you* left it there," Brie reminded him with a knowing look. Nacho reluctantly agreed that it had been the right choice to leave his mobile kitchen behind, but he hoped that it would be okay while they were gone. He hated the idea of replacing it. He'd spent a *ton* of credits on the spices and ingredients, and he'd made specific modifications to the original design. Starting over would be no fun.

Shoving his concern for his pack aside, Nacho quickly explained what he'd seen, knowing they were under an incredibly tight deadline. Reuben squinted at the cook, a half-grin on his face. "A Brewer, huh? Do you think she can do root beer? I'm only risking my life for some random lady if she can do root beer."

Brie didn't respond to that, nor did Nacho. The Berserker did give the cook a long, studious look. With a sly girl, she leaned in close and stage-whispered, "Did I hear you use the word… 'pretty'… in your detailed description of her?"

"I can't tell you for sure." Nacho wasn't going to go down that road, not right now. Auburn hair swaying gently in the breeze meant nothing to him with so much at stake be. "This isn't helping us get to her before Nibbles and Henry get back to their camp. We need to go, now."

Reuben chuckled and nudged his wife. "He never said the word, but we both heard him *not* say it. Lots of details. *Luxurious* auburn hair. A remarkable sparkle in her *green* eyes. Sarcasm and sea shanties…"

"Not helping," Nacho hissed quietly. "Also, I'm nearly positive I never used those words."

"Look, lover boy…" Brie's eyebrows knitted together as she frowned. "I know rescuing a damsel in distress sounds good on paper, but we came here for our friends. Taye and Abby might be in real trouble in the CrossWorld. Shouldn't we go there first?"

Nacho grunted in frustration. "It's not just the damsel in distress thing. We *need* a Brewer. If we get someone who can make us Mana potions, then we can stay in Active Combat indefinitely. With plentiful Mana, Reuben can keep us healed. When we find Kristie, she can use her Death Blossom ability without worrying about dying from lack of Mana. Trust me. We *need* Jennifer."

"We, or *you*?" Reuben winked broadly at the cook, getting a flat stare in return. "We. Got it. *Totally* 'we'."

"Maybe." Brie took a fresh grip on her lacrosse stick and

squeezed it hard enough that the wood audibly creaked. "I just hope we don't die trying to rescue her. Our friends would think we abandoned them."

Nacho soberly pushed his friends to start moving. While they were fairly quiet, he didn't think they would be able to sneak by all the zombies he'd seen. He wracked his brains, trying to think of where they could flee after Brie charged forward and smashed that chain. They were going to be chased by hundreds of people, both alive and dead. Or possibly… made of cake? Nacho was still trying to figure out how Nibbles had turned a human's arm into cake, but he was leaning toward a magical artifact and not a class ability for one simple reason: no other Necromancer he'd ever met could do the same.

His eyes were continuously drawn to the Portal, about a mile south of their current position.

Simon Spear had claimed there was a dungeon near the Portal, and his description of it made it sound like a Skill Box dungeon. But where? Most likely, it was situated somewhere between the Portal and the Muddy River, if they had already been able to scout it even slightly.

They were out of time to run any further reconnaissance. Their best chance was to grab the Brewer and escape into the dungeon. They'd have a higher chance of survival in a dungeon than running through a forest full of the undead. If they could escape the zombies, they might just make it through the Portal. Ideally, Nacho wanted to return and gather reinforcements from his guild members down in the Bove's Lair, but it seemed that the necromancers were not only anticipating that; they were *hoping* for it. That was enough to ensure that Nacho fought against his instincts and pressed onward.

The dungeon might make the… Nacho tried to think of what the guild name could possibly be. The Walking Zombies and the Order of the Fist? Sounded a little too slice of life for him, too long. Walking Fists? That was fairly likely, and he felt like the Brewer had mentioned something along that line in her 'rambling'.

He could only hope that the Mind Players would think twice about braving a dungeon without a surplus of Body Players, though they possibly had plenty of bodies to throw at any issues that arose. At least in a dungeon, the Dinner Party would be able to use the narrow corridors to their advantage and fight their enemies one person at a time. The Necromancers would be fools to chase them into the confines, where their swarm tactics would be utterly useless.

The only thing that made the slapdash rescue plan even *slightly* plausible was Brie's ability to run at super speeds and bash anything that got in her way, *out* of her way. She was practically a hammer tornado. If he didn't have so much faith in his team, he would have absolutely attempted this on his own instead of putting them at risk. Nacho offered some snacks to his team, but they grimaced and indicated that they had enough on hand.

That left him with *plenty* of food that *he* didn't mind eating. After the Donut Disaster, Nacho had a surplus of leftovers. Brie was also wearing a brand-new belt which contained a pouch for peanut butter balls and a bandolier of the strawberry cottage cheese 'Life Hack' yogurt tubes. Nacho pulled out a round, rubbery bug strip and got to chewing. Eventually, he was able to get it down by drinking nearly half a liter of water. "A cross between jerky and bubble gum. I love both of those, so I guess I'm just not seeing the issue other people have with it."

When they came within reach of the one undead guard closest to Jennifer, Nacho motioned his friends lower to the ground. "Brie, charge forward and get the Brewer free. Reuben and I will start pounding zombies over here to cause a diversion. Once she's ready to go, we'll head to the southeast. I'm hoping we can find the dungeon that Simon Spear described, and we can use it as a fallback point to limit how many enemies can come after us at the same time."

Reuben nodded and curled his hands into fists. "Blood and cheese, bro."

"Careful, love. After he made donuts, I'm worried that your

battlecry will give him bad ideas." Brie winced as she realized what she had just said. "Doesn't Muenster cheese have lamb's blood in it? Ick. Speaking of ick, we're going into Active Combat. I hate to do this to ourselves, but… I'd take a donut now? I didn't realize just how *many* enemies were around."

"Sure. Also, you're thinking 'Head Cheese', and it isn't really cheese. It's a meat jelly." Nacho removed six of the donuts from a Storage Slot, tossing one to her as he tore off a chunk and started chewing. It gave his jaw something to do, and he liked the feeling.

"Urrgh. Flat, greasy hockey pucks. Also, I don't know why you know that head cheese is a meat jelly, but if you make it for me, I'll hurt you." Brie gagged as she forced the food down.

"It's like sugar mixed with sawdust, cooked in rancid duck lard. The consistency is reminiscent of beach sand mixed with an oil spill."

"I sometimes forget that you grew up in a house where your parents would critique the food in front of a server and make them bring the report back to the cook." Once his bite hit his stomach, Nacho had officially eaten a full portion of food, which allowed him to boost one of his stats. He chose his Fitness, since this battle was going to be equal parts fighting and running. He also equipped his armor directly from his Storage Slot and was immediately ready to go—pot on his head, wok on his chest, skillet on his back, knives poised and ready to strike.

"You're too harsh, sweets." Reuben started chowing down on a donut. "Once you get past the texture and the taste, they aren't that bad."

"This is *food*." Brie eyed her remaining few bites like the bread might come alive at any moment and try to wiggle down her throat. "What *is* there besides texture and taste?"

"If you think eating them is bad, you should've tried *cooking* them." Nacho shuddered at the memory of the Donut Disaster. To be fair, after he'd rolled out the dough and cut out the donuts, the cloud of floating millet particles hadn't seemed to impact the final product too badly.

He had no prior-world experience with cooking, so the concern and assumption that things were going to go wrong was just his natural state. Things had usually turned out okay, once he'd gotten the hang of using a recipe. Not this time. The grease had spat and **hissed** like a living animal, as if the millet flour was personally insulted by his lack of experience baking. The donuts at least *looked* correct, but no matter what he had done, he had been unable to raise the rarity to anything higher than 'Common'.

Brie steeled herself. She was a realist, and the reality was that forcing the food down was going to help keep them alive. The Berserker ate two donuts without pausing, chasing the gritty discs with a tube of yogurt. She glowed a bit as she increased her Fitness Stat by one hundred and ninety-five percent of her current maximum, winding up with a Fitness of sixty-five. Some quick calculations revealed that her strikes would impart an additional thirty-two and a half percent damage, and her health jumped from fifty-four to one hundred and forty.

Frankly, Nacho preened a little at how effective his concoctions were. It was clear that ultimately, she agreed that a little suffering up front was far better than a lot of suffering during combat.

He chased the miserable pastries down with some Life Hack of his own. His Fitness was jacked all the way up to seventy-three, which gave him an additional thirty six and a half percent on damage. With his knives, further amplified by Reuben's Positive Vibes and their Special Tier one WarCry ability, he would be dishing out twenty-six Health Points with each flick of the wrist. Small Blades likewise gave him a bonus, but it was the fact that he could attack four times in a single second, two attacks with each knife, that really put him over the top.

Reuben doused them all in his happy magic, and they glowed in response.

"Brie, go!" Nacho directed quietly, not wanting to reduce her ability to take the initiative in combat.

"Can do. Stay fresh, cheese bags." The Berserker took off in a blur of Combat Dash, heading directly toward the tree where Jennifer Ales was chained.

"I love that woman more every single day," Reuben chuckled as he watched her go. The closest zombie in armor shuffled forward, sword raised awkwardly. There was no surprise on its ruined face, and Nacho could only mentally shrug. If there was one thing that undead were famous for, it was attacking with nearly no lag time as soon as they found a target.

Now it was their turn. Nacho decided that if he was going to be a distraction, he was going to be a big one.

Greetings, Player! During this bit of Active Combat, we ask that age-old question: how do you kill something that is already dead? The typical answer is usually with force, a lot of force, or maybe throwing those dismal excuses for donuts that you made for your guild as if they were rocks. Either way. No Store, No Regens, no kidding. May your future be delicious!

Reuben charged forward to intercept the zombie that was trying to slice at Brie. Throwing a single punch, he liquified the rotten face, destroying its entire head thanks to the Sausage Clips of Striking around his wrist. "Killed the thing with one blow; they have less than twenty-eight health!"

Other zombies shambled forward, and something about them changed. Judging by the way their vacant eyes suddenly started darting around and the visibly more fluid movements, Nacho knew that the Necromancers were seeing through their eyes and taking direct control. The Mind Players were zeroing in on the intruders and would likely arrive any minute now. Nacho called out, "Gotta get out of here before the fluid guzzlers get close enough to buff their meat toys."

"There's a better way of saying that, I just *know* there is." Reuben threw punches left and right, killing any zombie that came close and laughing the entire time. "This is awesome! I've never gotten to see what my level *really* means compared to other people."

One undead warrior hacked into Reuben, but he only took a regular sword's worth of damage—ten Health Points, minus a point, because of the terrible yet effective donuts.

"Trust me when I say that it's better to be punching up at monsters than testing yourself against humans." The undead surrounded Nacho, and a wild smile rampaged across his face. "I love being surrounded. That means I can kill in every direction. Let's dance, zombies… I wonder if there's a delicious secret you're hiding."

He struck out with his blades, each strike ending the unlife of another walking corpse. Hopped up on defense-boosting donuts and strawberry yogurt, he realized that he could fight creatures at this level indefinitely. In fact, as he hadn't activated a Skill yet, he wasn't even losing hunger points.

Congratulations! You have killed Four Novice Zombies!

Tier 0 Standard Summoned Creature = 0 Credits!

You get nothing for killing these zombies except a vague feeling that you should wash your knives before you prep your next meal.

"Huh." Nacho looked down at his blades and blinked in surprise. "Never really thought about that. If I use the same knives for fighting *and* cooking… is that unsanitary? Let's try cleaning them next time and see if that impacts my prep work."

"You don't *usually* wash them?" That, more than fighting meat puppets, seemed to be making Reuben's stomach churn.

"I clean the blood off. *Ow*! Stop distracting me!" Another zombie had come up and hit him. Nacho whirled and hacked his cleaver into the head of the offending undead.

. . .

Health remaining: 147/156. Pathetic, rookie numbers.
Damage dealt: 18/18! Instant kill!

Reuben punched the heads off two others with a single motion, apparently just to see if he could. "Woo! If you can blast the heads off of two zombies with one punch, why use two punches to blast the heads off those zombies?"

As they stood in the midst of a rapidly expanding circle of gore, Nacho scanned the forest and noticed that all the trees in the area were rustling as *things* moved past them. It was time to run. "Reuben, we need to get to Jennifer. I'm hoping your fitness-focused girlfriend has lacrossed the silver off those chains."

"Fitness-focused *wife*, not girlfriend!" Reuben reminded him at maximum volume. "Lead the way, boss man!"

A spell exploded near them as robed fingers rampaged through the foliage. Nacho whirled and ran, but they weren't out of Active Combat yet. Zombies were everywhere, and Nacho felt a surreal jolt, as though he was running in a horror-themed forest after dark. Firming his resolve, he grounded himself quickly. "The stink is bad, the danger is real. Keep it together!"

One undead guy stumbled out in front of him, and Nacho tumbled into a midair somersault, swinging and neatly severing the head off its shoulders as his momentum took him past the corpse. The System flashed another message, cheerfully informing him that he'd killed a zombie but got nothing for doing so.

Nacho and Reuben made it to Jennifer's glade with minimal effort, the Guild Leader trying not to feel annoyed at how slow the Healer ran. It wasn't his fault: Nacho had gained a total of fifteen more points in his stats than Reuben at the same level. Everything, from his vestibular sense to his ability to process input and react, was just *better* as a result. Adding on the buffs from his food, there was simply no way to make a comparison to other humans anymore. Maybe gorillas? Cheetahs?

They burst into the clearing and found a strange sight awaiting them. Brie's face was bright red with rage, but not at the zombies. Those she could, and did, kill nearly contemptuously using Mr. Lacrosse Stick. No, the Berserker was glaring at Jennifer Ales, who was free of the chain and rushing back and forth packing up her brewing supplies.

"We don't have *time* for that," Brie told the woman firmly as she loaded up a glowing orb and sent it hurtling into a dense cluster of staggering dead people. "Leave it, or I leave you."

"This stuff is too expensive to just *leave* here! I'm almost done, please!" Jennifer frantically flung a long spoon and glassware into her Brewer's pack, then slung it onto her shoulders. She gripped a nearly three-foot-long spoon in one hand and an equally long paddle in the other. "There! Ready, let's go!"

Nacho knew from experience that fighting while wearing her backpack wasn't going to be easy. "This mission just turned from a rescue to an escort mission. Ales, start running!"

Brie blitzed into the middle of another throng of oncoming zombies, drawing them to her and using her Defensive Whirl to block every single one of their attacks. Her counterattack *mowed* the group down. Reuben moved to her flank to punch the ones trying to attack from her blind spot.

A scarlet spell grenade exploded near their feet. With a shout, Nacho grabbed Jennifer by the arm and started half-running, half-dragging the Brewer. 'We need to go! I hope you can run with your backpack. If not, we're going to have to dump it."

"I can run, don't you worry. I have a Brewmeister ability that allows me to do all *sorts* of things with my gear." She threw him a confident smile as she got her legs situated and started running on her own in the direction he had been guiding her. "Keep them off me, yeah? Not a huge fan of the whole not-getting-paid-for-the-work-I-do thing we had going on here."

Nacho was a little taken aback. A ton of bravado was suddenly rolling off this person who had been a captive less than five minutes ago, for who knew how long. With Brie and Reuben covering their backs, they sped through the forest, stumbling unexpectedly across another path that cut southeast through the trees. Nacho could smell the Muddy River, and he altered their angle slightly: this path just might take them to the dungeon.

"We might have a problem!" Brie's voice carried perfectly to the front of the group as they ran, her years of being captain of the Lacrosse team shining at that moment. "Tier one zombies coming in *fast*!"

CHAPTER FIFTEEN

Nacho still had plenty of health, so he assumed that the fact they were still in Active Combat wasn't a big deal. He and Jennifer had already started down the path in the hopes of quickly reaching the strange dungeon his people had tried to explore.

The Satiation duo skidded to a halt and ran back to help Brie, who was currently facing off against the six undead Cross-Human soldiers that Nacho had seen escorting Nibbles. They still wore the cheap Juxtaposition helmets and sunglasses, slashing at Brie with the otherworldly long-bladed spears in their rotting hands. These zombies were of the fast flavor, and they were far too well-coordinated.

Brie spun and knocked away all the spears, managing to whack the agile corpses in the noggin at least once each. Unlike the Novice Zombies, that didn't mean a one-shot kill. Either the helmets were extra-effective, or the puppets themselves could withstand a much higher level of punishment compared to the base models. Perhaps a bit of both, since the zombies took the blow without even losing their helmets or cracking their cheap sunglasses.

The first creature slashed into Brie, the blade bouncing back in kind, thanks to her unfashionable armor, basic Tier one mana protection, and the donuts cutting the damage she took by ten percent. In all, the dead man's weapon stopped as though it had hit a wall; the zombie's light opening attack had interrupted its own battle rhythm near-perfectly.

For a second, Nacho contemplated pulling the Sewer Skewers from his Storage Slot and staking the fighters to the ground, but he knew that his knives would serve him better in combat against the multitude of weak enemies that were closing in. He was still fueled by his Cooking Magic and glowing from Reuben's Positive Vibes, so he decided it was time to get involved. His blade struck one of the zombies in the back, sinking in with practically no resistance. "Mmm. *That's* a familiar feeling that I haven't missed all that much."

The System let him know that they were up against some serious opponents as Nacho slammed his cleaver into the unprotected neck, right near the brainstem.

Damage dealt: 96/200. Plenty of meat in this puppet!

"These are pretty tanky!" The CrossHuman zombies were fast, powerful, and carried ten times as many Health Points as their Tier zero equivalents. Was it because of the power of their summoner? Or was it because they were CrossHuman corpses? "Keep an eye peeled for the Mind Players controlling them; I think these are the Guild Master's personal Elites."

Jennifer ran up with her backpack clanking, joining him in bashing the same zombie that Nacho had wounded. She smacked the zombie's helmet off with her spoon and swept off the glasses with her paddle, simultaneously taking off a good amount of face with the strike. The Brewer smiled at the cook. "I thought he might have a nose for beer, but it seems he's lost it."

"Was that a joke? Tell me the Brewer just tried to joke." Reuben stepped up and punched another zombie, his fist going *through* the thing's sunglasses to crush its sinus cavity. "In combat? Hey, Ales! Nacho is single, and I think you should-"

"No more talking, Reuben," Nacho demanded darkly. He immediately waded back in to finish off the undead Cross-Human that he'd hit, but he took a spear in the side for his trouble.

Health remaining: 117/156. Aww, did you get speared? Is somebody not as good at combat as he thought he was?

The Tier one zombies were dealing thirty damage a pop, which was three times what a spear could normally do. Nacho's eyes narrowed. "I think it'd be the best thing for everyone involved if we made sure these things were dead-dead instead of undead."

Between them, Reuben and Brie were able to take down another of the zombies. Brie used her devastating Combat Dash strike, which hit for seventy-six damage per hit. Reuben managed fifty-six damage with his one-two punch, but that meant he had to land five full blows to take one of the slippery opponents out for good.

Mind Players were congregating on the outskirts of the brawl, throwing spells with no concern for the controlled meat puppets. Purple streaks of light hit Reuben and Brie one after another, almost seeming to curve around the undead to seek living flesh.

The Berserker grunted in pain as her health began to nose-dive, but she swept Mr. Lacrosse Stick into the leg of a zombie, cracking it off at the knee and sending it tumbling to the ground. "One less zombie coming after us; now get back!"

Jennifer ignored the demand, slinging a pouch forward and digging through it. "I can keep these guys back for a minute! As long as you all don't mind a *small* forest fire, anyway."

"How small? Wait, I don't care. Do it!" At that moment, Nacho wasn't worried about the ecological effects of whatever Jennifer damage might inflict; they needed an escape.

Brie's Defensive Whirl protected them for a moment, knocking the nearest zombies aside and opening a corridor of escape for the Dinner Party to run along. Jennifer followed behind them after a moment, fiddling with *something as she scurried in their wake.*

Nacho glanced back just as a purple streak hit his cast iron armor squarely in the center of his back. His Skillet of Turtling saved him from any third-degree burns, the innate fire resistance mitigating some of the possible secondary damage. He didn't look back again, deciding that any choices made by Ales were her own problem now.

It was rather disturbing to accept that other humans were attacking them. Even with the atrocities that they were clearly committing, Nacho *still* didn't like the idea of getting back into the habit of killing other people. Monsters and zombies were one thing, but taking out living people was a road under construction that he wanted to leave blocked to all through traffic.

Jennifer hurled something above her head, and moments later, a wall of flame exploded behind them. It was as much smoke as it was fire, completely cutting off all visibility. Even so, the dry trees caught aflame in no time flat, and the brittle leaves went up like torches. The Dinner Party trotted to a halt after a few long seconds of no noticeable pursuit, and Reuben grabbed hold of his wife to heal her with a tight hug. Her wounds immediately began to close, but Reuben didn't let her go.

He just kept mumbling, "Too close. I don't *want* you to be a zombie."

"Ow. *S*ss**." Jennifer hissed as she felt at the skin where her face had been seared by spell fire. "I hope it's okay to burn the forest down."

"More than fine; this place sucks. A little cleansing flame is the best thing that could happen to it." Brie struggled free of her husband and gave him a slight shove. "Let's get out of here!"

They sprinted down the path, hoping that they'd fall out of Active Combat and get their Health Regen back once they put some distance between themselves and the monsters masquerading as humans. Slowly they moved into a more familiar, distance-eating run, and Nacho threw more than one glance at the Brewer before finally finding his voice. "Did you brew up whatever you threw?"

Jennifer was in good enough shape that she could talk while they ran. Or was that because of her 'Brewmeister' skill? "No, it was a Potion of Instant Firewall. I'm pretty sure you get special Satiation Player mob drops, right? Mine all come in liquid form."

"That's true. Items change when the System realizes I'm a Satiation Player. But how often are you getting mob drops? I've gotten, like... one. Even then, it was from a boss, and a quest item to boot." Nacho watched curiously as she shrugged, ignoring the mysterious smile she wore. She must have gotten that question more than once in her time, if she had a set expression ready to go. Out of nowhere, a thought occurred to Nacho. "Hey, when you kill things, do you get credits?"

"Not one!" Jennifer clutched her spoon and paddle as she ran. "I just get some snotty message from the System that I should be hidden away like a delicate flower instead of risking my wilting petals on the front lines."

"Ugh." Brie grunted in sympathetic annoyance.

"Totally," Jennifer agreed as they broke from the trees to find themselves on the bank of the wide Muddy River. A stone trail led up from a dock on the riverside, running up to the forest, where the trail shot south down a decline to the bottom of a ravine.

In the distance rose the Portal—Nacho could see the top of the stone arch rising above the smoke that was starting to form a haze in the air. That Portal had to be at least a hundred feet tall, if not two hundred. Happily, the pungent smell of the burning leaves blocked out the otherworldly stench, even at this distance.

Nacho coughed as the wind shifted, blowing ashes their way. He looked over his shoulder, watching the raging wall of blazing smoke that rivaled fires he only used to see on the news from California. Forest fires were certainly devastating, but they could also be handy. All those flames had probably made the Walking Fists abandon the Portal, and it might even be unguarded on this side. Still, getting to the Portal through the forest fire wouldn't be easy. Despite being at Tier one, his lungs still required oxygen to breathe, and that might prove to be problematic, given the amount of smoke in the air.

Congratulations, Player! You've created a great fire for roasting marshmallows! Active Combat is over, so you can buy hot dogs from the Store! Enjoy your Regens! May your future be delicious.

Nacho led his friends down the cobblestone path and down the steps into a ravine that cut across the landscape. It was getting harder to breathe, and they could feel the ambient temperature soaring. Reuben pointed wordlessly into the distance, and Nacho followed his index finger to the bottom of the ravine, where the crumbling stones of a dungeon entrance were visible through the swirling smoke.

At the top of the archway was a sculpted face, and at first glance it looked human. Upon closer examination, the eyes of the face weren't round, they were crosses. Was this a Cross-Human dungeon, and if so… what did that mean? Were they barred from entry?

Nacho didn't know, but he cared not one bit. His attention was fixed on a cloaked figure emerging from the fire. The cloak wasn't burning, and neither was the Player. In fact, he was *holding* flames. That wasn't great. More fire-resistant Mind

Players emerged from the forest shortly and started running toward them with hoarse, exceedingly *miffed*, shouts of fury.

The four of them hurried down the steps, with Nacho motioning for Jennifer to enter the dungeon. "Okay, this is probably either a really good idea or an utterly terrible one. Fingers crossed!"

"Like the eyes!" Jennifer pointed upward as she passed underneath the arch and scampered down more steps.

"She's funny. I like her." Reuben patted Nacho on the arm, gripping him when Nacho tried to pull away. "Don't be like that. I'm married; let me live vicariously through you."

"If we survive her rescue, I'll like her." Brie scowled at the swaying mane of auburn hair as it progressed further into the dungeon. "Got a few points against her right now. Even *you* knew enough to leave your mobile kitchen behind."

Nacho could only shrug, not wanting to admit that he *had* nearly made them go back for it. Reuben and Brie hurried under the arch, and Nacho swung in behind them. He paused under the arch and reached into a pouch on his belt, allowing one of his Firefly Potstickers to buzz out and hover around their heads to provide a light source.

A ball of fire exploded behind him before he could release the rest, his skillet keeping him perfectly protected. Nacho was deeply impressed; wearing cooking gear as armor had proven to provide him with more protection from fire than he had ever expected. "Time's up! Run!"

"Hope you're ready for leg day, bud." Reuben pointed at the small, shallow steps that disappeared into the darkness. They started down as quickly as they could go, taking the steps three at a time. The slippery stone didn't make it easy, but each of them had high enough stats that the risk was minimal.

Active Combat faded away once more, and their aches and pains vanished without a trace within a few steps. Most of the time, being in the Juxtaposition was awful, without a doubt, but the ability to heal even the most grievous wounds in a matter of mere moments was nice. Jennifer called back over her shoulder,

"This place isn't up to code. I'm not getting the welcome message yet."

Reuben laughed too loudly, just glad he had a new person to bounce inane topics around with. "I'll put a complaint in to the building inspector. Bad steps. Delayed welcome message. Got it."

"*Naaa-chooo*!" A new voice rang out behind the group, echoing off the walls from far above them. "We know it's you!"

The cook swept his Skillet Shield off his back and turned, ready for another fireball. It never came. He and the rest of his gang were already about halfway down the spiral staircase, rendering any attacks that required line-of-sight useless.

From the entrance, that same voice called down. "Nacho! We can hear you! It's time for you to give up! Come quietly!"

"No can do; we're funny people. If we come quietly, that precludes joking. Sorry, but that means it's a no from me!" Reuben called back. "Oh, and also, you shouldn't kill us. Dead people don't make for good conversationalists."

"We want the Brewer back!" the voice called down. "If you give her back to us, you can go in peace."

"No thanks!" Nacho joined in on the upward shouting. "She likes us better. Something about access to deodorant and toothpaste? You know toothpaste is practically free, right?"

Some quiet murmuring filtered down from above, but one of the loudest comments was, "Abyss, he's right. It's like a single point for a six-pack at the Epic-"

"Shush! Nacho, we're coming after you! There's no escape," the angry man screamed, clearly unhappy about the taunting. "We'll just add you to the ranks and *take* the Brewer back."

"You know I can cook, right?" Nacho questioned practically conversationally, trusting the echoes to deliver his words. "Shouldn't you kill my friends and take me into custody? I mean, if you lock up one Satiation Player, you might as well lock up two."

The resulting pause grew so quiet that Nacho swore he could hear the crackle of the burning forest outside. After an unnaturally long silence, heated whispers started to build, accompanied by the swish and clank of robed and armored limbs waving emphatically.

Nacho motioned for the others to keep going, and they tried to be as stealthy as possible in their descent. No one in their group was willing to speak, which was clearly the smart call. While the geniuses up top debated who they should kill and who they should capture, Nacho was hoping to make a clean getaway.

They followed the dim glow of the single Firefly Potsticker to the bottom of the steps and scurried under a *concerningly* thick portcullis. The huge metal gate would've been impossible to pass if it had been locked into place, but currently, the bars were secured in a recessed area of the ceiling. Even so, they wasted no time in sprinting under it, *just* in case it was a trap.

Once they passed beneath the gate, they finally received the welcome message to the dungeon. A single glance at the message confirmed that Arriod and his CrossHumans had already plundered this particular dungeon, and the Patrons weren't shy about bragging about it.

CHAPTER SIXTEEN

Firefly Potstickers danced overhead, lighting up the room as Nacho and his friends gaped at the ruins of a See's Candy store. Shattered glass from ravaged display cases crunched beneath their feet as they eased across the cracked floor tiles, highlighting the fact that all of the candy was gone. Yet wrappers, boxes, and other packaging littered nearly every surface. The place had clearly been ransacked, even though the sweet, lingering scent of candy remained. Two oversized wooden doors offered them choices for further delving, one on the left, the other to the right.

A System message blasted into their brains, causing each of them to flinch, and a slight trickle of blood erupted from Jennifer's nose.

Welcome, Player, to the Sweet Skillz Welcome Dungeon! It's not a Welcome Dungeon for you, Earthlings. This is a big warm welcome dungeon for the friends, strangers, and murderers visiting from what you call the Cross-World. They call it CruxTerra, which has a certain irony to it.

All you need to know is that the CruxTerrans have beaten their

Welcome Dungeon and acquired a bunch of cool new abilities. To be totally fair, a certain CrossHuman with a cool curved sword cleared out much of the place himself, so there aren't many monsters or loot deposits left.

Even so, there are some goodies still waiting in the deeper levels.

But you don't want the deeper levels, do you?

You want a quick trip through.

We can offer that, and we can sweeten the pot.

Get through this dungeon without making even a single kill, and we'll give you twenty-five thousand credits each! When we say kills, we mean no kills—no murdering monsters, other humans, CrossHumans, or each other.

P.S. They didn't find the entrance to the Starvation Dungeon. Not yet. Are you able to do it?

Be warned: the Starvation Dungeon is the next big event! Your Worlds hang in the balance!

"Ah, blast it." Jennifer snapped her fingers with a dramatic swing of her arm. "I was going to murder all of you in your sleep. Now it's not profitable. Hey, you guys would have gone to sleep if we'd found a bed in here, right?"

"*Edgy* jokes from the new girl." Reuben's characteristic laugh carried a hint of concern. "Still waiting to find out whether they're actually jokes, or if she has been genuinely threatening us since she first met us?"

Brie was less optimistic about the dark humor than the guys were. "Say something like that even one more time, and I'm going to have to take the threat seriously. Don't make me do that."

Jennifer choked out a small noise that *could* have been a nervous laugh. 'You got it. Not joking."

Nacho couldn't help but smile smugly. "You're not joking? You *do* have a plan to murder us."

"Not a good one," Jennifer sighed wistfully, her tiny smirk replaced by a pained yelp as Brie's lacrosse stick swung out, took her legs out from under her, then whipped up and around to crush the downed woman's head.

The cook casually blocked the strike with his knives braced in an 'x' pattern to disperse the force. "Sorry, Brie. That was my fault; I goaded her."

"I warned her," the Berserker reminded them coldly, eyes still on the dropped newcomer. "Next time, I *won't* stop after one hit."

"That would have cost us a hundred thousand credits cumulatively if it landed," Reuben pointed out casually. "Blood and cheese, absolutely. Gotta protect your friends; I'm on board. Still, maybe we *all* take a nice, easy step back, and relax into the dungeon theme."

From further up the stairs, the clank of armor reminded them that they were neither alone nor safe. Almost immediately, the stink of zombies swept over them in a cloud of aerosolized decay. Grimacing, the cook grabbed Jennifer's hand and hauled her to her feet. "Necromancers likely have skills to heal their creations, which means they have probably recharged their army and are sending them down. No time for relaxing, it seems."

Without a thought, Nacho chose the door to the right, shoving it open and leading the others through a corridor lined with smashed glass shelves. He directed half of his potstickers into the darkness—revealing a grimy dirt corridor with a dusty packed floor, glittering with piles of pulverized glass.

"Marching orders, big boss man?" Jennifer questioned with a wary glance at Brie.

Yoo-hoo, Player! Did someone say marching orders? People listen to you? On purpose*? Would you like to add Jennifer Ales to the Dinner Party?*

Yes / No

. . .

Jennifer knew what message he'd just gotten, and she could see the hesitation in his eyes. "You don't have to add me to your party. You don't know me; I get it."

"No, that would be pretty sucky of us not to add you in." Nacho made the call, and a moment later, Jennifer's basic status information appeared in their party view. Not much else changed, except she could see how many credits they had pooled together, and it would be easy to show each other their Stat Sheets when the time came.

Nacho motioned for their Berserker to take point. Up front, she could protect them, though they had to try not to kill anything they came across. That reward was *tempting*. He paused mid-step, realizing what was really going on. "Everyone, I think that we need to be extra careful, and if it comes down to it, don't hold back from killing anything that needs to die. Those credits aren't a reward… they're a challenge to make the dungeon harder. *Way* harder. If we can't do it and keep all of us alive, don't bother."

"Now that you mention it, that seems like a *lot* of credits for a quick stroll through a cleared dungeon," Reuben affirmed consideringly, nodding at Nacho in clear approval.

"I'll be in the back." Nacho slammed his Skillet of Turtling into place. "If those zombies come up faster than we expect, I can tank the hits. Any fire blasts will fail against me as well."

They crunched across the shattered glass for a few steps before Reuben paused and looked back the way they had come. "Make sure to close all doors we go through. That way, they might get lost, or otherwise be unable to follow us. At minimum, it will slow them down."

Judging by the clamor filtering through the wooden door, the Walking Fists had made it down to the entrance room. Armor-clad zombies clanked, and the whispers of the Mind Players echoed way too loudly for it to be a natural effect.

Nacho wondered what kind of offer the Walking Fists had gotten as a Welcome message. Were they promised the same twenty-five thousand credits each for no killing? Or did the

Patrons make them an offer to end Eli 'Nacho' Naches for the same amount?

It wasn't clear, but one thing that the cook did know for sure was that the Patrons weren't throwing them a bone. Something else was going on in these tunnels.

The corridor of brutalized shelves ended in a four-way intersection. The packed earth gave way to a blank concrete floor. The walls had become plain, white drywall. Overall, the dungeon so far felt like walking through the back hallways of a local shopping mall, only, the ceiling above was still hard-packed dirt, and the sweet smell of chocolate and cookies lingered in the air.

"Lot better than undead stink, smoke, or whatever filth was seeping through the portal. Kinda hard to believe this place can smell so good when literally everything else in the area smells terrible. Jennifer, sorry to say you are included in that list, through no fault of your own." Reuben warily regarded the bare earth overhead as Jennifer held herself back from sending a cutting remark his way. "Speaking of things all around us, while I'm not exactly claustrophobic, I don't want to be buried alive. You know, it's something I've tried to avoid nearly as much as making the IRS angry."

"No money means no IRS, and also the tax is applied to our guild automatically, so there's no need to set up anything similar in this world," Brie reminded the group quietly. "Please keep your head in the game, guys. We need to decide which tunnel to take. Or do you all prefer we fight the zombies and necromancers behind us? If so, we should grab a bite to eat first."

"Let's not fight," It took Nacho an uncomfortably long time to settle on his final choice. "We should save our food for our CrossWorld trip. We just need to hurry, and avoid killing anything if we can get away with it."

"Right, good call." Reuben shook the sausage clips on his wrists. "No Cooking Magic and No Positive Vibes means less of a chance that we'll kill something if we need to slap it out of the way. I'm only doing seventeen damage per punch without any buffs. Wait… I forgot, I do double damage against any food-related monsters."

"Which we're bound to run into in the Sweet Skillz dungeon." Jennifer smiled as she caught where he was going with his leading statement.

"Good, love the rapid choices we're making." Brie tapped her foot impatiently. 'All of this is fascinating. Back to my original question: which way are we going?"

Nacho tried to picture where the entrance of the dungeon stood in relation to where the Portal should be. "Straight. Go straight."

Brie jogged ahead as silently as possible, with the rest of the group falling in behind her. The central corridor widened, and the cement floor ended only twenty feet after they'd entered the passage. Nacho and his friends abruptly found themselves standing on the edge of a slimy mud pit with crystalline stones placed in a path crossing the room. The white walls were gone as quickly as they had appeared, replaced by thick mud and crumbly dirt. The ceiling expanded into a stunning array of jagged crystals, each one gleaming in the light of the fluttering Potstickers.

The sugary smell was almost stifling. Nacho paused, taking a closer look at the area they were in. "Those rocks look a bit too brightly colored… that's not mud on the ground. Look. The particles are too grainy, and there's a white substance mixed in."

The crystal pathway through the murk ran straight across the wide room before splitting into passageways, once again offering a choice of going to the left or the right.

"Let's keep to the right," Brie directed, taking Nacho's points into consideration. "But we're going to have to cross on the stone path, so be wary."

"You know what this looks like?" Jennifer tapped her chin with her combat spoon, then swished it at the ceiling. Even with the tool, the lowest stalactite was too far up for her to reach. "Rock candy, not real rocks. Maybe that's where the smell is coming from?"

"Then… could this be…" Reuben crouched and stuck a finger into the mud bog. He sniffed the sludge, then licked it, making everyone wince, and Brie gagged. "This isn't a mud bog. Well, not *just* a mud bog. This is made at least partially from Oreos… we called it dirt cake, and-"

He cut off with a yelp as something shot out of the murk at his face. It was anaconda-sized, and it wasn't alone. Others wriggled up from the sweet depths of the cookie pit, and Nacho and his friends were unexpectedly thrown into Active Combat.

Even Nacho, terrible cook that he was, remembered dirt cake. He had been able to buy it fully made, after all. It was a mixture of chocolate sandwich cookies, fudge-flavored pudding, whipped cream, and powdered sugar. He'd heard complaints that the recipe didn't call for powdered sugar, but he'd dust it on top anyway. That way, he could claim that he had 'made it' for anyone that wanted a bite.

There was one final ingredient that usually made its way in: gummy worms.

"Get across; I'll keep them busy!" Brie spun her lacrosse stick in her hand and sent a wave of energy cycling across the roiling cookie bog. Her Defensive Whirl deflected giant gummy worms around her husband—barely in time to save him from getting mauled by the round mouths full of jagged teeth.

"What kind of gummy anatomy do these worms have?" Reuben had recovered and was racing across the room, shouting his confusion for all to hear. "Is the stomach acid of the monster sweet? What about the brain?"

Brie's thrown Defensive Whirl had stunned a bunch of the monster worms, but another one appeared at the other end of the dirt bog. Reuben waited until it slithered close enough and threw a punch, hitting the worm so hard that it dropped and began to flail and flop around, flinging cookie dirt everywhere. Reuben laughed darkly as he cracked his knuckles. "Instant concussion on Tier one monsters! Seventy-nine Health each, just as a heads up. Have I mentioned that I *love* double damage?"

Reuben cleared the way with a flurry of jabs, quickly reaching the other side where the rock candy path split. He hurried to the right, then held back to let Jennifer and Nacho run past him. It was clear that he wasn't going to leave the room without his wife.

The cook started to calculate whether he needed to join in the action, but Jennifer kept her paddle and spoon ready in case something came for them out of the darkness that lay ahead. Both were unneeded, as Brie Combat Dashed across the room, clearing the way by directly knocking aside anything that got in her way.

"Getting across the dirt cake is going to be a real challenge for the Mind Players and their zombies," Jennifer commented as she watched the worms writhe a little more before sinking back into the delicious danger dessert. She pulled Nacho down the passageway to the right so that Reuben and Brie had enough room to stand on the rock candy stones in the cookie dirt.

Brie snatched a tube of Life Hack yogurt and pinched it, sucking it down with a single gulp. When she caught Nacho staring, she shrugged. "Don't worry. I won't double-stack the Fitness increases. Just the one."

"Love that you're able to open your throat like that." Reuben whistled softly. "Not a skill many people have, being able to take a full portion with such ease."

Brie squinted at him as she retrieved a peanut butter ball. "Why do I feel like you're being gross?"

"Was that Go-Gurt?" Jennifer questioned as Brie tossed the used tube to the side. "Still can't get over the fact that littering is fine now."

"I do love how clean everything stays." Brie made a face as she considered the food she had just taken in. "It's kind of like Go-Gurt, with cottage cheese added. All prepared by someone that doesn't understand flavor profiles in the slightest."

Jennifer wrinkled her nose and stuck out her tongue. "Yikes. Back on Earth, I was lactose intolerant. That sounds bad enough even without your cook measuring it out to keep things balanced."

"Careful, now..." Reuben cautioned her as Nacho winced and slapped his forehead. "You're around the three cheeses here. Let's all try to be very lactose *tolerant* of the people around us."

"Is *that* what I've been missing? Measuring cups and stuff?" Nacho's mutter wasn't nearly as quiet as he had thought it was going to be.

"What do you mean?" Reuben, normally the voice of reason, sounded cold. "Have you just been *eyeballing* your recipes?"

"What's the real difference between a teaspoon and a tablespoon anyway?" Nacho was still lost in his own thoughts. "You use both of them to stir a cup of coffee. *Either*, I should say."

"I can help him, I think. Brewing is all about exact measurements as well." Jennifer's offer earned her a warm smile from Reuben, and a much kinder considering gaze from Brie. "Also, they're catching up."

The first of the armored zombies shuffled into the room, only to immediately step foot into the bog and get swarmed by gummy worms. Nacho's stomach fell as he watched: he knew two of the zombies. Remy Radix, and Stephen Grote. They must've died during the CrossHuman attack.

Reuben recognized them at the same moment. "Nacho, I'm sorry, bro. Those two... we knew we took casualties, but to actually see the casualties walking around after we lost them is pretty messed up."

Nacho watched as the bodies of people he once knew were turned into worm food. His jaw tightened, "At least now we know that the Necromancers can turn regular people into their Tier one zombies, not just CrossHumans."

"Let's go. We can't do anything for them here." Brie soberly led the way, and Nacho followed after one long moment where he considered taking out all the Necromancers as they crossed the bog. Only the fact that he was alone made him turn and follow.

The rock candy path brought them into another cavernous room, where the floor, walls, and ceiling were all made of the glistening rock candy. A surprisingly ornate rock candy fountain burbled a bright yellow liquid into a ruby red basin. From the smell, it was lemonade, and they all hoped that was the case, since Reuben walked right up to it and took a **slurp** with no hesitation. He gave them a thumbs-up. "Not a sewage line!"

The ceiling and walls were a swirled mixture of lemon candy and lime candy, yellow and green, though the floor was pink and the fountain dark red. A bright blue door waited on the other side of the room, and the sheer number of clashing colors hurt Nacho's eyes.

A menacing **sucking** sound echoed off the hardened candy surfaces as a lime-green slime monster reminiscent of a living Jell-O salad peeled off the brightly colored ceiling. Inside its translucent mass, instead of marshmallows and fruit chunks, floated the remnants of other players. Brie held up one hand and took the measure of the monster. "Those look exactly like those grubling sacks from the Deep Buggy Darkness. You think those are real bodies inside, or are they just a thematic thing?"

The System threw up the Active Combat message as the Jell-O monster's tentacles lashed out, catching Reuben around one arm. He took the damage and swung his other fist into the tentacle. The food-related monster took a *whole* lotta damage, and the remnants of its tentacle splattered across the room.

"Same plan as before!" Brie shoved Jennifer forward to get her moving. "I'll clear the way, and then I'll use Combat Dash to join you. Run!"

"I wanted to taste that lemonade, too," Jennifer joked as her feet started pounding across the sugary surface. "I'm sure it's delicious."

"It was," Reuben confirmed cheerfully. Another Jell-O slime, this one yellow, peeled away from the wall and lashed out with jiggly tentacles, only for Jennifer to smack them away with her spoon and paddle.

Nacho had his cleaver and skillet out, and he hacked into the tentacle of a third monster, this one another lime green. His blade struck, but the monster's limb wobbled away without any visible damage.

Damage dealt: None! This creature is immune to slashing damage!

The Patrons had straight-up lied about the dungeon being mostly dead. Two rooms had already unveiled two sets of sticky-sweet monsters. The Sweet Skillz Welcome Dungeon was definitely alive and kicking.

Between the boosts they could bring to bear, Nacho and his friends would have dealt with the slime monster easily enough, but… the reward *was* tempting. Brie threw her Defensive Whirl across the floor, which slapped away all the tentacles with a cyclone of energy. Nacho, Reuben, and Jennifer sprinted along in its wake and flung open the bright blue door, followed easily by Brie, who used a Combat Dash to join them.

The Walking Fists' forces would have to fight their way through the gummy worms, the Jell-O slimes, and whatever else had spawned. It was unlikely that they would be able to avoid the fight like The Dinner Party was managing to do, which allowed Nacho to relax slightly. If the four of them could just focus on the dungeon, and not worry about the people chasing them, everything would be that much easier.

They passed through multiple other treat-related rooms, culminating in having to duck away from rocky candy golems. They kept moving the entire time they traversed the dungeon, all the way until they discovered candy mosaic steps that led up through a back exit and emerged into the forest above. Once again, Nacho noticed a huge portcullis that had been retracted into the ceiling. If that had been closed, they wouldn't have been able to escape the dungeon. He wasn't sure what the gates were for, or what was required in order to close them.

In the end, they emerged from the Sweet Skillz Welcome Dungeon without killing a single saccharine assailant, resulting in a clamorous *cha-ching* as each of their balances grew twenty-five thousand credits richer in an instant.

It was a sweet little bonus, and the shortcut had helped them lose the necromancers. However, they found themselves in the middle of the forest fire, and they were forced to walk up candy steps that were half-melted from the heat. Jennifer had a pained look on her face as she observed the flaming devastation she had set off. "I feel bad for this. Should I feel bad? I mean, it's not an Earth forest, but it is a forest."

"A *monster* forest, filled with zombies, Necromancers, and CrossHumans. Probably some trees corrupted to the point of becoming actual threats in their own right as well. Feel bad for nothing that died in the fire," Nacho gently reminded her. "Only thing is, everything has Putrid Mana in it. Cover your mouths, and try not to breathe in the smoke. All those trees had the chance to grow into Tier three monsters someday, so I think a forest fire is just fine if it actually manages to slow them down."

Reuben coughed, going slightly pale as he clutched at his chest. "Okay, while I love our banter, we need to get going before this smoke makes me puke."

"It's this way." Brie pointed for effect, but all of them knew where to look. Even with the stifling smoke assaulting their senses, the unmistakable stench of the Portal was far stronger. As they walked through literal fire toward a new world, Nacho couldn't deny he felt nervous. No human had ever gone through the Portal and returned to tell the tale. He shook off the worry and steeled his mind. "I've already survived one new world. Just have to make sure we survive another."

CHAPTER SEVENTEEN

Nacho led the way through the blazing forest, following the chemical stink to the CrossWorld Portal. Before long, they managed to find a road relatively clear of flames, though they had quickly learned that the ash and deadly fumes were more of a problem.

The forest fire had already burned through the trees around the Portal, so by the time they reached the source of the nauseating smell, they didn't have to worry about hidden sentries. They even gained the unexpected luxury of being able to inspect the distortion in its entirety as they approached.

A hundred feet tall and thirty feet wide, the CrossWorld Portal displayed various designs cut into the heavy frame, which was otherwise flawlessly crafted from white marble. Some friezes mimicked Celtic knots, while others were a mixture of dragons, griffins, hydras… but also tacos, popcorn boxes, Bucky Cups that were almost exclusive to Texas, and various other food-related items. That was the Juxtaposition alright—monsters and food, with neither more important than the other.

A wavering purple light extended from the top of the rectangular structure all the way down to the dirt. Lavender sparks **snapped** and **popped** within the purple energy field. All of the theatrical details highlighted one simple fact: crossing over to the other world was easy.

They simply had to walk into the light.

Nacho and his friends took a moment to consider the Portal in front of them, relieved and slightly concerned that no one was attacking them yet. Brie laughed as she a realization dawned. "Jennifer's forest fire helped us more than just granting us an initial escape."

"Glad we can joke about it." The Brewer was still unsure of where she stood in Brie's eyes, and it showed. "Jokes are okay again? I'm not used to mass destruction."

"You don't have to come with us, Jennifer," Nacho informed her as gently as he could manage, which ended up still sounding slightly sharp. "That is… you don't know us, and this is monstrously dangerous. People who go through that Portal don't come back."

"'Monstrously dangerous'?" Jennifer shifted her backpack, tightening a strap and smirking. "If you wanted to warn me away, you're failing gloriously. I want to see another world, just like anyone else would. I'm coming, as long as Brie eases off the 'kill me at a moment's notice' vibe she has going on."

"No promises." Brie pushed her nose into the crook of her elbow to fight the smell. "I don't mind the help, but if we're going to go, we need to go now. Kristie, Taye, and Abby might still be alive, but for how much longer?"

"Then I'm going," the Brewer announced with surprising force. "For one, you guys saved me from making beer for humorless Necromancers. There was *zero* fun to be had there, and they kept telling me they'd eat me if I messed up. The way they said it, *that* didn't sound very fun either. Second, I don't know all the rules of the Juxtaposition, but I do know that food and drinks play a key part in allowing us to succeed. I want to try your nasty cottage cheese Go-Gurt. Call me curious."

"Seems strange, but I'll call you whatever you'd like, Ms. Curious." Nacho was pleased with her choice, but he felt the added responsibility of keeping her alive at the same time. She was correct; drinks *were* incredibly important, and he intended to figure out what her unique abilities could do for the survival of the human race. Plus, she'd mentioned being able to brew decent soda. He knew that alone was enough for Reuben to add her directly to the inner circle for life. "Welcome aboard. Now, let's get through this Portal."

"Wait." Brie accessed the Store and bought four pairs of sunglasses, a single Credit dropping two in her hands at a time. "We'll need these to cover our eyes. Like the Patrons said, our round pupils will stick out."

"You smarty-pants. It isn't game mechanics; it's a social construct! I would have totally forgotten." Reuben gave her a peck on the cheek as he collected his eyewear.

"Thanks. One more thing." Brie held up a hand to stop them from charging in headlong. "We have the Patrons for Earth, right? Do the CrossHumans have Patrons, and if so, are they the same Patrons, or are they different?"

Nacho shrugged slowly, unable to answer her question. "I don't know much about the Patrons and their relationship between worlds. I would assume that they would be different, but… I mean, if it's just betting, then the Patrons would simply bet on the world they thought would have the best chance of winning. All I know for sure is this CrossHuman named Arriod made it pretty clear he was fighting a war against all humans. Well, it was as much of a buffet for them as it was war. The CrossHumans didn't mind eating humans–to tell you the truth, we, uh, ate them right back."

Jennifer choked, looking shocked and a little confused, and Nacho blanched as he realized how that had sounded. She had no context, and didn't know about his boon. Stumbling over his words, Nacho tried to correct himself, "That is, not now, not in *this* reality! I had a-"

"Explanations later; finding our friends now." Brie marched forward, though she did throw him a lifeline. "He's right, it's not what it sounds like."

Nacho found himself completely unable to think, and decided to act instead. "Okay, see you on the other side!"

Purple sparks continued to crackle out of the Portal with a light popping sound, ignoring the fact that Nacho's fingertips were touching the purple wall of light. The cook had been expecting it to feel hot, to feel like *something*, but he may as well have been touching air. At first. Between one moment and the next, the energy clung to him like he was shoving his hand through cotton candy—he *could* pull away, but decided against it.

All four of them were shoulder to shoulder with one hand inside the Portal, so he made the first move, pushing his face through the light and into the cotton candy energy field. With a lurch, he stepped onto the ground of a new world, full of amazingly fresh-smelling air. If this world had ever had pollution as an issue, that was gone now. He felt *rejuvenated* after only a few deep breaths.

The Portal, now behind them, continued to snap and pop. For a long moment, Nacho simply experienced the CrossWorld—or CruxTerra, as the locals apparently called it.

The sky was a burning orange and full of smoke, just like theirs… no. It had seemed like smoke at first, but Nacho quickly realized the swirling plumes were composed of pollen wafting off the trees around them in waves. The trees' outer bark was blue, and they were devoid of leaves; instead swollen pods hung from their azure branches. Suddenly, Arriod's threat from Nacho's last vision came back to him like a face full of freezing water with cubes of bad omen ice floating in it.

'It's us or it's you, Nacho. This is a zero-sum game, and I can guarantee you, we are not going to lose.'

Blue sunshine cut through the orangeness around them, painting the alien scenery in colors completely unnatural to them. Jennifer immediately noticed something was wrong and grabbed Nacho's arm to march him forward. "This is all normal for us, *right*, Nacho? We're just walking out of the Portal after scouting Earth. We're just walking right through these blue trees, under the blue sun, with enough pollen in the air to kill your average asthmatic. Home. Yup, this is our planet."

Reuben and Brie followed smoothly behind them, and all four moved away from the Portal and through the bizarre forest. It took no time at all for two men in bright lacquer armor to hustle up to them, weapons at the ready. It was hard to tell what color their gear was, given the odd nature of the light on Crux-Terra. Both men wore fashionable cloaks and gripped familiar long-bladed spears.

On the left chest panel of their armor, a letter and number had been painted in a highly visible manner. The cook took this in with narrowed eyes. "D-Three?"

Neither were wearing sunglasses, leaving their cross-shaped pupils visible. The leftmost guard spoke clearly. "All Portal traffic must check in immediately, as per statute fifteen-point-one-eight-six. Name, rank, unit designation."

Nacho immediately realized they needed to trick these guards, or they would have to kill them. If that happened, they would be on a time limit right from the start. It was clear that this place was far more disciplined than their own world, so he decided to introduce some of Earth's specialty: chaos. Urgency and yelling usually worked to freak guards out no matter where he went, but he'd really have to sell it.

Luckily, he had plenty of experience infiltrating places that he wasn't supposed to be. He channeled some of that energy into his performance. "Move, fools! We're obviously A-ones. We were wounded over in the round world, and we had to wait for our regenerations to kick in. Even then, it was madness over there. *Madness*, I tell you! There was a forest fire, and Arriod left us unexpectedly. We need to catch up to the prisoners that were carted in; it's a matter of utmost urgency! They have the location of an artifact, and only *we* know that *they* know!"

While gesticulating wildly, Nacho wondered if anyone outside of movie villains had ever shouted 'move, fools' unironically. He also wondered if he had gone too high with his rank.

Claiming A-one was a risk, but if these D-threes were anything like standard human guards… they'd be fine.

On top of that, if the guards didn't buy Nacho's story, they were about to get a hands-on lacrosse lesson.

The guards looked shocked at the mention of A-one-ranked beings talking to them. But what *really* made them jump was that name: Arriod. It seemed he was a big deal on the very blue and orange CruxTerra; just as much, if not more, than on Earth.

Nacho figured their appearance might've helped sell the lie as well. He looked like a walking kitchen. Jennifer was practically dwarfed by her huge backpack, with her paddle and spoon stuck haphazardly into her belt. Reuben looked like a warrior knight, except for the sausage clips around his wrists. Then there was Brie, with her lacrosse stick and her circus clown collection of brightly colored armor, which coordinated strangely well in the bright blue sunlight.

They were an odd collection, all right. But to be fair, they had just escaped a Necromancer who wore a hydration backpack and chewed on a human arm made of cake dangling over one shoulder, so oddities were becoming more commonplace.

"A-ah. I see." One of the CruxTerran guards began to hem and haw, until he was jostled into action by a nudge from his partner. "Uh, the roundie prisoners escaped captivity and disappeared inside some kind of… welcome dungeon. Or at least that's what we're calling it. There was an uprising in Sector Seventeen, and Arriod was called in to put it down."

"You mean to tell me… the prisoners were left with *you*, and as soon as Arriod had to step away, you *lost* them?" Jennifer sighed, pinching the bridge of her nose as she shook her head. "I knew those Sector Seventeeners were no good."

"Why are you speaking for your leader?" The other guard glanced uneasily between Jennifer and Nacho, suspicious for some reason that the humans likely wouldn't understand. "I think it's time you lowered your sunshaders. You could be-"

Reuben stepped up, his Marketing Skill practically *oozing* out of him. "The roundies have critical information for the success of our world. The very lives of every man, woman, and child hangs in the balance. Now, if you'll tell us where this dungeon they fled into is, we can *hopefully* overlook the fact that you lost them in the first place."

Mr. Gullible Guard pointed with his spear. "Yes! Down that path to the dungeon. You'll see the gate, but… we can't get through it."

"Don't worry." Reuben smiled with all of his teeth showing. "We're A-one. We have our ways."

Both of the CrossHumans—or was it CruxTerrans?—smiled along with him as Brie and Jennifer marched past. Reuben trailed after, waving farewell at the two CruxTerran guards. Their eyes followed the group, and just as Reuben's hand was dropping to his side, Nacho casually stepped up to the rearmost guard and slipped his hand over the CruxTerran's mouth.

In the same moment, he slammed his blade point-first through the clavicle and into the guard's esophagus, guaranteeing that he wouldn't be able to make a sound over the blood pouring into his lungs. As the man's cross-pupiled eyes grew wide, Nacho glided around him and repeated the attack with the other guard. They sank to their knees nearly in tandem, suffocating silently, and Nacho used his massive Fitness to grab each of them and drag them into the foliage before finishing them off with a double chop of his cleaver.

Reuben watched the near-silent, brutal slaughter with a wide-open mouth, gaping at the clean kills done in such an efficient and casual manner. "N-Nacho…!"

"What?" The cook looked up and noticed the shocked faces of his group. "Did I make a mess? That first strike should have kept everything contained inside their-"

"You just *murdered*-" Jennifer started to shout, only to be cut off by Brie swatting her across the face.

The Berserker glared icily at the shaken Brewer. "Quiet. *Down*."

"They weren't fooled, guys," Nacho calmly informed them as he scattered some of the strange foliage over the corpses. "This one was already grabbing at his flare-looking thing. They were only waiting until we turned away to send up the warning. Sorry, Reuben. Your skill failed."

The unexpected slaughter effectively crushed further conversation, and they spent their efforts rushing down the dirt road that cut through the trees without trying to look like they were in a hurry. Time after time, they passed tents and sentinels outfitted in strong lacquer armor. Each and every one of them was marked with a letter and number identifier, everything from B-one to I-nine.

Nacho didn't know what any of those designations meant, and he wasn't going to do something as foolish as head over and *ask*. It was just as Jennifer had been trying to remind him with the first step through the portal—if they walked with purpose, and if they looked like they knew where they were going, most people wouldn't be too suspicious.

The cook had to forcibly slow his pace to get a better sense of things. All the tents, all the soldiers, surrounded a central archway. That must've been where the CruxTerran version of the Welcome Dungeon opened, which meant it was where the Breakfast Club would be. The Patrons had to be using some kind of powerful magic to keep the small CruxTerran army out of those tunnels.

Nacho remembered the gates he'd observed at the entrances to the Sweet Skillz Welcome Dungeon. Had they been closed when Arriod and his people were running it? That seemed... likely. His mind raced as he searched for a way to walk through those soldiers unobstructed and invade their welcome dungeon. The short answer was: they couldn't.

"There's gotta be more than one entrance. Keep an eye out for anything that looks System-made." Everyone stayed in step with him, and they had no choice but to keep on skirting past the encampment. The Dinner Party searched for a solid hour, eventually finding a small castle, not much more than a few low walls around a keep. A dirt path led right up to the portcullis. Over a shallow, dusty moat hung a sign, written in a language that Nacho didn't recognize, likely native CruxTerran.

Nacho started to slow, but before he could stop, Jennifer grabbed him. "No use stopping now, Nacho. Let's keep moving."

Arm in arm, he and Jennifer marched up to the gate with Reuben and Brie behind them. As they drew close, the sign shifted from the bizarre script into English. A simple word greeted them. A wonderful word.

WELCOME!

"Thank goodness… it's a secondary entrance." Brie huffed out a deep breath. "No idea why it isn't guarded, and I don't know how we're going to get back to the Portal when we return, but I've never been more relieved to see the entrance to one of these dungeons in my life."

CHAPTER EIGHTEEN

Nacho paused in hesitant contemplation under the blue sunshine of this other world as rivers of orange pollen, sweet and fragrant, filled the air. He didn't know how he was going to get himself and his friends through the huge portcullis of the CruxTerran castle. There was clearly a welcome sign above the gate, but so far, nothing about this place looked very welcoming.

Surprisingly, as the party approached, the bars of the portcullis lifted with the sound of chiming steel chains and stone grinding on stone. The moment they were inside the courtyard, the gate **slammed** down behind them, cutting off most of the light that had been filtering into the area. Their eyes adjusted rapidly, and soon they were able to make out stairs descending into the deeper darkness.

"Thoughts?" Brie called softly to the others.

"Either this is a new Welcome Dungeon, just for us, or it'll connect us to the existing Welcome Dungeon." Reuben had an answer on his lips the same moment that she asked the question. "We might've managed to find a secret way to get to the Breakfast Club, if the Welcome dungeon back on Earth is anything like this one."

"Good. Good." Brie took a deep breath and motioned at a side door. "Reuben, mind coming with me for a moment? I need something from your storage."

They vanished into the darkness without another word, opting not to enter into the dungeon, but instead taking advantage of what appeared to be a rest area. At least as far as Nacho could tell. He watched their departure quizzically but made no move to follow them. Jennifer turned to him a few minutes after the couple had left, once it was clear they might not be right back. "Hey, Nacho… so I know I'm the new girl here, but is Brie… okay?"

The cook knew there was only one answer to that question, and his brow furrowed as he tried to decipher what she could be getting at. "Without a doubt. She's the toughest of us, mentally. I'm completely unstable and far too dedicated to whatever I'm trying to be good at, and Reuben is too lackadaisical to really take anything into serious consideration. He's sharp, though. More than me, at far too many things."

"You think they're just blowing off steam?" Jennifer questioned knowingly as she peered into the darkness.

"Probably something like that." Now that he thought about it, Nacho realized that Brie *had* been more volcanic than normal. Even at the best of times, she ran hot, and she had *really* been leaning into the 'berserk' part of her Berserker class. "She's been getting into character and treating this more like a full-blown role play with every passing day. It helps her get through the tough parts, especially since she has to deal with the two of us guys constantly making jokes."

"I've seen it before," Jennifer quietly stated, a tinge of sadness creeping into her tone. "It's amazing that more people haven't completely lost it. In the end, the Juxtaposition is more mental than anything else. Sure, it's physically demanding, and there's the whole Hunger and Thirst aspect, but ultimately, it's your mental attitude that makes the difference."

She spoke with an unexpected air of authority on the subject.

"Nope, you're wrong. Sorry if it goes against your therapist instincts." Nacho selected a solid chunk of wall, leaned back, crossed his arms, and stretched his legs out in front of him. "This place is the *opposite* of mental-strength-required. In fact, it's all too easy to get lost in the physicality of the environment. As soon as you hit fifteen points in Mind or Fitness, your brain is automatically protected against sudden wild mood swings. The Mana inside of you will give you all the drive you need in order to survive, and it acts as a safeguard against most mental issues that would normally come with the danger and loss of adjusting to the Juxtaposition. The *real* issue is that if you hit those numbers while you're in a bad place, it'll take even longer than usual to get out of it. Luckily, most people that level up and reach those points are riding the high of survival when they do. It's a nice buffer."

"Interesting. How do you know that?" Jennifer threw him some side-eye and laughed with only a tiny hint at her underlying fear of this trio, slipping off her enormous pack and joining him on the floor after a brief pause. "Also, um, why did you talk about eating people?"

"Right, that." Nacho winced as he ordered his thoughts. "I was granted a boon from a Patron that allowed me to experience three years in this world before coming here. I'm not a serial killer, or a cannibal… anymore. Technically, I never was. I just got to experience it."

"That's an interesting boon." Jennifer studied him with a slight frown on her lips. "Is that why you chose to class as a cook? How you earned enough points to buy it? Why you could kill those guards and not even realize that we were upset that you did it?"

"Yeah… look. I have lots of experience surviving, and even more experience in killing. I was an Assassin in my initial vision, boon, whatever. Spent years in the game and learned *exactly* how Hunger and Thirst Points become critical. As for the mental stuff, I had access to a lot of information packs that other people bought, even if I had to take them off their bodies.

You have to hone your survival instinct down to a fine point, and the Mana in our bodies makes that... not easy, but it takes the edge off."

"Thank you for sharing." A mischievous smile played across the Brewer's face, all traces of concern melting away. "Also, no therapist instincts here, I was a bartender before the Juxtaposition, which is *like* being a therapist, except pretzels are more important, and you get paid a lot less per hour."

"You think you know about apocalyptic stress from bartending?" Nacho chuckled at the comparison.

Jennifer gave him a strange look. "Uh, *yeah*. Staff calls in sick, it's Mardi Gras, and your bar is hosting the Kappa Epsilon Gamma fraternity. Anyway, yes. *Stress*. Bartending is only one of the many hats I'd worn in my life before the Juxtaposition. I've done plenty of other things that were stressful."

Nacho attempted to ask her what those things were, but she cut him off. Perhaps she wasn't too happy about his smirking, but he couldn't even pretend to care.

She nudged him. "I want to know more about your boon."

"I don't mind; it's not a big secret, even if I don't usually start conversations with that information." Nacho launched into the whole story of his Probability Vision, though he kept the murder talk down to around fifteen percent, and he included only about *two* percent of the cannibalism. Too late, he realized that if he'd wanted to make a good impression, he should've included *zero* talk of cannibalism.

Jennifer didn't seem particularly shocked. "You did what you had to do. I can see how losing Reuben and Brie would've torn you up. Yet, you survived... because of the boon. Of course, everything is different now. You've helped so many people, and according to the Patrons, you have the most powerful guild in the world. That's nothing to laugh at. It was why me and my people... oh... right. Why we came south. It's unfortunate that we came across the distasteful alliance of the Midnight Fists and Walking Freds first. I lost *everyone*, and now I have some... survivor guilt. At least, thanks to you, I know that

I'm not a monster. It's the Mana in my head that is protecting me from spiraling like a Christmas ham into despair."

He let the silence stretch for a moment, but eventually Nacho tried to put some of the mystery together. "You did some brewing and you bartended. That explains why you decided to be a Brewer, but it doesn't tell me how you could survive so well in the Evaluation World."

"That is an aspect of my mysterious past. Suffice to say, I did really well in League of Legends."

Nacho perked up at the admission and tried to draw the connection from one to the other. He failed. After a long moment, all he could say was, "...Really?"

"*No*! How would that help me? With my past, becoming a Brewer was a no-brainer, and I'm passionate about soup." Jennifer scoffed at him, though a smile was clearly trying to fight its way out. He waited patiently, and after an extended pause, she made a decision. "You know, since I'm part of the Dinner Party, and since I just know that you're dying to talk about soup recipes... I could show you my character sheet."

"Are you sure? That's very personal." Nacho didn't even try to hide his surprise. "I didn't want to be pushy."

"You've been a perfect gentleman," Jennifer informed him agreeably. In a blink, the Brewer sent the information over.

Jennifer Ales
Class: Vat Attacker
Level: 11
Experience Points: 23,300 to Level 11!
Current Credits: 27,345 (106,975 total Dinner Party pool)

Build Type: Balanced, Instant
Body:

- *Fitness: 19*
- *Metabolic efficiency: 18*

Mind:

- *Mental energy: 18*
- *Circuit: 18*

Satiation:

- *Hunger: 100*
- *Thirst: 100*

Total Health Points: 48
Bonus Physical Damage: 9.5%
Health Regen: 18% Health Regen/minute
Total Mana Pool: 37
Bonus Spell Damage: 9%
Mana Pool Regen: 18% Mana Regen/minute

Skill Slots (4/4)

- *Boot Camp Brewmeister (Passive) Level 19: Can use any Satiation Player item as a weapon to generate 10 HP per strike. Bonus damage: one point per skill level (currently 19 HP of damage).*

Tier 1 Enhancement: Hurl any Satiation Player Item at your enemies!

0% Mana, Hydration, and Metabolic Cost

- *Purify (Active) Level 19: Remove Putrid Mana from all sources of water everywhere! Make one gallon of delicious and nutritious water per level (currently 19 gallons).*

Tier 1 Enhancement: Process water from 15 feet away!

Mana Cost = 5%
Hydration Cost = 5%

Metabolic Cost = 5%

- *Mana Pop (Active) Level 19: Create a soda in a Juxtaposition bottle that restores 38 Thirst Points and 95 Mana Points!*

Tier 1 Enhancement: Brew Soda from 15 feet away!

Mana Cost = 10%
Hydration Cost = 10%
Metabolic Cost = 10%

- *Stone Soup Mistress (Active) Level 19: Increase any food source by 38% by dropping a stone (along with actual food) into your deliciously purified water. Note: Soups/Stews increase both Hunger Points and Thirst Points.*

Tier 1 Enhancement: Soup it up from 15 feet away!

Mana Cost = 5%
Hydration Cost = 5%
Metabolic Cost = 5%

Nacho had to take a moment for all of the information to sink in. "Let me get this straight… when you hit someone with your big spoon, it does sword-like damage. Then, since you have the skill at level nineteen, you're doing twenty-nine points of damage? *Per strike*? You can literally kill a man with a spoon."

"Right," the Brewer agreed with an evil smile. "Or I can use my paddle, *or* both. I can also throw them, but I don't want to lose my spoon. I really like it."

Nacho let out a low whistle of appreciation as he continued down the list. "Purify takes the Putrid Mana out of water. That makes sense. You don't have to pay for the bottled water, which gets exponentially more expensive as we go. Gotcha. Mana Pop looks really useful; also tasty."

Jennifer furrowed her brow and shrugged. "I mostly traveled with Mind Players. It might have gone better if we'd had more brawn when we got hit by the zombies, but I didn't really have a way to help them much."

Nacho tried to find some silver lining. "You did have soup for your people. That must've helped to stave off the starvation."

"Yeah, with even a little bread, I can basically turn a quarter portion into a half portion. It helped with Hunger and Thirst Points, but… not enough."

He gently elbowed her to pull her from her reminiscent sadness. "I can't wait to try some. I haven't even tried tackling soups or stews. I did make bug gyros, but… it didn't go well. People just don't like the idea of eating insects."

"I'm sure *that's* the issue." Jennifer smiled and locked eyes with him. "Or maybe they just haven't gotten hungry enough. Or, maybe—just maybe—your friends are correct, and you don't know how to make things taste the way they should. I can help, I'll make a sauce that you can add to your food that makes it edible for anyone."

"Wait. That's a thing? What kind-"

"It's ketchup, Nacho." She laughed at the dumbfounded expression on his face. "Seriously? You make enough food at a time to feed thousands, and you never thought to offer condiments?"

"It didn't seem important?" was the only excuse that he could offer. Nacho felt gratitude fill him up completely. "That'll help a *lot.* Also, you should join the Chips Guild. You do have to pay a tax, and there is this oath of loyalty, which sounds pretty hardcore, but we're a reasonable lot. No pressure."

"Let me try your cooking first." Jennifer tried to laugh, but found that she was too somber after their heavier conversation. "You'll have to try my fresh water and potent drinks. I'm pretty good, but… I have to admit, I'm a little nervous about you trying my soup, since you are a master chef."

"Yeah, no. Common Cook here, extra emphasis on 'common'." He stood up and offered her a hand. "You're probably going to try out my donuts first. Just… the bug gyros were so much better. I have never tried to use this type of flour, so don't judge me too harshly."

"Never!" she mockingly promised as she settled her pack back on her shoulders and walked with him toward the dungeon entrance at the center of the courtyard. As if the couple had been waiting for them to finish their conversation, Brie and Reuben came out of the room where they'd been talking, holding hands.

"Ready to continue on?" Reuben questioned, a bright smile on his face. "I know we are. Nothing quite like getting a co-op bathroom break to make a couple *truly* close."

"Well, don't hoard the toilet paper in your Storage Slots, and you won't need to come with me," Brie scoffed at him without a hint of shame.

Nacho stared at Reuben, and the silence stretched until he was finally able to get his question out. "You're using an entire Storage Slot for *toilet paper*? *That's* the reason we were forced to leave my mobile kitchen behind?"

"Well… I mean, if life on Earth right before the Juxtaposition taught me anything, it was that you could never go wrong stocking up on ultra-soft." Reuben dove out of the way as one of Nacho's knives whistled through the air at him.

CHAPTER NINETEEN

Basic needs covered and tension broken, the group started heading slowly down the stones of the circular staircase. At first glance, the steps looked like regular stone rectangles, until Nacho noticed that the small platforms were actually a combination of triangles and circles that fit together well, but not perfectly. After descending down half a dozen of the unusual steps, Jennifer was the one that finally voiced her concerns. "Do the words 'non-Euclidean geometry' mean anything to you guys?"

Reuben turned to stare at her, the whites of his eyes showing clearly. "No. We don't speak words like that here. I took Statistics to avoid opening myself to that insanity."

Nacho glanced at the architecture one last time before asking, "Is this pertinent to our success or survival, Jen? Or are you just making conversation?"

"No," she slowly acknowledged, then immediately amended her opinion. "Maybe. The circles and triangles on the steps are definitely different, and I'm thinking... you remember how everything was candy on our side? Maybe it's a theme from our worlds, to introduce or 'welcome' us to this new society.'"

"I love that idea. Not sure how we're going to defeat *math*, but I will admit that it's been a dream of mine since I was a child," Reuben promised the group far too seriously, just as the System chimed in with a long message.

Welcome, Player, to the Skillz Slammer, the Welcome Dungeon for you round-pupiled humans who've come traipsing through the Portals set up between your Home Sweet Home and CruxTerra. This is a classic Crux-Terran dungeon, which means you'll encounter things both beautiful and strange to your chaotic minds.

You'll want to fight your way to the Skillz Cube. There, we will offer you Rare or complex abilities that will blow your mind and ruin your purse! This is going to be a special experience that you will treasure for the rest of your lives.

However short that may be!

Guess what, sports fans? With the CruxTerrans finding their Welcome Dungeon, and you Earthlings finally locating yours, you have unlocked the Starvation Dungeon! You won't be able to start the Starvation Dungeon until your rivals, the CruxTerrans, are in position on the Earth's Starter World, and then it's a race to the end!

Both of your worlds are Starter Worlds, and in the Starvation Dungeon, you'll be competing to see which world gets to move on to the next round of happy-fun futures!

This is a zero-sum game, Player! One side can't win if the other side doesn't lose. We didn't make the rules; we're just enjoying them.

Good luck, brave Player, and may your future be delicious!

They collectively stopped in the middle of the strange triangle-and-circle adorned chamber to take in what all that might mean. The Brewer seemed to be the kind of person that couldn't keep their internal thoughts private for long, and she naturally spoke up first. "All this talk about Starvation Dungeons is making me hungry all of a sudden. Can I have one of these donuts you guys keep mentioning?"

"You're gonna want something else," Nacho admitted with a grunt as his friends snorted at him. "I have an old pocket pancake left? Those weren't bad."

"Are you being serious right now?" Brie rested one hand on her face, her elbow supported by her other arm braced across her stomach as she sighed.

"Yeah, nothing sells a pancake more than pulling an 'old' one out of your pocket and offering it to me with a creepy grin." Jennifer joined Brie in shaking her head, while Reuben and Nacho locked eyes and shrugged.

"Food is food." Nacho was having trouble understanding the issue. "Am I wrong?"

Brie flatly replied, "You're wrong."

"You're right, Nacho. I don't get it either," Reuben commiserated with him at the same time his wife spoke.

"*You* don't get an opinion on this." Brie pulled Mr. Lacrosse Stick from storage and rested it on her shoulders. "Might I remind you that I've seen you pull pizza from under a couch, get really excited because it was a 'surprise from past you', and eat it?"

"It was still in the box," Reuben protested earnestly. "Can we talk about this dungeon, please? I'm thinking it's your classic dungeon-nested-inside-a-dungeon situation, kind of like the UnderFun. We go through the 'Skillz Slammer' first to get new abilities, and then we have to find the entrance to the Starvation Dungeon, which sounds like some kind of endgame event. I'm hoping that with both a Brewer and a Common Cook, we might be able to get through this without, you know, actually starving?"

"Still hungry," Jen muttered softly, intentionally *not* looking at the pancake Nacho was holding out for her.

The cook shook his head. After dealing with the Juxtaposition longer than anyone else, he knew better than Reuben on the subject. "Not so sure it's going to be that easy. When the Patrons talk about starving, I think they mean it. Most likely, they're going to change the rules regarding how our Hunger and Thirst Points work. We'll just have to cross that buffet line when we get to it."

Jennifer sighed and rubbed her growling stomach. "Can someone either feed me, or let us move on? I was held captive by those necromancers for a long time…"

"Have a peanut butter ball." Brie handed over the treat and started progressing down the stairs. "Let's get going, everyone. It's not going to get any easier if we wait around. Everything is getting stronger, and we need to stay ahead of the curve."

"Would you say that we need to do… anything in particular?" Reuben poked at her. "Something that, perhaps, we dairy sacks should consider being in order to prevent ourselves from rotting?"

"Seriously, Reuben? We aren't in a comic book, I don't need a tagline, and I certainly don't need to shout it every five minutes, do I?" Brie let out a huff of annoyance as he shook his head in mock incomprehension, eyes gleaming. "*Fine*! Stay fresh… cheese bags."

"I am so incredibly motivated to be fresh right now." Reuben practically skipped down the stairs with a chipper spring to each movement. "Let's go solve math's problems instead of letting it work things out on its own!"

They descended farther down the stairs with the Firefly Potstickers fluttering about to light the way. They weren't in Active Combat, so Nacho considered taking a few minutes to make more peanut butter balls and Life Hack yogurt, but he was also well aware that every second counted. They were on CruxTerra to rescue their friends, and apparently something in here held the fate of their entire world in the balance. He'd just have to hope that he'd get Store access again soon, and that his current supplies would be enough.

The circular staircase culminated in a landing that opened up onto a grand hallway with a sloped ceiling. The floor continued with the imprinted triangles and circles, but the walls and ceiling were covered in small, colorful tiles to create a mosaic of images.

It was also strangely warm in the room, though there was no discernible heat source. Too warm. Nacho found himself sweating, and not from nerves. He'd delved down into any number of pits on his own Starter World, but he didn't know what kind of horrors awaited them here. "How different do you think things really are in this world?"

"I mean… the people cheerfully live with a number and letter designation in lieu of names. I think things are *very* different." Reuben shook the sausage clips around his wrists, letting them jangle against his armor. "We should watch out for traps, if we can even recognize them. I also wouldn't recommend touching anything. Ya just never know."

"Good thinking." Nacho cautiously approached a wall on his right, inspecting the tiled mural curiously. The mosaics depicted two people, a man and a woman, emerging from the blue pods of a tree. Following the design up, more people joined the two people to create one big happy kingdom, complete with a castle on the left wall.

Jennifer sidled up to him, leaning her head back to look at the ceiling. "It tells a story, right? This world's Adam and Eve, emerging from those weird trees, and they have kids, and they get a big castle—it moves right to left, like Japanese mangas."

"If we're thinking of it like that, as their world history," Brie pointed at the next section, "then the people join together in a big happy kingdom, until they get unhappy and split."

The next mosaic displayed a collection of castles, each with a different flag. Some flags showed two hearts, others showed eyes with a vertical slit, very reptilian, while still others showed a tree with the odd pods. It was obvious that the symbols indicated the different kingdoms.

Seven kingdoms in total had spread across seven continents. Nacho was surprised at the eyes—the pupils very clearly weren't crosses in these images. Did their crosses come later? Was it a natural evolution, or had it been done for some other reason?

His eyes traversed the ceiling, locating a massive display in which armies started crossing oceans, each bearing a different flag. The wars seemed epic in scale. Some of the soldiers brandished curved swords, while others wielded strange half-moon axes, but most carried the long-bladed pikes that they'd witnessed the undead wielding back on Earth.

Reuben clutched his leather Helm of Helming with one hand as he craned his neck. "Those weapons are called naginatas back on Earth. The CruxTerrans went through their own warring feudal period here, it seems."

On the far wall, a small boy pulled a naginata out of a stone, and all of the various armies bowed down to him. The mural seemed to indicate a time of peace that followed this.

The Healer randomly laughed. "You think King Arthur transmigrated? How about Merlin?"

"I don't understand." Brie glanced back at her husband, smiling softly as she observed the sheer happiness on his face, "What is transmigrating?"

"It's what we just did—no, actually, this is a classic portal fantasy now." Reuben chuckled and rubbed his hands together in glee that he got to explain the concept. "It means someone that unexpectedly travels to a new world and has to learn all the new customs, even though they get to keep their memories. Usually."

"Ah. Fiction. Books." Brie returned her attention to the tiled artwork as Reuben glanced at her with a complicated expression.

"*Fiction*? Are we living through the same Armageddon?"

Nacho ignored their good-natured bantering and walked to the next section, finding more modern-looking cities, though again, each city had distinct banners, though there seemed to be a general culture of growth and peace. All the way until war broke out, again. The main difference was that this section included guns, tanks, and fighter planes. They were definitely at least into the Earth's modern age.

Each of the warring nations had a name now. Were they nations or families? Nacho wasn't sure. He read through the list

—the Qua, the Mac, the La, the Sno, the PewJack, the Bus, and the Ye.

The fighting shifted into a single image that left a chill in Nacho's heart for some reason. The single-eye banner—still with a vertical pupil—was carried by a man wielding a long-bladed spear. The figure had a name displayed in golden tiles under his combat boots—Ridiquool PewJack, the very first of the PewJack leaders, it seemed.

PewJack soon had all the other banners at his feet, allowing his alone to stand. It seemed the different societies on the planet, across all seven continents, now had a definitive ruler.

Down the wall to the left, PewJack the Second stood with the same banner, only with the addition of a horizontal line on the eye that created the cross-shaped pupils. But why? What happened with the subsequent rulers and the eyes?

"Okay, so are you reading that like I'm reading it?" Reuben tapped on the tile, blatantly ignoring his previous recommendation to touch nothing.

Jennifer was catching up to them, having taken more time to look over the details. "The PewJack family won, but where did the cross-shaped pupil come from? Did you guys notice that?"

"I didn't. But it looks like the CruxTerrans had a modern age like we did." Nacho had progressed to the end of the grand hallway and was inspecting a very solid-looking wooden door with a huge iron bar across the middle. He wasn't ready to open that door just yet. Something told him that it was the only reason they hadn't needed to deal with monsters as they studied the murals.

"Well, they are up to PewJack the Fourth," Jennifer walked to the last part of the wall, where the heroic-looking leader stood not with a rifle, but the banner and a curved sword, while monsters poured out of a radically changed world of blue trees and medieval soldiers wielding naginatas.

"Interesting that he has a sword, and not a spear," Nacho mused aloud as his attention was pulled to the image.

Brie pointed at the final mosaic with her lacrosse stick.

"That's the Juxtaposition. These guys had the same thing happen to their planet that we did."

"Looks like it." Reuben took another pass under the more modern history. "Only, they had a one-world government and they liked eggs. Is it me, or is there a ton of scrambled egg action up there? Look… anywhere an egg shows up, it's scrambled. I wonder why? Are eggs different in this world?"

Nacho joined the big guy and took a look, his professional curiosity roused. He hadn't noticed it before, but yes, he could see now that under the rulership of the one-world government, yellow-feathered chickens were everywhere. The murals had included a surprising surplus of odd, orange-colored eggs, and he spotted more with every glance. Chefs in different buildings stood over stoves that looked *exactly* the same, handing out scrambled eggs to people in lines. "Now that you have my attention on this, I admit that it'd be interesting to buy a CruxTerran cookbook."

"Let's just get going." Brie was clearly done with the history lesson. "There haven't been any monsters, and there haven't been traps. Let's count ourselves lucky and try the door so we can save our friends. They aren't some sort of side quest that we can ignore until we're ready to get to it!"

"Whoa!" Reuben pulled Brie back as she grabbed at the iron bar. "If there *is* a trap, I'd imagine it's there. Wish we had a rogue with a trap-finding skill. Or a secret door skill. But—"

It had been quiet, but suddenly, beyond the big door, came the rattle of chains. It was the typical spine-tingling poltergeist sound, and it was close. It also sounded rather angry at being kept waiting.

"Prisoners maybe?" Jennifer looked a little pale, the unknown sounds messing with her imagination. "You think people are locked up in here?"

The small group went quiet, trying not to insult her with their answers. Sighing, Nacho decided to explain for her benefit. "How much dungeon diving have you done?"

"Never did spend much time playing video games. Now,

during the last… almost a year now, huh? I mostly stayed back at camp, and, you know, brewed. Brewer here, and all that. The Patrons warned me it might be boring, but boring was kind of nice after all the fighting I had to do in the Evaluation World."

"Hurray for boredom," Nacho agreed calmly. "Now, to be clear, there are only monsters in there. If it looks like captive people, all they're trying to do is lure you into an ambush. Believe nothing and suspect everything. Absolute paranoia is the only way to stay alive in dungeons like this. All set?"

"Sure?" Jen seemed slightly confused still, but she decided to cover for it by eating the peanut butter ball that Brie had given her. She clearly had not been expecting a screen to pop up in front of her face, judging by the way her eyes went wide and flashed blue.

"Ah, right. Good point. I think we should *all* eat and raise our stats before we try the door. I have a feeling that Active Combat is in our near future."

"Care to sample my balls, love?" Reuben offered his food pouch full of peanut-buttery goodness to Brie, getting a punch in the arm for his phrasing. "*Ow*! What! Why?"

CHAPTER TWENTY

Nacho watched nervously as Jennifer choked down her first *real* sample of his cooking. For some reason, the fact that she had eaten a peanut butter ball first made it even worse for her when she tried to bite down on the fried millet circle. The cook could only wince as her expression went from excited, to confused, to grim and determined.

"I guess I now understand why you all called it the 'donut disaster'." She eyed the tube of strawberry life-hack yogurt suspiciously as she worked to force her molars through the dense bread-like substance. "Is *everything*-"

"No, it's *not* all that bad." Nacho flung out his hands in annoyance. "Just wait, I can explain. As it turns out, millet doesn't work like normal wheat, so the recipe was practically guaranteed to fail. Even so, ten percent off any damage you take is pretty good, right? Also, think about the Stat bonuses?"

"Yeah, yeah, yeah." Jennifer couldn't stop grimacing. "I get it. Stats good. Donuts bad. But… Nacho, *how* do you mess up a donut? Fried bread has been around in every civilization since they figured out how to fry things!"

"If I knew how to do it *right*, it obviously wouldn't have

come out like this." Nacho wasn't going to be using Mana or doing any cooking, so he upped his Fitness as usual and relaxed into the moment. He shook off the criticism; the results were undeniably positive, and that was all that mattered to him. In all other things, practice makes better. So long as he lived long enough to get there, he'd eventually become a gourmet chef.

Reuben stepped toward the door. "Let me go first; I can soak up the worst of the damage if it's a trap. Everyone else, get back. Can I borrow your Mr. Lacrosse Stick, babe?"

"Um… *can* you?" Brie handed it over apprehensively, and released a small sigh of relief as neither her husband nor her weapon exploded. "I guess you can? Huh. Maybe because we're married? Wait… does this mean that our fates are tied together?"

"I mean…? That's what marriage means, right? Odd way to put it, but I guess it's a neat trick that you can use magic that was meant for her, but I'm in no rush to join you in marital 'bliss', even if I could expand my list of weapons." Nacho pulled his Skillet of Turtling off his back, then moved to stand in front of Brie and Jennifer; decidedly *not* looking at the latter.

Reuben braced the lacrosse stick under the bar and *shoved*, leaping back as the door dissolved into a viscous fluid and exploded toward them as though someone had tossed an ice cube into a deep fryer. An unbelievable wave of heat washed over Nacho, and the scent in the air confirmed that the door had disintegrated into boiling oil. Specifically, rancid oil that stank of three days of non-stop fish frying.

The Healer had managed to leap back, but given the fact that the room now smelled like rank cheese, he'd been coated pretty heavily by the deadly trap. "Bleh! I guess… I'm a cheese curd now?"

Most of the expelled oil had splashed against Nacho's skillet shield, but the trap was designed to slosh over everything; it did its job far too well.

. . .

Damage mitigated: 17!

Look at your fancy Tier one-ness keeping you safe. That would have really *hurt you back at Tier zero. But* no~o, *you had to stay on yo~our side of the portal.*

Brie and Jennifer were completely unhurt, which Nacho took as a win. The door itself was now a slick puddle on the floor, and the oil swiftly cooled and began to congeal into a pungent yellow slime. A long hallway of doors was revealed, a classic dungeon if Nacho had ever seen one. Before anyone could react, one of the nearest doors in the corridor opened, and a hand grasped the doorframe.

Welcome to Active Combat! Nice job surviving our oil door trap! This is the big leagues; you're running an alien dungeon. Who knows what you might find? Actually… we do know, we just aren't telling!

Nacho didn't like the sound of that, but he couldn't spare any attention to parse the message. A shambling humanoid staggered out of the dungeon cell, slopping through the congealing oil on the floor.

The man-shaped thing was wearing rags, as expected from a dungeon denizen, but the clothing wasn't the odd thing. At first, the humanoid appeared to be covered in scabs, but the texture was too well-formed for that. Only after Nacho inspected the creature did the strange skin make sense.

Lightly Breaded Prisoner

Effective Tier/Level:?

HP:?

. . .

"There's a layer of, what, *breading* covering him? He looks like a person turned into a walking chicken tender." Jen gagged as her stomach growled. "Ew, *ew*. I knew I should have eaten more before we came down here."

Every inch of the strange monster had been covered in batter, then fried. At the end of the drumstick-shaped arms and legs dangled chains, explaining the clanking they'd heard before the door had opened.

Brie stormed forward, one hand held out to Reuben. "Toss me my stick. I'll take care of this thing."

He threw his wife Mr. Lacrosse Stick without hesitation, which was perfect, as Brie was already sprinting. She grabbed the hilt of her weapon and half-turned to maximize her impact, striking the ghoulish monster square in the chest with devastating effect. The Lightly Breaded Prisoner was torn in half upon contact. Breading went flying, revealing diseased skin and congealed-grease-filled organs.

As the top half of the humanoid went flying, the other cell doors creaked open and a dozen more of the prisoners came limping toward them. Reuben was ready, slamming his fists together as he charged in. "*Finally*! I've been going *crazy* waiting for a chance to get some combat in!"

Brie didn't slow down to let him catch up, "These things are going to be easy to take care of. They only have thirty points a pop. I'll get their attention, and you hit them from behind."

The Berserker Combat Dashed right through the middle of the crispy combatants. When they tried to lash her to death with their chains, she didn't even bother to block, trusting her Tier one mana to take care of the attacks. Two of the fried monsters hissed with pure fury as the chains bounced off her without a *hint* of damage. She reached the other end of the hallway, where another spiral staircase dropped down to the next level, just as Reuben bowled into them.

He almost casually slugged prisoners in passing, each punch popping their bodies like he was fighting particularly nasty water balloons. Reuben *howled* with laughter as he worked his way through them like a professional boxer fighting younglings. "Ha, they count as *food*! Not sure who would eat tall, dark, and breaded here, but-"

The Healer drove his fist through the crispy face of another prisoner with a delighted peal escaping his lips, "who cares? Is this what it's like to fight Tier zeros as a mid-Tier one?"

"Exactly correct, buddy. This *right here* is why it's supposed to be a terrible idea to fight up Tiers. Remember this feeling; I don't think our experiences up to this point really drove that point home well enough." Nacho maintained his position behind Reuben, staying relaxed but wary.

It was good that he did, as a second prisoner leapt out of the nearest door—one that had already released a monster—and tried to tackle him. His blades flashed out, the cleaver stopping the momentum entirely as the chef's knife opened up a trio of lacerations at almost the same instant. The body dropped to the ground, neatly sliced into four chunks.

Congratulations! You have killed a Lightly Breaded Prisoner!

Tier 0 Standard Creature = 0 Credits

Good job!

"Celestial *feces*! Why aren't *you* on the front line?" Jennifer gaped at him as Nacho casually strolled after the natural disaster that was Brie and Reuben fighting as one.

"Careful guys, they're getting slightly stronger with each kill, I think! Why am I not…? Oh, you know. Gotta let them get some experience with just… slaughtering enemies." The cook could only shrug at the Brewer's baffled frown. "What do you expect? At a certain level of strength, you're not hitting above your weight class all the time. If you don't keep your edge, you get dead real fast. Wanna kill a few?"

"I'm good, I think." Jennifer swallowed hard, her eyes clouded with confusion. She watched the battle for a minute, and her face firmed up and she went into full cheerleader mode. "Get 'em, guys. Show them no mercy! I bet they're sorry they crawled out of the oil this morning!"

In the end, it wasn't much of a fight. After a quick ten minutes of combat, the hallway was littered with monster parts and fried debris, and the only resources it had cost were a few Hunger Points from Brie dashing into them during her initial test. Unfortunately, just as they thought combat was ending, another prisoner lumbered *up* the stairs near the Berserker. She casually whipped her stick around with a single hand and splattered the monster across the wall without even looking. "Everyone ready to move on, or… Nacho, wanna process those things?"

He considered it for a moment, but ended up shaking his head. "Too close to human for comfort. Let's hope things get a little more beastly as we move on. What did she call it? Non-Euclidean monsters?"

"Processing them…?" Jennifer stood at the doorway of a cell, staring at the crispy, severed parts with a strange look on her face. "They count as *food.* That's just wrong. Also… this."

Nacho joined her, peeking curiously into the small cell. It seemed to be a complicated cooking area. A bubbling pit of oil lay on one side of the small room, which could have been mistaken for a hot tub, if it weren't for the smell. The other half of the room was dominated by a table covered in mashed apples and flour. Connecting the two areas was a dipping contraption that could lift the prisoners by their chains from the table and drop them into the boiling oil hot spring.

Jennifer looked puzzled. "Was this a torture area? Or were they re-animated and then fried?"

"It's best not to think about it all too much," Nacho admitted, his voice full of exhaustion. "The Patrons created this whole setup. Most of the time, the Juxtaposition just throws us a weird amalgamation of animals corrupted by Putrid Mana. But sometimes, they like to include a little bizzaro-bonkers action to mess with our heads. None of these were real; they were animated meat puppets controlled and created by the dungeon."

"I think I figured out the trick to this place." Brie was still at the entrance, killing each prisoner or two as they shuffled up from below. "The Patrons are going to keep us in Active Combat by poking us to death with these low-level monsters."

Reuben went to give his wife a long hug. "Thanks for sharing with us! I'd likely have gotten there soon, but I love when I get to skip steps in my mental processing."

Jennifer pointed at them with her spoon. "Do they do that a lot?"

"It's part love, part healing," Nacho explained with only minor discomfort. "He's very into the whole love and affirmation thing. He *really* gets into it. Great way to break the ice with him if you ever need a conversation starter. Everyone, let's get down to the next level while we can."

Brie surged forward, smiling and ready to go. Reuben was ready to back her up, and Jennifer hustled to get to her position in front of Nacho, inspecting the others critically. "You okay on Mana, Reuben?"

Brie barely paused to reply before she crushed two more breaded skulls.

Reuben bobbed his head cheerfully. "Yeah, I've only used about four Mana points. I'm good. If we run into something really bad, I can use Positive Vibes. That takes five percent, but we can manage."

"Let me help out?" Jennifer pulled out a red and yellow bottle, Store colors, and offered it to Reuben. "If you get low, drink some of that. It'll go down a bit more smoothly than Major Millet's donut recipe."

"Pretty sure if he had ever earned a rank, it would have been stripped after the last two debacles." Reuben chuckled as he took the bottle, looking at Nacho expectantly. The cook didn't react, resulting in a mild shrug and moving on. The staircase took them down to another long hallway of frying cells, organized in the same setup as the floor above, though each of these held more prisoners, with some still on the table, others being lifted out of the boiling grease as the doors opened. The freshly dipped prisoners slipped forward on slimy feet, breading still sizzling.

Still, the quantities didn't matter. No matter how many of the fried monsters there were, only three of the prisoners could attack Brie at a time without hampering each other significantly. She'd put down the first one, then bop the other two to force them back. From there, the first one to surge forward again was crushed with an overhead blow, and the momentum of the rebound was used to bash the other, spreading their internal organs across the walls and floor.

It was kind of messed up, but the dungeon was starting to smell… not *good*, but perhaps appetizing? Nacho found himself thinking fondly of french fries on more than one occasion. These crispy critters didn't deal much damage at first, but their attacks were growing slightly more dangerous the further the Dinner Party descended. The chains hitting the humans directly wasn't a big deal, yet. But when a blow *did* land, it applied a burning damage-over-time effect from the hot oil that splattered out. Strangely enough, that minor damage was able to bypass their protective mana, but only when enough had accumulated in one spot over a short enough time.

"It must be like environmental damage," Reuben hypothesized as he bounded forward to relieve Brie. "The damage is accounted for differently than a direct attack. Makes sense, but it's something to watch out for—*ow*! That's not the kind of fast food chain I'm into!"

"Which is why you don't get hit!" Brie grumpily fired back, unable to hide her concern for his safety. She kept her stick ready to bash anything that came near him, but she also made sure that she didn't get in his way enough to stifle him.

Jennifer joined combat for the first time, hurling her spoon into the forehead of one of the monsters. Apparently her Brewmeister ability had kicked in, and the spoon went *through* its body. "Why did I even do that? Now I'm going to need to scrub and sanitize the spoon before I can do any brewing with it."

Brie and Reuben both paused their fighting to stare pointedly at Nacho and his knives.

"Yeah, *yeah*! Sure, it makes sense when you *think* about it. I just didn't know it mattered," Nacho huffed as he was relegated to the back of the pack until the hallway was clear. Killing every single creature they encountered wasn't really worth the effort, given the stakes of this particular dungeon run. They'd eliminated nearly fifty of the things already, earning twenty credits each. Two entire floors of combat had only generated one thousand credits.

Since he wasn't taking kills unless they needed him to intervene, Nacho spent his time considering the newest addition to their team. If Jennifer decided that she was going to join them more permanently, they should also start investing in and leveling up her Skills and Tier. Nacho and his friends were already at level fifteen, and the party information indicated that she was still stuck at level eleven.

The cook slowed slightly and pulled his *Aria* out of his Storage Slot. He slapped it open, flicking rapidly through the pages. "What could I possibly cook using what I have on hand? Hmm… Colonel White Beard has a chicken tender salad I might be able to make. I'd need lettuce, tomatoes… and maybe a nice ranch dressing? Wait a second… I already decided I can't cook these things. Ugh. I think the grease in the air is making my thoughts think on their own or something."

He left his cookbook open and looked up, only to come face to face with another walking cafeteria reject. The prisoner, still crackling from boiling grease, whipped the surprised cook directly across the face with its chain.

Critical hit! Stealth attack!

Health Remaining: 90/156!

Wow! You pulled out a <u>book</u> mid-combat? You're <u>bored</u>?!! We can help!

Increasing difficulty!

"Son of a biscuit!" He cleaved the prisoner to death in under a single second, then hurried to catch up—after bending to scoop his cookbook up from where he had dropped it, stashing it safely back into a Storage Slot. Straightening, he noticed that wasn't the only monster near him, and a loud clanking from the stairwell revealed that increasing numbers were swarming down the stairs behind them. "Coming from behind! Beat your feet; let's get moving!"

He started trotting backward and utilizing his knife skills to protect their rear from the prisoners as Brie, Reuben, and Jennifer slashed their way along the corridor, only to find another spiral staircase at the end of the hallway. Reuben called out, "Seems like the jail cells are some kind of monster generator, yeah? We got the breaded dudes coming at us from all directions. That's a… pain."

"Ha!" Jennifer laughed as she recognized the French wordplay. The others only rolled their eyes, as he had already used that joke recently.

"I'm so happy we took on another person," Reuben enthused conversationally as another fried prisoner came running down the hallway, hobbling faster than any other before. Nacho dodged the whipping chain, then cut it into flat chunks like a country-fried steak as Brie took a moment to reload with a slurp of Life Hack.

Jennifer had retrieved her hurled spoon, but she was still trying ineffectually to shake the yuck off it. "I'm so sorry… that you have to keep eating his food, Brie."

"*Nice*." Nacho hustled them down the next stairs, knowing that if they weren't careful, they might get overwhelmed, no matter how weak the monsters were. "Try to do a sweet thing for people, and all they do is whine! That's it. Bug-based meals for everyone, for the next three days after I get back to my kitchen!"

CHAPTER TWENTY-ONE

They fought their way down several additional levels of the fry pit dungeon cells. On the third floor, they started encountering 'Extra Crispy Prisoners'. Those weren't lightly breaded, instead having layer upon layer of batter that provided them with decently thick armor.

The new batch of fried monsters had fifty Health. They were also exponentially faster than the earlier versions, and their chains were able to deal damage through the humans' mana barriers. Each ECP hit for a walloping *thirty* damage, even before their sizzling hot iron added on the damage-over-time effect. The Dinner Party was fortunately able to barge through by making sure to keep Brie fed, all so that she could use her Defensive Whirl to keep the attacks at bay while the rest of the party waded into battle.

"I thought that this was supposed to be some kind of math dungeon?" Reuben complained as he expended more Mana to heal his teammates, as well as to give them some Positive Vibes. With the extra thirty-eight percent bonus damage, they were still moving fast enough to keep from being overwhelmed. "Let me give you a heal, Nacho. Your face is freaking me out. I can't leave it like that, 'cause I can't look away."

"It is a math dungeon! Don't you see the enemies *multiplying*?" Luckily for all the living people in the area, one-hit kills were still the norm for Brie. "All the way until I *square root* them into the floor?"

"It… that… an effort was made, and that's good enough for me." Reuben chuckled cheerfully as a one-two punch turned his target into a slowly dissolving mess. Nacho and Jennifer were starting to have to ramp up the number of blows they landed to achieve the same effect as the heavy hitters. It was taking multiple strikes for them to take down an opponent due to the thick layer of extra crispy armor protecting the strangely beguiling meat underneath.

The Extra Crispies at the front were the main concern, but Nacho remained at the rear to keep the variations of Lightly Breaded Prisoners at bay. He was enjoying himself; there was something darkly satisfying about cleanly slaying his opponents. "Just gotta make sure I don't accidentally take a bite of them."

"You say something, Nacho?" Jen queried in confusion.

Nacho shook his head in sharp denial, feeling at his face. The raised welt had vanished, thanks to the Healer, but he swore there was still lingering pain. "Sure didn't."

Eventually the Dinner Party managed to fight their way through to the fourth level of the dungeon, finding that the interior had changed from the previous iterations. This hallway of cells ended in a colossal iron-reinforced door that sported the same iron bar construction as the door in the mosaic tile entrance room.

"I need a donut." Brie gingerly accepted the fried disaster from the smugly smiling cook, turning his frown upside-down when she loaded it into the net of her stick and launched it into the bar as though it were one of her explosive orbs. To his disappointment—as well as piquing his experimental side—the circle of food impacted hard enough to force the bar off its hooks. As they had expected, the door sloshed outward as a fountain of rancid canola. "I think I found a solution for your failed recipes, Nacho."

"Food as *weapons*? Are you kidding me?" Reuben was practically vibrating with excitement. "What can we do with this? Baguette swords? Lacrosse meat-ball projectiles? No! I got it! *Pound* cake!"

"Like… a cake golem that goes and pounds stuff for you?" Jennifer questioned with nearly as much excitement. "Can food be used like that?"

"I think so, I mean… look at those potstickers flying around and providing light?" Reuben stated consideringly, rubbing his chin twice as he continuously nodded. "I think he is *more* than just a cook, or he could be, at least. I think he is actually some kind of crafter class. I've been wondering why his class is so completely expensive, and the most rare of them all. If it's *really* just food and nothing else. Nacho, I think the class selection was a double red herring. The first decoy was making the class seem unappealing; the second was making your class look like a one-trick pony! We need to look for recipes that let you make weapons, items-"

The oil started to congeal on the stones, allowing them to cross the threshold as Reuben waxed eloquent about the possibilities of the Common Cook class. Stone stairs circled down to the fifth level of the dungeon, and for some reason, none of the monsters they had encountered thus far followed them down. Happily, instead of a series of fry rooms like previous floors, the stairwell deposited them into a cavernous chamber.

On the walls hung iron shackles, empty for now. Nacho noted them warily and hoped they wouldn't find themselves strapped to the stone. The center of the room was dominated by a slightly rusted iron cube with seams welded along its edges. Nacho recalled the welcome message, and how it had said they had to fight their way to the Skillz Cube. That iron was certainly cube shaped… it looked promising.

That was the *only* happy thing he could note. Three devices dominated the space—an iron maiden that looked suspiciously like Mrs. Butterworth, a smoking cauldron of boiling oil, and a rack made from long pieces of wooden planks that Nacho was fairly certain were used to smoke salmon. There was something strange about the rack, something that stood out to him: on it were several shelves full of herbs he didn't recognize.

"Hey, look, a *spice* rack!" Reuben cackled nervously. As though his words were a trigger, the sound of the fried prisoners parading down the stairs filled the air.

"Abyss, I knew it was too good to be true. They were just gathering their numbers." Brie loaded up another donut in Mr. Lacrosse Stick, making Nacho's face fall, though she kept a proper exploding orb on hand as well. "This is either a trap, or we're going to be facing some bad things."

"Some kind of pepper?" Jennifer worriedly offered as she pointed at the rack. "I think the spices just moved."

Just as she spoke, the 'furniture' wrenched itself up by its chains, metal legs unfolding from the bottom. From the top emerged long arms that gripped the chains and manacles, giving the metal lengths a practice **snap** and using them as flails.

Spicy Cuddle Rack

Effective Tier/Level:???

HP:?

"It's a Tier two monster!" Nacho warned them, his Sewer Skewers materializing in his hands. "Watch out; we don't know what kind of effect its aura will have on the area."

At that moment, the smiling iron maiden came to life, the kindly metal face opening and silently screaming; revealing rows of nails instead of teeth. Nacho sped forward to hunker down in front of his team as the iron maiden's body opened to showcase the fact that it, too, had access to spikes.

Those fired off like railguns from old Earth.

Nacho raised his shield and barely deflected the sharpened metal. One wasn't properly shifted and managed to catch him in the side as it **whizzed** past him.

Health Remaining: 134/156! 25 total taken; ten percent mitigated by donuts!

Look at that! I guess you <u>are</u> what you eat. You've got a hole in you, just like your donuts!

Reuben leapt in front of Brie and took the next spikes, which clattered to the ground like metallic rain, sending the pungent aroma of his cheesy protection into the air. He howled in pain as he looked down, "*Ahh*! Spike in my thigh. Ring of Cheese is *already* maxed out for damage absorption?"

Right off the bat, Nacho and Reuben were wounded, and their troubles didn't end there.

The biggest fried prisoner they had yet encountered crawled out of the cauldron and slopped onto the ground, spilling an oil slick that washed out to coat nearly a quarter of the floor. It had been so heavily egged, battered, and cooked that there was very little human about it any longer. The monster was so crisply armored that it could hardly walk, and the breading glowed an ominous neon orange. Two gargantuan chains hung from its arms, also encased in a bright orange crust.

Jennifer called out, "I got a lock on both! The iron maiden is a 'Mrs. Syrup Spiker', and our big, fried friend is a Flamin' Hot Cheetos UltraPrisoner! Both are Tier two."

"What is with the power scaling in this place? The other monsters were all Tier zero or early Tier one!" Reuben ineffectually complained as the tantalizing scent of Cheetos filled the room with a nostalgic aroma, which was rapidly overpowering Reuben's Ring of Cheese stench.

Nacho mentally went through their inventory in an instant. Two disaster donuts, two Life Hack yogurts, and a single pocket pancake. Reuben had cast three Healing Hugs and two Positive Vibes, so he was down forty percent of his Mana and thirty-five Thirst Points. He had extra water stored away in his Storage Slots, along with the mysterious bottle from Jennifer.

As for the cook, he had Mana and Thirst Points to spare. He'd been healed after taking the chain to the face, so his Hunger Points were also fine. A plan started to form, so he quickly yelled to the others, "Brie! We can't have that iron maiden throwing spikes at us. Take that one out first. I'm going to get the UltraPrisoner between us to soak up any more spikes until then. Jennifer, Reuben, keep the spice rack busy, and—if you can—try not to break all the spices. I might be able to use them."

"Fight the thing *without* breaking it?" Jennifer wondered sarcastically. "That sounds great; why not just feed ourselves to it at the same time?"

"If he thought that would defeat it, he would have already fed himself to it. Probably." Reuben waded into combat, fists leading the way. "Nacho leads by example. Great quality. Best not to ask too many questions. I'll take it head on;, you hit it from the back."

There was a real chance they wouldn't be able to 'hit' it at all, since it was a Tier two monster, and the two of them wouldn't get any damage bonuses against it. They also needed to account for the still-unknown Tier two bonus that it carried.

Nacho wouldn't have that problem with the UltraPrisoner. His knives allowed his damage to stick so long as he was only attacking one Tier higher, so he got to work. He flung his skillet shield onto his back and drew his cleaver and chef's knife, **clicking** the Sewer Skewers to his chest in a bandolier formation for easy access. He danced forward, glowing slightly from a fresh dose of Reuben's Positive Vibes, and whirled into chopping the bright orange UltraPrisoner.

Damage Dealt: 26/26/52! Nice!

Total Damage Dealt: 104/400!

With every attack, breading went flying as though an ornithologist had just found the favorite snack of ducks. The effect was concerning at first, until he realized that the HungerCry Knives prep effect was activating, giving him fifty percent more yield. Apparently, that included the crunchy, crackling Cheeto-enhanced batter of the prisoner. He accepted the oddity of it when he realized that the crumbs were soaking up the spilled oil wherever they landed.

Nacho's eyes watered as spicy dust filled the air, and he blinked away the tears. As though waiting for the disruption, the Flamin' Hot UltraPrisoner let out a muffled roar and lashed out with huge chains. Nacho ducked one, but took the other right across his shoulder.

Health Remaining: 94/156! 45 damage at once? Ow! Good thing you scarfed those donuts. Aren't you happy you front-loaded your misery?

Losing forty health in a single glancing blow *hurt.* Nacho danced back and positioned Mr. Flamin' Hot right where he wanted, blocking the door and any spikes that might be hurtling through the air between them. "Speaking of spikes…!"

Rolling forward, he slammed first one, then a second skewer through a foot, nailing it to the ground. Avoiding the Retaliatory attack, he dodged to the other limb and did the same. Behind the enormous boss monster, the smaller fried critters tried to push the Cheetos goliath out of the way, but the bright orange chicken tender was too big and bulky.

. . .

Damage Dealt: 25/27/30/33! Wow! 25 damage was the base damage, and it was increased by 10% per skewer correctly inserted into a single target! What a shafting legend!

Total damage dealt: 219/400!

Target is effectively rooted! Can you keep stacking those percentages?

Mr. Flamin' Hot struck back with one of his chains, the links crashing into Nacho's Helm of Boiling and sending him flying into a wall. He felt blood splash down the side of his face, and an instant headache formed as he tried to get his bearings.

Health Remaining: 44/156!

Coughing blood, nursing a concussion, and knowing another hit would likely kill him, Nacho went on the defensive. "Reuben! I need a heal!"

The cook knew that he was doing pretty well. In two rounds of fighting, he'd halved the monster's Health. He just needed a bit more time. Just then, the sound of glass breaking pulled his attention, an indication that many spices had been lost. Even if he hated the idea of losing any of them, it was nearly the last thing on his mind at the moment.

"We can't hit it," Jennifer yelled over the sound, "but Reuben and I are keeping it busy."

Along with the shattering sound came metallic banging that reminded Nacho of their time fighting the Rave-ins as Brie pounded rhythmically on the iron maiden. She must've been keeping it busy, because they hadn't needed to deal with any more of the miniature ballista bolts.

As he took a step forward, Nacho felt himself embraced by Reuben from a distance. It was a ghostly hug, mostly just the sensation of pressure, but the pain in Nacho's head dissipated as he felt his Health Points fill.

. . .

Health Remaining: 139/155!

That made Nacho feel much better about finishing the fight. He went back and focused on one of the UltraPrisoner's arms, hacking and slashing at the arm until the sheer weight of the meat tore the limb off entirely with a satisfying **squelch**. The length of chain clanked to the ground, mostly missing him as additional puff of Cheeto dust filled the air.

Total damage dealt: 318/400!

That last chain struck Nacho in his left arm, and he was back down to ninety-four Health. A small part of him railed against the idea of being the one to kill the Cheeto UltraPrisoner—they wouldn't get any credits—but he couldn't exactly pull Brie away from the iron maiden.

Two more Sewer Skewers slammed into the chest of the massive chicken strip.

Total damage dealt: 394/400! Do it! End this abomination! After that, we suggest sampling it. Yummo!

"Brie! Take down the UltraPrisoner with one strike! Four health left!" Nacho called out as he retreated from the chain that shattered the stones of the floor.

The Berserker backed away from the iron maiden. "Not a problem, Nacho! *Hup*!"

A glowing lacrosse ball blitzed through the Mr. Flamin' Hot's breading, then drove onward into its mass before detonating; unveiling the fried ECP's that had built up on the stairwell behind it. The Tier two monster fell to the side, already dead. As soon as it was truly slain, the other prisoners on the stairs shrank to half their size with a whining *hiss* as its aura effect on them ended, only to be blocked from entering as the corpse rolled at a sharp angle thanks to its skewered feet… crunching to a stop and fully blocking the doorway once more.

The Dinner Party was down to two monsters in the chamber.

"Look out! Spikes!" Brie twisted her stick, throwing a swirling vortex of energy right into the center mass of the Iron Maiden. Mrs. Syrup's spikes were caught in the whirl, and ten of them ended up falling onto the floor. Two flew off course, their wild trajectory driving them into the walls.

"I'm out of action," their Berserker called out, moving only half as fast as she had been moments before. "I have to eat!"

Jennifer was pounding on the spice rack with her spoon and paddle, leaving no damage. Reuben was in the front, fists up, trying to block the *cracking* chains, but it was obvious he hadn't been too successful with that strategy. He fell back, panting, "Heals for everyone, starting with myself!"

He glowed a buttery color, then Jennifer was given a long-distance Healing Hug as Nacho sheathed his chef's knife and pulled his skillet from his back. Knowing he was going to have to play defense for a minute, he rushed the iron maiden.

Mrs. Syrup lunged for him, trying to rip him apart with her terrifying metallic teeth. For being made of metal, she had surprising speed and flexibility, and he only managed to keep those teeth out of him with careful usage of his shield and a whole lotta dodging.

Brie took some distance, then sucked down two tubes of the Life Hack, one after another, for fifty of her Hunger Points. That was the last of the remaining food, beyond two donuts and the pocket pancake Nacho was carting around. The cook *clanged* his cleaver into the iron maiden, leaving behind a deep dent as he dove out of her way.

. . .

Total Damage Dealt: 94/400.

"How does she still have this much health?" Nacho called almost accusingly over to Brie.

"Her aura effect! It drains Health based on damage dealt, and she gets bonus Health for all the damage done when it's full. I've been *beating* on this thing just to take out the health you and Reuben gave it!" Mrs. Syrup opened her belly to reveal a fresh round of spikes prepped and ready to fly. "Also, she can re-grow her spikes super fast!"

Nacho didn't know how he was going to protect himself and everyone else, until another warm feeling swept over him. Healing Hugs. He was back up to full Health Points… until he took the spike attack at close range.

He protected his head and chest fairly easily with his shield, but his legs were tattered remnants after four spikes hit him one after another.

Health Remaining: 66/156! Wowzers! You lost over half your health in less than a second! Only 90 after mitigation, but you should run—oh wait, your legs are shredded *cheese!*

"So… many… cheese jokes." He struck the iron maiden twice more with his cleaver. Didn't have to be standing to get the job done. Mrs. Syrup had regained a bunch of health thanks to the successful attack, though it still looked like she'd been hit by a series of motorcycles—there were more dents and crushed metal than smooth patches by this point. Even as he watched, some of those dents popped back into place, and the metal reformed. "Brie! I'm dying here!"

"Coming as fast as I can!"

Nacho rolled away, painting a smear of bright red arterial blood across the floor behind him. He heard Reuben gulp down the last of his water, and an instant later, the big guy was granting another heal, boosting Nacho's precious Health Points by ninety-five and instantly repairing the damage to his legs.

The spikes that had been embedded in his limbs clattered to the floor, and he took stock of his personal situation. His wounds were mostly healed, but he was still covered in blood. "They say it's better to be covered in your *enemy's* blood than your own, but maybe this is the more hygienic option?"

Healed up near full, Nacho switched targets and charged the Spicy Cuddle Rack as Brie swung back into combat with the deadly metal monster. Only two shelves of spices hadn't been destroyed—one at the very top of the rack, and one at the very bottom.

The cook caught one chain on his shield and pushed it aside as he moved in. For some reason, the chain smelled faintly of rosemary. The other chain grazed his formerly holey legs, but Nacho fought through the pain and chopped his cleaver twice into the side of the spice rack.

Damage Dealt: 52/400.

*A *screech** of tortured metal arose, and a moment later, Brie dashed into combat and hit the rack with a full force *thwack* from the rear. A huge slab of the rack was smashed off, and Nacho smelled cayenne pepper, or something close to it, filling the air. Jennifer dropped back, keeping her spoon and paddle ready.

"Almost outta mana! Drinking the drink!" Reuben tipped back the bottle Jen had given him at the entrance, letting out a happy yell after the first sip. "Jennifer, this tastes exactly like cream soda! You're a genius!"

The spice rack didn't turn, but the shouting had distracted

Nacho; he paid dearly for that by taking both chains across his chest and belly, then being grabbed and slammed into the ground.

Health Remaining: 8/156! Hey! That should have killed you!

Nacho could barely feel his head swimming. Every part of him hurt, but distantly. He was riding the knife's edge of unconsciousness… when a happy Healing Hug from his best friend brought him back up to one hundred and three Health. He turned his head and vomited as the massive concussion was eradicated, then sprang to his feet to kill the beast once and for all.

Brie Combat Dashed into the Spicy Cuddle Rack, and Nacho followed, attacking with everything he had in him, chopping wood and crushing spice containers left and right. He must've hit this world's version of cinnamon and curry powder, because he suddenly felt like he was fighting an Indian food restaurant. With all that hullaballoo, they only managed to bring the killer Spice Rack's Health down to sixty-eight.

All Brie had to do was hit it one more time with her Combat Dash ability… but to manage that, she'd need food. Nacho dropped his chef's knife, produced his last pocket pancake, and frisbee-d it to Brie, who caught it and shoved it into her mouth with a grimace and a growl.

Jennifer charged into the gap with spoon and paddle both, slapping the chains away just before they could injure Nacho once more. The Spicy Cuddle Rack vented its rage by flinging her back across the floor with a sudden backswing.

Brie noisily gulped down the last bite of pancake, and with a sudden burst of speed, she slammed her lacrosse stick into the back of the spice rack, shattering a huge hole in the wooden body, which froze oddly in place before falling to the ground.

Long moments passed, and the System finally admitted that

Active Combat was over. Jennifer rejoined them with a few pitiful noises as she felt her distorted broken nose, which set itself with a wet *crunch* as their Health Regen kicked in. Nacho made sure everyone had survived… then started snatching up spice bottles, as many as he could carry, and tossing them into the Brewer's backpack.

Reuben barked out a laugh from a short distance away. "You are not going to *believe* what I'm seeing."

"Oh, that's *so* gross." Brie gulped in a breath, sounding like she was about to be sick all over the floor. Nacho realized he could hear the sounds of chewing, and his rampant curiosity induced him to turn in time to see the Lightly Breaded Prisoners, the extra crispy ones, chomping their way through the Flamin' Hot UltraPrisoner's body. The smaller ones had ripped off the breading covering their faces and were using yellow-stained teeth to try and eat their way into the room.

Worse yet, they were succeeding.

The problem was, there was only one way out of the room: through the hordes of fried monsters that clearly had filled up the stairwell.

Jennifer's laugh in the sudden silence sounded disturbing. "Looks like our victory doesn't taste so good. How are we going to get out of here?"

Nacho searched around the room and pointed to the center. "Let's hope that the big iron cube in the middle of the room has more than just 'skillz' in it."

CHAPTER TWENTY-TWO

Nacho hurried over to the iron cube, trying to glean as much information about it as possible. It wasn't flat on the ground; instead one tip was set into the floor, with the opposite corner pointing at the ceiling.

Dealing with the stress of the situation in his own way, Reuben waxed eloquent about drinks. "I would've loved that soda you made even if it had been fruit punch or grape or lime, but you really knocked it out of the park with the cream soda. If you can do root beer, or even sarsaparilla, I think you'll have me as a customer for life."

"How much did it help with your Mana?" the Brewer questioned, professional curiosity keeping her polite as the swarms of monsters continued to chew their way into the room. "Not that the taste doesn't matter, but the important part is combat effectiveness, as Nacho's donuts proved."

"Mana…? Right, yeah, it totally refueled me," Reuben answered with a dismissive wave of his hand. "My max Mana is only forty-one points, but your brew packs a walloping ninety-five. I'm swimming in the deep end of the Mana Pool. You don't happen to have another one?"

"If you're thirsty, *please* drink from your Yeti horn, not from a currently-rare Mana potion." Brie's interjections were curiously quiet during their conversation. Likely because she was busy braining the Fried Prisoners that were managing to eat through the blockade. Moments after having her attention called to the creatures, Jennifer joined Brie in bashing at the newfound credit farm.

Nacho called over his shoulder to his buddy. "Reuben, come and help me out? I'm losing all the fluid that I want to keep in my body, and regens cut out when Brie started killin'."

"Ah, yeah. Whoops." The big guy came up and wrapped the cook up in his arms. "There you go!"

Nacho's health shot up to full, and Reuben took his hugs to heal Brie, so everyone was running at maximum capacity. All of their Fitness Stats had dropped back to normal, and only two of the disaster donuts remained for emergency nourishment.

The cook needed to find some time to fulfill his duties and refill their larder, but if that time failed to manifest, they had to get out of combat long enough to at least *buy* some food for Brie. It wouldn't have Cooking Magic, but at least it would help her with her Hunger Points and keep her able to fight.

Reaching for the cube, the first thing he did was try to lift it. The chunk of iron didn't move one iota. Not unexpected, but annoying nonetheless. Nacho gave Reuben the penultimate donut. "Here. Upgrade your Fitness; I don't think we have to open the cube, but we probably lift it. You and Brie should have about equal stats, but she's busy."

Nacho forced himself to eat the final tragic pastry while Reuben was choking his down. Then, with their Fitnesses effectively doubled, they hefted the cube together and almost leveraged it out of the hole. Reuben grunted as they strained, "Nice… one… Nacho. This has to be the answer!"

"Brie! There's a way out!" Jennifer realized what they were doing, and the two women moved away from the door. With all of them working together, they were able to heave the Skillz

Cube to the side, and a metal ladder dropped down through a chiseled stone hole into the gloom below

"No upgrades?" Jennifer looked to the others for confirmation. "Huh. I thought the Skillz Cube would contain the Skills."

Nacho snapped his fingers, and his Firefly Potstickers went zooming down into the depths. The ladder extended down that hole, far beyond the maximum range of his light source. "There's no opening that iron cube. Let's see where the ladder leads."

Brie spun and beheaded a Lightly Breaded Prisoner that was sprinting at them. More and more were wrestling their way into the room now that no one was actively working to keep them out. "I'll hold these guys off for now! You three head down, and I'll be right above you. I don't think these crispy guys are able to climb down a ladder, but we need to plan as if they will just drop on top of us!"

"Let me try something. If it doesn't work, um… don't do it?" Nacho sheathed his knives and stuck his skillet on his back. He led the way down, thankful for his glowing food products that buzzed around him as he eased down into the blackness. Something about the descent made him deeply uncomfortable, and he had heard horror stories of ladders failing or disappearing altogether. To make matters worse, this ladder was extra-long, hundreds of feet at the minimum. But all that meant to him was that he should move *fast*. Keeping his lights below him, he gripped the edges of the ladder and *slid*.

Down, down… he picked up speed, trusting that his heat-resistant oven-mitt-gauntlets would keep his skin from being damaged by the friction.

The ground rushed into sight, and he *squeezed*. Almost too slowly, he came to a complete stop with only two rungs between him and a stone platform that was a good fifty feet wide and ten long. On his left was yet another ladder going down a different hole. He sent his potstickers down the next ladder until he couldn't see them flicker. "Abyss, how far down does this go?

Getting back to the surface is gonna *suck*. Anyway… guys! Secure area down here!"

He only needed to wait a short while for the others to join him. Even though they didn't perfectly replicate his strategy to reach the platform, they did slide as much as they could, then scoot out of the way as fast as possible so the others could land safely. There was enough room on the other side of the platform, next to the second ladder, to allow them to comfortably stand. Just as Brie landed and moved out of the way, a mindless body dropped at terminal velocity, only to turn into a smear on the platform as it exploded into batter, bones, and mostly-cooked white meat. Most of the mess went flying away against the cave walls, but Nacho still had to wipe some of the sloshing viscera off his face. One of the fried guys had jumped, and more were bound to follow. It seemed that while the Prisoners couldn't climb, they could fall.

Another one came soaring down to erupt like a rotten melon.

"We can't wait here. If those things can aim, they might just try to jump on us. I do *not* want to be killed by falling Fried Prisoners." Jennifer started toward the second ladder, her swaying backpack appearing large enough to block the entire hole. "If enough come down, they'll eventually have a soft landing. Let's hurry."

Nacho swung in ahead of her, followed by Reuben, then Brie. This ladder was disconcertingly long, and the group stared down its length with growing trepidation. Offering his friends a too-serious salute, Nacho stepped into open air and dropped like a stone, to a shocked gasp from the Brewer and a taunting call from Reuben, "Show off!"

The cook chuckled as he reached out and grasped the ladder, slowing his fall until his lights swooped below him once more. He relaxed his grip and increased his speed until he caught the first hint of light reflecting off the ground below. He slowed and stopped himself, hopping to the ground and peering around the gloomy cavern curiously. They were out of

Welcome Dungeon, that was clear enough. "This… *has* to be the CruxTerran UnderFun. Skyscrapers disappearing into the stone, check. Windows flickering with light. Could electricity work here? Did they even use electricity?"

There was enough illumination for Nacho to see a forest on the outskirts of the buried city. At the edge of downtown, a small park offered a tidy square of hot pink grass to break up the metric tons of concrete. That solitary square of gently rippling foliage brought to his attention the fact that concrete was a theme in the city, if not *the* theme. Every single one of the buildings were gray, square, and only interesting if you were a connoisseur of cement.

"Did an architect want to design the most boring buildings imaginable?" Reuben's comment was practically a bellow as he joined the others on the ground. "It's not just me that's happy that these were buried underground, right? I have to assume their whole civilization is pretty cheerful about it."

Bits of breading and Prisoners came raining down every so often when one of the crispy monsters hit the overhead ledge just right, but the team of four felt unconcerned about being overwhelmed by the mindless fried fiends any longer, to say the least. Nacho pondered his friend's question for a moment, then nodded sincerely. "Frankly, I couldn't agree with you more. This looks like the architecture of an entire world of people that are still constantly at war. These might be bunkers, if they're at all reinforced."

The minute Brie touched down onto the roof of the building, the happy System messages burst into view.

Congratulations! You beat the monsters and unplugged the Skillz Cube, and now you get your reward! Not only that, but you also found the entrance into the CruxTerran Continent 4, Urban Zone 3, UnderFun A! You are one step closer to the Starvation Dungeon, the lightning round where scores change by the moment!

Fun fact: some humans are already waiting at the entrance to the Star-

vation Dungeon. The minute Arriod QuaJohn finds his entrance, we'll start allowing people to risk it all in the final game between the two Juxtaposed worlds. Who will win? It's so exciting!

But first, the Skillz we promised.

Follow the torches to the rooms below. Each room is individually created for your comfort and entertainment.

Congratulations! You cleared your Welcome Dungeon! Each person gets three million tax-free credits to spend! These credits cannot be shared, given to a guild, or dropped on death. They are only for you, and by the way… Arriod earned this same payout over a month ago! You guys are real far behind.

Jennifer staggered, then laughed far too loudly for the near-silent area. "I'm *loving* hanging out with you guys. I've never gotten so many credits! I really enjoyed the 'credits hitting the account' sound, even if it did nearly knock me out."

A second later, Nacho heard the same **cha-ching** as three *million* credits flooded his account. Frankly, if it were a physical sound, his eardrums would have been blown out. He wanted to admire his account balance gleefully, but he knew that the Patrons might use his distraction as an excuse to pull their special Skills away. "Don't stop and shop; we need to get to the Skills first. Spend money *after* that! Hurry!"

"What the…? Why?" Jennifer stared in bewildered concern as everyone else instantly grew serious.

"Go, go!" the cook ordered as a torch bloomed to life near a door into the building. They took off running with Nacho leading the way, Jennifer trailing just a tiny bit behind. "It could be that the Patrons are throwing heaps of money at us because they think we won't survive. Especially since we can't combine or transfer them."

"Wow," Reuben sighed as he kept pace with Jennifer just to make sure she didn't feel *too* much slower than the others. "What a Debbie Downer. Here Jennifer was, all impressed with our luck and fortitude, and you're grabbing at the skills like a paranoid, starving dog."

"I'm siding with Nacho on this one. The last time we were in an UnderFun, we got *branded.* I have no interest in having a scarlet letter on my neck ever again." Brie corralled her husband, relentlessly pushing him toward the door framed by the torches. Nacho strolled inside and eased up a concrete staircase, plain metal railing included. They were moving slower now, wary of traps. He was carefully making his way forward, shield and cleaver at the ready.

The top level of the building was an underwhelming passageway of industrial beige carpet and taupe walls, the depressingly bland corporate version of 'comforting'. A total of four doors awaited them, two on either side of the hallway; next to each door, a single torch burned a bright, phosphorus green. Reuben noticed a name plate on the first one on the left. "Hey, so this is cool. It has my nickname on it: 'Reuby Tuesday.' Should I be honored or afraid?"

"*That's* your nickname?" Jennifer was the only one pulled into his tomfoolery. "I've never heard them call you that."

"Inner circle only, sorry to say." Reuben pointed across the hall. "How do you feel about 'Ranger Jenny'? Is that someone you know?"

That was, in fact, what was printed on the door in red and yellow letters, and Jennifer blushed a deep crimson, refusing to elaborate.

Brie was already standing by her door, marked with 'Bash 'em Bloody Berserker'. That label instantly changed the group's humorous mood over the plaque nicknames, as no one had ever said those words around Brie.

Jennifer glanced over to Nacho's door, as it was right next to hers. "Oh, this is rich. 'Chef Boy-Har-Hardy'. Funny. From what I've seen, it's also accurate."

Nacho felt the heat rise in his cheeks. He wasn't used to compliments from people that were *not* his oldest friends. Not for his attitude, and *certainly* not from his cooking. "Uh, right. Reuben likes cheeseburgers. I have… had, I guess… a desire for highly processed ravioli products served in a can. Before the Juxtaposition, obviously. I was *very* good at operating can openers. Think that impacts the names?"

"It's true. The fact that he's fine with eating his bland, tasteless, or even gross cooking? That's all because it was his entire diet before he came here. Nary a flavor packet in sight." Reuben raised a finger. "Nothing like what *you're* making, sweet Jennifer Ales. Please… for all of our sakes… teach him why taste matters."

Jennifer affected a mock faraway look in her eyes, playing along far too much for Nacho's liking. "Carbonation and taste is essential to a civilized society."

"Enough of this! Why did we even rush here if we were just gonna stand outside the doors and jabber?" Brie growled as she opened her door without any further preamble. She took a step forward, went pale, then took a wobbly step back. Before her foot even landed, her eyes glowed. "I'm getting a System message. Okay. This is fine."

Nacho hurried forward and glanced inside Brie's room. It was just bare concrete and drywall, like it was still under construction. Yet in the middle stood a life-sized Brie McCurdy statue. She was in her wedding gown, arms crossed, and looking as angry as she had been when Nacho had forced them to put their survival packs on just minutes before the Juxtaposition began.

"Get *moving*, people!" Brie blinked away the glow and walked briskly into her room. "I'm going to do a little window shopping, but let's not buy anything before we formulate a plan to create as much synergy as possible."

"Oh. I love that word. 'Synergy.' Almost as much as 'dynamic' or 'agile'." Reuben smiled with nostalgia as he reminisced over his college career, learning to market people and products.

Nacho rolled his eyes and opened his door. There he stood:

a year younger, wearing a tuxedo with a look of wonder on his face. Seeing a perfect sculpture of his own body was strange, especially since it was from such an eventful day.

A blink later, he couldn't see his statue, because the System was already chattering at him.

CHAPTER TWENTY-THREE

Welcome, Cookie, to the Skillz Box! Not to be confused with the Skillz Cube, which you had to move to get here. Fun fact: this room is also cube-shaped, and it contains a variety of Skillz, so it's kind of like a Skillz Cube as well. Anyway, would you like to go over what you can already do?

Yes / No

From the other room, he heard Brie yell, "I'm not reviewing my Skills. I know what I can already do. I'm just going to cut to the chase."

"Same!" Nacho yelled back. He chose the 'no' option, only for the system to directly ignore him. He heard a frustrated grunt from another room, and knew that he was not the only one dealing with this issue.

No, Cookie, really, let's review your Stat Sheet together. The statue wants to do it! It'll be fun. Don't do it for us; do it for the statue. Stat Sheet coming in hot!

Eli 'Nacho' Naches
Class: Junior League Chef
Level: 15
Experience Points: 159,700 to Level 16!
Current Credits: 3,027,700 (12,136,225 total Dinner Party pool. 9,000,000 unavailable for use!)

Build Type: Balanced, Delayed
Body:

- *Fitness: 25*
- *Metabolic Efficiency: 25*

Mind:

- *Mental Energy: 25*
- *Circuit: 25*

Satiation:

- *Hunger: 100*
- *Thirst: 100*

Health Points: 60
Bonus Physical Damage: 12.5%
Health Regen: 25% Health Regen/minute
Total Mana Pool: 47.5
Bonus Spell Damage: 12.5%
Mana Pool Regen: 25% Mana Regen/minute

Skill Slots (4/4)

- *Small Blades (Passive) Level 19: 38% bonus damage on all knife attacks.*

Tier 1 Enhancement: Your blades can slice from up to 6 inches away from their edge!

- *Ingredient Processing (Active) Level 19: Remove Putrid Mana from monsters up to Level 21.*

Tier 1 Enhancement: Process ingredients from 15 feet away!

- *Cooking Magic (Active) Level 19: Create food that enhances a single stat by 95% of maximum.*

Tier 1 Enhancement: Throw magic into a food item you cooked from 15 feet away!

- *Feasting Feats (Active) Level 19: Cook 19 times the food you're currently preparing!*

Tier 1 Enhancement: you can choose up to five locations where people can use you like a vending machine! At the low, low cost of 15% of the sale price, people no longer need to come bother you directly for their food. It'll just appear in front of them in the location you specify, within 500 feet of the food source.

Caution! As this is meant as a feast for many, and not for one, only a single portion of each meal created through the use of this Skill can be eaten by each person!

It was all a review for Nacho, but he was a little surprised at how many credits the four of them had. Then he remembered they'd each earned the twenty-five thousand credits from the Sweet Skillz, and then there was the obvious three million each for the Skillz Slammer. The real surprise was the extra thirty-three thousand that Brie and the gang must've collected while killing the various fried undead. There had to be some bonuses included, since a lot of those Prisoners had been low Tier. Even for a Tier two monster, like those they'd fought in the final chamber, the maximum number of credits for a kill had only been sixty. That was practically worthless at this stage.

The other stuff was familiar. He was level fifteen, and getting to level twenty—becoming a Tier two player—felt like a long way off.

He double checked the handy table that listed the cost of getting to Tier two:

Lvl : EXP required : Credits required
16 : 159,700 : 319,400
17 : 258,400 : 516,800
18 : 418,100 : 836,200
19 : 676,500 : 1,353,000
20 : 1,094,600 : 2,189,200

Combined Totals: 2,607,300 EXP : 5,214,600 Credits

"Maybe not as far off as I thought it was." Nacho muttered softly to the empty room.

"Yes! Let's skip all the work and go right for the juicy upgrade!" Reuben called out from his room. "We have enough credits to get ourselves close to Tier two! It's not as impossible as we initially thought!"

"Skills first!" Nacho called back warningly. "Let's spend the money in the smartest possible way, *please*."

Purchasing an additional Skill Slot would cost him five thousand credits, which seemed incredibly cheap, only due to the fact that leveling took millions of credits, and he suddenly had a comparable balance on hand. In reality, that was equivalent to earning the maximum payout for killing eighty-three Tier two monsters. "Mm. I feel like my perspective is getting skewed. I shouldn't be thinking of that as 'easy'."

A mirror appeared in the room, giving him a view of

himself dressed up in his Sunday Brunch Armor, skillet shield on his back, HungerCry Knives sheathed on his belt. It was rather shocking to observe the change between his baby-faced statue in a tuxedo, and the scarred guy with hollow eyes wearing a pot on his head and frying pans on his shoulders. "I've come a long way in eleven short months."

Nacho barely managed to shake off the cognitive dissonance.

Let's review some of your Skill options, some of which appeared in the Evaluation Mall. You have three of the finest options available already: Ingredient Processing, Cooking Magic, and Feasting Feats. Here are some of the great options you have previously unlocked for purchase:

GOURMET LURES: Allows you to lure monsters to your location. If you like being the target of lots of unwanted attention, or you like drawing monsters to yourself, choose this one!

BLADE SHARPENING: You probably don't need this one since your HungerCry knives have permanent sharpness. But Tier 2 will be coming any time now. This skill allows you to keep your blades sharp enough to cut through a tin can!

CYCLONE WHISK: Mix things really well and fast. It's not exciting. But the name is cool. NOTE: You cannot use this ability in Active Combat.

MOTHER'S LOVE: This is like Reuben's Healing Hug, only you can put it in your mouth. Yes, you can bake cookies that heal. Or, as we like to call them, Mouth Hugs.

. . .

SUMMON STAFF: Trash Golems. They'll smell and they certainly won't be sanitary, but they can help you chop onions.

MANY HANDS: Cross a hit-show chef with a spider, and that'll be you! This will allow you to grow multiple appendages for cooking-related activities! Number of appendages based on skill level. Caution: this skill permanently mutates your body.

COMBAT CONVENIENCE STORE: Buy convenience store items from the Store during Active Combat or Active Cooking.

There were a handful of other options, but Nacho had gone over all of these before. The Many Hands skill was pulling his consideration the hardest—even with the knowledge that it would actually alter his physiology—but the Mother's Love ability *would* make his food even more valuable. If he cooked his disaster donuts again, they would reduce damage, heal damage, and give the consumer a boost to a Stat of their choice.

But… the Patrons seemed to want to tempt him to buy from that preexisting list. There had to be more.

Nacho, those are some cool abilities, right? Would you like to purchase an additional Skill Slot and a Skill for the low, low price of 10,000 credits?

Yes / No

Nacho chose 'no' just as Reuben shouted from his stall. "I'm not buying from the existing list. I want to see what's special. Is that what we're doing? Do we think there's something special that we don't see?"

"Almost certainly!" Jennifer yelled back from her room, voice brimming with excitement. "I'm way ahead of you there!"

Luckily, the walls were thin, and there were no wandering monsters coming to check out why there was so much shouting. They'd be easy pickings, all four of them alone in their respective rooms, vision obscured by System messages. Nacho likewise chose not to take the offered deal, and the next message confirmed the wisdom of the decision.

I see you are playing hard to get. Would you like to see the special Skillz Box abilities we've opened up for you, since you successfully completed your Welcome Dungeon?

Ow! You don't need to hit that 'yes' button so hard every time.

Here are three extra Skills that we're offering just to yo~ou… until you buy them and make them publicly available! We hope you like them!

GMO MINIONS: Have you dreamed of commanding a deep-fried army? Did the Lightly Breaded and Extra Crispy Prisoners make you oddly hungry? Do you want to convert enemies into your unwilling allies? Well, this skill will give you the ability to fry up humans, CrossHumans, and monsters to use against your enemies! We'll provide the recipe, the vat, and the canola oil. You provide the questionable moral decisions. Note: Any minion that makes a kill will automatically transfer the credits for the kill to your account!

GASTRONOMIC TELEPATHY: Many people order their steak well done, then are upset when they receive a charcoal briquette. Others want theirs rare but complain about the blood. This ability will grant you magical insight regarding exactly what people want when it comes to their meat, as well as other items on the menu. Is the pasta too al dente for the snob who said he likes chewy noodles? Are people complaining about the consistency of their oatmeal? Are you tired of people requesting blended soups when they really want chunky? You'll know, every time, how to please your most picky customers. Note: automatically teaches you how to flavor the meal to your target's liking.

. . .

BABY BIRD(ING): As you know, during Active Combat, things can get dicey very quickly. Most of the time, you're too busy to dice onions. You've done well in providing your troops with Strawberry Life-Hack Yogurt, Pocket Pancakes, and Peanut Butter Balls. Still, we can't tell you how many times your party members have nearly choked to death while trying to eat in the middle of combat. Actually, there's a tally: 412 times. Now, with BABY BIRD(ING), you can satiate your people from across the room! You eat the food, and they get the Hunger Points! At Higher Tiers, you will be able to BABY BIRD Hunger Points at multiple people, then stand back and chow down while your friends kill the monsters! Yum, yum!

Nacho read through the skills, and he was impressed by two out of the three new abilities. Yet, a second later, the System sent a new message with a timer at the bottom, ticking down from thirty seconds.

Here comes the hard sell, Cookie!
Please make your choice now:
10,000 credits for the extra Skill Slot and normal Skill
20,000 credits for the extra Skill Slot and special Skill
Please make your decision in thirty seconds!

"We might have a problem!" Nacho shouted. "I found two skills I really like, and I only have thirty seconds to choose-"

"Same!" Reuben and Brie shouted nearly simultaneously. Jennifer was silent, but she was probably already in the middle of her own impossible debate.

"The special version costs fifteen *thousand* credits, twenty total for the slot-" the cook tried to explain, only for Brie to bark at him.

"We trust you to make smart choices, so *do it*!"

Nacho thought having his own army of crispy combatants would be incredibly powerful. He could march his army of sizzling Prisoners across the land and down into dungeons, taking in all the credits they gained from fighting while he stayed home and cooked away. It would open up a whole new revenue stream for him! The downside? There was bound to be a limit, and he'd have to use living beings. He felt a weariness take hold of him. The idea of having to drag trussed-up enemies through egg and breadcrumbs and then throw them in a big vat of boiling oil felt exhausting. "This one's out. Too… serial-killer for me."

Also, he was absolutely not going with the Gastronomic Telepathy option. With the fate of the world in the balance, he didn't really care if people liked his food or not. Most of the time, they were eating during combat, so taste wasn't that big of a deal. That made the final decision easy.

Nacho chose the extra Skill Slot, and for his fifth Skill—Baby Birding.

This particular Skill was a game changer. As long as he had food, his most powerful Body Players like Brie, Abby, and Taye could use their abilities all they wanted without needing to pause to eat.

A **buzzing** started in Nacho's stomach, growing until he had to close his eyes as he rose from the ground. Leveling up a Skill felt good and left him feeling powerful, but adding a skill was even better.

He smelled baking brownies.

He tasted almond Christmas cookies.

A glow rose from within his skin, sparkling like fireworks on the Fourth of July.

Then he mentally grounded himself, opening his eyes as Reuben yelled from the other room. "Hey! Everyone! Hey! Come quick!"

"What's wrong?" Nacho didn't wait for the answer. He burst out of his room, sprinting to Reuben, where he found the big guy glowing like a lantern as he earned his fourth Skill. Reuben settled back to the ground and pointed at his statue, which wore the piecemeal armor and the Leather Helm of Helming. He pointed at the terrible helmet. "Why didn't you tell me I looked so good? I mean, I was never one for hats, but this helmet? *Awesome.*"

Brie had joined Nacho in the doorway, and scowled her most ferocious expression at her husband. "Don't *do* that, Reuben. If you're going to joke, tell us. I'm already on edge from being down here. I thought you were under attack."

Nacho turned and peeked into Jennifer's room, noting that the Brewer's glow was just fading away. Her statue showed her in her stylish black leather armor, with her spoons and paddle ready for battle. He wondered what her statue had looked like when she first entered.

A System message popped up.

Fair warning! The gates to the Skillz Slammer Welcome Dungeon, on both sides, have opened. CruxTerrans are coming, though they'll have to fight their way through a fresh batch of monsters. We like to keep our Welcome Dungeons fully stocked. Have fun finding the entrance to the Starvation Dungeon!

"That's just great." Brie marched back to the staircase. "We definitely need to talk about our Skills, but I don't want to do it up here. Let's just go."

Jennifer frowned, clearly a little troubled. Reuben looked conflicted, but he took a few steps after his wife, his stride becoming stronger as he moved. "I want to be happy about my new ability because it's awesome. But she's just… so right, all the time. C'mon, guys."

Following Brie down a floor, into the bureaucratic frightmare of CruxTerra, Nacho smirked as he thought about how differently combat was going to be for the Berserker… all thanks to his new Skill.

CHAPTER TWENTY-FOUR

As they made their way down the stairs, Reuben explained that his new Skill had cost him seven thousand and five hundred credits, and Brie paid the same. Jennifer had paid twenty thousand credits for her new Skill, proving to Nacho that Satiation Players' Skills were considered more potent.

Exiting the stairwell, they found themselves in the entrance to a room that could have easily been the Internal Revenue Service's main lobby, or any standard DMV. Nacho carefully ran his eyes over the room, noticing that the lights clearly weren't powered by electricity. Instead, a glowing moss covered what would've been a typical office fluorescent light hanging over a cubicle.

Nacho was a little surprised that CruxTerra looked just... super boring. Every computer on every desk was a chunky plastic monstrosity. Each workstation seemed to be made of old tank metal. The equally metallic chairs were similar, though they had a scant half-inch of foam cushion that would offer bureaucratic butts a bit of padding.

The cook crept into the room and eased over to one of the cubicles. While the CruxTerrans had clearly used computers, they also had kept paper ledgers, calendars, and various manuals. A variety of old-fashioned ink stamps were visible on numerous deals, and it was clear that they were used a great deal. CruxTerran written language seemed to be perfect for stamps—big blocky letters with lots of straight lines. Each stamp included the symbol that PewJack had chosen for his empire: the cross-pupiled eye.

Nacho couldn't read any of the words at first. Once he attempted a System View, the System obligingly translated the text. The document he'd found was a Test Procedure Specification report, and he dropped it as soon as he figured out how useless it was. Then he shuffled some papers to find a calendar, all marked up by an L-three district manager named Pecu Leer. He'd had time set aside on his calendar for interrogations, coercions, and a section of his day for stamping important documents.

Reuben joined Nacho in the cubicle farm, rolling open a filing cabinet the color of boredom. "I think we can be confident that we can beat the CruxTerrans. All we have to do is intercept their TPS reports, and we'll halt their entire civilization."

"I found an actual TPS report," Nacho muttered with a gesture at the document that had landed on the floor.

"Why wouldn't you?" Brie stood at the door, refusing to join them in rooting through documents. "I'd like to get down to street level and rest. We'll probably have some fighting ahead of us, and we're running low on food. Nacho, that means it's on you to do some cooking."

Jennifer walked over to a desk where a barcode scanner was connected to one of the terminals. "From the logbook, it looks like they wrote down the names and corresponding ranks of dissidents, recorded the type of 'persuasion' they used on them, and whether they were killed or incarcerated. That was all noted, but it's also fairly apparent that there was a second database for tracking all the methods and information. Why do something once, if you can do it twice? Ugh. Bureaucracy."

"No joke. Let's get out of here while we still can." Reuben headed to the door with his wife, only to halt as the Brewer called to them.

"Hold on, there's more." Jennifer shook the scanner. "I looked at an old manual using the System View. I'm pretty sure that they scanned people's eyes to identify them. Could it be that they based their entire civilization based on UPC codes in their pupils?"

"Bar codes? Really? You think that's what the line is across their pupil?" Nacho stepped away from the reminder of what his life would have been if the Juxtaposition had not happened, both physically and mentally putting distance between himself and the cubicle. "I suppose that makes sense; they have to be something that was added on. Their history shows them without it, and we had already worked out that it was a recent addition."

"Why *wouldn't* a totalitarian world government force people to get tattoos on their eyes?" Reuben shook his head sadly as his wife gently but firmly pulled on his arm. Brie wasn't verbally hurrying them along, but Nacho could feel her anxious impatience. He understood why. The Kansas City Under Fun had contained multiple dungeons, very dangerous bosses, and a puzzle that had led to the death of Richard Crave and his strike team. The CruxTerran UnderFun likely also had hordes of deadly monsters for them to face.

At the same time, Brie was smart enough to know that the more they knew about the CruxTerrans the better. Only one world would win, and they needed to make sure that winner was Earth.

"Here's what I'm seeing." Jennifer easily summed up what they'd found. "Centralized world government. They have networked computers, but it seems like they also used paper backups. Judging by this ledger, it seems that all food production was for large groups only. Nothing was ever made or allowed to be customized just for one person."

"What does that even mean?" Nacho wondered out loud. "How would that even work?"

"Look." Jen's finger trailed down a list of expenses that were subdivided into dining facilities and the food allowed in each one. "Depending on the rank, the quality of food was better. However, even the A-one leadership like Arriod ate at a buffet for breakfast and dinner. Then, over here, you can see that the only food allowed for excursions are meals ready to eat, or MRE's."

"Scrambled eggs, toast, pancakes, sausage." Reuben had gotten interested in the conversation for some reason and ambled back over to read the ledger. "No waffles? Not even at the highest echelon of society? Scrambled eggs only? No sunny-side up, no additions to the basic protein? I *need* to have onions and a little bit of milk in my eggs. Makes them fluffy and delicious."

"They take longer to make, and more effort, than mass-production." Nacho stated with dawning realization. "It isn't about keeping them from having good food; it's all about efficiency and maximizing return. If you can pay a cook for an hour and get as much food as you could with three different cooks making specific meals over the course of three hours, why wouldn't you go with the faster, cheaper option?"

"I need to ask…" Reuben jokingly poked his friend in the side, "Did the CrossHumans teach you how to cook? Because you prepare food *exactly* like this. Bland, but does the job of filling Hunger Points."

"I think we're done here." Jennifer crumpled up a piece of paper and threw it at Reuben. "Come on, friend. Let's get outside, and then we can talk about Skills. I used some of the credits to buy myself a brand-new Skill Slot and a very nice new talent."

"We should level up as much as possible as well, once we are safe," Brie added, as though they were all having a perfectly normal conversation. "I know it's not going to be pleasant, but I need to improve my Fitness and Metabolic Efficiency before we go too deep. It'll also allow us to bump our Skills to a higher Tier… abyss, I'll need to upgrade my weapon."

The Berserker led the way down the stairwell and through the building. They passed other cubicle farms, as well as a floor that was nothing but filing cabinets to hold all the reports and memos. The building seemed strangely devoid of monsters and any other living thing. Nacho particularly noticed the odd absence of dungeon welcome messages from the System. Crossing the bottom floor took them past another scanning station, then a guard room where a wicked-looking assault rifle hung on the wall.

Reuben stared longingly at the nifty weapon. "I wish gunpowder worked. I'd love to use that machine gun on monsters."

Jennifer went over, quickly figured out the gun, and pointed it at the computer and pulled the trigger. It **clicked**. She tossed it on the ground, shrugging easily. No one had expected it to work in the first place. Reuben went and put an arm around Brie, who patted his hand distractedly and led him through the glass doors, which were reinforced inside with blue metal wire; probably the most colorful thing they'd seen in the place.

Outside, other gray, square skyscrapers rose into the rocky ceiling above. Every window glowed with mossy bioluminescence. There were no cars, but large ancient-looking buses, kind of like a cross between a San Francisco cable car and a Soviet-era commuter train, sat abandoned on nearly every block. More blacks, grays, and whites, though there was a bit of frill to the bus design. The street signs were mildly interesting. Nacho used the System View to read them: Third X Axis North. Second Y Axis West.

"We did it!" Jennifer pointed at the signs as the others flinched at her sudden shout. "I don't want to go on a *tangent*, but look at the street signs! Do you remember when we entered the Welcome Dungeon and thought that we were going to be fighting math? I think this is why! It was a clue! I'm reading the sine over there, or… maybe the cosine, but I think if we can figure this out, it'll lead us to the Starvation Dungeon!"

Reuben took a few steps back. "Wait just an abyssal minute, Brewer. I can do puns, but *actual* math has no place here."

"No, I think she has a point. We need to figure this out so that we aren't just aimlessly wandering for the next two days." Brie pointed with Mr. Lacrosse Stick. "Let's find that park we saw from the top of the building. Once we set up camp, we can level up, talk about our Skills, and try to calculate where we need to be."

The Dinner Party passed between the government buildings, paused at an intersection, then crossed a deserted street to get to the collection of dead alien trees growing out of the square rectangle of grass surrounded by a sea of cement. Nacho checked the rooftop of the building that they'd just been in, finding that the ladder leading up into the ceiling remained clear of CruxTerrans. If the armies up top had found the castle and noticed the gate open, they would likely still be fighting the fried prisoners.

"Man… anyone else ever get hit by a wave of 'what the abyss is happening'?" the cook grumped as they found a bench out in the open, away from the shadows thrown by the trees. Nacho frowned at the clear outlines of his footprints in all the grit and watched as the others nodded solemnly.

Brie leaned Mr. Lacrosse Stick against the bench. "I'm not going to mess around. We're going to use our credits to level, because getting to the edge of Tier two is important now that we have all these skills to play around with. Nacho, can you make sure to have recipes and food ready to go for us at that Tier? I have no interest in starving when we finally make that leap."

"I'm already on it," Nacho promised her easily. "It won't be an issue."

"Good. I'm that case, I'm going to go ahead and upgrade right now. Everyone please be prepared for issues while I'm indisposed. Okay, I'm feeling my blood starting to boil. Joint pain is next. This one is going to be bad, I can feel it." Brie shut her eyes and started sweating as her entire body began heating up and glowing. Reuben attempted to hold her hand, but she eased him away without looking at him. "Nothing you can do, and I really don't want to crush your hand as my muscles tense."

Seeing the Berserker in so much pain, Nacho wasn't exactly excited to be leveling up, but she was right about it being important. For just a single moment, he hoped that he would be able to handle the physiological changes at least as well as she was, if only to impress Jennifer. He paused and forcibly relaxed. He didn't *need* to impress the Brewer. They were becoming friends, they were adventuring together, but that was it. He just needed to stay alive, keep his people alive, and keep using his Skills until he had perfected them.

A light exhalation was followed by Nacho firming his resolve and whispering, "Practice makes better."

CHAPTER TWENTY-FIVE

"This is *awesome.*" Jennifer focused on her screen, then spent credits like a lake being evaporated with a single flash of light. She went from level eleven to level eighteen for the princely sum of two million, one hundred thirteen thousand, eight hundred credits. Since she wasn't crossing Tiers, it was a much faster process. She was clearly happy with the results, as she was smiling even while wiping sweat off her face. "Yes! Much more Mana. Much more Health. My Fitness is up to twenty-four. I could get used to this. No hours in the gym. No early morning runs. Just kill monsters, get credits, level up!"

"Wanna share your new Skill?" Nacho prodded once it seemed she was done bragging.

"I'll show you mine once you level." She shoved him playfully, but with her augmented strength, it wasn't gentle. Even so, she was barely able to move him. "Sheesh, I'm three levels above you now, and you *still* have higher Fitness? What kind of a monster are you?"

"Our kind of monster." Reuben grunted as his bicep muscles literally boiled and burst before reforming into a unified whole. "*Ugh.* Yeah… the kind of monster you want to be with, not against. This hurts so bad; why do I always want to jump as many levels as possible at a time?"

"It's not just you." Jennifer shrugged and sipped from a red and yellow bottle of something she'd brewed up. "I don't know. It kind of makes sense. Leveling up hurts, but it does feel… special?"

Reuben, by that point, was completely oblivious to the outside world. Nacho took the moment of silence to go through some numbers on his own. He was going to be a little short for all the things he wanted to upgrade, since he'd spent twenty thousand credits on his new Skill Slot and Skill. Because of the unplanned expense, he took what amount he was able to siphon from the party pool and went shopping.

Not allowing himself to think about what he was doing, the cook spent three million, twenty-five thousand, four hundred credits to purchase one million, five hundred twelve thousand, four hundred Experience Points. His character class leapt from level fifteen to level nineteen. He squeezed his eyes shut, waiting for the pain… only to recall that he only got stat point effects every five levels. Opening his eyes, he shrugged at the others. "Money spent, no change in attributes. Slightly anti-climactic, but that's okay."

The leveling was over, so the Stat Sheet fun could begin. Nacho realized that he hadn't leveled his new Baby Birding Skill, and it was still at zero percent. To upgrade their new Skills to level nineteen was a paltry three thousand eight hundred credits, which seemed so… cheap. By contrast, getting his Character Class to level twenty would cost two *million* more credits. "Times like these make me wonder how in the *world* Crave managed to reach Tier two back in our UnderFun."

"Killing, murdering, credit-siphoning, and extorting his hundreds of guild members," Reuben gently reminded his friend. "Remember how they were forced to do whatever he told them? The fifty percent tax rate? That's how."

"Ah. Right. That. Anyway… wanna see my new Skill?"

Nacho spent his money, then shared the information on the new ability.

- *Baby Bird(ing) (Active) Level 19: You eat food, and one person of your choice within 15 feet gets 38% of the Hunger Points from the consumed food. Note: Player performing the Baby Birding reclaims zero Hunger Points from the food eaten.*

Tier 1 Enhancement: up to four people of your choice within 30 feet get 38% of the Hunger Points you consume.

Mana Cost = 25%
Hydration Cost = 25%
Metabolic Cost = 0%

It was Brie's turn to laugh. "Oh, this is great. Nacho eats a full portion of his disaster donuts, and I get thirty-eight Hunger Points. Do you know what this means?"

"It means you don't necessarily have to eat during combat," Nacho replied with a cheerful grin. "It doesn't say anything about the buffs that the food offers, so you'll still want to eat whenever we know there's a fight coming. Once we figure out our Skills, I definitely need to do some cooking."

The Berserker hurled herself over to Nacho and gave him a huge hug, then remembered herself and stepped back. "Yes. This is good news."

Nacho wiped pollen off his pants. "I get to stand back and eat while you guys do all the fighting. I can help Brie, Abby, and Taye all at the same time, as long as they are within thirty feet. When we get to Tier two, we don't know what else we'll get. Tier two Skills come with an additional ability."

Reuben's eyes flashed and he leveled his own mysterious Skill before sharing. "The good news doesn't stop there. Just watch what I can do now."

Reuben Colby

Class: Merchant of Soothing
Level: 19
Experience Points: 2,189,200 to Level 20!
Current Credits: 0 (883,626 total Dinner Party pool)

Build Type: Balanced, Instant
Body:

- *Fitness: 25*
- *Metabolic efficiency: 24*

Mind:

- *Mental energy: 24*
- *Circuit: 24*

Satiation:

- *Hunger: 100*
- *Thirst: 100*

Total Health Points: 60
Bonus Physical Damage:12.50%
Health Regen: 24% Health Regen/minute
Total Mana Pool: 46
Bonus Spell Damage: 12.00%
Mana Pool Regen: 24% Mana Regen/minute

Skill Slots (4/4)

- *Healing Hugs (Active) Level 19: 95 Health Points Restored Upon Hugging.*

Tier 1 Enhancement: Hurl your hug 30 feet!

- *Positive Vibes (Active) Level 19: Weapon blessing: (applies to whole party, lasts 10 minutes) Adds 38% physical damage.*

Tier 1 Enhancement: Longer duration! Double the love!

- *Marketing (Active) Level 19: Able to lure creatures to a location. Impacts up to Level: 20.*

Tier 1 Enhancement: Maximizes the four principles of marketing (Product, Price, Place, and Promotion).

- *NEW! Every Slash Has a Silver Lining (Passive Ability) Level 19: Being a Healer means rushing into the fray and putting your own body on the line to help the damage sponges in your party. However, with this skill, every time you take a beating, your party gets healed!*

Tier 1 Enhancement: For every point of damage you take, four people of your choosing get 38% of the damage added to their Health Points!

No Mana, Hydration, or Metabolic Cost

"Nothing says I can't target myself, right? I'll heal a third of the damage I take! Lawyered." The big guy made a fist, showing off his Ring of Cheese. "I can absorb damage with this magic item, up to three times my Health Points. I finally have a Skill that is also going to make my pain count for something. It's automatic, baby. I get hit, and I get to choose who gets a portion of those points."

"I don't know about this." Brie shook her head, thinking through the Skill applications. "You already take a lot of risks, Reuben. I hate the idea that you'll run into a fight just so we get Health Points."

Reuben gathered his wife's hand gently in his. "Don't worry, I love you too much to die."

"Love you too." The Berserker finally nodded, unable to

come up with anything else to say. "It *is* pretty powerful. One-third of the damage you take, we get back in Health Points. Between this and Nacho's ability, I'll be constantly fed and healed in Active Combat. This is good, especially paired with my new Skill."

Brie McCurdy
Class: Battle Babe
Level: 19
Experience Points: 2,189,200 to Level 20!

Skill Slots (4/4)

- *Athletic Endurance (Passive) Level 19: 38% reduction to hunger loss penalties when using physical skills.*

Tier 1 Enhancement: Eating food considered 'Healthy' will offer an extra portion per three portions.

- *Combat Dash (Active) Level 19: 38% Damage on Dash Attacks, 10-meter dash.*

Tier 1 Enhancement: Throw your attack up to 15 feet!

- *Defensive Whirl (Active) Level 19: Spin toward your enemy, auto-blocking up to 10 strikes.*

Tier 1 Enhancement: Throw your Whirl up to 15 feet!

- *Melee Munchies (Passive Ability) Level 19: Oh, brave Body Player, going out there and murdering monsters works up quite an appetite. With this ability, the more damage you take, the less hungry you'll be. It's the combat diet! Get stabbed? Get food! Avoid getting stabbed? stay hungry! For every Health Point you lose in combat, you get 38% back in Hunger Points.*

Tier 1 Enhancement: All Hunger Points from Melee Munchies will taste like cherry pie.

Brie winced. "I probably would've chosen a Berserker Scream if I had known that Nacho had his… Baby Birding. *There's* a lovely image to have in my head. But that thirty second timer. Gah! I had to choose–I'm sorry, but I'm really tired of trying to eat while I fight."

"It's all a net positive." Nacho offered her a smile, though he was curious about the Berserker Scream. "Whatever we can do to keep your Hunger Points up is *excellent*. You're already doing a tremendous amount of damage, and that's only going to improve now that you can get fed twice."

"All I need to do is get whaled on." Brie looked like a weight had been lifted off of her shoulders. "Also, I have no idea how to say this politely, but… I'm relieved to finally be as strong as you, Nacho. I'm the front liner, and we both have a Fitness of twenty-five. I know, I know, you'll zoom ahead again at level twenty, but I hate it that our *cook* can outrun and outfight me."

"Aw, you don't need to worry about that, Brie. You are definitely the number one fighter in our hearts," Nacho informed her with a crooked smile, not bothering to point out the fact that he had *never* been a better fighter; he was just a better killer than she was.

He excelled at dodging and dealing massive damage, but as soon as he started to take hits, he became disoriented and lost a lot of his combat effectiveness. Still, explaining that in a way that kept her ego satiated was going to be too difficult. He understood her concerns: Nacho generally found himself in combat, whether he wanted to be there or not. Having knives that could cut through monsters a Tier higher than his level came with a certain amount of responsibility for keeping other people alive.

They collectively turned to Jennifer, who suddenly turned shy and began stammering. "W-well, with what you guys have,

I'm a little, um, *nervous* to show you my new ability. It's kind of a work in progress."

"Wait a sec on that." Nacho pulled up a few numbers, comparing them side-by-side with their total credit pool. "Let's get you to level nineteen no matter what. We've done dungeon runs before like this, and the more power we all have, the better."

Jennifer waved her hands in a stopping motion. "No, I couldn't ask that of you. We would need five hundred thousand credits to get me to level nineteen. I'm practically a stranger-"

"*Hey*!" From out of seemingly nowhere, she was interrupted by a familiar voice as Taye came pounding across the pavement toward them. "Guys! You're *here*! I can't believe you're here! I *knew* you'd come for us!"

The teen archer sprinted into the park and swept Nacho into a hug, before doing the same with Brie and Reuben. The Healer patted the jubilant teen on the back and whispered, "That's what she said."

Taye was stunned for a moment, though he quickly burst into laughter as Brie smacked Reuben on the chest and glared. "You are *ridiculous*! I'm so glad to see you guys."

"This is Jennifer, a Brewer," Nacho explained as the archer turned to take in the new member of the team. "She's cool. Can you tell us what's going on down here?"

Mood turning serious, Taye nodded a few times, as though he were trying to find the words he needed. "Nothing good, that's for sure."

CHAPTER TWENTY-SIX

Brie interrupted the Archer before he could go any further. "Is everyone in the Breakfast Club okay?"

"Yes, for now." Taye swallowed and gestured back the way he had come. "We jailbroke Kristie, then ran for the entrance to the Welcome Dungeon. We had to kill… a *lot* of CrossHumans. It was… we were killing actual *people*, and we earned a lot of credits for it. But I hated it. I hated it so much. They were going to *eat* us!"

At that, his strange expression turned into a fierce glare as he searched the group for any judgment in their eyes. All he found was a slight sick look on three of the four, while Nacho merely met his anguish with eyes full of understanding; perhaps also a slight hint of boredom. The cook nodded, reaching over to grip Taye's shoulder in a firm grasp. "These things happen. Don't beat yourself up about it. What happened then?"

"Abyss, you're *cold* about this stuff, dude," Reuben muttered, earning a droll look from Nacho as Taye calmed down enough to move on.

"I'm sure you saw the message about the gate up there being open? Don't worry about our side. We had to fight our way through this, like, super old medieval dungeon, and fought some weird stuff. Between Kristie and Hazel, we managed to cause a cave-in and made it so the caves that connect the dungeon to the UnderFun are impassable."

Nacho felt a wave of relief. Not only were all of his friends still alive, but they didn't need to worry about the CruxTerrans coming at them from multiple directions. "Spectacular job, my friend. Everything you did *had* to be done. How did you find us?"

Taye itched the side of his head with his bow as his body slowly deflated; the tension he had been holding while preparing to defend himself seeped away. "I was doing some scouting. When I heard voices, I got ready to fight more Cross-Humans. I was so surprised to see you guys that I nearly thought you were an illusion! It's really, *really* good that you're here. We didn't want to do the Starvation Dungeon without our big hitters. We were going to try anyway, but we all knew we'd fail. C'mon!"

"Starvation Dungeon?" Nacho felt icy dread start to build up inside him as the Archer guided them through the maze of streets. Out of all the crazy names of dungeons he'd encountered over the years, this one felt like it would be the worst. Starvation meant loss of Skills and a rapid death. "You found it, then? Apparently, it's the key to the entire Juxtaposition."

"I saw that." Taye nodded but didn't slow. "Just so you know, we can't go through the entrance until the CruxTerrans are in place. It seemed like a really bad idea to go in on our own, but the alternative was going to be fighting our way back up and then out past the army."

"Back up a tiny bit." Brie finally spoke up. "Did you say something about getting a ton of credits?"

Taye's face paled slightly, and his reply came out a little quieter. "Yeah. Killing the CruxTerrans was... profitable. I don't... I can't spend those credits. It feels disgusting to think about. Oh! We got three million credits each for completing the Welcome Dungeon! There was also something called a

Skillz Box, and some of us got the chance to buy new abilities."

Nacho thought the Patrons were being uncharacteristically generous. He didn't like it: if he were in a video game and had found a healing fountain and a bed in a room, he knew that the next fight was going to take everything he had. This situation was giving him the same vibe. "Was any of that taxed?"

"Only the killing," Taye sheepishly informed him, though Nacho waved off his worries as he opened his guild management sheet.

Chips Guild Stat Sheet

Total Guild Credits: 664,900 credits

Total Number of Members: 6,511

Guild Master: Eli 'Nacho' Naches

Alternate Guild Master: Daniel 'Mayor Dan' Chronour

Third Alternate: Reuben 'The Sultan of Sauerkraut' Colby

Nacho was pleased that they had enough to bring Jennifer up to level Nineteen. He just had to convince her it was the right thing to do. It sparked a lively debate, which only ended because *Taye* of all people insisted. "Look, ma'am. I don't know you, but you're with us on this quest. From what I understand, if we don't win this, humanity dies. Please don't fight us on this. I earned a lot of those credits, and I want you to have them."

Jennifer groaned but finally moved her pride out of the way. "Fine. I can't believe you guys are throwing credits around like this. I'm sure you're making your guild treasurer furious."

Reuben rumbled with laughter, "Old Bill is going to be angry about something anyway. He's not in charge of anything, but he gets all uppity about taxes."

"To be fair, we *do* keep treating all the tax money like our personal piggy bank," Brie pointed out.

Her husband only shrugged and showed off his lopsided

grin, "Let's just win this game, and then we can take a few months off and spend money solely on city development."

Nacho grabbed credits from the guild's coffers for the Brewer's upgrade. He also pulled forty thousand extra credits for himself and the team as a safety net. Jennifer upgraded as begrudgingly as the Guild Leader himself spent money, her internal pain turning to actual pain as her characteristic upgrading set her mind and body alight for a few long minutes. The Brewer's eyes finally flashed and she straightened up, panting heavily. "Okay, I'm upgraded, thanks to your generosity. I hope it was worth it. Here's what you bought."

Jennifer Ales
Class: Vat Attacker
Level: 19
Experience Points: 2,189,200 to Level 20!
Current Credits: 10,000

Skill Slots (5/5)

- *Boot Camp Brewmeister (Passive) Level 19: Can use any Satiation Player item as a weapon, adds 10 damage to base weapon damage. Bonus damage one point/per skill level (currently 19 HP of damage).*

Tier 1 Enhancement: Hurl any Satiation Player item at your enemies!

No Mana, Hydration, or Metabolic Cost

- *Purify (Active) Level 19: Remove Putrid Mana from all sources of water everywhere! Make one gallon of delicious and nutritious water per level (currently 19 gallons).*

Tier 1 Enhancement: Process water from 15 feet away!

Mana Cost = 5%

Hydration Cost = 5%
Metabolic Cost = 5%

- *Mana Pop (Active) Level 19: Create a soda in a Juxtaposition bottle that restores 38 Thirst Points and 95 Mana Points!*

Tier 1 Enhancement: Brew Soda from 15 feet away!

Mana Cost = 10%
Hydration Cost = 10%
Metabolic Cost = 10%

- *Stone Soup Mistress (Active) Level 19: Increase any food source by 38% by dropping a stone (and actual food) into your deliciously purified water. Note: Soups/Stews increase both Hunger Points and Thirst Points.*

Tier 1 Enhancement: Soup it up from 15 feet away!

Mana Cost = 5%
Hydration Cost = 5%
Metabolic Cost = 5%

- *Mighty Mixology (Active Ability) Level 19: The subtle art of Mixology is only practiced by the bravest of Mixologists, and it's a rare Brewer indeed who will risk their sanity and stomach to concoct a variety of potions, tonics, elixirs, and philters. To make the juices that Players crave, you must be un-philtered. This Skill allows the Brewer to create potions that can do all sorts of things. But like the best bartenders, you must have a recipe and at least three ingredients.*

Tier 1 Enhancement: Mix your potions from 15 feet away.

Mana Cost = 99%

Hydration Cost = 99%
Metabolic Cost = 99%

Nacho skipped the characteristic points of the Stat Sheet quickly, since it matched Reuben's and Brie's perfectly with the round-robin method of upgrading. When he got to her last Skill, he paused, unsure what he was reading at first. Jennifer saw his confusion mirrored in the faces of everyone reading her sheet. "I can purify water, and I can make some soup, and I can brew the soda that Reuben likes so much. However, I was always a little disappointed that, as a Brewer, I couldn't do more potions. Finally, I have a skill that allows me to do just that."

The cook tried to think of a few options for her Skill, but nothing was coming to mind. He was already lost in his own class, and he had no desire to figure hers out as well. "Do you have a cookbook? I keep my recipes in a central cookbook that I had to buy, and… it was pricey."

Jennifer snatched a slim leather volume out of thin air, far smaller than Nacho's *Coquinaria*. "I bought my Cocktail Menu, though I don't have much in it. My Mana Pop was the only real magical drink, and the rest are just non-magical beer, some ginger ale, and some pretty good root beer."

"Blood and *cheese*, baby!" That got Reuben's attention. "I would argue that root beer has a magic all of its own."

Jennifer grinned at him, the nervousness in her eyes fading. "Maybe. But with my Mighty Mixology skill, I think I can start making any number of powerful potions."

"I don't mean to interrupt, but I'm sure Abby and Kristie are wondering where I'm at," Taye broke in, trailing off as he became the center of attention. "We don't want to keep them waiting?"

"You're right," Nacho agreed easily as they started moving again, having paused to upgrade the new addition.

Contrary to what he had just asked of them, when they started moving past a few specific buildings that blocked their view, Taye warned them to slow down. "We made a few mistakes here in the UnderFun. We didn't know, though we should've. We came across these huge buffalo beasts called Resent-o-potamuses. They were fine until we killed one, but then the entire herd came after us. It's like they have some kind of telepathy—kill one, and the rest of the species goes hostile and hates you forever."

They came across several of the carcasses, huge, horned beasts that were in the process of melting into puddles of Putrid Mana on the street. Nacho was disappointed he hadn't been there; he could've processed the ingredients and grilled some of the meat to refill their empty food pouches. "Once we get to the rest of our people, I'll see what I can cook up. While I'm not a good cook *yet*, I'm getting better all the time."

"Practice makes better, right?" Jennifer gave him a little grin as a sly smile appeared on his face. "I guess I can only hope for the best. Your donuts didn't fill me with much confidence."

"A-hem." Nacho coughed into his fist and quickly changed subjects. "I would imagine you can buy potion recipes from the Store, right? Have you had a chance to look?"

"A little. But the recipes are devilishly expensive. There was *one* I found that might be good. It's called a 'Missile Margarita', and it doubles the damage of any ranged weapon. Meeting Taye, I think it might be good for the Archer, though I'm not sure it's legal for him to drink? Ha! Just joking… those laws went out the door with the electricity. It's single-use, though. You drink it, and then your next attack carries the bonus. There's another one like it called 'Root Beer Bash', for melee attacks. I'd love to get both, and then I can brew them up for the Body Players. But, I'll readily admit that the description of the Skill has me worried. It says it's dangerous to brew potions; do you know what that means, exactly?"

"I'll risk it!" Reuben dashed forward and caught up with them specifically to volunteer. "Root Beer Blast, Jennifer? Please. I am a connoisseur of the rootsy non-alcoholic beverages."

Brie, up front with Taye, agreed with the sigh of someone who had seen far too much. "He actually is."

"The danger likely comes from the actual creation of this stuff. I can't imagine that a Mana potion stored near a fire *wouldn't* explode, right?" Nacho shrugged and moved on easily. "If this were a game, I bet you'd be more like an Alchemist than a Brewer. That means you need to make sure you aren't poisoning people you don't mean to poison, like yourself."

"I guess that makes sense." She went silent as they stepped around the corner of a stocky building. On the other side of the tenements, the asphalt cut through a forest of more dead trees. They finally left the city behind and traveled through the trees until Taye brought them to an ugly concrete bridge spanning a mere trickle of a stream.

Across the bridge, the road ended in a wall of solid rock. Another Portal broke up its blank expanse, but unlike the one on the surface, this one didn't stink. In fact, it smelled like a Thanksgiving dinner: everything from the roasting turkey, to the smell of coffee, to the definite aroma of pumpkin pie baking. Or was it apple? It seemed to change—just when they thought they smelled the most delicious thing possible, a new fragrance made their taste buds go crazy. Sparks constantly erupted from the waving purple light spelling 'Starvation Dungeon' atop an archway.

Kristie, Abby, and a smattering of other people were camped out on the banks of the stream. They all leapt to their feet and came storming over to give the Dinner Party hugs.

"It's so good to see you, Bucko! I knew, I just *knew* that you'd come for us. Who's the new girl? A big backpack, spoons… you found yourself a lady cook? Good for you!" Abby had tears in her eyes when she pulled Nacho into a crushing embrace. She turned and pumped Jennifer's arm like she had found her new best friend. "Don't know who you are, lady cook, but we are glad to have you with us."

"Brewer, in fact." Jennifer smiled and extricated her hand from the iron grip. "You're a frontliner as well? Very cool. I've seen Brie in action. Can't wait to see what you can do. Once I get the credits, I might have a cocktail that will really help you bring the heat!"

Kristie stepped forward with a troubled expression as she focused on her Guild Leader. "Thanks for coming for us, Nacho. I'm sorry I got captured."

"*Not* your fault." Nacho tapped his fingernails against the sheaths of his knives as he tried to move past the teary welcome. "Can you fill me in on the situation?"

"Did I hear she's a Brewer?" Another Mind Player, Hazel, brightened. She was an older woman, middle-aged, who'd lost her husband in the Kansas City Downtown UnderFun. "That is great news! I got this new shield spell to keep people safe, but it costs a huge hunk of Mana."

Nacho smiled warmly, trying to remember that even though dealing with people could be a challenge, he liked his guild members. He *also* loved discussing Skills. With his knowledge of the Juxtaposition, he was particularly good at providing people with different paths for optimizing their abilities. His eyes never left Kristie, and she nodded to indicate that she would be ready to tell him what she needed when they were done catching up.

Taye then introduced five Body Players that had also been part of the group grabbed from the Bove's Lair. Taye referred to them as the Five Sword Guys, though one of them laughed at that. "Yeah, that's us."

Though Nacho waited patiently for an explanation of the joke, none was forthcoming. Those Five Sword Guys did look intimidating—all of them were fully kitted out with red metal armor, hand-and-a-half swords, and kite shields, and they clearly knew how to use them. All were well on their way to Tier two, though nowhere near the inflated levels the Brunch Force was bringing to bear.

After introductions, and just before he started getting annoyed by all the too-relaxed conversation, Nacho couldn't help but try to enter the Portal. He and his friends approached the sparking panel of light, their senses inundated by delicious scents the closer they came. The cook felt his stomach rumble and his mouth salivate as he slid a hand into the light, pushing through.

Hey, Player! We love that you are excited to run the Starvation Dungeon! You're so plucky! However, you can't start until CruxTerrans are on the other side, on your world, and in position. Arriod QuaJohn is probably your best bet. Just be patient, and before too long, you'll be running that dungeon down! May Your Future Be Delicious!

The cottony light around him hardened, squeezing him out of the Portal. He staggered back and stumbled right into Jennifer's arms. The Brewer caught him before he managed to right his balance. "Easy, buddy."

"My turn!" Reuben pushed into the Portal, only to come staggering back. "Yep. We're going to have to wait. It definitely feels like a race."

Nacho knew right where he was going with that line of thinking. "Well, if we're running a race, we need to carb load. Jennifer and I will start on the delicious snacks."

"I can't wait to mix it up," the Brewer laughed as everyone except Reuben rolled their eyes.

Reuben shook his head at the reactions commiseratingly. "No one appreciates us like they should."

CHAPTER TWENTY-SEVEN

Nacho helped Jennifer get her mobile brewery set up and started a fire, which was easy because the wood was dry and dead. He was deeply missing his own mobile kitchen, and he tossed a glare in Reuben's direction each time he thought about it. Being so far away from the government buildings and their bioluminescent light, the fires were necessary for both peace of mind and security, but unfortunately, all the flickering light might have been the reason the monsters came in full force.

Six huge Resent-o-potamuses came storming toward them, trying to exact revenge on the Breakfast Club. The bulky beasts were huge, without a doubt, and as ugly as a bad drawing of a water buffalo from a first-grade art class. Distended bellies swayed above furry, muscular legs, and a collection of mismatched horns jutted from their giant skulls. Unlike prototypical herbivores, these things had fangs and seemed ready to put them to use.

Too bad for them, they were only low-level Tier one creatures with around one hundred Health. With a damage threshold of only fifteen points, even Reuben could have enjoyed using them as punching bags until they collapsed and turned to goo.

Brie ran out front as Taye started sending ranged attacks that ripped through the creatures. Reuben stayed right next to his wife; in other words, he wasn't afraid in the slightest. He punched one monster right in its big, mutated snout as it tried to gore him with a crooked horn, sending its face crunching into the dry river bank. The horn managed to scrape him on the way down, and the stink of the Ring of Cheese wafted over the camp. In the same instant, Brie and Abby glowed a light green, demonstrating Reuben's new passive healing Skill.

Brie tossed Mr. Lacrosse Stick around like it was a three ounce twig, smashing the creatures like rotten tomatoes. Watching a mutant buffalo being tossed like pizza crust by her whirling attacks was actually rather entertaining. The minute the first one slumped to the ground, Nacho stepped forward and prepared to use his staple recipe of salted and peppered meat.

"This is just… wow. Wasn't long ago that the Bove was considered a Calamity-class monster, and now I'm practically sneering at creatures around the same level of power. Welp. I'm not needed in combat, so I'm gonna start cooking. Brie, that okay with you?" He had learned his lesson, and he knew better than to ignore combat if other people were feeling pressured. He got a thumbs-up from the Berserker between kills. From fifteen feet away, the cook flipped his knives and *slashed* downward, watching as the meat parted smoothly and cleanly, Putrid Mana flowing out of the severed chunk.

Brie called over to him as she casually swung her stick like a golf club, sending the impacted creature a few feet into the air, "I'm going to be hungry once we take care of these things. Not from this fight, but just getting here. These things are as easy as the Extra Crispy Prisoners."

Jennifer didn't bother to fight at all, and Nacho realized that they'd need to talk to her about where to focus her attention during combat situations. Currently, she was setting up vials, tubes, and a complicated chemistry set of brewery implements. In no time flat, she had a whole mad scientist's lair set up on a folding table. A massive metal cauldron swung above the fire, clearly one of her magic items.

"Steak *ni~ight*!" Nacho sang out happily. "Hope no one here is a vegetarian, or else I won't be able to help you!"

Taye lined up a shot with his Eagle Eye ability, sending out a piercing arrow that went straight through one Resent-o-potamus only to hit another. "Buy one, get one free!"

"You've been practicing," Nacho noted approvingly as he sized up the meat that was waiting for him. He thought he'd only be able to process the meat off one of the beasts, but then he realized that Mana wasn't a problem anymore. He was in Active Combat, but he bought a bottle of Jennifer's Mana soda from the smiling Brewer and tipped it back. He wasn't sure what he had been expecting, but it tasted like the very best of a typical highly processed, high fructose corn syrup infused, sugary drink.

Thirst: +25!
Mana: +95!

With a delighted grin, Nacho got back to processing the Putrid Mana out of the Resent-o-potamuses once all the beasts had been dispatched. Once the clean piles of meat were neatly stacked, he took off the Wok of Blocking, which was his chest plate, as well as the Skillet of Turtling, and filled both with… steak. He wasn't sure if the meat was considered steak, but that was what he was calling it. Carting the meat to his cooking area, he used his Pauldrons of Frying to season the steaks—applying a generous helping of salt and pepper.

When the first of the steaks hit medium rare, he decided to be a good leader and try it before anyone else had to suffer through his cooking. He chewed the first bite, looked at the meat, and shrugged. "*I* like it, so I hope everyone else does too. Huh… it only got to Common rank, so that's not a *great* sign."

With the Resent-o-potamus meat sizzling away, Nacho took his Helm of Boiling and washed it out thoroughly using Store soap, remembering his promises to his friends to attend to the cleanliness of his tools. He whistled to himself as he used it to whip up some pancake batter, pausing intermittently to flip the steaks.

Jennifer sauntered over and laughed as she watched how careful he was being with every step. "Is it *really* so strange for you to have to wash your gear before you use it to cook? You were just *sweating* into it. This seriously it looks like you're constipated with how hard you are staring at that helmet."

"I *wash* things," Nacho protested mildly as he swished batter around halfheartedly. "It's clean… ish."

"Nice." Jennifer took her cauldron to the stream for a quick scrub and lugged it back over to the fire. "Using tainted gear means you're including ingredients you don't mean to add. That means the quality can't increase. Here, I processed the Putrid Mana out of the water. We'll be able to drink this no problem, but do you wanna try it for cooking? Anything is better than Store bought, right?"

"That'd be perfect, and I bet you're right." Nacho cheerfully accepted the higher-quality ingredient and smoothly got back to work.

"It's kind of amazing how boosting our characteristics can have such a profound effect on the most simple things, like mixing batter for you, or drinks for me. Also, the first rule of cooking back on Earth was to make sure that your ingredients tasted correct. Try some of the water?" Jennifer handed him a Juxtaposition cup, and Nacho tossed it back with a smile of thanks.

The smile froze in place as he processed what he had just put in his mouth.

Jennifer's purified water tasted like life itself. It had a slight mineral aftertaste, but that only made it better. It was also ice cold, and as refreshing as a rainstorm on a hot day. "That is, by far, the very best water I've ever tasted."

He heard a tiny **cha-ching** sound and looked around in confusion. Pulling up his balance, he learned that the cup of water had cost him thirty-eight credits. He had never been charged for food or drink before, and he wasn't sure that he liked the experience. Nacho let it go after a moment, since that was his main way of earning credits as well: one of his level nineteen meals cost people one hundred and fourteen credits for three servings.

"That was a single serving of Tier one water? Worth it. My Thirst Points are full just off that." His Cooking Magic cost ten percent of his Thirst each time he added bonuses to his food, so having access to excellent water was a massive boon.

"Right, forgot to warn you about the cost." Jennifer squeezed her eyes shut in an embarrassed wince. "Sorry. But it's good, right?"

"It's a *perfect* cup of water. If all water tasted like this, I don't think I would ever drink anything else. Is the river that cold?"

"My fluids just come out cold, no matter what the temperature is." Jennifer bent placidly over her equipment as Nacho did a double take at her phrasing. "When I'm using my skills, I go into Active Brewing, and it's like Active Combat. No Store. No Regen. Does that happen to you?"

"Active Cooking never gets boring. I highly appreciate any Mana you can give me so that I can keep everything moving the way it should." Nacho piled all of the meat into his skillet and poured water into his Wok of Blocking. "That's why your Mana soda is such a miracle. I have always been stuck at only nineteen safe rounds of ingredient processing. Now, the only limit I have is how fast it takes the meat to dissolve into puddles of Putrid Mana, and how many Mana sodas I can purchase."

"Speaking of, I really need to find some new recipes so that I can aid other people in being useful as well," the Brewer mumbled as she continued fussing with her mobile brewing stand.

"Jennifer, please let the Chips Guild finance your first potions? If we can double a single attack, that might mean the difference between life and death."

After thinking for an uncomfortably long moment, clearly wavering back and forth, the Brewer acquiesced. "Fine. I won't argue. Especially if what I've heard of this Arriod guy is true. Nibbles and Henry said he has this sword that can do all sorts of things. Nibbles laughed, claiming that if he couldn't kill Arriod, he'd join him. Henry wasn't so sure. I mean, Henry did have some lingering sense of Earthling pride, or maybe morals, remaining. Not Nibbles."

Nacho poured his pancake batter into one Pauldron of Frying while the steaks sizzled in the other, adding Cooking Magic to both. The rest of the Chips Guild was staring at him hungrily now that the threat had passed and the scent of a hot meal had begun filling the camp.

"I have to warn you, they aren't cheap. Epic Tier one Class Items. They're eight hundred credits per potion." Jennifer shook her head. "It's a lot. I found them in their own special category in a Mixology Menu I can access through the Store. If it's too much, I'll understand."

"Not too much." Nacho tried to smother his inner skinflint as he accessed the Chips Guild and transferred the credits to the Brewer. Her eyes flashed as she made the purchases without hesitation, and two pages appeared in her hands. Those were directly integrated into her Cocktail Menu, which was enviably small; Nacho's cookbook was the size of a small encyclopedia.

Humming a familiar shanty with a slight smile on her lips, Jennifer immediately got busy working on her new Missile Margarita. She measured a surprising variety of ingredients with an expert hand and poured them into a tall shaker. By now, most of the other people had gathered around them, wondering when dinner would be ready. The Breakfast Club made nine people, if they were including the Five Sword Guys. The Dinner Party had four, capping the group at thirteen people total.

Almost everyone cheered when Nacho started passing out plates.

Reuben was the first person in line—he'd been at the front of many a food line, and he knew how to throw elbows to get the room he needed. "You know, Nacho, to make things easier, we should form a single party, like when we ran the UnderFun. Remember? We were the Brunch Force. We should do something different for the Starvation Dungeon. How about the High Tea Terrors?"

"No. What?" Nacho cocked his head. "Is that a British thing? Why?"

Jennifer took a break from brewing and tossed in her idea. "What about the 'Snack Attack'?"

Brie unexpectedly laughed, and that settled it in the minds of Reuben and Nacho. People tucked into the steak and pancakes with gusto, and Nacho was inordinately pleased with how well the pancakes had turned out. Crisp on the outside, warm and fluffy on the inside, just like they should be. With a little Epic syrup, they went down smoothly and were considered a Rare food, allowing for an additional stack of Nacho's Cooking Magic if eaten at the correct time.

The cook didn't stop working until everyone had stashed four servings of both the Resent-o-potamus steaks and the pancakes in their storage. It was easy to make his food in large quantities because of his Feasting Feats ability, and he continued to abuse that as much as possible. Nacho wanted everyone loaded down with tons of food before they entered the Starvation Dungeon.

Thanks to Nacho's Cooking Magic, they all boosted their Stats with the evening meal. They might not need the buffs for a while, but they needed the sustenance, and it never hurt to have a stronger workforce. Jennifer ate intermittently while she puttered around. The Brewer did admit that the steak was pleasant to eat, and not gamey at all. The salt was enough to bring out its meaty flavors, even if Nacho had only been able to raise it into a Common item. "My water is good, Nacho, but your pancakes are *great.*"

Nacho couldn't help but be thrilled, though he kept his excitement to himself and merely nodded at her gratefully. "Lots of practice."

Two things happened suddenly, and very unexpectedly.

Jennifer's vials exploded one after another, and she was thrown back a few feet, clearly wounded. Not a second later, the Portal's purple waver shifted into a shining white beacon that sent a shockwave of radiance across the dark forest.

The Patrons flooded their minds with a message.

The Entrance to the Starvation Dungeon is open! Come one, come all, to your doom or boon! Enjoy your last minutes, while making your future delicious!

Jennifer hit the ground and rolled once, then laid face down… far too still.

CHAPTER TWENTY-EIGHT

Nacho ignored the blinding light of the portal as he scrambled over to Jennifer. He slid to her side and was relieved to find that she was still breathing. He helped her sit up, noticing a vial of lime-green liquid still clutched in her hand. It must have been the Missile Margarita she'd been attempting to create. "What happened?"

Jennifer's eyes fluttered open, and she looked around deliriously. "I'm so hungry, thirsty, and everything in between."

"How about some big, angry hippo steaks?" Nacho eased her back to lean against a nearby tree trunk, his eyes scanning hers to see if she had a concussion.

"That's a deal," Jennifer groaned as she wiped away a stream of blood that was flowing from her left nostril. "I'll wash them down with a bottle of my Mana Pop. I made a six pack in preparation for the Starvation Dungeon."

Everyone had gathered around them, except Reuben, who knew what needed to be done. "Pack your *things*! We don't know how long that Portal is going to be open, so we need to *move*, people!"

. . .

As the leader of the Snack Attack, you should approach the Portal. We're going to have ourselves a little chat about how the Starvation Dungeon works.

Nacho stood, realizing that he was only clad in his jeans and t-shirt, since he had been using his gear to cook. "Reuben is right. I just got a message from the Patrons. I've been called to a conference."

He grabbed his knives and sheathed them on his belt, then asked Reuben to take care of cleaning his armor. He did grab his skillet shield, the metal still hot and greasy, only for Reuben and Brie to stop him.

"Are you sure you need to go over there alone?" Brie questioned him with a glare that practically *dared* him to say 'yes'. "I think that's a bad idea."

"Yeah, what she said." Reuben was a bit pale. "Uh, be careful."

"I will." Nacho hurried over the bridge as Brie tossed her hands up in a 'why do I bother' motion. He approached the blinding radiance with his skillet raised to block some of the light, rapidly analyzing his status. He was at full Health, Hunger, and Thirst. He had magically enhanced food in his Slots—four full portions of Resent-o-potamus steak and pocket pancakes.

Unwilling to stall and risk ticking off the Patrons, he walked into the light and arrived… in a very cozy sitting room. Polished wood floor, gleaming panels, and velvet wallpaper ensconced the space with an air of understated elegance. Comfy couches were bookended by ornate end tables. On a central coffee table sat a colossal leather bound tome, its title glittering in ornate golden script, *The History of the Seven Hundred and Seventy-Seven Thousand Juxtapositions. Volume 1.*

Nacho would've gone right for the book, except that he found himself not ten feet from Arriod, who stood with his katana drawn. His sunglasses had been pushed rest atop his head. The CruxTerran had dressed to blend in surprisingly well with regular humans from Kansas City. Cowboy boots, jeans, skin-tight black T-shirt beneath a fur-lined vest. Where was his armor?

Next to Arriod stood a guy in a toga and strange boots. A toothpick jutted belligerently from the corner of his mouth. On his head was a helmet with an eye on the front—an eye with cross-shaped pupils. The helmet was more likely to fit in on a football field than a field of battle, but Nacho had no doubt that it was an item he would kill to attain for himself: this was obviously a Patron.

The next moment, Kronos walked out of the wall, adjusted his New York Yankees cap, and brushed some lint off his own toga. Kronos nodded at the other Patron. "Hey, Johnny, so glad we all decided that we could have this little meeting in person. I mean, we all know about the rules that get… bent."

'Johnny' nodded and chewed on his toothpick. "Can't break 'em. You know the Cultivator would know. As it is, he's busy lookin' elsewhere."

The Cultivator? Who was that? Nacho hadn't heard the name before, but it seemed the Patrons answered to someone else after all.

Johnny swept off his helmet to reveal a sweaty scalp, motioning to Arriod. "This is my guy, Arriod. That's Nacho?"

"That's right," Kronos replied as the tension ramped up in the room. He evidently *hated* Arriod's silent intensity, unnerved by those very strange eyes, despite his lofty status as a Patron.

Right then, Nacho had to remind himself that at one point, he'd been the Shadow Killer. He accessed and equipped some of that old bravado, anxious to move things along and get back to his team. "Hey, guys, great to see everyone. Firstly, if Arriod and I are going to fight, I'd like to get my armor on before his blade can get anywhere near my *flesh*."

Arriod was silent, though he took a fresh grip on his sword when Nacho stressed the word 'flesh'. Nacho laughed darkly and crossed his arms. "Yeah, Arriod, I know about your sword. How it deals crazy bonus damage to flesh, how you-"

"Enough table talk!" Johnny burst out, and Nacho found that his jaw had been forcibly clenched shut. "You two are going to go head-to-head in the game now. This is what *everything* we've done so far has been building up to. We're starting a bit early, but a certain Patron's boon messed up our build order-"

"You better watch your mouth." Kronos pushed his cap back, flipping the visor to face behind his head. "I played by the rules; I just went all-in on my boy Nacho. Sure, some Patrons aren't happy, but at least you can't say this round is boring. Action, romance, danger, intrigue, and high-stakes betting? Multiple worlds are on the line! The entire universe will one day hang in the balance, and it might all come down to which world wins… right here, right now."

"Zero-sum game," Nacho concurred as soon as the restriction was lifted. "Too bad it has to end this way. If things were different, I could've introduced you to personalized meals, Arriod."

"I'm sure it would've been a new experience." The Crux-Terran finally replied in a deep voice, very confident, not a hint of sarcasm to be found. "But as the Store has proven, it is highly inefficient."

"Let's cut the chit-chat," Johnny grumbled, clearly sullen that he was no longer the star of the show. "The rules are simple: You each will gather your parties and enter into the Pantry. Fight or don't, but the name of the game is to reach the Dining Room Table *without eating*. First one to reach the Feast Portal wins. If you eat, you lose."

"Uuugh. Your lack of details makes everything so boring!" Kronos sighed and shook his head. "Come on, Johnny. Let's *not* cut to the chase. Let's build this up more. I wanted you to brag about the Starvation Dungeon a bit."

"You *want* me to brag? Fine." Johnny plopped down in a chair and settled his helmet on his knee, Waving his toothpick around like a conductor's baton. "The Starvation Dungeon isn't on *any* world. It's an in-between place, a little pocket dimension we created between your two Starter Worlds. We really pulled out all the stops for this one. You'll see. It's not like any dungeon that you two have run before. Once you step inside, you're trapped. The only way out is through the Portal of Feasting. Even better, this is the *actual* bridge between your worlds. But the portals that let you cross over to each other's planets don't let you into the... fun part."

"Let me tell our lucky contestants what the spoils are!" Kronos selected a chair across from Johnny, their overwhelming power causing the air between them to spark and **snap** as if they were starting a fight too fast for the human eye to see. "The winning party takes control of the Portal you two have been zipping through. That's the one in Nacho's AKC, and Arriod's zone four, section three, subsection two-point-three-two."

"As soon as there is a winner..." Johnny took over, as though the explanation was all perfectly rehearsed, "all other Portals between the worlds close forever. The winner's world gains various bonuses. Additional credits per kill, some boons, and other fabulous prizes. What does the loser's world get? A Putrid Mana dump. That translates into a near-immediate doubling of the Tiers of all monsters. Tier twos become Tier fours. Tier fours become Tier eights. Bam. Instant death planet. Now, we've had losing worlds take years to finally fail, but once every sapient planetary native on a world is gone... the next round begins."

When it became clear that no other details were freely forthcoming, Nacho immediately started asking questions. "With the one Portal, the winner controls it completely, right?"

"Along with a brand-new castle to keep out unwanted visitors." Kronos nodded approvingly at his insightful guess. "The best, most Epic fortress that credits can't buy. It will make Armor Mountain look like a couch-cushion fort."

"Why do your people have so many competing convenience stores? They all sell nearly the same items." Arriod's questions took an abrupt turn into bizzaro land. "Why waste your time and resources on so many practically identical brands?"

"Free market capitalism," Nacho replied without pausing to wonder why he wanted to know. "It drives innovation and intellectual advances faster than any other system."

"That's a shame," Arriod whispered softly.

"Rules." Johnny cut in once more. "No eating in the Starvation Dungeon. If you eat anything, even an eighth of a portion, you forfeit *everything*. Drinking is okay, which will be good news for your Mind Players. They'll get their Thirst Points, but there's no way to regain Hunger Points in the dungeon. Your Body Players are going to have to use their Skills wisely-"

"Arriod and Brie recently acquired some Skills that allow them to regain some of their Hunger Points," Kronos interrupted the other Patron. "Those won't work until you're within three hundred feet of the Feast Portal, or fifteen elephants trunk-to-tail. Football is kinda like Quack Ball, for the CruxTerrans. We figure if you all get that far, then you should be allowed to use every Skill you have at your disposal for the battle royale."

Nacho had a bad feeling about all of this. Brie would be furious that she wouldn't be able to use her Melee Munchies. What kind of ability did Arriod have? The CruxTerran tilted his head, those strange eyes fixed on Nacho. "You seem troubled, round-pupil. You seem weak."

"Beating you will only double the pleasure," Nacho lazily retorted. "Also, your *face* is weaker than tea that's been left to steep for only thirty seconds."

"What does that *even-*" The CruxTerran's eyes narrowed as he tried to piece together the non sequitur.

"Nope, it's *odd*." Nacho kept up the inane drivel, trying to test whether he would be able to use his strange insults to gain an edge, "That's how you know it's number one. What's a 'peef'?"

"Large herd animal we use as a meat source," Arriod

answered quietly, apparently having completely let go of his emotions in order to focus more closely on the Patrons.

"Too bad." Nacho had figured as much, but he had been hoping to make the man miss something important. It hadn't worked. "Let's roll. We start in the Pantry, and we have to get to the Dining Room Table. I'm assuming this is going to be a foodie dungeon? There a time limit?"

"You know what happens in twenty hours if you don't eat," Kronos reminded him. "You start losing Hunger Points, and if your Body Players are using their Skills while starving... well, that's going to give them a bad case of dying."

Nacho hated how casually his Patron mentioned that particular mechanic. One of the reasons why he had decided to become a cook had been to prevent people from starving to death. He'd seen it happen, and it wasn't pretty. It had directly driven the entire world to cannibalism during the Probability Vision.

Johnny put his toothpick back into his mouth and his helmet back on his head. "That's already too much of a hint. Nacho, sorry you're going to die, but my guy is going to win this little race. I hope your round-eyed world is ready to fight unrelenting waves of monsters while CruxTerra gets all the goodies."

A twinkle danced in Johnny's eye, and Nacho figured that the Patron had some kind of secret plan.

"Not going to happen." Kronos took off his cap and waved it at the other Patron. "I've bet it all on Nacho, and I have a secret weapon. A little piece of intel just might change everything... but we're not here to discuss secrets, and we won't be taking any more questions."

"Agreed. Let the games begin." Johnny snapped his fingers.

An instant later, Nacho felt his armor in place, from his helmet-pot to his shoulder pans, to his Wok of Blocking protecting his chest. They *hadn't* been cleaned, and he grimaced at the fact that he was wearing dirty dishes. He found himself surrounded by Reuben, Brie, Jennifer, the Breakfast Club, and the Five Sword Guys. They weren't on Earth anymore; each of them had been transported directly into the Pantry.

Across from them, not twenty feet away, Arriod waited with his strike team.

Their Starvation Dungeon run had begun.

"Everybody..." Nacho took a deep breath, pointed into the distance, and bellowed, "*Run*!"

CHAPTER TWENTY-NINE

Welcome to the Pantry, and to Active Combat! You'll have to tell your people the rules after this session of Active Combat, if you survive it. No Store. No Regens.

No eating!

Happily for Nacho and his team, they had the benefit of having just eaten, and he'd put all of his Stat bonuses into Fitness. The cook raised his skillet shield just as Arriod's ghostly blade hurtled across the cavern, only to ram into his shield and rend his flesh behind the protection without the blade even touching him. The cook screamed as blood fountained from his body, splashing against the inside of his armor, only to rebound and coat him with the strangely hot fluid.

Health remaining: 32/156!

. . .

Just like that, Nacho was down to a measly thirty-two Health. Without his boosts and preparation, that would've been a killing blow. He'd taken a massive strike from Arriod, and the Crux-Terran was halfway across the room. The guy had thrown a copy of his sword, powered by some insane Skill. Dealing one hundred and twenty-four damage with one blow wasn't... natural.

Even as he forced himself out of shock, Nacho's mind registered and cataloged the area. The scale of the space made his mind spin as much as the pain: everyone on the floor was about an inch tall, their battleground hidden beneath vast shelves that rose up as far as the eye could see. They were in a Pantry for planet-sized beings!

The Pantry's shelves were full of towering cans of soup, packages of macaroni and cheese, and various building-sized bags of chips. Nacho idly considered that it would be kind of fun to find out how long it would take to eat a Dorito the size of a king-sized bed. Too bad if they ate anything in the Starvation Dungeon, they would lose everything. Not only would Arriod win the dungeon, but he'd also doom the Earth's Starter World by doubling its Putrid Mana.

That thought galvanized him to regain his faculties: anything even in the *vicinity* of Tier four would kill them all.

In the distance, two mountain-sized doors—easily larger than Mount Everest—loomed on either side of the Pantry. There was no way they could open the massive panels using the doorknobs, but perhaps they could slip underneath them.

One door was clearly designated for the Earthlings—a poster had been plastered on the front, depicting a cartoonish character with very round pupils throwing a peace sign and eating a taco. The other door displayed a poster of a Crux-Terran saluting and eating an unrecognizable goop that must have been their version of tacos.

Nacho felt the uniquely disconcerting sensation of his skin crawling back together and some of his blood being slurped back into his veins as a Reuben hug suffused him. Just like that, he was back up to one hundred and twenty-seven Health and ready for battle.

Perfect timing, as a balding CruxTerran with light blue eyes appeared out of thin air right next to Nacho. The CruxTerran swung out and lashed Nacho with a crackling red energy whip, sending the cook to the ground writhing in pain as the Mana coursed through his body.

Health remaining: 82/156!

Before baldie could vanish again—either teleporting or moving into stealth—Jennifer hurled her stirring spoon at him. The guy let out a yelp and vanished as the spoon clattered to the floor. An arrow exploded into another CruxTerran with gray rock skin as armor. A cluster of tentacles erupted out of his body—a whole *mess* of tentacles.

Before he could run forward with his wiggling limbs, the unknown combatant was stopped by another of Taye's exploding arrows. Other CruxTerrans engaged Nacho's people, and both sides were letting their powers fly. That wasn't a good thing—not when they still had to get through the entire Starvation Dungeon without eating.

Arriod strode forward with numerous copies of his katana churning in the air around him. Nacho realized irritably that to get to the man, someone would have to brave his blender curtain.

That wasn't a problem for Brie. She threw her Defensive Whirl in front of her and raced forward, ready to introduce Arriod to Mr. Lacrosse Stick.

"Dinner Party!" Nacho bellowed in fury as he struggled to his feet. "Don't use any more of your Skills! Trust me!"

The blond Berserker heard him and understood that a strange mechanic must be at work, so she didn't bring her full Combat Dash heat when she slammed her stick into Arriod's chest. His ribs didn't snap like sticks, indicating that he must have found some kind of magical armor. Instead, he simply staggered back, though he was still clearly annoyed and in pain.

"Mind Players," Nacho called to his troops. "Hit them with all you've got! Body Players, save your Skills! *Don't use Hunger Points*!"

They would need every last one of them. He'd have to explain everything later.

Kristie inhaled sharply, then launched her Death Blossom behind the CruxTerran soldiers. An explosion of pink energy tore holes through a couple of Arriod's soldiers, dropping them before they even realized they'd been converted into charred husks. Hazel hurled purple grenades one after another, striking down another soldier with the magical debris.

Brie was forced back—if she didn't use her Defensive Whirl, Arriod and his active Skills would chop her to bits. Nacho couldn't understand why Arriod was using his Skills. Did he not understand how the Starvation Debuff worked? Or… did he know something the cook didn't?

Nacho pulled Jennifer back from the fight, noting that she'd recovered her stirring spoon. "We have to get through that door. We might be able to take out Arriod and his strike team, but then we won't survive the Starvation Dungeon. Everyone! Pull back! What part of '*run*' was unclear?"

A sudden wall of purple light speared across the floor of the Pantry, cleanly separating the Earthlings from the CruxTerrans. Darker purple spikes jutted out across the strange wall, and one of the CruxTerran soldiers came too close; the spike telescoped out and impaled him through the throat.

That purple light looked familiar. Nacho wasn't sure if Hazel was responsible, but either way, they had to be careful. Arriod laughed callously as The Dinner Party regrouped. "Nacho, the *boy* leader! I'd thought you'd be older, but you're just out of schooling, yes?"

"Graduated college once upon a time, but not in this life," Nacho called back, hoping the conversation would buy his people enough time to find where they needed to go. "Didn't seem to be a problem when I built the Chips Guild. Correct me if I'm wrong, but you used at least two of your Skills. You hit me with something bad, and you also have your shower curtain of death. You're going to get mighty hungry, Arriod… and there won't be anyone around to eat. You know… except your own soldiers."

Arriod sheathed his sword as the Blade Curtain continued to storm around him. He muttered something strange, and a cut on his face healed over. Was he a Paladin?

A strangely familiar **crinkling** sound seemed to completely fill the air, to the point that it was impossible for anyone to hear their own voice. Nacho searched for the source of the sound, only to spot one of the mountainous Cool Ranch Doritos chips bags above falling onto its side. It was open, so bed-sized triangles began falling all around them, bouncing off the ground with enough force to cause miniature localized earthquakes.

Reuben pushed one of their guild members to the side just as a Dorito hit the ground, shattering and spraying everyone with bits of delicious-smelling debris. Another chip landed squarely on one of the Five Sword Guys, slicing through his body like an oversized guillotine. He didn't make it. Items in his Storage Slots appeared around his body. Nacho then realized they'd lost two more of the Five Sword Guys to the tentacle guy and the teleporter.

"UltraSoldiers! Retreat!" Arriod's voice was nearly inaudible, but no one had really needed any instruction. Both sides were already sprinting for the door. The air smelled like processed cheese, and a growing fog of Doritos flavoring swirled around them.

"I have to admit," Arriod's words reached Nacho, even though the man himself was running away, just like the cook was, "I am impressed. I hit you square with my Slice Sing, along with another of my Skills, and you're still… alive. Not one player in a thousand could've taken that much damage."

"Don't worry your pretty lil' head over me. I'm one in a

million." Nacho paused, utterly unsure if his opponent could even hear him. "You know we're just playing the Patron's game, right? Do you like being a puppet? What say we join forces?"

Arriod was silent for a long moment—just long enough that Nacho was certain that the other man hadn't heard him—then a whispery voice touched his ears. "Only one world can win this game. I don't like being a puppet. But."

Nacho looked over his shoulder, whatever was left of the message apparently unable to cross the distance between them. Arriod saluted him sadly, but firmly.

In reply, Nacho threw up a peace sign.

Arriod merely shrugged and continued his run toward his people that were already on their backs, pushing themselves underneath the crack in the door. Nacho hardly noticed, because he was too busy running full tilt until he reached the corresponding door. With barely a thought, he dropped onto his back and slid smoothly under the door, his skillet acting almost like a sled.

By the time he stood, Brie was on one knee, breathing hard, as were most of Nacho's people. The ragged team was gasping, chattering, and audibly wondering how they had all been pulled from the CruxTerran UnderFun and into the Pantry.

Reuben was still trying to catch his breath, but there was one major difference between him and everyone else: his absolute addiction to junk food. In one hand was an arm-length shard of chip, and he was already rearing back to chomp into it.

Nacho's knife **pinged** off the Healer's sausage clip, shattering the chip and scattering the majority of it as Reuben's teeth *clicked* together. The cook arrived just after the knife, grabbing the hand still holding the chip and shaking his friend until it was all on the ground. "Everyone! We *can't eat.* If we eat, we lose. Not this game, but *Earth.*"

"Wait… we lose the planet if we eat these?" Reuben eyed the massive Dorito hunk with hurt eyes. "But Nacho… *huge Doritos*. When will I ever get this chance again? Can I… can I at least lick the air?"

"Don't risk every remaining human life to lick the air, *please*. Someday, I'll find a giant food cookbook and recreate this scenario just for you." Nacho looked at the remnants of his crew and found his heart in his throat. The two surviving Sword Guys stood shaking their heads and sighing mournfully. Both had taken their red helmets off, allowing Nacho to remember their names. Steve, on the left, had a red shield and sword. Stephen, even further to the left, supported a two-handed claymore, just like Gustav back with the Ghost Pepper Brigade.

Nacho was about to gather his people around him, but the System interrupted his leadership moment.

Congratulations, you survived your first Active Combat session in the Starvation Dungeon! You still have Store access and your Regens. Perhaps you'd like to buy a treat to celebrate? All Epic food, for all Tiers, is free!

Good luck—may your future be delicious!

"What is going on?" Brie called out for answers, and Nacho knew that he wouldn't be able to give her a satisfactory response. "One minute, we're packing up, and the next, we're in the middle of Active Combat? Were we shrunk? Is this place just massive?"

"It sure seems like it." Nacho cast his eyes skyward, grasping for something, anything, to offer them. He stood with his people in the middle of a dungeon hallway, only they were the size of ants. The walls of rough-hewn stone stretched for miles out of sight. The polished wooden floor reflected the wavering torch-light. Even the matching wooden baseboards rose about a dozen feet tall. *Way* above them blazed torches as bright as miniature suns. Nacho was so tiny that he was having a hard time seeing the ceiling in any great detail—the hallway stretching out from them seemed endless.

Reuben was the one to approach the two remaining Sword

Guys and offer his condolences. "I'm sorry about Sean, Sam, and Silas."

Steve nodded sharply, his heartache leaking through every motion. "Thanks. We did well together. But at least they're free from the Juxtaposition. May they be eating burgers and fries wherever they are."

"Burgers and fries forever." Stephen solemnly bumped fists with his friend, though their own secret handshake seemed to wither away as soon as the knuckles grazed against each other. "Look, we should be okay. We might only be Two Sword Guys here, but we'll always be Five in our hearts."

Both the red-armored Warriors abruptly turned on Nacho. "Tell us about this Starvation Dungeon. We need to beat it. For the fallen triple-S."

Nacho held nothing back, explaining everything he had learned about the strange competition they found themselves in as the ragged team jogged just fast enough to be able to keep the pace up the entire day if needed. Once he was finished, Brie chimed in, somewhat concerned. "I used my Defensive Whirl twice and my Combat Dash once. Thanks to my Athletic Endurance, I have seventy-six Hunger Points left."

Taye chimed in with his stats. "I used Eagle Aim twice. I'm at eighty Hunger."

Abby banged her staff on the ground. "Uh, yeah, I didn't use any of my Skills in there. Glad I didn't. I hate being hungry… like, I *really* hate it. Anything else you can tell us, young buck?"

Nacho realized he had forgotten something important after all. "Brie can't use her Melee Munchies ability, at least not until she's within three hundred feet of the Portal of Feasting."

Reuben seemed more impressed than upset. "It makes sense. They want us hungry, and Brie wouldn't be hungry if she could turn damage into Hunger Points. Smart. They really thought of everything."

"Please do not congratulate the enemy." Brie clenched her jaws like she wanted to compress her teeth into diamonds.

Nacho wished he had better news. Both Brie and Taye were already down on Hunger Points. If they beat the Starvation Dungeon quickly, it wouldn't matter that much. But if it took even a little bit longer than twenty-four hours, those points just might prove the difference between life and death.

"I hope that there are food-related monsters in here, if there even *are* monsters." Reuben jangled the Sausage Clips of Striking around his wrists. "I get bonuses. Nacho, my main man, I have a question. What if we went back into the Pantry and tried to run the CruxTerran's dungeon instead?"

"Or what if we ambushed them?" Jennifer suggested darkly, fingers twitching as though she were imagining pouring caustic potions down their necks. "If we killed Arriod and his people, you think we'd win automatically?"

As if to answer her, an explosion of noise detonated from the other side of the door. It was no longer the brittle clatter of chips falling; cans of food had come crashing down to roll around in the mess. It was almost like something was pushing things off the shelves.

"Move faster!" The truth immediately dawned on Nacho. "The Patrons want us to run this dungeon like a race. The first team to the Dining Room Table and the Portal of Feasting wins; the loser probably gets *squished*!"

With how big the hallway was, and how small they were, they might spend all their time sprinting from one place to another. If that was the case, then food would become a real problem all too soon.

Reuben's stomach growled almost as loudly as a can of soup that crashed to the ground behind them. "Abyss! My clothes are *coated* in cool ranch dust. Does this place *have* to smell so good? I'm gonna accidentally *inhale* too hard and doom our entire race!"

CHAPTER THIRTY

Two hours into their run, even Brie was showing signs of mentally wearing down. As Nacho tried to gauge the distance they still needed to cross, he felt his heart drop. He could still see the Pantry door rising up in the distance behind them. There was nothing but an open hallway stretching in front of them. At this rate, they might walk two days and *still* not reach the next room.

Brie screeched to a stop, Mr. Lacrosse Stick appearing in her hands. Taye pulled out his bow, prepping an arrow and searching around frantically. "Where is it? What is it? You're nervous; that means the rest of us should be terrified, right?"

"Deep breaths, Taye." Nacho, the only other person that was used to pushing the limit on his stats, knew why she'd stopped. The insectile chittering, the scratch of spiked legs rustling across the polished wood floor. "Roaches. There are cockroaches scuttling around us. Form up, and let me check something."

"Where?" Kristie called, hunting for signs of movement around the massive, empty corridor that they were attempting to traverse. "Nacho, *where*? I hate those things."

He didn't answer, sliding under one of the nearby shelves and touching the polished baseboard. It felt solid, and whatever was on the other side of the wall never appeared. He pushed to his feet, shook his head in negation, and Brie marched forward, leading the way once more. She was considerably more alert, and by the way her fingers were gripping her weapon, the Berserker was ready for something, *anything*, to happen.

The roaches didn't appear, apparently never finding a hole in the baseboards. Still, the noises and concern had given them something to talk about. Time marched on in keeping with their feet, and eventually, the majority of the team had begun hitting their mental limits for continuous running. Nacho couldn't help but feel dissatisfied, knowing that it was highly probable that the well-trained CruxTerran UltraSoldiers would be able to push much further than they had been able to manage.

Four hours of jogging turned into eight... turned into twelve. After a short deliberation, it was agreed that they should seek to be more well-rested and alert than the other team by the time they reached their final goal, so the cook reluctantly allowed a two-hour rest. All around him, members of the group flopped to the ground wherever they were standing, either lying flat or sitting with their backs braced against the wall.

Reuben yelled out in frustration. "*Starvation* Dungeon? More like the boredom dungeon! Yeah, we can't eat. You know I eat when I'm bored, and I'm so *abyssal* bored."

Brie didn't respond. She simply laid down on her back, folded her hands across her chest, and closed her eyes. Mr. Lacrosse Stick lay next to her, ready to swing into action at the slightest provocation. With a fair amount of disgruntled muttering, Reuben laid down next to Brie, to comfort her if nothing else. Nacho watched them for a long, lingering moment, glad that his friends had good spouses in each other.

One incongruity stood out to the cook in the next moment: Jennifer was in the process of setting up her folding table and buying wood for a fire. Nacho strolled over and settled on the ground to watch her work. "Are you sure you don't want to rest?"

"There's no *way* I'm sleeping while we're in a dungeon. Sounds like a good strategy to get dead real fast. Besides, I'm going to brew up another six-pack of my Mana Soda." She poured a vial of liquid into the pot she'd hung over the fire. "I'm making the essential oils, then adding strawberries and lots of sugar, but I buy that. Normally, I mix the essential oils with my own water that I purify and carbonate with my Wand of Carbonation—a Rare magic item I got from a monster drop—but I'll need to buy common Tier one sparkling water, since we're in the dungeon. That means a bad aftertaste, and it goes flat in a few hours. But having the potion is what matters more than taste."

Nacho was glad Reuben already seemed to be sleeping, or else he might've argued mightily against such a sacrilege. The Brewer's pragmatic rationale just put a smile on his face. "I couldn't agree with you more."

"Someone needs to stay awake, and… is *everyone* else asleep? Has no one heard of a watch rotation? Also, I know you called a two hour break, but you may want to extend that to three. People sleep in hour and a half cycles, and getting two cycles of sleep might be more beneficial for everyone. Then again, that means we'll only have nine hours to finish this dungeon before we start feeling the effects of starvation."

"I'm… I don't think that's a good idea." Nacho was hesitant at first, but he finished his statement strong. "I understand better than anyone what it means to hit starvation, and we all have enough in Fitness to go an entire *day* with no sleep. This rest stop is, to put it bluntly, to compensate for a lack of training and mental fortitude. So *what* if we are a little extra tired for a tiny slice of time? Literally *every* human life is at stake."

"Even knowing that, you allowed a rest? I get it. You're frustrated as a leader, but being a good one means that you work with the needs of your people." Jennifer stirred her fruit and oils in the fizzing water, regarding him pensively. "I've always had enough to eat since we got to this world. Do you wanna give me a refresher on what happens if we don't eat for a full day?"

"The Starvation Debuff is... deadly. It also works way, *way* faster than people seem to realize." His tone grew dark, and his mind retreated to the not-so-distant past when he had observed literal hundreds of people dropping like flies, and the more recent occurrence when he had tried to sentence Zack to death by starvation. "You're only *required* to eat once every twenty-four hours. If you miss that benchmark, you lose one Hunger Point every minute that you don't eat, until you go negative. Negative Hunger Points mean that your *Health Regen* turns negative. From that point forward, you lose *percentages* of your Health, but... not for long. Ultimately, what that means is... if you're at max health, it still only takes twenty-eight minutes."

Nacho knew that number from experience. At a single negative Hunger Point, they would lose point two-five percent of their Health points. Minus two Hunger Points? Point five percent. At negative four, they lost the first full percentage point of Health, and each minute compounded that. To remove the debuff, not only did they need to eat, but they needed to eat until their Hunger Points were *positive* again. Sometimes, it just wasn't possible to make that happen in time.

"Thirst works similarly, only that's a Dehydration Debuff. If they don't drink a full portion of liquid once a day, their Mana Regen turns negative. Run out of Mana, and you go unconscious. Can't eat when you're unconscious, and there's no Juxtaposition equivalent of a feeding tube. Eventually, the Starvation Debuff kills you... wait." Nacho stared at her in astonishment. "You know, with my new talent, I could eat and give people Hunger Points, even if they were unconscious."

Jennifer shook her head. "Let's not get that far, okay? We're going to make sure we get to that Dining Room Table before Brie drops, because she and Taye used their Hunger Points, and they can't get them back."

"Great, they can be our canaries," Nacho chuckled darkly. "If they go down, we move that much faster. Speaking of dropping, aren't *you* tired?"

"I was in the army, then the reserves when I was working at the brewery," Jennifer replied easily. "You learn early on how to embrace the suck. A lot of people have never been pushed to their real limits. I have, and I know how far I can push myself before I *need* rest, even if the stat points we get have been messing with that a little."

"More like a lot." Nacho's grin settled into a more natural version as he considered the new information. "Every time you increase your characteristics, you need to push yourself to the limit to find what that limit actually is. Not a lot of people can do that, at least not over and over again."

A few minutes passed in silence, only broken by the clacking sound of Jennifer tinkering with her liquids. Nacho hesitated awkwardly, then opted to walk off, calling softly over his shoulder, "Listen, I'm going to patrol; try and get some rest when you're done."

An uneventful few hours passed, feeling longer to the cook than the entirety of the time they'd been running. But finally, he roused the group by borrowing Jennifer's wooden spoon and banging it on his skillet. Everyone quickly gathered their things, and Jennifer packed away her brewing supplies.

Brie called to them from her self-appointed patrol as she waited for the others to be ready. "Hey! I think I found something."

That got everyone moving, and they quickly hurried over to join her. When they reached the Berserker, they found her inspecting a jagged hole nibbled through the baseboard. The hole revealed a dim passageway between two stones, and… it looked promising, in terms of bypassing the expansive hallway and reaching the next area. The concerning part was that the hole was about five feet wide and ten feet high.

Nacho opened one of his pockets, summoning his Firefly

Potstickers and sending them through the opening. Moments later, they observed that it wasn't just a shallow cave, but a path too long to see the end of.

"Should we all check it out?" Taye stepped forward, ready to lead the charge. "Or maybe just send in a few people? I'll go."

Nacho reached back and fluidly pulled his skillet shield off his back. "We're not dividing the party, not in a place like this. Let's all go in. Brie, Abby, we'll put you up front. Hazel, be ready with your shields for them. I'm hoping this goes where we need, or else we'll have even less time to save the world."

"*Literally* the world," Reuben snorted as they shuffled into the hole. "We could just evacuate all the people into CruxTerra, if the CrossHumans weren't so ready to try 'long pork'."

"There's no way people would leave," Brie commented wryly. "Look at Old Bill. He's ready to fight another Bove head on if one threatens to knock over his shack."

That got a few chuckles from the group, though they quickly lapsed into silence as they explored the strange cave system, climbing upward the entire time. It wasn't too long before Nacho started worrying that they might have to turn back, but just as he opened his mouth to order a retreat, light gleamed up ahead. Brie pointed Mr. Lacrosse Stick at the near-daylight that was illuminating their path. "It ends up there, I think. I'll go slow."

"You're darn tootin' we'll go slow," Abby grumbled as her knuckles turned white from gripping her iron-shod weapon so tightly.

Brie reached the end of the passageway, and let out an involuntary gasp. "Nacho, front and center! I need you to see… *this*."

Nacho slipped through his people and stepped out onto a ledge with Brie. His eyes adjusted rapidly, and his jaw dropped.

"For abyss' sake, just tell us what it is!" Jennifer called from the back.

"It's a *kitchen.*" Nacho breathed the statement so softly that he needed to repeat himself. "A massive kitchen, and it looks like things are really cookin'."

CHAPTER THIRTY-ONE

Nacho found himself overlooking a kitchen version of the Grand Canyon. He and Brie had emerged onto a wooden shelf that spanned the entire upper wall of the gargantuan room. The shelf held various knick-knacks, plates, an odd spoon collection, and some picture frames that were too far away for the actual pictures to be visible.

The floor, more than a mile below, appeared to be cracked yellow linoleum. To the left sat a little kitchen table and chairs next to an unmarked door. That likely led to the hallway they had vacated, but there was no guarantee that was the case.

To the right was where the real action was. A refrigerator towered over the kitchen from the opposite wall, nearly level with the shelf they had emerged onto. It was with a strange sense of nostalgia that they realized the fridge was running. The familiar hum of the engine flew in the face of the whole no-electricity apocalypse to which humanity had been subjected. Speaking of flies, several fly corpses the size of a typical two-door sedan littered the countertop, and a few still buzzed around the fluorescent lighting far above the humans.

Down from the fridge—across a messy butcher block

counter—was a sink that could have contended with a lake in size. Only if the lake had industrial levels of pollution being dumped into it; the gargantuan reservoir was full of filthy dishwater, dotted with floating chunks of grease and rotten leftovers. That alone was filling the room with an eye-watering stink even at this distance.

Another expanse of butcher block covered the distance from the sink to the stove top—which appeared to be a combination of gas and electric. From so far away, it was hard to tell. Finally, a cabinet hung next to a door marked 'Dining Room'. Reuben shouldered his way out of the tunnel to stand next to Nacho, surveying the giant's kitchen. "Well, that's… fortunate, right? We found the Dining Room, at the bare minimum. Getting there isn't going to be easy, since the distances are all weird. Really gives me a new respect for spiders climbing through our houses."

"Let's not give the Patrons any ideas." Brie immediately clapped a hand over his mouth with a hiss, knowing that any damage was likely already done.

Abby shuddered in shared revulsion. "Amen to that, bucko."

"Let's head that way." Nacho pointed to the refrigerator and started moving along the dusty platform. "I think the easiest way off this shelf is to jump to the top of the fridge, though I don't know how we're going to be able to get down to the counter from there. Anyone have rope, or do we need to plan to buy some?"

"I have a hundred feet." Taye was the picture-perfect example of a good adventurer—carrying rope and expecting trouble.

"I have fifty feet," Reuben added. "As does Nacho; I made sure of it."

Brie and Abby moved forward to take point, followed by Reuben, Taye, Kristie, and Hazel. Nacho, Jennifer, Steve, and Stephen followed behind them to provide the rear guard, everyone settling into a fast jog as soon as they were comfortable with their placement. Even so, it took another hour of trotting across the shelf to reach the far edge, leaving them with only seven hours before the Starvation Debuff came into effect.

Nacho craned his neck to look back at the way they'd come as the group paused before tackling the next obstacle, only for Brie to tap the dusty shelf with her lacrosse stick and motivate the group to get moving again. "We're on the clock! No jokes or delays. That means you, Reuben. Let's just find a way down."

Below them waited the top of the refrigerator. A hatch, like something on top of a submarine, was in the center of the huge fridge. That hatch wasn't enormous like the rest of the room—it seemed to be comfortably human-sized. It was pretty clear that was where Nacho and his Snack Attack were expected to go.

Would there be another way out of the freezer? Or was it a trap?

Reuben saw it and was appropriately skeptical, launching into speculation even as his wife stared daggers at him. "It's a good bet that the freezer is bad news. Do we ignore it and try to get to the counter? Or should we try to find a way to the floor?"

Nacho gazed down to the nasty, dusty top of the fridge. "Let's see if we can get down there first. Then we can decide. The hatch might be locked."

"You know it's not," Jennifer prophesied in a sing-song voice. "We're being led. It's interesting that we happened to find that mousehole that brought us to the ledge, and now there's that hatch. The Patrons have laid out the path—fridge to counter, to sink, to that stovetop."

Now that they were closer, Nacho could just pick out the outline of a little door in the side of the cabinet on the other side of the stove, proving Jennifer's theory right. They had a precise path to follow. Taye was already coiling out his rope. "Okay. Let's see how far this reaches."

No one was surprised when the end of the rope somehow *perfectly* reached down to about ten feet over the top of the fridge. Jennifer tied knots to make it easier on everyone else, though each of them were over twice as strong as they had been at the start of the Juxtaposition. Still, climbing down a swinging rope wasn't easy. Kristie suggested buying rappelling gear, but no one wanted to waste credits.

Taye took a moment to consider the placement of his makeshift ladder and called out a realization worth mentioning. "If we use the rope to get the fridge, we're not going to be able to retrieve it, and it'll still be a bit of a drop. That means we're stuck on top of the counter once we climb down. Are we good with that?"

"I think we have to be." Brie stowed Mr. Lacrosse Stick in a Storage Slot and slipped over the edge, dropping as quickly as possible down the knotted length. Once she reached the end, she pushed away from the wall, swinging as far as she could with the rope before releasing and landing with a roll on the fridge top. Abby followed her over the edge next, and one by one, they replicated the feat of acrobatics their combat leader had performed.

Nacho was grateful for the knots as he descended. By the time he'd lowered himself to the end of his rope, he could already feel the fridge's motor running—the vibrations traveled up his legs. Before jumping, he got a better look at the butcher block counter that connected the freezer to the sink. The wood was stained, scored, and even burned. It looked like a battle had taken place there. The sink itself was even more disgusting the closer he got—it was nearly overflowing with decomposing sludge. The cook didn't know how to get his team across that slop without swimming, and he certainly wasn't looking forward to that.

Tumbling to the fridge's surface, Nacho smoothly rolled and got back to his feet. Without slowing, he made his way directly to the hatch, spun the handle, and hauled it open. A blast of freezing air hit everyone nearby, nearly sending them flying over the edge. After everyone was stable, they checked inside and found an ice-encrusted ladder.

Nacho sent his glowing potstickers down. The freezer was stacked full of frosty boxes—TV dinners, Hot Pockets, and a few frozen pizzas. The meals must've been there a *long* time. It resembled the neglected freezer at someone's office, full of frozen food from forgotten feasts. The cook put his foot on the top rung, "I'll go first-?"

His statement was cut off with a yelp as his main Berserker pushed him out of the way and took his place. "That would be my responsibility, even if I'm not thrilled about the cold."

"I'll back you up," Reuben offered as he pulled a scowling Nacho off the ground.

Brie dropped down the ladder with a speedy slide, mirroring Nacho's feat from their descent into the Welcome Dungeon. True to his word, Reuben followed, and then *Kristie* climbed down before the team deigned to allow Nacho to join the procession. He had never been quite as happy as he was at the moment he discovered that his Gauntlets of Oven Taming could keep his hands warm on the freezing metal that sped by.

They slid more slowly than they'd be comfortable with on a non-frozen ladder, as they were uncertain about being able to slow down as effectively on the ice-encrusted monstrosity. Nacho strained his eyes to search for another hatch on the counter side of the freezer as he moved, but there were too many boxes in the way to be able to tell for certain.

As the last of them landed in the ground that was in dire need of a good defrost cycle, something shifted around them. It was hard to tell where the sound came from, as the acoustics in the freezer were terrible. The frozen dinners were stacked like shipping containers, leaving only narrow spaces for them to run through, but if any one of the boxes of Weight Watcher fudge bars came tumbling down, they'd ironically get crushed by their massive size.

"Anyone else hear the one about the frozen pizza?" Reuben chuckled in a normal tone, even if his teeth were chattering. "Never mind. I'm too cold, and that joke is too cheesy."

As the group let out a collective groan, the boxes around them went crazy, shaking and bouncing all over the place.

Nacho reacted instantly, shifting his body and pulling Abby

out of harm's way as a sharp edge of cardboard burst off a box to form an opening. "The monsters are in the boxes! Everyone move!"

Doughy hands, tipped with pepperoni claws and coated in half-frozen spaghetti sauce ripped out of a package of Hot Pockets. A TV dinner box let out a roar as congealed gravy tentacles tore through the front. A Blue Bunny ice cream tub blew off its lid, and a bestial ice cream bunny rose up: certain death to the lactose intolerant.

Reuben didn't seem too concerned, putting on a brave face and jeering, "Food-based monsters? Let me at 'em!"

"No." Nacho knew better than to let this slow them down. "It isn't time to fight. It's time to run."

CHAPTER THIRTY-TWO

As everyone sprinted forward in an attempt at pushing past the incoming wave of monsters, Reuben cast Positive Vibes on the group. "That should make it so you can hit hard enough to knock them out of the way, Brie!"

Welcome to Active Combat! This poor freezer food has been ignored for too long, and the food wants revenge!

"For Celestial's sake, concentrate on running!" Nacho shouted at his friends as he took the lead, surging ahead of the Berserker and doing a flying leap kick into what had to be an upper Tier two dinosaur-shaped chicken nugget. He was only able to knock it off of balance thanks to the fact that they were standing on a massive sheet of ice. It went skidding away, not entirely falling, but it was unable to scramble across the slick surface to rejoin battle before the rest of his team had bypassed it.

The ten remaining people in the group were fully cognizant that being caught by the various frozen foods in the arctic killbox was a death sentence. None of them could eat Nacho's food for a boost to their physicality, so they were running off of fumes as well as Positive Vibes. For the vast majority of them, it was completely unreasonable to assume that they could even land a blow that would leave any lasting damage on these creatures.

More mutated food monsters were joining the battle every few seconds, ranging from mid-Tier two, to finally rousing a low-level Tier three monster: the bunny ice cream golem, with its body shaped into round portions that looked more like armor than a tasty treat. Simply being near it was painful, as its Tier three aura was affecting the world around it in a severe way. Specifically, it was sending out waves of frozen air, lowering the overall temperature of the entire ice box, as well as generating icy armor across its own body and those of the other monsters. That same ice was attempting to coat the humans, freezing them up and locking their limbs in place.

"Detour, detour!" Nacho twisted and kicked one of the packages that several monsters had been crawling out of, imparting enough force that it started to tip over and crush anything in its way. He could only hope that it would slow down the ice cream golem, but frankly, he had very little faith that anything would be able to hold that creature back. In lieu of stopping it outright, he fervently wished that it was the strongest creature they would encounter, and now that they knew about it, they could avoid that monstrosity of an area boss.

The array of creatures appearing to attack them was dizzying: everything from partially frozen spaghetti creatures to bloodthirsty hot pockets, as well as hot dogs, chicken nuggets, and frozen fruit. All of them were twisted into abominations that, strangely enough, were *not* attempting to eat them in some sort of ironic twist. No... what they were doing was *far* more dangerous.

They were trying to force-feed the humans.

As had been clearly explained to everyone, if a single one of them ate *anything* in the Starvation Dungeon, they would doom Earth and everyone living there.

There was one nice aspect about fighting inside of an enclosed box. Namely, the end was always in sight and growing closer every moment. It wasn't long before Nacho spotted the side door that was their size, and each of them understood that they had found the exit that they desperately needed. With their destination set, each of them put on a burst of speed and hoped to be the first one to open the door for the others.

Attempting to crush their hope, a package of Fudgsicles burst open and spilled out icy warriors brandishing sticks that they had pulled out of themselves. Some of them still had portions of their body covered in their plastic wrappers, and Nacho just *knew* that they would be harder to defeat in direct combat; likely the packaging would act almost as a force field or another piece of armor. As far as he had ever been able to determine within the Juxtaposition, there were no coincidences or accidents when it came to the monsters. Sometimes they might look silly, or do strange things, but there was always a purpose behind the details; and that purpose was always to make the creature deadlier.

The Fudgsicles brandished their sticks and shrieked out of their fudgy mouths, looking for all the world like a defensive line that was merely trying to hold out until the cleanup crew had arrived. A burst of icy air followed by a strangely gurgling roar confirmed *exactly* what the enemies were waiting on: ice crystals had already begun thickening on their frozen bodies, and the ice cream bunny was thundering toward the Snack Attack, its massive stride eating through the distance that they had been able to build up.

"Defensive Whirl!" Brie shouted as she brandished Mr. Lacrosse Stick, sending a swirl of energy forward and guaranteeing the safety of her teammates as they shoved through the line and scrambled their way to the human-sized egress. Of course, it was frozen shut and crusted over by a heavy layer of frost. They began slamming their weapons and shattering the ice, completely uncaring if it would impact the efficiency of this freezer once they escaped it.

Even though it felt like it was taking a massive amount of time, the distance between them and the ice cream golem had barely decreased by the time Nacho pushed the door open. A gust of blazing hot air, which was most likely only room temperature, swirled into the frozen arena and nearly knocked the humans back to their doom. Fighting against the updraft, each of them desperately wrestled their way toward the exit.

Something they had forgotten, thanks to the situation, as well as the adrenaline coursing through their bodies, was the atrocious smell of the sink far below. For one long moment, Nacho considered shutting the door, but the chill running down his spine created by the approaching Tier three monster he could not defeat smothered all thoughts of avoiding something just because it was 'stinky'.

The only remaining consideration was how to get out of there safely, without simply diving into free fall and splattering on the floor. It took a precious few seconds, but Nacho realized that if they jumped at a certain angle, it was a forty-foot drop from the door in the side of the freezer down to a scuzzy kitchen sponge resting on an even scuzzier counter. "I found our exit! Aim for the landing pad, and prepare for the worst!"

Stephen reached the door and volunteered to test out the fall by diving headfirst out of the opening without a word or slowing down. The cook did an involuntary double take, as he had not been expecting anyone to risk themselves so nonchalantly. Watching the man land with a **squelch**, bounce slightly, then pop up and wave at them, Nacho knew that he had chosen the correct path that the Patrons had laid out for them.

One after another, the team started jumping. Over half of them were out, but the Fudgesicle soldiers were closing in, furious that their prey was escaping. The sticks that they had pulled out of themselves had shifted along with changes in their own sludgy bodies to make them better and more efficient at fighting—now they were threatening the remainder of the team with hockey sticks with a splintery blade on the bottom corner edge. Brie, Reuben, and Steve were providing security against them, blocking their attacks and shoving them away as the other members of their party escaped.

Soon only five humans remained, and Reuben was chosen to go out first. He nodded at Nacho as he sprinted to the exit and did a flip, while the cook moved forward to help with defense as Jessica prepared to jump. It was at that moment that things went horribly wrong.

A rebound from a blocked blow twisted and smacked into Steve, who stumbled and was unable to block the follow-up from the Fudgesicle warrior that he had been battling. The stick sent him tumbling deeper into the freezer, and he landed at the foot of the ice cream golem. Everyone thought that was the end for him, but instead of crushing the human with a single attack, the boss monster of the freezer reached down and picked him up surprisingly gently.

"No! *No*!" Steve struggled as hard as he could, but he knew what was coming. The tip of the ice cream golem's rabbit paw shifted into a spoon offering a delectable, heaping portion of fragrant ice cream. It started moving slowly, inevitably toward his mouth even as the man struggled against it. "It's going to make me eat it! Make sure I don't! Don't let me be the reason humanity—**urk**!"

Nacho had tossed a Sewer Skewer to Jessica, then pulled out another one of his own. Without hesitation, both of them hurled their weapons at their friend as soon as it became obvious what was going to happen. Just as Steve had started to beg for them to end him, the attacks landed, dealing a total of fifty-two and a half damage with just the weapon's base damage, more than enough to instantly kill him after the strike he had taken from the Fudgesicle warriors.

The remaining humans turned and scrambled for the door, completely ignoring the damage that they were taking from behind. Nacho was the last one out. The only reason tears weren't streaming down his face was that they were freezing as soon as they touched his skin.

He soared from the open door, diving to the sponge below him. He landed, he bounced, and he stood up… ready to finish the mission.

CHAPTER THIRTY-THREE

"It's hour eighteen in the Starvation Dungeon, and no one is losing Hunger Points yet." Nacho looked around to confirm the accuracy of his assertion. "It's only a matter of time, so we need to hurry. We can… we'll honor the fallen after we make sure that *we* are going to make it through this."

Brie and Abby both had used their abilities, which meant they had fewer Hunger Points to spare and would suffer a faster death than the others if they failed to reach safety in time. The Berserker was lucky that her Athletic Endurance ability reduced the Metabolic Cost of her skills by thirty-eight percent, but that wouldn't mean a thing long-term if they were too slow.

With those cheery thoughts in mind, they started filing across the filth-encrusted butcher block countertop, which led to the putrid lake they'd seen from the top of the fridge. As far as they could tell from here, there was no way to get across the sink except for swimming; and that seemed… inadvisable.

Brie jogged to the edge of the counter as the others were mentally preparing to continue their forced run. The Berserker came back with bad news, her grim expression set in stone. "Even if we had our rope, there's no way it would reach all the way down to the linoleum. It looks like we need to head for the sink."

"The sink, it is." Reuben's acquiescence was uncharacteristically mellow, bordering on depressed. Nacho's arm snaked out and he grabbed his friend, pulling him in for a quick, quiet talk.

"I totally get it. Right now, we're running on minimal sleep, no food, and we're losing friends." Reuben began to squirm in the Guild Leader's grip, but Nacho wasn't letting go. "But let me tell you something. If they see that their leaders, the people they are looking to for direction, are starting to collapse under the weight of all of this… it will break them."

Only then did he let go, and even if Reuben glared at Nacho, he understood and took the advice. Taking a deep breath, he forced a grin onto his face and called out heroically with a dramatic point "To the sink!"

"Onward! To the sink!" Jennifer echoed him with a raised Sewer Skewer. That reminded Nacho that he could recall the ones that they'd… used… to his bandolier. Holding one of the weapons in his hand as a focus, he was able to recall all of the others directly to his person. The Brewer observed the process with blatant excitement. "*Whoa*! What? *I* want some recalling weapons!"

"I know, I know." Nacho preened under the attention, glad to have a new topic to latch onto. "It's amazing. Take half of these to use with your throwing ability, would you?"

The Brewer gladly accepted the skewers, and Nacho watched them go with a smile. Having someone with a skill dedicated to throwing satiation items guaranteed that they would be put to good use. It didn't hurt that he had demonstrated he could get them back whenever he wanted.

They hurried forward with renewed determination, and Nacho knew that even though people wanted to talk about Steve, they needed to focus on the living first. Due to their minuscule size, it took them a full two hours to cross the cutting board and reach the sink. Kristy's voice was stressed as she pointed out that a countdown timer that appeared in their vision, now intermittently flashing red. "Only four hours to get into the Dining Room? Are we-"

"We'll make it," Brie interrupted her firmly. Just then, they came within hearing distance of the **ploink, ploink, ploink** of a leaky faucet the size of Niagara Falls.

When they reached the sink's edge, they found that the sink took up the entire width—from the wall to the very edge of the counter. It was a vast expanse of weeks-old dishwater and backed-up drains, if the smell was any indication. Disturbingly multihued scum mottled the surface, like artwork dedicated to the world's most beloved molds and funguses.

There was one counterpoint to the mess: the faucet was reminiscent of a piece of modern art, hanging over them like the sword of Damocles. Crystal clear fresh water dripped into the morass at regular intervals. The cook noticed that Brie was studying the rhythmic dripping with a considering expression, and she finally turned to Nacho with concern written across her face. "I can't fight and swim at the same time."

"No one could ever expect you to do that." Nacho winced even as he voiced his next question. "Jennifer, is there *any* possible way that you would be able to purify all that water?"

"Not at that quantity." The Brewer grimaced apologetically. "I can only clean my level in gallons: in this case, nineteen gallons. Add on the fact that it would take Hunger Points, and I'd rather not play around with it."

"Look out!" Taye pointed with an arrow that he let fly in the same motion. "Incoming monsters!"

A yellow-green *something* was streaking toward them through the murk, followed by congealed pools of grease following in its wake.

Greater Grease Slime

Effective Tier/Level:???

HP:?

. . .

"Another set of Tier two monsters! Everyone back!" Nacho called out as calmly as he could manage. The System sent them the Active Combat message just as the closest Grease Slime threw out a tentacle faster than a whip crack, grabbing Stephen and hauling him toward the edge.

Kristie flung pink missiles that sizzled through the grimy appendages—which simply reformed and continued pulling without even slowing down. "We're in trouble; I can't do enough damage to hurt this thing!"

Stephen was about to be dragged into the water when Jennifer stepped forward and impaled a Sewer Skewer through the tentacle with perfect aim. It dropped Stephen, and Reuben strode forward, ready to heal their friend if needed.

Slimes started **slopping** out of the water, then **slurping** onto the countertop, doing nothing to improve the overall ambience of the location. Stephen had just begun to scramble back when another tentacle latched onto him and dragged him forward. He tried to hack through the tendril, but his sword couldn't pierce the Tier two protective coating of the greasy slime.

No matter what was thrown, whether lacrosse balls or Mana-made grenades, nothing seemed to work against the collection of slimes. Then came a moment that erased all other thoughts from their mind: They had been so preoccupied with the slimes that they had forgotten to account for the yellow-green something that had been originally leading the charge.

It broke from the surface and slowly slithered onto the counter, draining enough dirty dishwater to wash away the nearest of the slimes. It took a few moments for them to recognize what its original shape had been, simply due to the sheer scale of the creature: a towering kitchen sponge. Moldy yellow in the front, scratchy green matting on the back. It was nothing like the crusty sponge they'd jumped onto—this was *visibly* full of bacteria and would've been thrown away weeks ago in a real house. Yet, here it was, attacking them.

Scratchy green claws extended from yellow spongy arms; oversized webbed hands meant for swimming were instead reaching for their frail human bodies. Obviously pus-leaking legs carried it forward on webbed feet, and it screamed as though its mere existence was pain.

Abby dashed forward and swung her staff, bashing it as hard as she could. She may as well have not bothered to spend the energy with how spectacularly her strike managed to fail, dealing no damage at all. Abrasive claws slashed down her armor, shredding the metal as effortlessly as though it had a second job as a can opener.

Scratch-Bite, the Godking of Scrub Sponges
Effective Tier/Level:????
HP:?

"Those are a lot of question marks… Tier three boss monster!" Nacho called out just in case someone wasn't looking at it the way he was. Just as the warning left his lips, a tongue lashed out and encircled Jennifer, dragging the Brewer toward its main fanged maw.

At the same time, extra mouths opened across its entire body and coughed out a white phlegm, an explosion of mucus that dealt acid damage—which Nacho found out the painful way. He raised his Skillet of Turtling to catch the worst of it, but a few flecks of the goo struck his arm and sizzled away his skin, leaving his muscle fibers exposed to the open air.

Health remaining: 42/60!

"Nacho!" Jennifer screamed for help, scrabbling frantically against the tongue as her outer layer of flesh was being dissolved by the acidic mucous coating that appendage. She started stabbing her Sewer Skewers into Scratch-Bite, but the

Godking of Scrub Sponges shook her savagely, forcing her to drop all the weapons she had been handed.

Nacho sped forward and chopped his cleaver down onto the tongue, only for it to rebound like he had hit a rubber band reinforced with liquid steel.

Damage dealt: 0!

Sorry, Cookie! The Godking of Scrub Sponges requires you to do at least 150 damage in a hit, and you aren't even close. Your knife's ability only guarantees damage on creatures one Tier above you! Sad little Tier one Nacho. Womp, womp.

"Didn't need the reminder, System. I noticed the lack of gushing blood all on my own, thank you very much." Along with being unaffected by their attempts, the Tier three monster had one thousand Health. *None* of them were going to be able to do any damage against it with their standard attacks: they only had one weapon that could piece the creature's sponginess. "Still… gonna try and inflict some pain. Even if there's no guarantee that I will be able to hurt it, I'm going to act like I can. Practice makes better."

Nacho's only hope was to scoop a Skewer Sewer off the counter and try to stab the tongue. His hand slipped on the metal, his damaged muscles failing him, and the weapon ended up clattering to the counter once again. Scratch-Bite pulled the Brewer closer to its fangs as its other mouths hurled acidic nastiness, dealing damage to the fighters while they tried to beat back the Grease Slimes.

"Brie! I need help!" Nacho yelled in pure desperation as Jennifer was dragged into range of the monster's monolithic mandibles. "Fast!"

Brie Combat Dashed over but didn't try to involve her weapon. Instead, she used her momentum to grab Jennifer and yank her away from the Sponge God's tongue, leaving behind a sheet of flesh melted to the muscular appendage as Jennifer was ripped loose.

Jennifer screamed in agony, which transformed into rage as she stood and snatched up two of the Sewer Skewers, one in each hand. Somehow, the furious Brewer rammed both of them into the Godking of Scrub Sponges. The brobdingnagian sluice roared in pain and surprise as Jennifer danced back and hurled two more skewers into the moldering mass. "I knocked off over a hundred Health, but we're not going to win this fight by bashing our heads against it. Anyone have a good idea?"

Scratch-Bite spoke before they could. It didn't use words, preferring to speak with its acid mucous attack. Goo spewed from its many mouths, falling slower than it seemed it should, but still nearly too rapidly to react. Nacho leapt instinctively in front of Jennifer, his skillet shield blocking *almost* all damage.

Health remaining: 10/60!

"Reuben!" Brie yelled across the slashing hubbub. The Berserker swung Mr. Lacrosse Stick into the sponge, failing once again to do any damage at all. "Nacho needs healing!"

Nacho was desperate for a solution as he stumbled away from the boss monster, only to feel a Healing Hug encircle him and send his Health back to sixty. Reuben ran up behind the Godking of Scrub Sponges and hammered his fist, one after another into Scratch-Bite's fuzzy green back. "*Ow*! Hitting this thing is hurting me as I pull away—it's officially not food-related! The Grease Slime's were, but I can't hit them. We have got to take out the big daddy!"

"But how do we-?" Nacho gazed up at the faucet, his mind whirling as he remembered that this place was full of what had been modern conveniences in his world. His eyes were locked on the light switch on the wall, partially hidden in the tile. "The sink has a *garbage disposal*!"

Reuben took a splash of acid to the face, and due to taking the damage and his Skill stepping in, Jennifer, Brie, and Abby were instantly healed. Hazel took the momentary respite to throw up a Spike Wall, saving her own life, but also managing to save them *all* by accident. The Grease Slimes on the counter didn't take spike damage from the wall, but seemed confused by the spell. To them, the humans had simply vanished without a trace.

Nacho left the sponge battle behind, finding Taye firing arrows that exploded around the Grease Slimes. He grabbed Taye's Archer hoodie and pulled the younger man along with himself. "Taye! You're our best chance here! We need to turn on the garbage disposal; it's the only way we're going to be able to get through this."

"What the…? A garbage disposal?" Taye already had an arrow nocked and was searching for the target.

"Right there!" Nacho had to point for the Archer to notice it. "It's in the down position for now, and obviously the disposal isn't running. Aim below it, and blow the switch *up*. Turn it on! You're the only one with the range a shot like this requires!"

"Keep them off me. I need total focus." Taye eyed the distance, easily five hundred yards. "I'll have to use Eagle Aim, and I can't do both."

"Drink!" Jennifer passed a potion to the Archer, and he chugged it down without a thought. "That'll maximize your damage, believe me."

"I'll aim for the tile underneath and a little to the left. We don't want to destroy the circuits." The archer drew back his arrow to its maximum draw, holding it in place as he spoke softly to himself. After what seemed like *far* too long to Nacho, Taye loosed. A bright purple glow was yanked off his body and onto the arrow as the potion's magic was expended, and the feathered shaft went arcing over the water. It hit the tile right below the light switch—exactly where the Archer had intended. The resulting explosion of dust and debris blocked Nacho from seeing the results. That was fine; he could *hear* their success.

The world shook with sudden droning, a grinding that soon sent the lake of dishwater swirling around the sink. The counter rumbled underneath their feet, sending Taye tumbling, though Nacho caught him.

The big sponge toppled down onto its belly as its back half was dragged by the suction. The Grease Slimes were swept away from the edge of the sink as the water turned into a whirlpool. Countless monsters warbled in fear and agony as they were sucked down into the garbage disposal, which began screeching as it tore up the hardened grease, bubbling and puking up bits of the monsters.

The rumbling, screaming, and sucking continued, and the humans were forced to wait until Nacho saw the sloped walls of the sink appear. The layer of scum on them would act like lubricant, but it was the only way forward. "Slide down to the scum line! *Carefully*! We're not going to be able to turn off the garbage disposal anytime soon, and we're burning time."

Nacho didn't like leaving his people, but he also knew that they all had to get away from Scratch-Bite as soon as possible. It wasn't very likely that Jennifer would be able to finish Scratch-Bite off with her Sewer Skewers attack, as it required her to leave the skewers *in* the monster for the stacking damage effect to be used. That, and the monster was still struggling to fight back.

The cook went careening down the side of the sink, going faster, faster, and still picking up speed. He hit the bottom, and it was much like any water slide he'd ever been on, except that he landed in water that was murky and stank. He went skittering across the bottom until the water was still deep enough to slow his descent, leaving a wake that saved his life by pushing the muck away from him. Nacho was up on his feet in calf-deep water, fighting a current that was trying to pull him toward the roaring motor of the garbage disposal.

Losing his balance meant certain death.

He turned in time to see Reuben, Brie, and the rest of the Snack Attack come sliding down the grimy porcelain, slowing once they hit the deeper water in a big woosh of waves… but that was where the good news ended.

Scratch-Bite slid in after them, hitting the water with a slap and rising up on its webbed feet to awkwardly toddle after them. The thing might be Tier three, but it sure was slow. It *exhaled*, and grease started pouring off of it.

"Don't look back!" Nacho shouted, putting action to words as he began run-hopping through the remaining liquid. "That thing is creating more slimes!"

Fortunately, all of the current slimes were long gone, shredded in the garbage disposal. The bad news? Not only was the Godking of Scrub Sponges coming after them, but the sink was filling up once more.

The faucet had just 'mysteriously' turned on at full strength. The downpour could fill up the sink faster than the garbage disposal could suck the gushing influx down, thanks to being clogged with slimes and likely other, even *less* pleasant things. Nacho sputtered out a long, calming heave of air. "I can only hope the CruxTerrans are having a worse time than we are."

CHAPTER THIRTY-FOUR

Reuben and Jennifer were yelling about something that no one could hear, thanks to the calamitous noise of the garbage disposal. Nacho calculated their odds of escape, briefly letting out a whisper of relief that the Godking of Scrub Sponges couldn't run very well: it had been made for swimming through dishwater and for scraping the burned stuff off of pans.

It took forty-five minutes of wading through the water, even with their enhanced physiques pushed to the very limits, to reach the other side.

"What now?" Brie shouted at the top of her lungs, directly into Nacho's ear—the only way to be heard. Scratch-Bite roared behind them and dove into the water, trying to swim, but luckily the water level was still too low for it to be able to move well. The monster ended up flopping and flailing around, trying to find water deep enough for it to use its webbed hands and feet.

Nacho fished a glob of the shredded Grease Slime out of the water, squishing it in his hands and feeling it congeal and start to harden. He hurried over and slapped the grease on the side of the sink, where it stuck. A moment later, he hopped atop the glob and found that the dried slime could hold his weight. "We can use the grease to create a ladder!"

Reuben and Taye understood exactly what he was trying to do and rushed over to slap more grease on the sink wall. Nacho started climbing, slapping tossed greaseballs onto the wall. All in all, it was no different than a climbing rock wall all at any given YMCA. He created a series of little hand and foot holds as Kristie climbed up behind him, and soon they had an efficient supply chain sending the sludge upward.

Stephen was at the very bottom, which made every single person except for the man himself nervous. They didn't want to lose an entire subgroup on a mission, and those guys had an eighty percent death rate already. Higher and higher, Nacho climbed, until Stephen had to grab grease from the water, climb up halfway to the hall, hand it off to Brie, and scurry back down. All the while, the faucet continued to pour water into the sink… and it was finally deep enough for the Godking of Scrub Sponges to swim.

Rasping out a phlegmy roar of success, it splashed toward them, picking up a massive amount of speed with every stroke.

Stephen dumped his backpack and used it to scoop up as much slime as it could hold, then climbed as fast as he could. He had barely reached a high enough point that when the sponge took a swipe at him, it bounced off the dense porcelain instead of his weak flesh. Just as they started to celebrate, a whip shot out and wrapped around the man.

Scratch-Bite had missed with his claws, but hit with his tongue.

Stephen smiled gently and tossed the backpack of grease to Brie. He closed his eyes as the tongue started to pull him down, only for a skewer hurtle past him; Jennifer had his back.

It was the shot of a lifetime, striking the Sponge Godking in the back of its mouth and forcing it to gag, releasing the last Sword Guy.

Stephen scrambled out of range of Scratch-Bite's tongue as Nacho accepted the greasy backpack. Using the goop provided, he slammed the last lumps of their improvised climbing wall onto the sink and waited impatiently as it dried —all the while the monster was trying to scrabble up the perfectly smooth wall below. Finally, the cook was able to haul himself over the edge and gasp cleaner air, fully amazed that his plan had worked.

Nacho hurriedly stood and helped Kristie out of the sink, then the two of them pulled each person up the last little bit until they were all looking down into the half-full sink, where Scratch-Bite bellowed in impotent rage. The Sponge Godking would have to wait for the sink to fill, which would take a bit, as long as the garbage disposal's motor held out. The fresh liquid covered the bottom, but now that the humans were out, the whirlpool in the center was somehow working properly enough to suck the water down.

Active Combat is over! Regen and Store fun await you—hey, that was quick thinking! In previous iterations, people were powerful enough to kill the slimes and sponge, then use them as a raft to paddle over. But you used your modern-day conveniences to outwit the stink sink—don't worry, we also noticed how well you handled yourselves in the freezer. We're impressed! Here's a bonus of two million credits each (tax free) for your efforts! We're looking forward to a truly impressive showdown at the end.

Happy Starvation Dungeoneering, and may your future be delicious!

Nacho led the party across the counter until the sound of the faucet and garbage disposal faded to merely annoying instead of all-consuming. Stephen couldn't dispel the wide grin on his face as he took his greasy backpack away from Nacho. "That was a close one! At least it looks like we can do some upgrading. Are we going to upgrade our Tiers? Two million credits apiece is about right."

"It isn't enough for all of us to upgrade." Brie shook her head regretfully. "It's closer to two million, two hundred thousand credits to break the Tier barrier. Not sure where we're going to get the extra."

"Some of us will have to wait." Reuben held up his hand before anyone could protest. "I'll volunteer to remain at the peak of my current power. At this stage, my Healing Hugs are overkill anyway."

"I can stay-" Nacho winced as Brie started shaking her head to cut him off, and he went quiet. The thought of upgrading his class ahead of the others made him annoyed, but... he *could* utilize the stats he would get better than almost anyone else. He understood this, intellectually, though it felt like a waste when more combat-oriented people were needed in a place like this. If additional Tier three monsters were waiting for them... well, they had already determined that they couldn't beat them as they were now.

"Should we be doing this now, or wait until after the next challenge?" Taye's question hung in the air as the group turned to survey the next area to tackle. The stovetop was waiting for them, presenting a seemingly straightforward path toward the Dining Room. Still, something told Nacho that the next arena they had to fight through would in no way be *easier* than the ones they had started with.

They had three more hours until the Starvation Debuff hit.

Nacho checked on his Body Players who'd used their Skills as Jennifer offered a swig of Mana Soda to anyone that needed it. Brie was at sixty-six Hunger Points. Abby was at seventy. Taye was now down to seventy as well, thanks to using his Eagle Aim to save their life.

"Not to be a downer, Nacho," Reuben took off his eye-wateringly out-of-fashion helmet and scratched his head, clearly uncomfortable with delivering bad news, "but if we advance to Tier two, sure, we get bonus abilities and Stat Points, but we lose our magic items. We'd have to try upgrading them, and I'm not sure that's a good idea. In a place like this, so close to the Patrons who are watching every little interaction? I would set our chances of success at a negative percentage."

"Oh, abyss." Taye froze in place as he considered the ramifications of upgrading. "I don't want to give up my gear just yet. My bow, quiver, armor? It's all Tier one, and it's all connected. If upgrading one piece goes wrong, all of my stuff could go **boom**."

Nacho considered his own gear. His knives were guaranteed to be successfully upgraded—one of the reasons why he'd wanted them so much. As for his armor, he would have to upgrade each piece individually, and that would be both expensive and dangerous. There was always the risk that a piece of his armor would explode, throwing shrapnel. Or in the case of his Gauntlets of Oven Taming, filling the air with a magical version of asbestos.

"I'm going for an upgrade. I don't think we'll need my Wand of Carbonation *or* my Collapsible Cauldron. Those are my two biggest magic items." Jennifer waved one of the Sewer Skewers around. "I also have these now, if it's okay that I borrow them?"

Nacho nodded at the request. The skewers were more of a novelty to him, especially when his knives would be more than capable of getting the job done, and he could always recover the skewers when necessary. "They suit you well, since you have a skill that allows you to throw them properly."

"Sounds great to me. But *this* cheese doesn't have time to age right now, so how many credits do you need to get to Tier two?" Reuben transferred over the remaining credits and gave her a thumbs up. The total cost of going from level nineteen to twenty was two million, one hundred eighty-nine thousand, two hundred credits.

Jennifer let out a breath. "Okay, how about I try leveling and walking at the same time? If I can't, you guys keep walking and maybe someone carries my steaming body back until I cool off enough to get a good boost?"

Nacho agreed to help her out, keeping his mouth shut about what she could expect. In his past life, he had seen plenty of people attempting the breakthrough into the next Tier. He knew that sharing the knowledge he carried would only build people's anticipation and make it harder for them to make the leap.

Achieving level twenty meant reaching the first bottleneck in advancement: fatalities could, and would, occur if the player wasn't mentally strong enough to survive the process.

CHAPTER THIRTY-FIVE

Nacho lifted Jennifer in a Princess carry, clasping her hand and trying to reassure her—even though he knew there was a chance, however small, that she would be nothing more than a burned-out husk in the next few minutes. "It always feels like death when you upgrade your Character Class a Tier higher. You'll get through this."

She gasped, gagged, and nearly convulsed out of his arms onto the countertop. His reflexes were enough to make sure she stayed safe, but it was a close call. A strange secondary effect caught his attention as well, though he would likely never be able to tell her directly to her face: As the energy changed her body, she became significantly heavier. Her bones gained density, as did her muscles. If he had to guess, her nerves underwent a process that moved them further from normal human fleshy nerves and more into something like fiber optics.

As the process began to slow down, Nacho huffed out a long sigh of relief. The conversation regarding some people not being able to reach Tier two could wait a little bit longer.

Jennifer blinked a few times, then motioned that she wanted to walk. Nacho stuck close, ready in case she stumbled, and he watched her test out her new limits, as well as upgrading her Skills at the same time. She finally grinned at him as she adjusted to her new features. "That's… so cool. I had Purify before, but boosting my skill gave me a Tier two Enhancement: Corrupt. Here, read it for yourself. Let me bold this… there. I hid most of it, since I only really want you to see these two upgrades."

Jennifer Ales
Class: Soda Pop Priestess
Level: 20

Skill Slots (5/5)

- *Boot Camp Brewmeister (Passive) Level 29: Can use any Satiation Player item as a weapon, adds bonus damage of one point/per skill level (currently 29 HP) to base weapon damage.*

Tier 1 Enhancement: Hurl any Satiation Player Item at your enemies!

Tier 2 Enhancement: Triple Strike. When attacking with a Satiation Player item, you can attack with ***three*** *of the same item at the same time. Must have the items in your possession!*

- *Purify/Corrupt (Active) Level 29: Remove Putrid Mana from all sources of water everywhere! Make one gallon of delicious water per level (currently 29 gallons).*

Tier 1 Enhancement: Process water from 15 feet away!

Tier 2 Enhancement: Corrupt! Use your new Corrupt skill to add Putrid Mana back into people's drinks and spoil their food. Note: Consuming corrupted drinks will add on a ***hidden*** *Putrid Mana debuff!*

"Huh. Didn't know you could intentionally bold things,"

Nacho muttered as he read over the abilities. "You know, this practically makes you a frontline fighter if I let you hold on to the Sewer Skewers. With that bonus of twenty damage to an item, that allows a single one of them to land for forty-five damage by itself. Then, if that stacks as well? Abyss… this is awesome."

"Before I forget, Reuben transferred his entire two million to me." Jennifer brightened up and flashed Nacho a dazzling smile. 'Let me give you everything that I didn't use. That is… are you going to upgrade to the next Tier?"

"I…" Nacho paused to *really* consider it. If he did, he'd have more Health and be stronger. Still, there was a good chance he'd lose his armor. It wouldn't stop him from using it to cook, but it would leave him more vulnerable than he would be otherwise. There was one major issue with keeping his armor: Arriod's first strike when they entered the starvation dungeon had flat out *ignored* the protections that he had in place. When it came down to it, his armor needed to be stored away so that he could be as mobile as possible. There was no stopping attacks at that level, apparently. There was only dodging them.

That line of thinking was more than enough to set his decision in stone. Nacho caught up with his friends and called out, "I'm going to level, and then see if it's possible to bring my Sunday Brunch Armor up to Tier two."

Brie shot Jennifer an inquisitive look. 'Did you manage to upgrade your magic items?"

Jennifer's smile didn't waver a bit. "Yeah, I did! I'm carbonating at Tier two."

The Berserker let out a frustrated grunt. "I'm happy for you, but for some reason you seem to be a darling of the Patrons. Not to sound mean, Nacho, but it looks like they really want *your* head on a silver platter."

Nacho bought the remaining Experience Points to bring himself from level nineteen to level twenty, mentally firming his will and preparing for the agony. He had experienced this once before, and understood *exactly* what it was going to take to survive as well as succeed. Moments later, his joints felt like they were full of broken glass. His blood flow slowed, as it had seemingly turned into condensed tomato soup on the verge of boiling. He cried out and staggered forward blindly as hands reached out to hold him.

His thoughts swam back into focus an indefinite amount of time later, and he found himself swaying gently back and forth as Reuben carried him across the butcher block countertop. Various System messages flashed through his brain, sending bright red warnings about everything from his HungerCry Knives, to his Sunday Brunch Armor.

He tapped his friend on the side and was gently eased to the ground. Nacho glanced at his feet and noticed that his metal boots had gained an extra piece of metal—a square-shaped tube up the side of his leg. Opening his mouth to tell his people what he had learned, the words caught in his mouth as the world went quiet. His eyes swept the area, homing in on where the constant white noise had been coming from. That was when he realized: the garbage disposal had shut off.

The faucet continued to gush, meaning there was a good chance that they'd soon be seeing Scratch-Bite leveraging his way out of the sink. "You guys keep going; I'll boost my skills real quick, then catch up. I shouldn't have to say this out loud, but going up Tiers is the *worst.*"

Reuben stubbornly stayed right next to him as Nacho watched the rest of his team hurry across the countertop toward the stove in the distance, which was rising like a mountain to meet them. He hurriedly dumped credits into his upgrades, then took a look at the portions that mattered to him.

Eli 'Nacho' Naches
Class: Subpar Sous Chef
Level: 20

Build Type: Balanced, Delayed
Body:

- *Fitness: 30*
- *Metabolic Efficiency: 30*

Mind:

- *Mental Energy: 30*
- *Circuit: 30*

Satiation:

- *Hunger: 100*
- *Thirst: 100*

Total Health Points: 70
Bonus Physical Damage: 15%
Health Regen: 30% Health Regen/minute
Total Mana Pool: 55
Bonus Spell Damage: 15%
Mana Pool Regen: 30% Mana Regen/minute

Skill Slots (5/5)

- *Small Blades (Passive) Level 29:* ***58****% bonus damage on all knife attacks.*

Tier 1 Enhancement: Your blades can slice from up to 6 inches away from their edge!

Tier 2 Enhancement: Razor-Sharp Wit! With your Razor-Sharp Wit Skill, you can permanently increase the sharpness of one of your knives! Adds your skill level in HP damage (Currently ***29****). Can only be recast if the current blade is lost, sold, or stolen.*

- *Ingredient Processing (Active) Level 29: Remove Putrid Mana from monsters up to Level* ***31****.*

Tier 1 Ranged Attack Enhancement: Process ingredients from 15 feet away.

*Tier 2 Enhancement: Prep Work! With your Prep Work skill, start processing monster meat before the monster is even dead! Removing Putrid Mana from a living monster will inflict this skill level in damage (Currently **29**).*

- *Cooking Magic (Active) Level 29: Create food that enhances a single stat by 145% of max.*

Tier 1 Enhancement: Tier 1 Enhancement: Throw magic into a food item you cooked from 15 feet away!

Tier 2 Enhancement—Make your dishes irresistible! Increase the pleasure and power of what you cook by enhancing taste and perfecting texture by 29%!

- *Feasting Feats (Active) Level 19: Cook 29 times the food you're currently preparing!*

Tier 1 Enhancement: you can choose up to five locations which people can use like a vending machine! At the low, low cost of 15% of the sale price, people no longer need to come bother you directly for their food. It'll just appear in front of them, in whatever location you specify, within 500 feet of the food source.

Caution! As this is meant as a feast for many, and not for one, <u>only a single portion</u> of each meal created through the use of this skill can be eaten by each person!

Tier 2 Lure Enhancement—All Feasting Feats-created food <u>can</u> act as a lure for creatures up to level: 31. All resulting food odors and aesthetics improved by 58%.

- *Baby Bird(ing) (Active) Level 29: You eat the food, and one person of your choice within 15 feet gets 58% of the Hunger Points consumed.*

Tier 1 Enhancement: Three people of your choice within 30 feet regain 58% of the Hunger Points you consume.

Tier 2 Enhancement: Speed Eating! Speed Eating allows you to down a full portion of food in the same time it takes others to finish a quarter portion. Impress your friends! Eat more of their food faster!

Nacho wasn't sure about his new Tier two Enhancements, even if two of them *really* got him excited.

"Those upgrades are *awesome*!" Reuben exploded with unbridled excitement. "Your Tier two Small Blades enhancement is giving you more bang for your buck; which knife are you going to choose to bless with supernatural sharpness?"

"My cleaver," Nacho decided instantly. "It's the easier weapon to use in combat. Nice, simple, chopping motion."

Hey, there, Cookie! Welcome to Level 20! You are Tier 2 wonderful! Your mana is still adjusting, so we'll let you know when it settles into a nice, new, aura effect. In the meantime, would you like to upgrade all of your equipment?

Yes / No

Note: Items might explode. There are no guarantees. Upgrade costs fluctuate via market rates.

Nacho chose the 'no' option, as that was a trap. At least… something inside him was telling him to wait. Reuben laughed and tiredly called to the others, "Did you know that we thought he was insane when he first started obsessing over knives? To be fair, we didn't know the world was about to end. Look at him now, using knives and making them as strong as a claymore!"

The cook was focused on his other boosts. Frankly… the Tier two Cooking Magic enhancement was disappointing. He did care that his food wasn't always tasty. The important part was that it helped people, and he'd hoped that he would've been able to find something that would allow him to more easily stack *three* foods together, so he could increase people's stats by an utterly massive amount.

Now he would need to put in effort to learn how to *properly* cook, in order to make higher rarity foods with less effort.

At least his Baby Birding would allow him to eat more, faster, but how much could he shove down his gullet? There was no way to test that skill, given that they were in the Starvation Dungeon. Third, and most exciting to him, was that Ingredient Processing had taken on a distinct combat-oriented aspect. He could remove Putrid Mana from live monsters, and that would cause them damage? Nacho *loved* the idea of starting to prepare the meat while the monsters were alive. It would speed up killing them, draining them, and once they were dead: cooking them.

Dead last, both in order and in value as far as he was concerned: the Feasting Feats enhancement. Smell? Aesthetics? Who cared about that when you were trying to stay alive?

"Look at it like this." Reuben had a different opinion, and he wasn't going to leave it alone until he had his say. "You add a little bit of allure to your feasts, I turn up my Marketing Skill, and we can really attract people to our guild. We'll be able to bring them in from hundreds of miles around, and you'll be able to feed all of them with a flick of the wrist."

Nacho could only force a smile and a nod, then finally looked away to upgrade his HungerCry Knives. All that mattered right now was his damage output, and the last fight had proven that he didn't have nearly enough.

. . .

Wow, Cookie! You've come so far, and so have your HungerCry Knives. As you know, they are special objects; they can be upgraded for money, with no risk!

Let's review what these special knives can do!

- *Get 50% more of everything you chop!*
- *Chop things twice as fast! You use this in Active Combat, and it's why you get four attacks. You should use it more during Active Cooking. You are a cook, after all.*
- *Cut through the Mana barrier of any monster one Tier higher than your current level.*
- *The Tier 1 WarCry enchantment doubles your base damage, so your knives hit like swords.*

With that nice little reminder, here's a list of the Tier 2 abilities that can be yours if the price is right. Note: You can only choose from this list:

Silent Cut (500 credits)—Chop things 75% quieter.

Bountiful Beauty (500 credits)—Improve your Increased Yield to 75%

Hunger Dance (1000 credits)—You know those Japanese restaurants where you can watch the chef cook? This is like that, only when people watch you use your knives during Active Combat or Active Cooking, they become ravenous. This will make onlookers very hungry, directly reducing their Hunger Points by a certain percentage.

Knife Blind (1000 credits)—33% chance of blinding your opponents for 30 seconds because of the beauty of your knifework. If you have chopped an onion in the last hour, this improves to 66% for 60 seconds upon activation.

. . .

Garlic Crusher (1000 credits)—Peel 100% of your garlic bulbs in seconds by using the 'crush' method. Never run out of garlic. Ever.

Forever Sharp (2000 credits)—The HungerCry knives will automatically sharpen any knives around them to match their degree of sharpness.

Nacho immediately knew which one he'd try. It was a long shot, but he figured he'd give it a try. Most of the time, the Patrons hated anyone trying to mess with the rules in their favor, but in this case, the cook thought he might have a chance.

CHAPTER THIRTY-SIX

They ran to catch up to the group, and Nacho called for everyone to stop. A few of them were so tired that simply standing still was enough to make them collapse to the ground, barely awake. "Put all your swords, daggers, pocket knives—anything with a blade—down on the ground. I'm going to try something."

Brie was the first to move, though all she had was a tiny dagger. Jennifer produced various little knives she used for cutting up the ingredients she put into her drinks. Taye set out his backup dagger, and soon the pile was fairly substantial. Seeing everything was ready for him, Nacho laid the Cry Chef's Knife onto the counter, and held the Hunger Cleaver in the air. He slammed the cleaver down, choosing to use his Razor-Sharp Wit enhancement on it, boosting the base damage by ten, along with an extra twenty-nine because of the level of his Small Blades ability.

Nacho quickly bought the Tier two Forever Sharp enhancement and added it to his knives. The Hunger Cleaver flashed... as did the Cry Knife! Flakes of metal fell from all the other blades in the pile. "Did it-"

. . .

Clever for yourself, Cookie, but ultimately futile for the others. The Forever Sharp enhancement has been added to the Cry Chef's Knife, complete with the Razor-Sharp Wit bonus. You might even call it the Forever Razor-Sharp Wit boost. Both blades are supernaturally sharp, and those other knives will never get dull again, but the fact is: they aren't ancient artifacts of saucy slicing. No juicy damage bonus for them!

Stephen picked up his huge two-handed sword and swung it around. "Uh, I think it feels sharper? I guess I won't know until I hit something with it."

Even though his experiment had failed to help his team very much, Nacho was feeling good. He now had *two* weapons that could deal as much damage as Mr. Lacrosse Stick.

Nacho quickly described the results of his upgrade to the rest of the Snack Attack, but Brie merely closed her eyes and shook her head. "Nacho… we don't have time for all this. It's at *least* another hour to the Stove. We're going to get hit with the Starvation Debuff."

The cook was suddenly completely somber, staring into the haggard faces of his friends as he remembered the situation they were in. They were stuck on an endless countertop, probably halfway between the sink and the stove. Taye got a wistful look on his young face. "The Patrons created this entire pocket dimension, every aspect of the Starvation Dungeon. They planned this. They made this place so enormous that they could keep us walking for hours on end, so we'd start taking Starvation Debuffs. They *want* us to get to the Dining Room Table on the edge of death."

"We can't eat," Nacho reminded them as everyone started running. "No matter *what*."

"Zero-sum game," Kristie breathlessly called out between massive strides. "I hate those. I *like* it when everyone can win."

"That just isn't natural, kiddo," Abby grunted in reply, "It's not enough for some people to win. Some people can only feel like they've won if someone else loses. Sad but true."

Nacho had a couple of more things to do, remembering that an effect of his boots had unlocked, now that he was level twenty. He took a look, only to have tiny fireworks explode above his head.

Congratulations, Nacho! You've hit Level 20 and discovered the secret of your boots! Fill your boots with gravy, then fling that gravy with deadly results! Yes, you can kick your enemies to death up close or from a distance! Both attacks are valid, and both will include a deadly gravy spray! You'll deal twice your class level in gravy damage. To use, you must first fill your gravy boats with Store Gravy based on your level, or maybe you'll find a recipe to make scalding hot gravy on your own!

Note: Your boots have been automatically upgraded to Tier 2. Any piece of the Sunday Brunch Armor exposed to—and coated in—the gravy from the Gravy Boots will enjoy protection from destruction while upgrading!

Nacho browsed the Store while they moved, easily finding the military-grade gravy from the Store. He bought the Epic rarity version from the Store and loaded the Tier two class item into the tubes on the side of the boots, finally realizing what they were for. Moments later, he felt the hot gravy soak into his socks and warm his feet. It actually felt... good, if slightly stomach-churning. "Where was this when we fought our way through the freezer?"

He took a minute to practice flinging gravy, twisting his back heel and loading the little cups on top of his feet. Nacho then kicked the gravy out, and a wave of brown went gushing across the countertop; leaving wood that smoked and **sizzled**. If he dealt twice his level in damage, that meant just the gravy attack alone would hit for forty Health Points. He'd only get one kick per can of the sauce, but it was a nice little sneak attack.

Stripping off the Sunday Brunch Armor, he stopped

completely and set it out on the counter as the rest of his team continued running. He kicked gravy out of his boots onto the various pieces, getting at least two cups out of each boot. He felt… very silly.

He watched as the gravy cooled on his Helm of Boiling, Skillet of Turtling, Wok of Blocking, Pauldrons of Frying, and Gauntlets of Oven Taming. It took a few interminable seconds for the gravy to cool off enough to touch, and he smeared the fragrant juice across every surface. In one moment, he almost instinctively licked his finger, but he froze in horror with the digit almost in his mouth. "No. Eating."

Choosing to pay the exorbitant fee to upgrade his gear, Nacho winced in expectation of an explosion.

Like your armor, Cookie? We do too! We like a cook in heavy metal, but you aren't a cook anymore. You are a Subpar Sous Chef. Keep that gravy on, and let it do its magic. We'll work on getting your armor to Tier 2.

Trust us.

What could go wrong?

Nacho glowered at his gear. He would never trust the Patrons.

However, his team was getting further away with each passing second. He strapped everything back on, feeling super gross. He didn't just smell like old Resent-o-potamus meat; now he was covered in a layer of greasy meat sauce. Sighing at what his life had turned into, he bought more of the magical gravy and re-loaded his boots.

Sighing in mild disgust, he tested out his full thirty points in every characteristic, hurtling toward his team so fast that a normal person would have had their skin distended from the G-forces he was generating. Each step was a leap, every leap was a ballista bolt being released. In only a few moments, he was not only past his friends; he was in front of them and needing to slow down.

Taye sniffed the air, eyed the cook, and decided against saying anything. By the time they reached the Stove, they only had a half an hour before the Starvation Debuff would go into effect. In thirty minutes, they would start losing a Hunger Point every minute until they went negative. Most of the Snack Attack would have an hour and forty minutes of life from that moment on, but Brie, Abby, and Taye were literally *and* figuratively on the chopping block, with only an hour and ten minutes before they permanently collapsed.

Using his speed, he rushed forward to survey the landscape in front of them and choose a path. There were nine burners in all—three rows of three. The middle row was completely black, but Nacho could faintly see a glow of red swirling heating elements underneath the glass. A moment later, he could see it even better: that red glow was getting brighter. Even from here, the cook could feel the heat, and it was quickly growing uncomfortable.

To his ever-increasing annoyance, Nacho was both gravy-coated and sweaty.

Both the front row and the back row were gas burners, but they were off. For now. Six aluminum-foil covered pans occupied the dormant front and back burners. They looked *so* familiar, but Nacho couldn't quite place them. Brie pointed with her lacrosse stick. "I don't see any controls, and I don't like those pans and that aluminum foil. What are they?"

"Jiffy Pop!" Abby called loudly and happily. "That's popcorn in there, and… well, I'm betting some monsters as well. We have to get across the burners, but I don't know how. I guess maybe we should try walking down the front or the back? Brie's right. I don't see the controls; Patrons musta learned from the sink."

Stephen marched forward, headed toward the back row of gas burners with the covered pans there. "Let's just see what happens."

Before they could stop him, the red-armored Body Player

approached the first pan, and gas exploded with blue fire both in the front and the back.

Stephen was thrown back, and he lifted his wrist, displaying a nasty burn that covered him from finger to elbow. Even his hair was smoldering a bit.

Hello, Players! It's Active Combat again! There won't be Store access, and you won't get your Regens. You just might get a hot, greasy treat! Or something cold and somewhat moldy. Scratch-Bite is mad that you killed his Grease Slime friends, so we're giving him a speed boost until he catches up! Better hurry; we're pretty sure you are all getting hungry, and that's <u>not</u> the way to make your future delicious!

Nacho felt the big guy's Positive Vibes give him a nice, cozy glow. Everyone else felt it too, going by the way their skin illuminated. The cook turned back to discover the Godking of Scrub Sponges skating toward them, only with each step, it was squirting water, enabling it to slip and slide across the countertop.

The sink had clearly overflowed, because a good portion of the counter was wet. In the distance, Nacho could hear water hitting the floor. Soon the sound of the overflowing waterfall was eclipsed by the popcorn heating in the first two Jiffy Pop pans, one on his left and one on his right.

Pop!

Pop!

With every explosion that could make a hardened artilleryman grin, the aluminum-foil expanded a little further. It took mere moments for the entire place to smell like a movie theater as a mist of hot buttered popcorn blew in on the wind.

Nacho crept forward and cursed Uber his breath when he spotted the controls embedded in the glass of that treacherous central electric stove lane. To his surprise, there was a diagram explaining how to turn on the front and back burner, which would turn off the central burner. But… the read-out was marked by a single exclamation point burning a cheery crimson.

He understood the diabolical nature of the trap: Stephen had accidentally attempted to circumnavigate the System by deviating from the path. That set off the gas burners, and now the heat blazing across that first burner would kill them if they tried to cross. The same could be said about the gas burners in the front and back row.

Stephen hadn't known what he was doing, and Nacho tried not to hold it against him… but the man might've just killed them all.

CHAPTER THIRTY-SEVEN

Nacho stood sweating in front of the giant electric stove that continued to glow red-hot. To his right and left, the gas burners spewed bright blue flames. The situation seemed utterly hopeless; at least if they hoped to get past this without getting burned to *near* death, at the very least.

Kristie was the only one to put forward an idea. "Scratch-Bite! That sponge is going to be releasing torrents of water. If we can kill it, or at least use it, I think we can use the body to cross the burner."

"Good thinking! I think I figured out the rest of the traps." Reuben had to yell to be heard over the sound of the popcorn popping, but he was clearly putting his years of gaming to good use. Before he could explain further, both of the back rows of aluminum foil that had formed a big bulging dome blew open, and butter fell like rain. Popcorn followed; huge kernels landing with as much force as individual boulders in an avalanche.

Some rolled into the burner and caught on fire, but the blue flame didn't destroy the fluffy kernels. Instead, it bound them together until a six-foot-tall gorilla-shaped creature emerged, made of blue fire and popcorn, each fused segment bigger than a basketball.

Lesser Orville FireCorn
Effective Tier/Level:?
Health:?

Based on the falling popcorn, and how more falling kernels were already attaching to the strange amalgamation, Nacho didn't think the Orville FireCorn would stay Tier zero for long. The Jiffy Pop pan on the front burner exploded, and moments later, another Orville FireCorn rumbled to life. As one, both monsters strode forward on their long popcorn legs. The cook considered adding his Prep-Work enhancement to his Ingredient Processing ability, stopping himself only because it would cost five percent of his Hunger Points.

This close to getting the starvation debuff, losing even one point of Hunger was a bad idea. Beyond that, he had to face the Godking of Scrub Sponges. Now that he was Tier two, his knives were guaranteed to be able to exact damage on the beast, and he was excited to see how quickly he could topple the sopping Boss with his Forever Razor-Sharp Wit HungerCry Knives.

The two Jiffy Pop pans kept on exploding, throwing popcorn and creating monsters. The first Tier one Orville enhanced itself by gathering more kernels and adding flaming clubs to its hands. Brie blitzed forward and engaged one with Mr. Lacrosse Stick, while Abby mauled another.

Scratch-Bite roared triumphantly as it swept up behind them, interrupted as Jennifer hurled skewers that **thunked** into its body. Three hit the beast, one after another. Normally, between the base weapon damage and her bonus twenty-nine from her throwing skill, she would only deal fifty-four damage.

But between all boosts, as well as the stacking damage, those three skewers landed for two hundred and fifty-two.

The Tier three was *chunked*, instantly losing a quarter of its health, and Jennifer had three skewers remaining.

Nacho rushed to help her, a grin spreading on his lips. His tongue flicked out, proof of his utter concentration as he rushed a powerful enemy that he knew he could kill.

The two Jiffy Pop pans belched out a fresh blast of popcorn, but these kernels weren't the pristine white the others had been. They were golden brown, mingling with other half-burned kernels to form four more Orville FireCorns, all burning with the same distracting bright blue flame. They gripped unpopped kernels and flung them at Nacho, only for Hazel to intercept them with her spike wall.

Taye's shout reached Nacho's ears as the cook closed in on the sponge. "These four new monsters are still Tier one, but they have a lot of health! Hurry; the poppin' ain't stoppin'!"

Nacho understood that this stove scenario was very similar to the freezer. The longer they tarried, the more powerful the creatures would become. They'd soon be facing *eight* Tier two Orville FireCorns, then sixteen Tier threes. If they were still around by then, it would be as corpses.

Scratch-Bite wasn't standing idle, waiting for them to beat on it. Dozens of its s smaller mouths coughed up gobs of acid spew that **sizzled** through Nacho's gravy-smeared armor and onto his thigh: somehow failing to hurt him. It seemed the Juxtaposition was not done surprising them today.

His upgraded armor had reduced the damage nicely, but a strange feeling of sturdiness and dependability welled up from the human as his Mana finally settled from his recent breakthrough. Nacho got to experience the effect of his Mana-boosted Tier-based aura before he ever got to read over it, watching curiously as the mouth that had spewed the acid received a deep laceration, as though he had personally slashed its face.

. . .

Health remaining: 70/70! Acid damage mitigated.

Tier 2 aura effect determined: Your Mana thickens, becoming dense and harder to penetrate. It now takes a blow dealing at least 20% of your total health to inflict Health Point damage. At the same time, your Mana has gained some of your spiteful will! When you are attacked, if the damage is not high enough to break your damage mitigation threshold, the strike is returned to the attacker as slashing damage that will stick even if it isn't enough to otherwise injure your attacker.

Leaping into action, Nacho brandished both of his supernaturally sharp Tier two knives, slashing with his chef's knife and chopping with his cleaver. He struck the Godking of Scrub Sponges four times, generating very satisfying results.

Damage Dealt: 644/1000.

After a quick calculation of how much damage he knew Jennifer should have been doing, Nacho felt a thrill at the realization that he had hacked off over a third of its health in one go, and a glance at his combat logs revealed that he had dealt three hundred and ninety-two damage in total.

The Brewer threw her last three skewers in a single Skill-determined burst, the stacking damage of the skewers causing more damage with each skewer that landed. "It has less than fifty health left! Finish it!"

An oily tongue darted out of its fanged mouth and wrapped itself around Nacho's arm. The tongue went right through his Mama barrier to sear his arm, dealing twenty damage every other second. Nacho couldn't help but drop his chef's knife as his arm was shaken, and every one of the mouths not occupied by holding him spat acid in every direction.

. . .

Health Remaining: 50/70!
Health Remaining: 30/70!

He was dragged into the teeth for another mess of damage, his armor only able to rebuff *most* of the teeth.

Health Remaining: 5/70! Caution: death is imminent! You should eat something and get out of this situation!

Jennifer was out of skewers, and she scrambled to grab them, only for Scratch-Bite to **slap** her with a mighty blow of scratchy green claws, flinging her backward. Nacho was a bloody mess… until he felt a hug wrap around him, and he was instantly restored to full health; the tongue was even pushed out of his arm where it had dug in. The Healer whooped, "Ninety-five health per awkward remote embrace!"

Nacho had dropped his knife, but he had retained his cleaver—and it *loved* to cleave. Nacho whacked the tongue once, cleanly severing it.

Damage Dealt: 994/1000

Scratch-Bite let out a whimpering, pain-filled mewl, then bent and tried to gulp Nacho down in one bite. The cook found himself trapped in the mouth of the thing as teeth closed down on him. The fangs slammed around Nacho like a hydraulic press, and he thought he'd be bitten in two.

Health Remaining: 20/70!

. . .

"Not dead… yet." The Sponge Godking roared in blind fury at Nacho's taunt, opening its mouth to chomp down on him again. "I'm *no one's* hors d'oeuvre!"

Reuben tackled Nacho out of the way as the teeth snapped together. Nacho felt a warm glow fill him, but his face sank. He had been gifted twenty Health because of Reuben's Silver Lining ability, but that meant that his friend was getting chewed on.

The Godking of Scrub Sponges was at single-digits Health, and it looked it. Its tongue had been cut off, multiple slashes marred its dirty yellow body, and six skewers poked out of its flopping midsection.

Nacho flipped to his feet, grabbed his chef's knife and **clanged** the blades together to make sure Scratch-Bite only had eyes for him—and it had so *many* eyes.

"Follow me, you used-up dishrag!" he yelled at the beast. He wasn't sure if it could understand him, or if it was simply following its aggro attacking patterns, but Nacho was able to lead the Godking of Scrub Sponges over the burned popcorn bodies of the fallen Orvilles, closer and ever-closer to the heat of the electric stove top.

Nacho flung off his gravy-coated Gauntlets of Oven Taming, then jumped and slipped the mitts over his feet to skate across the deadly-hot surface. The Sponge Godking lumbered after him, lurching to a halt and looking down to see its yellow sponge feet burning. All its many, many eyes rolled around in their spongy eye-sockets. With an agonized shriek, it fell forward, losing its last six health to heat damage.

Congratulations! You have killed Scratch-Bite, the Godking of Scrub Sponges.

Tier 3 Epic Creature = 0 Credits

Do you smell that? It's the smell of victory! Victory has often smelled like burning, but this one feels distinct for some reason.

. . .

Scratch-Bite fell face first onto the stove and immediately started cooking. It didn't smell like victory; the stench was of a bacteria-riddled sponge superheating.

Thick smoke boiled out of the top of the Jiffy Pop aluminum domes. The popcorn that blew out next was charred black, forming eight Tier two Greater Orville FireCorns. These new monsters were eight feet tall and covered in the same blue flames. Not a single person even attempted to distract them, and Jennifer was the first across the sponge bridge.

Nacho couldn't slow down for people to catch up; he needed to get to the controls in the middle row of the black glass, surrounded on all sides by red-hot glowing coils. Now that he knew where to go, it was simple to turn off the central electric burner by stamping his foot on the power logo. The moment his foot hit, the gas burners on either side of him clicked on, and the butter at the bottom of the silver pans began to sizzle.

"Great, I can turn off the electric stove, but that turns on the gas burners?" Nacho shook his head at the rank unfairness of this place as he ran for his life.

The others were scrambling over the kitchen sponge, Brie and Reuben bringing up the rear. A Tier two burned FireCorn snapped a butter whip, cajoling another to throw its club—landing a blow on the back of Brie's head. She went down hard, and Reuben was forced to pause to heal her.

Stephen saw it, and pure determination set his face as he dashed past the couple and brandished his two-handed sword. "Go on! I'll buy you time!"

"No!" Nacho yelled at the fool. "I'm not losing anyone else!"

Stephen laughed maniacally, already blocking strikes one after another. "I knew this was a one-way trip for me the minute Steve bought it. Remember us as heroes, and *run*!"

Brie and Reuben were given just enough time to escape over the body of the Sponge Godking; by then, the central electric stove panel was already cooling. Nacho and the rest were able to safely run over the surface, and the Guild Leader slammed a foot down on the power icon of the final electric burner. The electricity blinked off as the gas ignited on the front and back set of burners, and he led the charge across the cooling electric burner.

It was a good fifteen-minute run to get to the cabinet. He glanced back to make sure the surviving Snack Attack fighters were following him, when his vision was assaulted with a System message.

Active Combat is over for now. You're still alive, so you can shop, and you can regenerate your Health and Mana. Looking a lil' hungry! You should probably find something to eat soon. Good luck with that.

No one said a word as they ran across the final stretch of countertop, Nacho reaching the little human-sized door in the end cabinet first and pulling it wide. Inside, complete darkness awaited them, though it smelled sweet. He sent his four remaining Firefly Potstickers inside as he took one final look around the room they were leaving. A door taller than Olympus Mons to his left, marked 'Dining Room', remained closed, but it would open in the same direction they were moving.

Nacho let his people enter the cabinet first, and he watched as the army of popcorn monsters—each varying levels of burned—charged across the countertop toward them. Wasting no time, as soon as the last human was safe, he leapt into the cabinet and slammed the door, locking it permanently closed.

Over the next few seconds, he could hear the grain golems roaring outside with impotent frustration.

Nacho exhaled Wd a deep sigh of relief and exhaustion as intense hunger hit him like a physical blow. The System threw him a terrible message that brought the soul-shattering taste of human flesh to his mouth unbidden.

. . .

We have some bad news! You've been hit with a Starvation Debuff! You will lose one Hunger Point per minute until you go negative—then your Health Regen will follow suit. After that, you'll die hungry. Your future won't be delicious, because you won't have a future. Better figure something out fast.

Nacho had one hundred Hunger Points. That gave him over two hours to live.

His eyes turned on his teammates. Taye was trembling, Brie's eyes were bulging, and Abby seemed appalled. At Nacho's best guess, they collectively had an hour to live, if nothing changed.

CHAPTER THIRTY-EIGHT

Nacho winced as the first hunger pangs of the Starvation Debuff twisted his guts. The smell inside the cabinet seemed tailor-made to enhance their discomfort: every last inch was crammed with a variety of candies. From knee-high Sweet Tarts to Reese's Peanut Butter Cups the size of tractor trailer tires, packages of Twix bars stacked like cordwood tempted the ravenous group as they picked their way through the sugary gloom. Entire bags of gummy bears had melted onto plates—surely ruining the dish—tossed next to sacks of off-brand Halloween candy.

Reuben grabbed his wife as soon as he could pry his arms off his own midsection. "Brie, how many Hunger Points do you have?"

"Sixty-one," the Berserker spoke nonchalantly, immediately changing the subject. "You know that every time I take damage, the System reminds me that I have Melee Munchies, but I can't use it until I'm within three hundred feet from the Feast Portal?"

Taye wasn't able to maintain his calm nearly as well. "Abby and I both have sixty-five Hunger Points left."

Reuben was completely silent, uncharacteristically not

making any kind of joke. They were literally counting down the minutes, with no plan in sight. In sixty-one minutes, Brie would lose vital percentages of her Health Points every minute.

Jennifer furrowed her brows. "I have a question about the Starvation Debuff. Can you use your Skill and go negative on purpose? I mean, what if Taye had five Hunger Points left and used his Eagle Aim?"

"Yes." Nacho wished he didn't know the answer to the question. "The System will let you go negative. In your scenario, Taye would have negative five Hunger Points, so he'd immediately start losing one-point-two-five percent of his Health Points. Since he has sixty Health, he'd only lose a fraction of Health Points, like point-seven-five or something."

"No eating," Brie commanded as they wound their way through the treat-cluttered shelves, "No matter what happens to *any* of us. We've come too far to lose now."

It took twenty minutes to get to the end of the candy cabinet at a dead sprint. Every five minutes, they'd get a message from the System about the Starvation Debuff. They finally reached another human-sized door on the other side of the cabinet, and Brie bashed it open—Mr. Lacrosse Stick at the ready. On the other side, dimly lit by flickering candlelight, lay a vast table of food. At the center was a turkey, though it could've easily been the carcass of a Tyrannosaurus rex roasted to a perfect golden brown.

The entire table was packed with food of all kinds, but mostly it resembled American feasting food: hams, turkeys, green bean casserole with the fried onions, a variety of potatoes and casseroles of all persuasions.

It truthfully wasn't that far from the cabinet to the table. They could probably run it in ten minutes if there was a path. Unfortunately, only open air hung between their position and the table itself. Worse, the floor was a mile straight down from where they were standing.

. . .

Starvation Debuff! You've lost another 5 Hunger Points, Cookie. You're at 75 Hunger Points. Better eat something quickly! Your future won't be delicious otherwise!

One glaring issue dominated this moment: namely, the fact that they were in a cabinet, and the table was in the center of the room. Monsters spilled into the room, hundreds if not thousands of the various creatures they had previously fought within the dungeon. One saving grace was that the monsters were milling idly about, seemingly confused at what to do next.

Nacho knew one thing for certain—they could get to the table across the floor, but there would be too many monsters to fight. "We have to create some kind of bridge… maybe we can use the Nerds Ropes I saw in there? We'd have to attach one end in the cabinet, and somehow get the other end to the table. I'm… not exactly sure how to do that."

"Oh! I know! C'mon!" Taye turned and ran back into the cabinet. "I was right! On the Nerds Rope package, I thought I saw something about a special prize, and look!"

Two boxes of Nerds Ropes were stacked on top of one another, not far from the mid-air exit. The words 'Special Prize' dominated the packaging, but the rest of the message was buried behind a pile of giant Kit Kat bars. Nacho pushed the heap aside to see what the special prize was, and he smiled as the words gave him a spark of hope. 'Miracle arrow inside! For when your Archer is determined to sacrifice hunger points and probably themself to save the day!'

Jennifer's laugh came out sharp. "Well, that's oddly specific and ominous."

"It doesn't matter." Taye wasn't smiling, but there was a fire in his eyes that hadn't been there a moment before. "Let's just push the box back to the door. The miracle arrow must work with the Nerds Ropes."

Nacho had the most Fitness, and he was able to push the

top box off the other one. Together, Jennifer, Taye, and Nacho shoved the Nerds Rope box across the floor.

Once they got it moving, it wasn't hard at all. Stopping near the door, Nacho flayed the packaging open with a flick of his knife. Everyone helped to lift out the lengthy Nerds rope coiled within, setting it carefully to the side. Nacho's Firefly Potstickers fluttered about inside the box until the cook saw a plastic package 'prize': an arrow and length of steel cable.

Nacho slid the package over to Taye and turned back to face the table. "Get that figured out."

"I... I just..." The kid was sweating and pale. "I've never been this hungry in my life. I can't believe how good these Nerds smell."

"I understand more than you could possibly believe." Reuben swallowed a mouthful of saliva and gestured into the distance. "I do have some good news. On the nearest corner of the table, there's a metal loop. I think the Patrons are finally giving us a break."

Nacho wasn't sure if they could trust that or not. He *did* know that if the Kronos had given them a gift, that same gift would be given to the CruxTerrans. The Patrons would want to keep things fair, so the betting couldn't be disputed. Kronos said the stakes were high, and the cook felt that all the way down to his soul.

Taye remained quiet as he went to the doorway and prepared the arrow. A slim silver cable connected to his arrow via a little hoop above the fletching. "It's a boomerang cable arrow. I got a System message about it. Eagle Aim to hit that loop... here goes ten Hunger Points."

Like Stephen, Taye was making the sacrifice play. He fired the arrow, and the cable spun out. It streaked down through the metal loop on the table and then came zooming back to them, only to be snatched out of the air by Brie, who held the other end of the silver cable so they wouldn't lose it.

Brie and Reuben attached the cable to the end of the Nerds

Rope, and then the entire crew took hold of the cable and pulled, stretching the Nerds Rope out of the candy cabinet.

Starvation Debuff! You've lost another 5 Hunger Points, Cookie. You're at 60 Hunger Points.

Which meant Brie only had twenty-six minutes left, and Taye… Taye was down to twenty minutes.

Nacho focused on pulling the Nerds Rope through the metal loop on the table. Jennifer moved a package of Twizzlers to make more room and found a metal loop hidden inside the cabinet; the weight of the rope dropped precipitously as soon as they began using it as intended. Every pulley they could manage to include would make the job that much easier.

The rope reached the table, Kristie secured both ends of the cable, and just like that, they had their bridge to the Dining Room of fate.

The Feast Portal had to be somewhere in the middle of all that food, and they needed to run for it. Nacho started directing people, "Brie and Taye should go first-"

"No. You and Jennifer should go first," Brie countered instantly. "You're our Tier twos, and you need to find that portal, not wait on us. No argument."

Nacho wasn't about to disagree with the Berserker—especially when she was correct. He looked down at the Nerds Rope. His first instinct was to crawl across the candy, but he needed to move, and move *now*. "Time to put these ridiculous stat points to good use."

Slicing open a ring pop candy, he smashed the candy portion and sprinted at the nerds rope with the plastic ring held above his head. He didn't look down, only jumped over the rope and used the split in the bottom portion of the ring to form a makeshift zipline. Having used his momentum to good effect, he clattered down the rope faster than he could have hoped to run, dangling underneath the sweet candy cable as he shot across the chasm.

Deciding against looking down and amping up his anxiety over hungry monsters watching him and hoping he would fall, Nacho surveyed the room instead, and his eyes took in a bittersweet sight. The CruxTerrans were in view. Nacho could see Arriod and his people standing in their corresponding little doorway on the opposite wall, but they hadn't created their bridge yet. "Finally, some good news."

Nacho made it to the table and swung himself up. A whole variety of giant, mouthwatering dishes confronted him with incredibly potent, enticing scents.

Congratulations, Cookie! You made it to the Dining Room Table first. You get a million credits! The game isn't over. The first player through the Feast Portal wins their World's First Round of the Juxtaposition! Good luck!

Nacho barely listened to the **cha-ching** of the credits hitting his account, not caring about them even one little bit in that moment. He spun to check on his people, relief flooding him at the sight of them following as quickly as they could. Jennifer led the way, followed by Brie, Taye, and Abby. Those three had to get over before they lost all their Hunger Points and passed out.

Nacho felt a wave of hunger hit him, and his knees buckled.

Starvation Debuff! You've lost another 5 Hunger Points, Cookie. You're at 50 Hunger Points. Better eat soon! Or your future won't be delicious!

Nacho unclenched his body, and saw something that made his blood run cold. One of Arriod's people *flew* through the air clutching a length of candy rope. He soared down and threaded it through the metal loop on the CruxTerran side of the table.

Arriod and his soldiers had a bridge of their own.

Their teleporter was making his way back across the gap, flashing through the air until he managed to get to the other side.

Arriod and his soldiers didn't crawl across their Nerds Rope. They *sprinted*. The teleporter and the flying guy ran for the big, roasted carcass of the main dish at the feast, drawing Nacho's attention to the purple Portal in the backside of the giant stuffed turkey. He'd found the Feast Portal—only about a quarter of a mile away—but so had the CruxTerrans. They would both need to run the same distance on an intersecting path to reach the portal, but only one person needed to get there in order to win.

Leaving his team behind in a flash of desperation, Nacho *ran* for all the worth he could get out of his stats, faster than any other human at his level… on the ground.

Even so, he could tell that the flying guy would get there first.

Nacho didn't exactly have a lot of ranged attack options, but he did have something new up his sleeve; or rather, near his pant leg. As their paths came closer together, he timed Mr. Wingsuit's trajectory and kicked out his foot right as the flying guy passed overhead. A wave of boiling gravy arced into the CruxTerran's flight path, and time seemed to pause as the System let him know that Active Combat had started.

The brown gravy splashed across the face of the highly-focused man, who let out a surprised yelp, falling to the ground in a splash of gravy and red-hot armor.

Damage Dealt: 40/60.

. . .

Nacho saw that the man only had twenty Health remaining, and he knew he could practically kill the downed CruxTerran with a thought. The flying guy struggled to get to his feet, nearly managing to straighten until an arrow **thudded** into his back. With a grunt, he fell face first onto the dining room table. Everything he'd stashed in his Storage Slots came spilling out, proving he was dead beyond a shadow of a doubt, and that Taye had earned the credits for the kill.

Before the cook could get excited about the small victory, the teleporter appeared about twenty feet in front of him. Apparently, he couldn't just *jump* to the Feast Portal, revealing that his range seemed to be limited. Still, he had a slight advantage.

Nacho chased after him, thundering between a quivering plate of canned cranberries and a massive tray of Stovetop stuffing. He felt a wave of gratitude at the familiar sensation of Reuben's Positive Vibes as his best friend helped from afar.

His Gravy Boot attack was all used up, so there was only one thing he could do. He snatched his Skillet of Turtling off his back, tacky with congealed gravy, and flung it like a vertical frisbee. "I cast *iron*!"

The skillet went spinning through the air, powered by his superhuman strength, and struck the teleporter in the back of the neck, sending him reeling into a plate of canned cranberry sauce.

Damage Dealt: 12/60.

Using a skillet as a weapon was only really effective as a means to knock someone over, but that was all Nacho needed. The teleporter tried to regain his feet, but he slipped on the gelatinous cranberry sauce and fell onto his back.

The cook didn't bother finishing him off, scooping up his skillet and attaching it to his back as he continued running toward the Portal that was still probably about a football field away. The popping purple light of the Feast Portal filled the air with a tantalizing roasted turkey scent that any good marketing agent would desperately want the rights for. His stomach ground out a fresh wail of protest as the teleporter appeared right behind Nacho and pulled him down with a lasso.

His legs were exposed, and the teleporter had tangled his ankles with a scarlet energy whip, but the damage done was merely glancing.

Health Remaining: 70/70! Damage doesn't meet the threshold! Rebounding…!

Damage dealt: 12 slashing!

The CruxTerran screamed and turned to teleport as a bright line appeared on his face where Nacho's aura had returned the damage he would have taken. Nacho knew he couldn't let the man go: it might take a couple of jumps to get to the Portal, but he'd get there.

A glowing lacrosse ball struck the table nearby, sending both men flailing away as it detonated. Brie's attack had hurt Nacho, but he was still alive, even if slightly dazed. Following in the ball's wake, the Berserker sped toward Nacho with bare feet and shredded armor. Well, she'd always hated that armor anyway. His addled mind made him wonder what had happened, and he hoped he would get a chance to hear the story.

Nacho turned in time to see Arriod's katana slashing toward his stomach, almost in slow motion as adrenaline flooded his brain. A whirlwind of power swept around him, diverting the sword from giving Nacho an unwanted appendectomy.

Brie had used her Defensive Whirl to save Nacho's life, but now she had less than two minutes of positive Hunger remaining. She continued to run toward him, clearly hoping she could get close enough to the Portal to regain Hunger Points.

Arriod staggered back as his attack failed, but he pointed at Brie with his left hand and closed his fist. With that simple motion, she fell to the ground, sending Mr. Lacrosse Stick sliding across the table. The Berserker went pale and heaved for air. Nacho knew that look: she was starving.

Before he could follow up on his successful ambush, Arriod was sent staggering back as pink missiles and purple grenades began to rain down on his head. His was sizzling, but the Crux-Terran healed himself using his Paladin powers.

"That's fine. Just fine." Nacho unsheathed his cleaver and chef's knife. "I'm going to cut you into lots of little pieces all by myself."

"You can't hurt me," Arriod replied in such a calm tone that Nacho almost found himself believing his enemy.

"That's okay. I'll just practice cutting you until I *can* do it." Nacho sank into a predator's stance and stalked toward the Paladin. "Then I'll practice chopping your severed limbs up until I can get the meat cubes *ju~ust* right. Practice makes better."

Something in the cook's eyes must have unnerved the Crux-Terran, because he didn't waste another second on grandstanding. He made another fist motion at Nacho, and the cook doubled over as he suffered through a pain in his stomach. A new message, one he'd never seen before, flashed through his mind.

Warning, Player! You have lost 20 Hunger Points due to Arriod's Hunger Strike!

Damage done, and leaving Nacho trying to recover from the twisting pain in his gut, Arriod sprinted toward the Feast Portal.

CHAPTER THIRTY-NINE

There was one thing that Arriod had not been expecting: Nacho wasn't the kind of person who would let a little bit of pain stop him from fulfilling his goals. While Nacho wasn't entirely certain what it translated to, the fact that he had significantly higher stats than any other person around meant that the cook could move at incredible speeds with incredible endurance.

It took but a moment for his cleaver to swing down in a strike from upper left to lower right, his intent clear; if the blow landed, Nacho would directly cut the Paladin in half. Arriod was no slouch himself, and the prickling in his neck that warned him of imminent danger saved his life as he turned and blocked the heavy blow with his sword. With grim satisfaction, Nacho watched the CruxTerran's eyes widen even through his ubiquitous sunglasses; clearly the man had not thought that a simple chef could muster such raw physical force without even using a Skill.

Completely knocked off course, Arriod lost a little ground as Nacho sped forward. The cook knew that he did not have to defeat his opponent in battle; he simply needed to win the race to the Portal. An instant later, it was his turn to dive for safety as a ghostly image of Arriod's katana flew through the air where he would have been. Nacho turned as his opponent caught up to him, bringing both of his kitchen knives forward in an 'X' pattern to catch the overhead blow of the lethal blade.

"I can use that a few more times, easily." Arriod's threat was a deadpan, sincere promise. "You may be able to get ahead of me a little bit, but as soon as you turn your back on me again, I will cut you in half."

"Well then, I guess I'll just need to make sure that you can't move your arms. You know what? While we're at it, let's just remove you as a threat entirely." With no further warning, the former Assassin sent his chef's knife slithering through the air, sending sparks flying wherever it nicked the katana. The Paladin was barely able to move to the side before his neck would have been sliced open. "I'm no expert on CrossHuman physiology, but something tells me your blood flows pretty similarly to ours. Let's find out!"

"We're CruxTerrans!" Arriod growled, then flinched involuntarily as his opponent began to *move*.

Using his raw physicality, Nacho darted forward, slamming his blades one after another into the Paladin. The speed was so great that he was absolutely *certain* he would be cutting the man down in no time, but then it was his turn to be surprised by the defensive skills his enemy could bring to bear. A Paladin specialized in dealing damage and healing damage that their bodies took, so even when Arriod could not block a knife blow perfectly, the damage was fixed moments later, if it was enough damage that it required attention.

Three seconds after their first engagement, having exchanged seven attacks, the two leaders of their respective groups disengaged and took a short leap backward to reset their stances. Nacho was positioned with the Portal behind him, and he was able to watch as his allies fought their own battles.

Taye was facing off against the CruxTerran teleporter, sending arrows flying at incredible speed wherever the man popped into existence, only for his target to vanish before the attack could land. It seemed that the teleporter had a minimum distance that he could travel in an instant, because there were times where he moved backwards in order to blink forward and appear close by the Archer. I'm those moments, Taye proved that he wasn't a one-hit wonder. His backup weapon, a dagger that Nacho had sharpened, swung out in an attempt to fend off the melee range attack, and he used the hardened wood of his bow to block the short sword his opponent was using against him.

After each deterred strike, the CruxTerran would vanish once more, appearing far enough away that Taye would fire an arrow his way moments later. Brie was holding her own against a full three opponents, even though she was unable to bring her Skills to bear against them due to the starvation debuff and how close she was to going negative in their Hunger Points. Nacho realized that the debuff must be an issue that was affecting more than just his own people, as any Skill use was accompanied by a magical effect, not the standard extra damage or faster movement that came with physical-style abilities.

Of course, this meant that Kristie was having a blast. More specifically, she was *blasting* whoever she was targeting with purple grenade after purple grenade, sending magical shrapnel, wood slivers from the slowly destroyed tabletop, and even some discarded weapons flying with each detonation. No one could seem to get close to her, protected as she was by both Brie and Reuben, but the close-quarters fighting that the rest of her team was engaging in also meant that she could not use her best spell and send out a nova of pinkish-purple bolts.

The cook was fairly certain that if their enemies grouped up even once, she would be able to take all of them out with a single detonation. Before he could do more than run his eyes over the situation, Arriod had shot forward with a massive burst of speed, his katana dragging along the table and leaving a groove in the beautiful wood before swinging into an uppercut that would have bisected Nacho if he hadn't moved, and likewise would have stabbed him in the face if he had merely dodged backwards a little. Instead, Nacho leaped forward and over the blade's arc, barely able to stay ahead of the deadly edge as it came up toward him.

Arriod followed through on the attack, bringing his katana in a full three hundred and sixty degree rotation, but Nacho had sprung directly backwards as soon as his feet were planted on the ground, and the blade passed him harmlessly as he got too close to his enemy's arms for the blade to impact him. Tossing his chef's knife in the air, he reached backwards and grabbed his skillet. Iron handle in hand, he swung the much wider weapon down on Arriod's hands as the blade of the katana passed him again, smashing it into the hilt and guard of the weapon before swinging it to his back and catching the falling chef's knife.

The unexpected shock sent the longer ranged weapon clattering across the floor, and Nacho followed it up by planting a boot in Arriod's side. The man toppled over, though he used his momentum to swing back to his feet and scrabble for his weapon. He looked up, expecting a follow-up attack, only to see Nacho once again sprinting at the portal, which was so close, so *tantalizing.* If he had looked back over his shoulder, Nacho would have seen the rage and fear that crossed the CruxTerran leader's face at that moment. "*No*! I refuse to lose; not after all of this!"

Repositioning his katana, Arriod swung it and once more sent out a ghostly copy of his blade, this one spinning slightly as it flew through the air. It listed lightly and lazily to the left, the direction that Nacho had dodged previously. The cook spotted the approaching phantom blade over his shoulder and only had a moment to react. He collapsed to the floor entirely, fully arresting all of his momentum but managing to escape what would have been an otherwise sudden and messy death.

The portal was only ten strides away, but there was no way that he was going to be able to make a move toward it without leaving himself completely exposed to the ghostly metal that was whistling through the air toward him even now. Playing defensively, the cook searched desperately for another opportunity to hold off his opponent, but Arriod was wise to his tricks now and knew that Nacho would use any excuse to make a break for it instead of ending things here and now.

Arriod attempted to circle around Nacho, but the cook countered it by simply backing up closer and closer to the Portal. Even so, both of them were in a position to observe what was happening among their teams when a sudden scream of agony shattered the literally delicious air. Taye had finally managed to figure out the movement patterns of the teleporting CruxTerran and put a shaft through his left shoulder. "You *shot* me! You filthy round-pupil alien!"

Each person was focused on their individual battles, and each of them had been creating their own battle rhythm. When the furious teleporter unexpectedly appeared directly behind Reuben, no one was in a position or mental place to stop him from slamming his short sword into the Healer's back.

Time froze for Nacho as he watched items appear around Reuben, a sure sign that his Storage Slots were collapsing due to his death.

Then he realized that time actually *was* frozen.

Only Brie was moving, but it wasn't her body. Strange, iridescent energy was flowing off of her, as what Nacho could only assume was her Patron-given boon was activated. Her voice shook the air as she called out pleadingly, "Rejection of death, one free life, given freely to one whose fate is bound to mine, my husband: Reuben Colby! *Please* work…!"

Her voice broke in a heartrending sob as the energy flowed from her and into Reuben, dragging his items back into their extra dimensional space in passing. When the last mote of energy had dissipated, time resumed as Reuben spun around and planted his fist in the absolutely shocked CruxTerran's face.

The enemy dropped to the ground, rolling twice before coming to a boneless stop. Kristie fired a purple grenade at the man to finish him off, but one of his allies appeared next to the fallen teleporter and slammed his shield forward, causing the grenade to rebound and fly back at Kristy ten times faster than it had traveled originally. She screamed and dove out of the way, and the energy grenade flew faster than a Ballista Bolt… directly toward the portal.

Directly at Arriod.

Just before impact, the condensed energy detonated. It had never been meant to exist for so long, so the total output was much lower than expected, but it was still enough for the shock-wave to toss both Nacho and Arriod off of the ground and send them cartwheeling through the shifting light of the Portal.

CHAPTER FORTY

The cook blinked as he stared in shock around the empty space where he and Arriod had appeared. An instant later, Johnny Meat arrived, and Nacho began to despair. If the Crux Terran's Patron had arrived, that meant-

His concerns turned into confusion as Kronos also materialized next to him, the pair of mortals and Patrons staring each other down. Johnny was the first to speak. "Well, ain't this a pickle."

"They went through at the *exact* same time. How long has it been since this happened?" Kronos chuckled quietly as Johnny counted up on his fingers. Nacho noticed that every time he used his fingers to count, another finger would appear on his hand.

"If I am recalling correctly, it's been eighteen thousand, seven hundred and twenty-one iterations since the last time this happened," Johnny muttered with an unhappy scowl. " Your boy there sure packs a punch. You sure you weren't cheating?"

"You saw everything just like I did, and so did *they*." Weighty stress hung on that last word, as Kronos waved his hand into the darkness around them. No matter how hard Nacho tried, he could not see anyone else, and he had to assume that was for the best. These Patrons were not known for their kindness and cheery attitudes. They were known for callously gambling with life and doing terrible things to civilizations on a whim. It was best if he didn't see their faces, as some of them would likely have taken offense to his involuntary response to their presence. In fact, he stopped trying to look and focused all of his attention on the issue at hand. "You know what this means, right?"

"Sudden death," Johnny Meat stated grimly, even though his lips turned up in a slight smile at the thought. "If I recall correctly, the theme of this death match is 'home field advantage', correct?"

"Sure is." Kronos didn't sound quite as happy as he had a moment ago, and a wide grin was taking over the sullen expression on Johnny's face. "You want to explain, or should I?"

"Here's how it works, players." Johnny launched directly into an explanation without another word toward his peer. "All of the people that were in the dungeon with you are out and in stasis until your fight ends. Both of *you* are going to be restored to full Health, Mana, Hunger, and Thirst. At any given point during your fight, whoever has more current Health gets the home field advantage. That means that the fight will take place on their Starter World. Other people are not only able, but expected and *encouraged*, to help out their contestant."

"The very *instant* that one of you has more Health than the other, you will be relocated to some random landmark in your own World, near something that is significant to you. That could be people, a place, or even monsters. Whatever pops into your head might influence it, or it might not." Kronos took over the explanation, locking eyes with Nacho as he spoke, as if he were trying to impart as much unspoken meaning as possible. "There will be no warning; there will be no slowing or stopping. it will be a smooth transition, and all attacks will continue as they were. Abyss, you might only notice if you look around."

"You will physically be unable to retreat more than twenty feet away from each other. The fight continues until one of you is dead." Johnny stopped abruptly, earning himself a glare from Kronos.

"The fight is until death *or* submission." Kronos looked at Nacho with a hint of worry in his eyes. "If there is no escape, there is always hope where there is life."

"All rules are explained. The fight begins immediately." Johnny Meat snapped his fingers, and instantly, the two enemies were facing each other in a field with a strange-colored sky, pollen dancing around them, and the shouts of troops training in the distance.

"What the…?" Nacho glared at the Paladin standing across from him. "There is no way that you have more Health than me. We should absolutely be on my planet right now."

"Have you never heard of class bonuses? Items that give you extra health? Wait… you mean to tell me that you are working with only the amount of Health that your base characteristics give you?" Arriod attacked immediately, any smile on his face hidden by his cloth mask. "Excellent."

Nacho cartwheeled out of the way as a glowing afterimage of the sword blasted through the air to his left, avoiding the Skill, but unable to account for the Paladin's charge. The Crux-Terran had known that the cook needed to dodge to the right in order to avoid the Skill that would have otherwise been a one-hit kill. As soon as he had triggered it, he attacked, catching Nacho in mid-air with a vicious slash. Even though he blocked a good chunk of the blow between his own weapons and his armor, the cook took enough damage that it was able to pierce through his damage mitigation.

Health remaining: 51/70.

Landing roughly on the ground, Nacho used the momentum to roll backward into a handspring that sent him to the maximum distance that he could take from his opponent. He only discovered the limitation because as soon as he hit twenty feet, it felt as though he had stumbled into a wall, sliding down the open air as if a perfectly smooth physical object stood in the way. "Ow, and noted. Well, you know what? If the restrictions are off and everything is fair play, time for me to show you what a cook can do."

Running alongside the barrier that continued to move away as Arriod came toward him, Nacho pulled a Rare Resent-o-Potamus steak out of his meat-filled storage slot and started taking huge chomps, downing it as quickly as he could. He smiled when the familiar option for him to add a buff to one of his characteristics appeared, and he chose to boost his Fitness.

Instantly, his speed, health, and capability to deal damage rocketed upward. His maximum health increased to one hundred and two, and his Fitness was sitting at a behemoth forty-four points. Regardless, the terrain around them didn't change, which was a slight surprise to Nacho. Was this why the CruxTerran's Patron had been so confident in their ability to survive and win in the Starvation Dungeon? Did they just have a ridiculous amount of Health and capability to keep it high? The possibility existed, but all that did was summon a manic grin to his face. "Finally… someone I can really hone my skills against. I haven't been able to properly *practice* in ages."

Stopping his slow circling on a dime, Nacho whirled around and rocketed toward the CruxTerran, who could only flinch back in surprise and slightly angle his sword to defend himself before the cook was upon him. The cleaver chopped down, slamming the larger katana into its wielder and sending the Paladin skidding back across the ground. Before he could get his momentum under control, Nacho was in his personal space, plunging his chef's knife into an armored thigh.

Damage dealt: 47!

. . .

"Huh." Nacho felt a jolt of slight disappointment. "I was expecting a little bit more out of that. Also, it's a kind of annoying that the System isn't showing me your maximum health."

"Proper armor is worth the cost," Arriod spat out, reaching up and adjusting his sunglasses. That motion caused Nacho to realize that the light around them was different; they were on his planet.

"Looks like I'll just need to go ahead and form a hypothesis on your maximum health based on that amount of damage, and test it. Over and *over*." Nacho dashed forward, low to the ground, and swept Arriod off his feet with a rapid twist. Hefting his cleaver up over his head, he brought it down full force on the man in mid-air, the blade penetrating deeply as the force of the attack slammed the Paladin into the ground.

Arriod coughed and murmured something so softly that Nacho almost missed it. "Johnny, mend my meat!"

Red and gold fire flashed across his body, and the brand new wounds vanished. They were also transported to another strange location, this one somewhere on the alien world that was CruxTerra. Nacho **tsked** in disdain. "This place is so bizarre, you know that? Why is there so much pollen everywhere? Does *no one* on your world have allergies?"

Arriod used the moment that he was being healed to dash away using some kind of Skill, only stopping and facing the human once he had reached the maximum distance he could take. "We used to have citizens weak to the air itself. Most allergens are formed due to pollution, and after the world government took over and reduced the population by four fifths, we didn't need to worry about it so much. Our world healed itself, and we focused on sustaining and maintaining."

"Cool story, but you just called out the problem with people in power. They *have* power. That means that they are not invested in growing, in changing, and being better than they once were. They just want to *maintain* the power they took for themselves." Nacho shook his head sadly as he readied himself for the next round of combat. "No government that enjoys such firm control would *ever* offer an education, or allow access to the necessary resources, to progress past what they can control perfectly. That leads to a society of stagnation and eventual collapse."

There seemed to be very little common ground that these two men could stand on, so no more words needed to be spoken. The cook dashed forward, knives held akimbo as he prepared to butcher the man in front of him. Arriod had seemed to realize that he wasn't going to be able to win a close range battle, so he sent one ghostly slash followed by another hot on its heels. Even though he was forced to back away, Nacho didn't miss the look of relief that crossed the face of his target.

"A-one priority mission! Assassin on CruxTerra!" The Crux-Terran bellowed into the air. Nacho winced as the call was taken up by people around them, who had kept out of sight until that moment but began bustling through the underbrush in search of whoever had been shouting. "Looks like you just *lost-*"

The smug assertion was cut off mid-sentence, as Nacho brought his blades down and slammed both of them into the armored side. Just like that, they were standing on Earth once more, materializing in the center of the Armor Mountain fortress.

Now it was the cook's turn to call for help, but he was able to manage it a bit more forcefully. "Guild Leader command! All available combatants, attack this CruxTerran! For the good of the Chips Guild, for the sake of humanity, take him down!"

The order went out, activating the geas that all Guild members were placed under as soon as they signed a contract to join a guild. First a trickle, then a battalion of humans rushed out of their homes, shops, and resting areas, weapons in hand and bearing down on the duo.

"So this is what it's going to be like?" Arriod snarled,

preparing to send another ghostly sword slash at his counterpart.

"Hey, man, *you* were the one that tried to get your people involved first." Nacho could only shrug.

"Then let's see what kind of a leader you are." The ghostly strike went out, just to the side of the cook's position. "Either you take the hit, or that will cut through half a dozen of your people!"

Nacho simply watched as the attack passed him by, blasting through a trio of humans and sending gore fountaining into the air before impacting a wall. "Yeah… you picked the wrong guy to try to convince to make a sacrifice play. I need to win no matter what, and I *will*."

He wiped a splash of blood off his face and prowled toward the now-trembling alien that was trapped in his world.

CHAPTER FORTY-ONE

Nacho didn't need any tricks; he bull-rushed Arriod, hoping that he would be able to beat the man down with his strength combined with the sheer force of numbers that he was able to bring to bear. Even as the human leader attacked, other guild members were flooding into the area, some firing arrows or magical abilities ahead of themselves if they were fairly confident that they would not hit their Guild Leader. However, the CruxTerran wasn't about to take all of that damage quietly. In one of the most well-funded moves that Nacho had ever seen, Arriod produced a flat piece of metal and bent it in his hand.

In an instant, a curved metallic wall surrounded him on all sides, except for a small opening that faced the cook. It appeared to have been designed specifically for the leader of the CruxTerrans, as there was exactly as much room as he needed to swing his katana around within its confines while having an extremely effective defensive capability. Still, the metal was fairly thin and was already beginning to warp and buckle under the barrage of guild member attacks.

It didn't need to hold for long; it merely needed to buy

enough time for the UltraSoldier Commander to pull out yet *another* item that he pointed at Nacho. This one appeared to be an oversized wasp's stinger, and when the man activated it, it shot toward Nacho faster than even *he* could dodge, following him as he tried. "You're *dead*."

"Seriously? Does *everyone* have more magical items than I do? I'm kind of feeling like things were stacked against me from the start-"

11 damage taken!

His words cut off as the flying implement slammed into his left butt cheek, injecting some form of corrosive poison that seemed to be generating pain more than dealing damage. It was an effective distraction, but that didn't stop the experienced corner Assassin from keeping on the move. In a high-level fight, staying still was a death sentence.

He took a moment to marvel at the fact that his aura allowed him to scale his Health higher and would create a more effective barrier even based on the buffs that he had added. He wondered if the effect would still work if he equipped other items that boosted his total Health, like Arriod clearly did, or whether it was limited to personal increases in base stat scores. Nacho shook off the strange, intrusive thoughts, knowing they were nothing more than his mind trying to find an escape from the pain that he was currently feeling.

A glance around showed that they had once again been moved, landing in a place that the cook recognized. They were facing off in a burned out husk of a forest, with the portal between worlds hovering in the distance. Thanks to the smoke in the air, it could easily have been the earth side of the portal, but the sheer amount of pollen that remained after a forest fire of this scale was a clear indicator that they were on CruxTerra.

"Wait… how did *this* place burn down?" was all he could get out before his senses screamed to him that death was trying to lick his ear. Nacho tumbled to the side, turning it into a roll, into a cartwheel, and ending with a backflip before he felt he was safe enough to reposition for combat. Turning toward the threat, he had fully expected to see a katana buried where he had been standing. Instead, arms holding various weaponry had shot out of the ground and were within inches of grasping on to him. "Zombies? Why would there be zombies here? Unless-"

Then the phantom katana from at him, and he parried it with his knives. Arriod's sunglasses had slipped off of his face in the last few moments, and Nacho took the opportunity to study as much of the man's visage as he could. A piece of fabric remained pulled up over his mouth and nose. Instead of a hat, the CruxTerran's head was adorned with a simple metal circlet that was not quite a crown, and not quite a helmet. His hair had turned white, likely from stress, as it was not white all the way down to the roots. More than anything, at that moment, the Paladin looked like an overworked—albeit fit—office worker that was trying to roleplay as a ninja.

"Arriod!" Nacho didn't take the opportunity to slay his opponent, who was wide open after having his blade knocked to the side. "Look around! Something went terribly wrong here. You practically had an entire army stationed here, but where are they? There are zombies popping out of the ground-"

"So you humans launched a sneak attack." Arriod didn't seem even slightly concerned over the environment that they were fighting in, focusing instead on swinging his sword as fast and hard as he could at the cook, who repelled the attacks unconsciously and practically *casually*, thanks to his wildly enhanced stats. With over forty points in his Fitness stat, even if his opponent was at his same Tier—and his same level—unless he had taken the same stat distribution style, it was highly likely that Arriod was currently sitting nearly twenty points over his maximum *possible* Fitness.

Thanks to the years of practice and training that Nacho had in fighting humans, especially humans that were stronger than him, this battle felt like child's play to him. Yet, if there was one thing that Nacho did *not* want to see happen, it was turning such a powerful opponent into a corpse that could be gathered by Guild Master Nibbles and his Necromancer allies. He had seen what that would look like, and the idea of having to fight Arriod again when he was even better equipped, able to be healed at a distance, devoid of the ability to feel fear or pain, with endless stamina and endurance to fight… even if Nacho won immediately, he would just be empowering another enemy that would eventually come for his head.

"Stop. Listen to me. Right now we are surrounded on all sides by zombies, which means they most likely have alerted their necromancer to our location." Nacho shoved the CruxTerran away from him, deliberately not using his knives to prove his point. "If they get one of our bodies, that is going to cause a big issue for all of our people down the line, win or lose. I can tell you right now, they don't care if their spells are used on humans or CrossHumans-"

"CruxTerrans," Arriod growled at him seemingly without heeding the deep concern that Nacho felt for the situation.

"Yes, yes. A *special* name for your *special* people. Feel *better* now?" Nacho winced as he realized that he was being abrasive, and that was no way to get this man to listen to him. "My apologies; there is no reason to be rude. Frankly, I don't particularly want to have to kill you. I'm just *going* to do it."

"Agreed."

The cook would have it no other way, especially not with their literal entire world and race on the line. "Among the people that I am certain are watching is their leader; he goes by Guild Master Nibbles. I have information on him, practically *legendary* rumors, that say he will stop at nothing to kill or control everything in his path. The more he kills, the more fodder he has for his army. Something about him attracts other dark magic users, and by this point, he has collected at minimum several hundreds of necromancers and other people that want to use their abilities for… let's just say not the good of Humanity. Or whatever you call it."

"CruxPhylumology."

"You sure do love your one word answers, don't you?" Nacho rolled his eyes, realizing his mistake in taking his eyes off his opponent only because the man tried to use that opportunity to skewer him through the heart. "You aren't taking this seriously. I get it. Maybe *those* will convince you."

He jumped back a few feet, waving into the distance, where undead CruxTerrans were sprinting toward them in perfect formation. Dozens, then hundreds, hurtled toward them across the burnt forest, knocking over trees that were little more than charcoal and kicking up enough dust to hide their true numbers, even more effectively than the acrid smoke hanging in the air already had. In fact, the ash on the ground had done such an effective job of muffling their approach, the combatants' focus on each other and the swirling smoke in the air had obscured the zombies until their plentiful ranks were practically right on top of the combatants.

Both of them turned to defend themselves immediately, destroying the incoming wave of Tier zero and Tier one opponents that were leading the charge. Neither of them stepped forward to help the other; in fact, they often grabbed and flung one of the zombies at the other instead of striking it down in an attempt to knock the other off guard and lower their overall health.

"You humans really suck at all this," Arriod called over at Nacho as the cook spun in a circle, felling eight of the Fell corpses at once.

"Yeah, I don't really think so. I've seen some of your history," Nacho fired back as if they were having a casual conversation while sipping coffee instead of fighting for their lives against an unending horde of the living dead. "Your people are just much more warlike. We had advanced to the point of practically lounging around every single day. It was more common to have a job where we sat for most of the day and stared at a screen—the vast majority of our movement coming from wiggling our fingers—instead of going out and fighting each other or joining the military."

"How foolish. Was service to your people not mandatory?" Arriod already knew the answer, and continued before Nacho could reply. "Of course it wasn't. I was the first to cross over to your world months ago, and it was clear there were no repercussions from your government for failing to maintain your bodies and minds at the standard required for survival in any situation. How did *that* work out for your world?"

"Yeah, not going to lie, I'm pretty sure we are down something like six billion people?" Nacho went silent with the acknowledgement, not having wanted to admit it to himself. Somehow, it had just slipped out. "Maybe there *is* something we can learn from each other, after all."

"No thank you." Arriod was at least polite about it. "We have learned everything we wanted from your world. It was a simple matter of interrogating prisoners of war. What we found was not worth pursuing."

At that moment, Nacho got an unpleasant surprise in the form of a peak Tier one zombie sneaking in among the cannon fodder and tackling him. Arriod sprinted over, and the cook was fairly certain it was not to help him out of his dire situation. The katana came down, positioned perfectly to remove his head with a single strike. "Die like a *dog*!"

Nacho slashed upward with his blades, pushing the zombie to the side just enough that both knives slammed into the Crux-Terran's armpits, cutting through flesh until they were stopped by the armor three-quarters of the way through.

Damage dealt: 80! This is one tough cookie, Cookie!

. . .

The zombies were gone, and the scent of freshly crushed greenery filled Nacho's nostrils as the CruxTerran Commander collapsed to the ground, agony the only expression in his eyes. "Whew, close one. Let's end this. I have an undead infection to excise… or maybe the Patrons will let me close the Portal and trap them over there. I guess I can only hope!"

CHAPTER FORTY-TWO

The Guild Leader of the Chip's Guild, the last and best hope for humanity, brought his blades above his head and slammed them down. His chef's knife was aimed at the exposed throat, his cleaver poised to chop into Arriod's ribs.

**Clang!*

Another metal dome appeared around the enemy commander, followed by a flash of gold and red fire that Nacho could only faintly see through the seam at the bottom. Nacho slammed his knives down on it twice more in frustration. "You have *got* to be kidding me! This is starting to get ridiculous! Tell me you at least *bought* these, and they weren't just dropped from monsters!"

His target was silent, opting not to poke out of the shell that he had erected to save his life. Nacho kicked the chunk of metal, and it moved back a few inches. That confirmed that it wasn't too heavy and also had not been attached to the ground. Prepared for some kind of trick, he shoved the toe of his Sunday Brunch-armored boot under the metal and kicked up, flipping it to release a katana traveling straight for his exposed inner thigh. Arriod screamed in exultation as his strike landed, bright red fluid spraying into the air and staining his face. Some even got in his mouth… and he smacked his lips in confusion at the unexpectedly sweet taste.

Nacho spun and kicked Arriod in the face, sending him tumbling to the ground. Clearly that had been some kind of last-ditch effort to win, as the CruxTerran's wounds were still seeping blood. He must have run out of Mana if he was unable to fully heal his wounds, or at least to heal them enough to bring his Health higher than Nacho's. The cook finally glanced down in confusion to see what had saved his life, or at least had kept him from singing as a soprano for the next few years.

"You…?" He reached down, resting his hand on the green dog-plant hybrid that had been haunting him ever since he had returned to the Juxtaposition. "Ever since I've met you, you've been trying to get in the way of blades around me. When I'm chopping vegetables, when I'm practicing my forms, and now you even take a strike meant for me?"

Reaching down, he scooped the little monster into his arms, noting that its weight had increased significantly. It was highly probable that the canine was now a Tier one monster, at the very *minimum*. "You sure have grown a lot, haven't you? Why, when I first saw you, you were only a puppy… now you're all grown up and able to survive direct hits from powerful aliens."

The green dog's tongue lapped out, trying to lick him across the face. Nacho avoided it by reflex, shaking his head lightly. "None of that, now. You are a good boy, aren't you? Who's a good boy-"

He turned to take stock of his fallen opponent, startled to see the Paladin tossing a small bottle off to the side. Arriod's arms were already in position, and a bright, ghostly glow was shining from his blade. He sucked in a breath and started to call out whatever his attack was, and at this range, it was highly unlikely that Nacho would be able to avoid it.

The cook had a simple solution in mind. He twisted and absolutely *hucked* the dog at Arriod. It arced though the air, tumbling end over end, and Nacho found his aim had been perfect. The sword came down and sent its ghostly counterpart forward, but both were caught and blocked by the rotund green dog.

Which promptly detonated as though a stinger missile had been sent in to take out a high-value target.

Health remaining: 22/102

Congratulations! You have been instrumental in defeating a previously unknown type of monster! Thanks to this feat, you will be granted some information!

Monster name: Melon Collie. This is a monster type that gets close to its target by pretending to be friendly, sad, and submissive; its true goal is self-destruction to propagate its species. If unable to clean up all of the remains, you will have to deal with hundreds of its spawn!

In case you were wondering, it evolved out of that watermelon that we tried to convince you to destroy about a year ago. Except this one was not filled with water; it was filled with hydrogen-jelly. Very volatile.

"Not you!" Nacho found himself in a new position; lying on the ground exactly twenty feet away from Arriod, blinking dirt and blood out of his eyes as strange black seeds rained down on him. He struggled to his feet, a slight concussion making the world around him distorted and unpleasant to look at. "I *knew* it! Bad dog! *Bad*! I knew that you were a monster! Why do I *listen* to people when they tell me that I'm being paranoid? It's only paranoia if they're *not* out to get you! *Abyss*!"

He stumbled over to the CruxTerran, breathing heavily and raising his knives. It was finally time to end this. Cleaver held high, he took one last step and stared at his fallen opponent. After a long moment, he let out a deep sigh and lowered the blade. Arriod was currently unconscious, and Nacho could only hope that it was because he had taken a blow to the head, and not because he had gone negative on Mana. The first was fixable, the second not so much.

Rifling through the man's gear, he found some steel wire that looked like it would suit his purposes perfectly. He grabbed the unconscious man, tied his hands and feet together, gathered his weapons, and tossed the CruxTerran up on his shoulder. Then he started running, trying to get his bearings. Frankly, he had no idea where he had ended up, nor *how* he had ended up here.

The answer hit him after a few minutes: each location in their respective worlds where they had been transported had been impacted by events happening mid-battle. Just before one instance of being transferred back to Arriod's world, someone had said something to the effect of 'you are dead', and it dropped them next to a whole swarm of undead nightmares. "Just before we came here… what did he say? Did he say…? Tha~at's it. He said 'die like a dog'. I guess the only thing that had any significance to me and was somewhat dog-like was that… Melon Collie."

It took nearly ten minutes of running while carrying his burden to come across an open clearing, and he found himself extremely high up the side of a mountain, almost near the summit. Nacho dropped Arriod like a sack of moldy potatoes, although frankly he hadn't exactly been too careful with the man up until that point anyway. Finding a thick tree, Nacho arched backward and swung as hard as he could, toppling it with a single strike, about three feet above his own head.

From there, he pressed Arriod against the stump and tied him there, pulling the wire tightly enough that it dug into the bark of the tree and wouldn't be easy to maneuver out of. He spent the next several moments trying to make the man regain consciousness. When the CruxTerran Commander finally awoke, he discovered pine needles shoved up his nose, his clothes wet from what he could only hope was a puddle, and pains all over his body.

"Why am I alive?" Arriod cut straight to the heart of the

matter as soon as he was aware that he had been captured by a human. *The* human. The human tasked specifically with killing him.

"Look." Nacho crouched down so that they were both seeing eye-to-eye. "Right now, between my mood and the day that I've been having, I really, *truly* want to kill you. I'm *going* to… as soon as I have a better reason than 'the Patrons want me to do it'. Give me a reason, *please* give me a reason… so that I can let out all of my frustration and anger over what you have done to my people."

The CruxTerran didn't say a word; apparently even *he* had a sense of self-preservation. Nacho decided to get on with what he really wanted out of this situation. "Listen, Arriod. This is until death *or submission*. What I want you to do is surrender; absolutely, unequivocally surrender. Swear that you will join my guild and follow our rules."

"Why in either of our worlds would I do something like that?" Arriod seemed like he had more to say, but Nacho's chef's knife flashed into his hand and shot forward, barely managing to stop just after breaking the skin on his neck.

"Shh… I need you to be *very* quiet right now." Nacho was trembling from the effort it took not to simply bury his enemy as catharsis for the last four years of his life. "I really don't like you, nor your people, though specifically I do not like *you*. But… that shouldn't condemn your entire population to death. I am certain there are bad apples out there, and that is easily proved on this planet by Nibbles. If *we* can produce monsters like that, and yet we can also produce people that are so good, like Reuben… the same has to be true for your world. It *has* to be true. Join our world and lead the effort to assimilate your people into mine. Pure amalgamation. We will live together, die together, as equals."

"Except for the whole 'living under your boot heel', correct?" Arriod hissed at Nacho. "You think I don't know what those guild contracts really are?"

"There is a reason I am a Guild Leader and not a Guild

Master," The cook softly stated, his cleaver having joined his chef's knife on the CruxTerran's throat without warning. Frankly, it was a total surprise to the cook, and he had to force himself to pull both of them away a little bit so that his emotions did not overcome him and end this conversation before it was *supposed* to be over. "I can guarantee that your people will have fair treatment and enjoy the same rights and freedoms that my people do."

"What of… me?" Arriod finally ground out, and that question more than any other shocked Nacho to his core.

"Wow. Look at that. You actually *do* want something for yourself underneath that hard shell of propaganda that you sell to the people on your world." Nacho tilted his head back and forth, "Although I suppose that wanting to live is fairly universal. Fair enough. If you agree, I will put you on the council in order to represent your people."

"But… why should I work with you?"

"Beyond living through the night?" Nacho chuckled softly. "It's a better life, Arriod. You can have things that are just for you. You can have *fun*. You don't even have to kill anyone else if you don't want to; in fact, that part is highly recommended."

"I don't understand. Why would I need things that are just for me?" Arriod shook his head in bewilderment, opening up new wounds on his neck as he swung too close to the incredibly sharp blades that Nacho was holding a *little* too tightly. "It is far more efficient to just-"

"Stop. Just stop." Nacho cast around for something that he could use as an example, and his eyes fell on a bird's nest that had come down with the tree. "We will start small, and eventually you will understand why all of us strive to have things in life that are good. It's unfortunate, but true, that resources are limited. But you know what? There are so few people remaining that *all* of us can have a taste of the good life."

Without saying another word, Nacho walked over to the nest and collected the eggs. Then he searched around until he found a few wild onions and mushrooms, though he had to kill them a little bit. They weren't very strong, but he still wasn't very comfortable with the idea of having to murder vegetation in order to make a meal. He collected some fallen wood for a fire and soon was heating his cast iron skillet.

With the fresh ingredients he had gathered, and his ever-present salt and pepper in his storage slots, Nacho made Arriod a meal. The first meal he would ever eat that was made *just* for him: a simple, scrumptious omelet.

It was literally glowing gold.

"Of *course* the first Epic rarity meal I make isn't even something I can eat. Here, try this." Nacho pulled down the cloth covering Arriod's mouth, exposing a bushy mustache. "*Ugh*. Uh, sorry… for some reason, I was not expecting that. Eat up."

"I refuse."

Nacho shrugged, a grin on his face. He didn't know why he was having so much fun with this, but he was. "I guess it's true what they say: you can lead one man's trash to another man's treasure, but you can't make it drink."

He had to force-feed the first bite to the CruxTerran, holding his skillet in one hand and making airplane noises as he tried to wedge the food into his mouth. After poking the man in the forehead, the lips, and maybe-not-very-gently in the eye, he slipped the mouthful in when a groan of pain exited his foe. After the first bite, the Commander accepted the rest of it easily.

When the omelet was fully gone, including any particles that Nacho scraped off the edges, Arriod closed his eyes and heaved a deep sigh.

"They might call me a traitor, they might revile me for being purchased with such a simple bribe… but I can see some benefit to this. I want this… for my people. I accept your terms. To save CruxTerra… and myself… I surrender."

EPILOGUE

Needless to say, that was *not* the ending that Johnny Meat had been hoping for. The Patron of the CruxTerran Commander was absolutely furious and was trying to scream at Arriod. In fact, he *was* screaming, his face going completely red with rage, but Kronos' power had apparently significantly increased upon Nacho's winning the first round of the Juxtaposition. With a mere snap of his fingers, the Patron from the opposing faction had been muted entirely.

"Congratulations to both of you, quite frankly, but especially you, Nacho. Here are your rewards; use them wisely. Upon this conversation ending, you will be placed in a brand new Mega Fortress, which will house the Portal between your two worlds. No one will be able to go through without your personal permission, or permission from someone to whom you have delegated power. Of course, you could always simply set a toll and allow anyone who pays it to move through. Really, it's all up to you at this point."

That was all of the information provided before Nacho and The Dinner Party were fully healed and relocated inside a massive structure that seemed to span miles. It resembled an old fortress back on earth, though the stone and metal walls and crenellations would also make the CruxTerrans feel right at home.

Nacho and Arriod were standing a few feet apart, face to face, with the remaining members of their respective groups arranged behind them. Before anyone else could react, the two leaders reached out and shook hands with each other. Arriod huffed out a long breath. "As per the terms of our surrender, I officially join your guild and surrender everyone in my guild to your command."

Congratulations! The Chips guild has gained 1,600,023 new members!

"*That's* how you had a disgusting amount of magical items that you could throw around willy-nilly." Nacho grumbled at the audacious number that had populated his view. "Next steps: I need a volunteer to return to Armor Mountain and get everyone relocated here immediately. There are plenty of dungeons in the area, and frankly, we're closer to Costco than we were at our last place."

"Nacho." Brie was the first to find her voice. "What's going on? What happened? Did you win?"

"We won," Nacho confirmed, much to the delight of all humans and the disappointment and fear of the CruxTerrans. "We created a peace treaty. They joined our guild; Arriod is now on the council. Also, in case you didn't see, we just gained over one and a half million new members. Members that we need to do everything in our power to rescue."

"What?" Reuben was peering around owlishly, and that did not surprise Nacho in the slightest. As far as they knew, the Healer had just died and been brought back to life, and suddenly everyone was healed and in a new place.

"I know this is all jarring, but let me put it like this." Nacho pointed at the Portal that was visible a few stories below, then directed their attention into the distance, where a discerning eye could spot Armor Mountain rising in the distance. "We need all of our guild members here as soon as possible so that we can set up a safe entry point. We have over a million of our people to evacuate from a world that is about to become twice as dangerous as it was, and that work needs to start now."

"Thank you." That was all Arriod could say as the humans sprang into motion, completely ignoring the fact that these people had been their bitter enemies moments ago. "Why are you able to… how can you so sincerely name my people as… 'our' people?"

"Buddy, let me tell you what." Reuben stepped in to explain. "I don't know where you have been getting your information from, but right now, you are in the Midwest, and we are nothing if not *hospitable*."

"Darn tootin!" Abby cackled as she waved a tall Crux-Terran over. "We're also not afraid to put people to work. You, teleporter guy. You should run to your world and start getting people moving this way. You seem like the speedy type, and I don't want to see you for a good long time. After what you did to Reuben, I'm not gonna be too sad if you don't come back from your mission."

"Watch out for the zombies," Nacho called gently as the man looked to Arriod for confirmation. "Oh, right, you guys didn't hear about that. Yeah, the necromancers went through the portal. Whole bunch of zombies living there now, and that whole forest is burned out."

Round one complete! Congratulations to: Earth! Yay! You win! All monsters are worth double credits, and every portion of food will serve as one and a half portions!

Warning to: CruxTerra! All monsters will double in strength over the next two weeks, and when the last sapient member on your world has been slain, the planet will collapse and all natural resources will be funneled to Earth to empower it for round two!

More monsters, a new theme, and a new race to fight a world that also won their first round, all with more fabulous prizes to come!

"Wait, round *two*?" Reuben groaned as he felt at the hole in his armor where his heart had been pierced. He shuddered deeply and reached over to pull Brie into a huge hug.

Her arms wrapped around him like steel bars. "Never scare me like that, ever again."

"You got it."

"What in the world *happened*? We need to know more!" Jennifer finally shouted, earning nods of agreement and rapt attention from the other people around the area.

"We fought it out, I fed him dinner, and we made nice." Nacho summed up as succinctly as he could. "Listen, there is lots of work to do, and not much time to do it. We need to set up an outpost on the other side of the Portal to make sure that we keep sapient people on that planet no matter what, to delay round two as long as possible."

"You will be leading us in round two, I assume?" Arriod stood straighter. "It would be my honor to stand with you against a new enemy and show them the folly of their ways."

Before the man had even finished speaking, Nacho was shaking his head. "No. I can't. Well, I can, but won't. Maybe I should, but I shorn't."

"Nacho-" Jennifer started to protest, only to be cut off by the Guild Leader.

"What part of 'shorn't' don't you understand?" Nacho waved his hands to quiet down the ensuing hubbub. "Listen, we have no idea if there are other cooks out there, if there is anyone else that can feed everyone that needs to be fed. No matter what else happens, I think my time out in the field hunting down monsters is over. My battles are going to be fought in the kitchen from now on."

"What are you saying?" Brie asked from her secure position in her husband's arm.

"Round two is not the only thing we have to worry about. Those necromancers don't care who is trying to help whom, or who they hurt in their pursuit of power. Dealing with that is going to take a lot of effort, and I can't do everything. I can't even do the primary thing I'm supposed to be doing very well. So… I need to buckle down. We all do. When round two starts, we need to be ready. Specifically… we'll need our replacements on the front line to be ready."

"You're sure it can't be us?" Even though Arriod was clearly ready to volunteer and had the respect and trust of his people as a Commander, one look at his now-white hair was enough to convince Nacho that this man would be better served training fighters or adding his voice from his seat of the council.

"If we are going to survive the next round, we need to select and train a group that can do it. It won't—it *can't*—be us. We just aren't enough, and now we have two worlds of people to prepare for what's coming." Nacho sucked in a deep breath and spoke the words that he and his entire guild would live or die by.

"We've done enough. No one can say different. We achieved my dream. Now it's someone else's turn. We've had my Omelet Endgame."

ABOUT DAKOTA KROUT

Dakota Krout, a heartwarmingly clever author known for weaving fun, punny, and clean humor into his LitRPG fantasy novels, brings joy and laughter to readers through his best-selling series: including Cooking With Disaster, Divine Dungeon, Completionist Chronicles, and Full Murderhobo! His work, celebrated for its wit and charm, earned him a spot as one of Audible's top 5 fantasy picks in 2017, alongside a top 5 bestseller rank that was featured on the New York Times.

Drawing upon his experiences in the Army, Dakota expertly crafts vast, imaginative worlds with intricate systems that captivate and delight. His background in programming and information technology not only infuses his writing with a distinct, logical flair; but also fuels his innovative spirit in managing his publishing company, Mountaindale Press. These unique perspectives shine through in his stories, making him beloved by fans of all ages who seek a wholesome and humorous escape.

Dakota's journey in publishing has been filled with gratefulness, and a deep desire to continue bringing smiles and laughter to his readers. "I hope you Read Every Book With A Smile!" - Dakota Krout

Connect with Dakota:
MountaindalePress.com

Patreon.com/DakotaKrout
Facebook.com/DakotaKrout
Twitter.com/DakotaKrout
Discord.gg/mdp

ABOUT MOUNTAINDALE PRESS

Dakota and Danielle Krout, a husband and wife team, strive to create as well as publish excellent fantasy and science fiction novels. Self-publishing *The Divine Dungeon: Dungeon Born* in 2016 transformed their careers from Dakota's military and programming background and Danielle's Ph.D. in pharmacology to President and CEO, respectively, of a small press. Their goal is to share their success with other authors and provide captivating fiction to readers with the purpose of solidifying Mountaindale Press as the place 'Where Fantasy Transforms Reality.'

Connect with Mountaindale Press:
MountaindalePress.com
Facebook.com/MountaindalePress
Twitter.com/_Mountaindale
Instagram.com/MountaindalePress

MOUNTAINDALE PRESS TITLES

GameLit and LitRPG

The Completionist Chronicles,
Cooking with Disaster,
The Divine Dungeon,
Full Murderhobo, and
Year of the Sword by Dakota Krout

A Touch of Power by Jay Boyce

Red Mage and
Farming Livia by Xander Boyce

Ether Collapse and
Ether Flows by Ryan DeBruyn

Unbound by Nicoli Gonnella

Threads of Fate by Michael Head

Lion's Lineage by Rohan Hublikar and Dakota Krout

Wolfman Warlock by James Hunter and Dakota Krout

Axe Druid,
Mephisto's Magic Online, and
High Table Hijinks by Christopher Johns

Dragon Core Chronicles by Lars Machmüller

Pixel Dust and
Necrotic Apocalypse by D. Petrie

Viceroy's Pride and
Tower of Somnus by Cale Plamann

Henchman by Carl Stubblefield

Artorian's Archives by Dennis Vanderkerken and Dakota Krout

Made in the USA
Columbia, SC
19 July 2024

38888814R00233